THE
VICE
SOCIETY

Also by James McCreet

The Incendiary's Trail

THE
VICE
SOCIETY

JAMES MCCREET

MACMILLAN

First published 2010 by Macmillan
an imprint of Pan Macmillan, a division of Macmillan Publishers Limited
Pan Macmillan, 20 New Wharf Road, London N1 9RR
Basingstoke and Oxford
Associated companies throughout the world
www.panmacmillan.com

ISBN 978-0-230-74796-8

1 3 5 7 9 8 6 4 2

A CIP catalogue record for this book is available from
the British Library.

Typeset in Sabon and Copperplate Gothic

Printed and bound in the UK by CPI Mackays, Chatham ME5 8TD

Visit **www.panmacmillan.com** to read more about all our books
and to buy them. You will also find features, author interviews and
news of any author events, and you can sign up for e-newsletters
so that you're always first to hear about our new releases.

For Dad

1937–2009

Author's Note

The name of Persephone would have been virtually unknown to the general population of 1840s Britain. Not until later in the century did a new wave of Victorian Hellenism raise the Greek names of the deities from academic obscurity to rank with the Latin versions.

PROLOGUE

It was not a crow that Alfred White saw taking flight from the railing of the Monument that gloomy London afternoon but a woman plummeting to her death.

Perhaps it was her black dress fluttering against the smoke-streaked sky that made him first see a bird. Or perhaps it was the curious trick of perspective that reduces a body when seen from two hundred feet below.

But whereas a bird rises or glides when it takes to the air, this was a dead weight falling soundlessly, impelled by nothing more than gravity and hopelessness.

It was the limbs that signified a person – arms not thrashing or reaching out to grasp the passing air, legs not wheeling for purchase or balance. She simply dropped: a limp silhouette beside the fluted column, turning slowly end over end as her bonnet came free and drifted away.

Alfred found himself unable to shout, unable to point. He was transfixed. She seemed to fall so slowly that he felt he could have served another customer with a cup of coffee from the copper urn, perhaps also buttering a slice of bread. He could have looked up and seen her still, descending – more like a spider on its thread than a body approaching death at unimaginable velocity.

His hand paused, holding out the change. His mouth stopped in the middle of a word. The business of Monument-yard rattled around him as it always did: ladies and gentlemen shopping, cabs and carriages passing, a dog yelping as it ran ahead of a group of boys. All was completely normal – for one second more, at least.

She did not fall unobstructed. One of the carved stone griffins atop the pedestal broke her fall around fifty feet from the ground, catching her foot and sending her wheeling madly so that one shoe was flung from the body. Her trajectory altered outwards and Alfred now heard the sound of her dress billowing madly against the air.

She crashed to the ground with a reverberating crack that filled the court as if it had been a dense bale of cargo tossed from the summit.

The impact echoed around the *façades* of the buildings, causing every person passing there to pause. A moment of silence followed, during which two dozen Londoners looked and made the identical realization. Then a strangled yell that might have come from any one of them:

'*My G—! Someone has jumped from the Monument.*'

The utterer of the cry was also the first on the scene: Mr Jenkins, the attendant of the Monument. And what he found there beside the iron palisades around the doorway was a grisly sight indeed.

The supine body had partially struck the railings, bending them with the tremendous force of the fall. Her left arm was severed at the elbow but for a tenuous remnant of skin. Her right leg stuck out sideways from the hip at a most unnatural angle. A considerable pool of thick, dark blood had already spread out from the back of her head, and more blood had been forced from her eyes, nose and ears. As Mr Jenkins bent close to her, a single spasm animated the frail body and she was dead.

Though the condition of the corpse was quite hideous to behold, her face had been undamaged by the fall. Mr Jenkins extracted his handkerchief and tenderly wiped away the blood to reveal the peaceful countenance of an attractive woman most likely in her early thirties.

She was dressed tastefully in a black silk dress – no doubt her best – and wore good silk stockings. One black leather shoe remained. Her light-blonde hair had been thrown into disarray by the fall, strewn about and soiled now in the thickening gore. She wore a simple gold wedding ring.

'Somebody fetch a surgeon!' said one of the crowd that had already formed around the body.

'She is dead,' said Mr Jenkins. 'She breathed only once. I . . . I took her money just a few moments ago . . . She smiled and commented upon the weather . . .'

People around him stared only at the body. Their expressions were of mixed horror and fascination.

'We need a casket,' said Mr Jenkins. 'Who will go and get one?'

Nobody responded. The body was the spectacle and the single focus.

'I say we need a casket. *Who will fetch one?*'

A voice of assent came from the rear of the group and a figure ran off to procure a receptacle for the body.

Meanwhile, the crowd grew, drawing people from the surrounding streets as the word went out. Upwards of two hundred people had congregated by the time the casket arrived: men, women and children staring first up at the brass-gilt flames atop the Monument, then following the path down with awed mutterings and pointed fingers to where the mangled corpse lay.

A shaken Mr Jenkins stayed close to the body, pulling down the dress as much as possible over the shattered limbs to cover the lady's modesty. Recently arrived policemen jostled the people back from the puddle of blood and made a path through which the coffin bearers could pass.

And fascination followed the body even as it was borne to St Magnus-the-Martyr on Upper-Thames-street and then to the watch house at London-bridge. There, it was examined by a surgeon and then – presumably to attempt some dissipation of the crowd – it was left in the open box for the clamouring public to view as they filed through in their hundreds. Not since 1810 had someone leaped from the Monument, when Mr Lyon Levi had been the first to take his life.

A queue trailed from that watch house well into the afternoon, with constables ushering people in for a few minutes at a time so that they could peer into the box and look upon that gentle face. If they expected to see a broken and bloody body, they were disappointed. Her splintered bones and torn skin now carefully arranged by the surgeon, she was as peaceful as if she had passed away during her sleep.

Only after darkness had fallen did the Lord Mayor himself, visiting the site of the precipitation, give the order that the shameful exhibition of the body should cease. A rumour was abroad that the husband of the deceased, missing his beloved and hearing the news, had gone to the Monument and had approached his honour personally to make the request.

As one might expect, the inquest upon the following day generated a veritable phrenzy of interest. The smoky taproom of the Old Swan tavern at Fish-street-hill was so crowded that constables had to force people out before the jury of twenty-four local inhabitants could be settled and sworn for the address of Mr Bowes, the city coroner. What occurred sub-sequently would shock and amaze them all.

The first witness to be called was Mr Jenkins, the Monument attendant. A short and unassuming man, he seemed most perturbed by the proceedings and by the attention upon him.

The coroner – How did the deceased appear when she paid her admittance?

Mr Jenkins – She was quite composed. We exchanged views on the weather and she said that she feared the view would not be very fine. But she did like to make the ascent.

The coroner – Have you, then, known the deceased to visit the Monument before?

Mr Jenkins – Quite regularly. She would come perhaps every fortnight, whatever the weather . . . save strong winds of course.

The coroner – For how long did she pursue this habit?

Mr Jenkins – Upwards of a year in my experience.

The coroner – And did you not think it strange that some-one would want to ascend even in poor weather and when there was little to see?

Mr Jenkins – Not at all, sir. It is only the tourists who complain of the poor views. The native Londoner expects to glimpse the city only through the smoke.

The comment raised a knowing laugh among those assembled there, and the coroner acknowledged it with a smile and a nod.

Mr Jenkins – I mean to say that there are many reasons to ascend, sir. The structure itself is of great interest, and some say that the upper air has medicinal properties.

The coroner – I dare say the air is less than medicinal when the breeze is from Southwark. But proceed – what happened after the deceased was admitted?

Mr Jenkins – She ascended, and the next thing I knew she had crashed to the ground.

The coroner – How long was she aloft?

Mr Jenkins – It is difficult to say. Perhaps thirty minutes, including the ascent.

The coroner – Is that period typical for visitors?

Mr Jenkins – It rather depends. Tourists are wont to return quickly if they are cold, or if the view is poor. The decea— the lady in question would often spend an hour taking the air.

The coroner – Were any other visitors aloft at the same time?

Mr Jenkins – Three gentlemen gained admittance shortly after the lady. They would have been on the viewing platform at the same time.

The coroner asked if the three gentlemen were present at the inquest and after a general hubbub it transpired that they were not.

The coroner – Did you see the gentlemen in question after the melancholy incident?

Mr Jenkins – I did not. My attention was occupied with the lady and with the gathering of people.

The coroner – Were they still aloft?

Mr Jenkins – No, sir. After the body was taken away, I ascended to find the viewing platform empty. Then I locked the doors early out of respect.

The coroner – So we may assume that the gentlemen you saw ascend left the Monument during the confusion after the fall.

Mr Jenkins – I suppose so. I did not see them leave.

The coroner – What did these gentlemen look like? We should bring them before this inquest at all costs.

Mr Jenkins – They were well dressed – not working men. They spoke civilly to me (or rather, one of them did) and paid the fee. I can think of nothing remarkable about their appearance. I see hundreds of people a day.

The coroner – Did you exchange any conversation with them?

Mr Jenkins – It is my nature to say a word or two to each visiter and I warned them that the aspect from the summit might not be worthy of the climb. The one who spoke thanked me for my solicitude but said they would ascend all the same because one of their number was in London for the first time.

The coroner – Did he appear to be a foreigner?

Mr Jenkins – The gentleman alluded to did not speak. He did not look particularly foreign.

The coroner – One final question, if you please. Did you find anything unusual when you ascended for the final time that day?

Mr Jenkins – I did.

At this revelation, a murmur thrilled around the room. Mr Jenkins must have felt his throat constrict at the attention on him. He willed his voice not to crack as he continued.

Mr Jenkins – I found a small Bible. Its pages were turned down at various pages and there was a note within. I handed both to the police.

The coroner – I have them here and will read the note aloud for the purposes of the inquest.

And here Mr Bowes cleared his throat. Only the barest noise could be discerned: the scrape of a shoe, a glass clinking in another room. The space might have been empty.

The coroner (reading) – 'I cannot go on. This life has become so intolerable to me that I must end it. I pray forgiveness from those who love me, and from my Maker who has set the weight of sin against self-murder. May His grace fall upon others more deserving than I.' It is signed 'Kathleen'.

Mr Bowes held up the letter for all to see and the silence seemed to intensify still further. He then passed it to the jury, who examined it closely. The writing was a strong and clear copperplate on fine paper.

The coroner – I draw the jury's attention to the fact that the note is not directed to a particular person. I also have the Bible Mr Jenkins has described. It has been examined and the folded pages relate to passages concerning the act of self-murder.

The Bible was handed to the jury, who handled it with even greater reverence and wonder than the note. No juror wanted to ask a further question, so Mr Jenkins was thanked for his testimony and allowed to sit.

The next witness was the surgeon, Mr Blackheath of Fish-street-hill. A sober gentleman with a balding pate, he seemed not the least cowed and had no doubt attended many such inquests.

The coroner – Could you give the jury your medical findings on the deceased?

Mr Blackheath – The body was quite extinct when I examined it. There was a compound fracture of the scull; the spine was fractured in multiple places and there were compound fractures of both legs and the right arm. The left arm was separated at the elbow and held to the upper arm by skin only. The right leg was also dislocated from the pelvis.

The coroner – Have you made an internal examination?

Mr Blackheath – I have not. The injuries are consistent with a fall from considerable height. The cause of death was the fracture to the scull combined with the spine fractures.

The coroner – Do you know whether the deceased was *enceinte*?

Mr Blackheath – I have not ascertained whether she is with child, no.

The coroner – Did the deceased have any other injuries that could not be explained by her fall?

Mr Blackheath – I detected nothing suspicious.

The coroner asked whether the jury would like to question the surgeon further, producing one rather inappropriate question from a man with a glistening red face:

The juror – I have heard that blood shot from her eyes, nose, ears and mouth. Is this normal in such a fall?

Mr Blackheath – The sudden impact of the brain inside the cranium causes colossal damage and haemorrhaging. The consequent pressure can indeed lead to dramatic bleeding from the orifices of the head. I understand that much of this was wiped away by the attendant, Mr Jenkins. [Mr Jenkins confirmed with a nod.]

Alfred White, a coffee-seller of Fish-street-hill, was the next to stand before the jury and explain what he had seen. As the only witness to have seen the woman actually fall, he was questioned closely by the jury.

A juror – Did the deceased jump, or did she step from the parapet?

Mr White – In truth, I did not see the precise moment she left the railing. She was in the open air as I first glimpsed her.

A juror – From her position, did she appear to jump from the top of the railing itself, or from the stone coping outside the railing?

Mr White – I cannot say.

A juror – Then, did she fly outwards from the edifice?

Mr White – No, she fell quite vertically and without movement for the duration of the drop.

The coroner – The deceased did not let out a cry or manifest signs of fear or distress?

Mr White – No, sir. The body seemed quite lifeless as it fell.

The coroner – Did you see the three gentlemen who entered the Monument shortly after the deceased?

Mr White – I did not. Nor did I see them leave. The fuss took all of my attention. I dare say it took everyone's attention.

The coroner asked if anyone present had seen the gentlemen enter or leave the Monument, but nobody came forward. He suggested to the jury that they might like to adjourn the inquest in order to find further information about these gentlemen, but that in the meantime there was one final person to call: the deceased's husband.

A respectful hush settled over the room and the red-faced juror who had asked the gruesome question looked most sheepish. The coroner explained that the husband, a Mr George Williamson, had volunteered to be examined by the jury in the interest of justice, but that the jury might choose not to submit the gentleman to questioning due to his distressed state.

The foreman consulted with his fellows and they returned the opinion that they owed it to their oath to explore every source of information on the incident and that they would keep their questioning as mercifully brief as possible.

There was a shuffling of chairs at the side of the room and Mr George Williamson stepped into the close, smoky space with his eyes downcast. His face was pitted with the scars of a previous attack of the smallpox and he walked with a heavy, shuffling gait as if grievously fatigued. He was clad entirely in dark blue, and, even in that brilliantly lighted room, he seemed to carry a darkness with him that was sufficiently saturated with sadness to repel any further feeling of pity bestowed upon him.

The coroner – Sir, could you tell us of the circumstances regarding your discovery of this tragedy.

The husband covered his mouth to cough and then spoke with a clear, authoritative voice.

Mr Williamson – I returned home to find my wife not at home. This was unusual, so I asked a neighbour if he had seen Katherine. He had not, but he had already heard of the incident and told me of it. Knowing that Katherine liked to visit the Monument, I felt a sense of foreboding and went there directly to see if she had been caught up in the *mêlée*.

The coroner – Then you did not assume that the decea— that your wife had precipitated herself from the summit?

Mr Williamson – No. Katherine would never do such a thing.

The coroner – What state of mind was your wife in when last you saw her?

Mr Williamson – I have told you that she would not commit suicide, whatever her state of mind. She was a good Christian and a happy woman.

The coroner – May I show you some items related to the case?

The jury foreman passed the Bible and letter to the coroner, who handed them to Mr Williamson. The unfortunate husband looked at them for a moment, opening the Bible at the marked pages. His face was a mask of impassiveness that belied the turmoil of emotion that must have been within him. Only a tensing of the jaw indicated his inner state.

The coroner – Do you recognize either of these items?

Mr Williamson – I do not.

A commotion here erupted in the room and the foreman had to shout repeatedly for quiet. Even after order had been retained, there was a constant muttering of speculation.

The coroner – Sir, do you mean to say that this Bible is not the property of your wife, and that the writing on the letter is not her hand?

Mr Williamson – Precisely that. Neither of these items is connected to Katherine. It is not her writing; it is not her Bible.

The coroner – I must say that your response has surprised us.

Mr Williamson – And I must say that the evidence here points clearly to a verdict other than suicide.

Disruption again fluttered through the room as the coroner and foreman struggled to subdue proceedings. Amidst the cacophony, a voice was heard to shout out a single word.

'*Murder!*'

At this, Mr Williamson's gaze darted into the corner whence the word had come and he speared a finger into the crowd. A sudden silence sliced through the noise and every pair of eyes fell upon the husband, his arm still outstretched.

Mr Williamson – Members of the jury . . . that, *that* is your verdict.

His face remained composed, but his intelligent eyes burned. Whether it was outrage or agony that was held within them, nobody could have discerned.

The coroner – It is the duty of the jury to decide on a verdict, Mr Will—

Mr Williamson – Will the foreman have me express myself freely?

The foreman acquiesced.

Mr Williamson – My wife did not kill herself. She had no reason to do so. There are evidently three gentlemen who could verify this, but the very fact of their absence should be a warning to us. A Bible and a note were left atop the viewing platform, but as neither belonged to my wife we must assume that they were placed there to create *the impression of suicide*. Quiet . . . quiet if you will . . . This was poorly executed: the note was addressed neither to me or to her mother. Why, even the name is wrong – Kathleen instead of Katherine – as if someone had misheard her. I would, indeed, like to ask Mr Jenkins if he saw my wife carrying the Bible as she entered.

Mr Jenkins (from the crowd) – In truth, I did not.

The coroner – What you say is certainly curious, Mr Williamson, but it does not, in itself, suggest murder.

Mr Williamson – I would like an internal examination to be made of my wife before she is laid to rest.

The coroner – We have heard from the surgeon that your wife was killed by the fall. Her injuries were quite consistent with—

Mr Williamson – No. We have heard that the injuries she suffered would have killed anyone – not necessarily that they killed *her*. The witness Mr White said that the body appeared 'quite lifeless' as it fell.

The coroner – A figure of speech.

Mr Williamson – I think not. I have seen the body of my wife and I believe I detected the faintest smell of prussic acid about her mouth. I have heard that other of the witnesses to her body at the watch house remarked upon the same thing. An internal examination would prove beyond doubt that—

The coroner – . . . that she took the poison before she jumped – a quite understandable act, I would assume, among suicides who fear the fall. Mr Williamson . . . we understand the magnitude of your suffering—

Mr Williamson – Hmm. Hmm. Understand it, do you?

Understand your . . . your love dashed to the ground before the whole city and then exhibited as if a curious fish in a shop window?

The coroner fell under that piercing stare, opened his mouth to speak, and was rendered mute by the drained, accusatory face before him. Its expression was held rigid only by a preternatural effort of will. Two constables moved closer to Mr Williamson and one rested a hand on his shoulder, saying something into his ear. At this word, the husband seemed to sag and let his head drop. He remained like this for a moment, shaking his head as all looked on with piteous aspect. Then he allowed himself to be led from the place without a further word.

The coroner suggested to the jury in sombre tones that the inquest should be adjourned until the three gentlemen could be located, and that if this proved impossible a verdict of suicide would seem the most sensible.

And though a search ensued over the coming days, along with an advertisement in *the Times*, no trace of the gentlemen could be found. Evidently, nobody had seen them.

Thus, suicide was the verdict and the body itself was shortly after interred in unconsecrated ground at the Spa Fields burial ground.

And that would have been the end of the story but for two further pertinent pieces of information. The first was that the grieving husband Mr George Williamson, a constable in the Metropolitan Police at the time, would become, in the intervening years, Detective Sergeant Williamson of the Detective Force: the most gifted and lauded investigator ever to work within those ranks.

The second would come seven years later, when the death

of Katherine Williamson would once again, in its own way, play its part in a story embroiling the husband and the police in an unprecedented case of murder, mystery and evil that would touch many with the cold fingers of death, from the most degraded gutter wretch to the finest personages in the loftiest positions . . .

ONE

---◆---

'Tell me everything.'

Metropolitan Police Commissioner Sir Richard Mayne closed the book he had been consulting and leaned back in his chair, looking over the broad surface of his sturdy oaken desk. His expression, as was invariably the case, was one of stern attention, fixing his interlocutor with a stare that doubted words before they were spoken and weighed them with a barrister's reasoning as they were. A virtual stranger to the physical world beyond that Scotland Yard office, his face had the pallor of one accustomed to meetings and hearings *in camera* rather than the vagaries of the elements. His eyes were sharp and missed nothing.

Before him in that modestly furnished room, as was invariably the case, stood the celebrated Inspector Albert Newsome of the Detective Force, erstwhile superior to Mr Williamson and a man who had worked through the ranks from the earliest days of the police. Of a wiry build, and with his unruly thatch of red hair, he was a man of the streets rather than a legal theorist. He might not have had the education of his commissioner, but in a midnight alley off Ratcliff-highway, his own particular 'schooling' would have seen him home alive. *His* expression was perpetually sardonic – something he took great care to restrain in this office.

'Yes, sir. As you may have heard, the incident occurred at three o'clock the morning before last on Holywell-street.'

'That stinking alley. It is a moral sewer and a disgrace to modern London.'

'Indeed. At that time, a gentleman named Jonathan Sampson fell from the third-floor window of Colliver's coffee house, sustaining a fractured thigh bone and a lacerated scull. He was found lying in the street by PC Cribb and taken immediately to King's College Hospital, where he died some hours later from his injuries. It is an unremarkable case, Sir Richard, and one that I am sure need not concern—'

'I will decide what concerns me, Inspector. That street has been the subject of much comment in the highest circles. It is a suppurating wound upon the fair complexion of our city and I am eager to cauterize it.'

'Yes, sir.'

'There are irregularities in the case that have come to light, are there not? On any other street, this might be the case of a mere drunk, but I am inclined to address any occurrence on Holywell-street with more scrutiny. What is this, for instance, about the victim's words when found, and later in the hospital?'

'The man was quite incoherent from his fall. He said to Constable Cribb: "What mystery is this? Why am I lying in the street?" Later, when questioned by the surgeon, he became increasingly reluctant to speak about the nature of his accident and said he would explain when he was better.'

'Explain what?'

'I do not know, sir. Presumably why he fell from the window.'

'Do you not find this evasiveness suspicious?'

'Not if the man was with a woman other than his wife.'

'Is there evidence to suggest this?'

'No, sir.'

'Do you suspect suicide?'

'I do not. There was no note, and the victim struggled for purchase as he hung from the window ledge. The scuffs can be seen there still where his shoes kicked phrenziedly in his attempts to save himself. Suicide was evidently not his intention – or he rapidly changed his mind after exiting the window.'

'Am I to assume, Inspector Newsome, that there was someone else in the room with him, or are you going to make me ask question after question? Tell me everything you know. What facts have been unearthed by today's inquest?'

'Very well, sir. The victim, Mr Sampson, was aged forty-three and was a stockbroker of North-road, Hoxton. He was unmarried and described by his sister – an attractive but clearly distraught young lady – as a quiet man who lived alone. This testimony was countered somewhat by the brother, who remarked that the victim had been rather more excitable than usual of late and that he had lived his bachelor's life "freely".'

'I dare say the brother had the more genuine version. Proceed.'

'The proprietress of the coffee house and the room above it, Mrs Colliver, admitted the victim and a fellow to the room at ten o'clock. Mr Sampson had arrived earlier and was joined by the other fellow shortly afterwards. They had eaten a light meal before taking the twin-bedded room together for a single night. Neither was intoxicated, and both were described by the lady as appearing "respectable".'

'Who was the other man?'

'Nobody recognized him and no name was taken. That will become relevant as I proceed.'

'Then do so, Inspector.'

'The next part of the story has the landlady awoken at around two o'clock in the morning by a loud moaning coming from the street. She looked out of her window and saw the victim lying upon the cobbles with a policeman, PC Cribb, bending over him.'

'Wait. Did not you say the incident occurred at three?'

'The constable says he found the man at three o'clock, and the victim's watch, which was smashed in the fall, registered at five to three. We may ascribe Mrs Colliver's confusion to being woken in the early hours.'

'Perhaps. It is interesting that the watch was not stolen. Even a broken one will fetch a price.'

'The constable, as I have said, found the victim insensible and bleeding from the head. At this stage, the victim was said by the constable to smell strongly of drink, though Mrs Colliver insists neither gentleman drank alcohol or had it taken to the room.'

'What of the other gentleman – the one sharing the room?'

'As the constable was seeing to the victim, another witness appeared on the scene: one Ned Coffin, a drunken mariner. Both he and PC Cribb saw the other gentleman, the room-mate, come out of the building in an agitated state and say: "O my G—, my friend has fallen out of the window! I must go and tell his friends," whereupon he rushed to a carriage that was stationary a little further down the street and fled in it towards St Clement Danes.'

'Was this roommate at the inquest?'

'No, sir. Nor did he return with any friends of the victim. I have had a man watching the coffee house since PC Cribb reported the case, and the inquest has been adjourned until further intelligence can be gathered about his identity or whereabouts.'

'Do we have a description?'

'No particularly good one. Mrs Colliver could think of little else to say but that he seemed a well-dressed man of good humour. Witnesses at the coffee house said the two spoke in quieted tones. Constable Cribb saw little due to the darkness and, presumably in the case of Mr Coffin, extreme intoxication.'

'Was this Coffin at the inquest?'

'No. I suspect he was in a deep state of slumber. I am attempting to locate him.'

'And do you still maintain that this is an unremarkable case? It seems to me that there is much that remains perplexing. Or have you solved the case already?'

'Sir, I have spent many years on these streets—'

'Without the preamble, if you please.'

'Well then, I will speak frankly. Perhaps the man was a sodomite and this good-humoured fellow was engaged with him in these unnatural practices. Naturally, neither would want to be identified as such by the police, even if it meant one of them was mortally wounded.'

'You do not shock me, Inspector. But you do disappoint me. My knowledge does not extend to sodomitical tastes, but I suggest that some manner of undress is conventional. The victim was fully clothed. And I feel sure such practices do not generally involve defenestration.'

'A simple transaction, sir. One fellow demands his payment, perhaps threatening the other with violence. With the door barred, our victim takes the only other escape route rather than be exposed. On being found, he naturally lies. The other fellow flees.'

'Supposition, Inspector.'

'The most likely explanation, I believe.'

'Have you made a thorough search of the room as Sergeant Williamson was wont to do?'

'I have a constable stationed there in case the young man should return.'

'But you have not searched it. Have you interviewed the family of the victim and the witnesses?'

'Sir, I hardly think—'

'Quite. That is precisely my point. If you have ambitions of taking the vacant post of Superintendent Wilberforce – so lamentably taken from us – I expect to see better work than this. I expect the Detective Force to be a torch exposing crime wherever it lurks, not brushing mysteries into the gutter like so much dung to clog the cleansing passage of water. I sincerely regret that Sergeant Williamson has left us.'

'He was not . . . he was no longer suited to his duties. I am sure he is quite content in his new position at the Mendicity Society, where he does not have to contend with the violence and danger of our job in the Detective Force.'

'Perhaps. Perhaps. I have heard good things about his work there. I trust *you* will now be proceeding directly to Holywell-street and thence to contact whatever witnesses may shed light on this case.'

'Indeed. There is only one other matter that may or may not be of relevance. On the same morning at around five o'clock, the body of a prostitute was found in a passage connecting Holywell-street with the Strand. She had taken prussic acid to end her life.'

'Do you see any connection between the two cases?'

'None, sir. I thought I would mention it.'

'Well, she was a prostitute. Such things happen. On with the case at hand.'

'As you wish.'

'Inspector Newsome – I perceive that you would have me perceive something is troubling you. Are you planning to tell me what it is?'

'Sir . . . this case seems odd in a way that I cannot specify. There are lies; there are secrets; there are private motivations in most lives. But I can see no evidence of a crime here, only of human nature. Why, even the newspaper reporters have shown little interest – and we know how they love a scandal.'

'To express it more frankly: you cannot see why I would assign the investigation of this, a seemingly insignificant case, to such a senior detective? I praise your diplomacy in raising the issue thus, and I suppose I should reveal my reasons. You are aware, I assume, of the Society for the Suppression of Vice?'

'I am. They are based at Lincolns-inn-fields.'

'Quite. What is your opinion of the Society?'

'In truth, they are meddlers of the highest order: holy hypocrites that will be happy only when every person in the country lives the same self-sanctified existence that they do. They are a bane to the working classes and finer sort alike, and their spies are the worst, most degraded people in this city. Even criminals have a code of honour, but those spies are blood-sucking worms.'

'I cannot fault your honesty, and I share some of your views. But the fact remains that the Society counts among its benefactors some of the most important people in this country: aristocrats, judges, Members of Parliament, even royalty. Shortly after this man Sampson fell out of the window, the Society contacted me through a person I am not at liberty to name – a person of considerable significance – and asked that I put my best man on the case. This person has also asked that I keep them informed of our progress. This, Inspector, is the political reality of policing, as you will no doubt discover if you become superintendent.'

'I see. But why this case in particular?'

'It is that street; you know its reputation. Everything that the Vice Society stands against is represented there, and they see it as a core of evil in the city. If there is illegality to be pursued there, they will do so with all their strength – and with any other power open to them. Let us conclude this case as quickly as we can; I am uncomfortable with the attention of the Society upon us. Go now to Holywell-street.'

TWO

London – city of impostors, false beggars, coiners, cheats, sham-goods sellers, double-tongued prostitutes and professional liars. The stranger to these streets can believe little of what he sees, and less of what he is told. Here, a man's identity is what he says it is, and his trade is whatever you will pay him money for. Nothing is quite as it seems.

Perhaps you are a generous sort and stricken with pity at the poverty you see. You can spare a few pennies for the beggar, and, if the case is particularly deserving, you might happily part with pounds to ease the sorry sufferings of those who dress in rags. Then the question arises: how does one know if the charity case at hand is genuine?

Respectable people look to the venerable Mendicity Society to see that their money goes only to verifiable cases. From its offices at unassuming Red Lion-square, the Society's roving constables – the doughty 'Red Liners' – ensure that acquisitive vagrants are dragged before magistrates, that the vocational beggar is put behind bars and that the truly mendicant are given work or Tickets of Entitlement to exchange for food. It is righteous work and zealously executed.

Indeed, for high-minded young men and sensitive young

ladies of the city, the Mendicity Society is a place for the devout to be associated with: an opportunity to do good work. Such people are constantly arriving at the offices with fine intentions – even more so during that period when a certain illustrious ex-detective had begun work there. Let us enter the building and see the upstanding people at work . . .

Here is the secretary escorting another earnest Christian volunteer through the various rooms and describing the activity of each. It is all highly organized and laudable, yet our young volunteer cannot help but become increasingly frustrated at the delay in approaching the most famed room of the building and of the Society itself – the one he has heard all about and in which he hopes to work: the begging letters office.

It is here that more than one thousand letters annually pass across desks to be verified according to the concerns of ladies and gentlemen, lords, dukes and earls who can never be certain that the piteous entreaties they receive in the post are truths or falsehoods. Only here can expert eyes examine the letters for the warp and weft of veracity.

Finally our volunteer is permitted entry. Within, there are shelves of ledgers containing the details of letter writers and their recipients across the country. Who is this sailor, for example, who claims to have fallen on hard times and purports to need ten pounds to release him from a debt? He has written to the Duke of —— with a story that would wring tears from the very saline ropes of an ocean-tracing brig. Is he truly a straitened tar of Ratcliff-highway, or a skilled literary gentleman in a base lodging somewhere sending off fifteen identical versions of the letter with a sly grin upon his face?

It is as quiet as a library, the silence disturbed only by the occasional shuffle of feet, the creak of a chair and the scrape of a ledger being withdrawn. Serious gentlemen examine letters before them, making notes and consulting endless columns of records for notable phrases, recurring names, prominent addresses, unusual vocabulary. By such means are the cheats trapped and brought to justice, and our volunteer is enthralled at the spectacle. He looks rapidly from desk to desk . . . at which one is seated the gentleman he hopes to meet?

There at the centre of the room, sitting at a broad desk neatly arrayed with piles of papers and books, was George Williamson, previously of the Metropolitan Police's Detective Force. He did not appear much changed from that grieving figure we saw seven years before – more careworn, perhaps; a little thinner about the face and with a harder edge to eyes that have seen more than any man should in the intervening period. Placed before him was a single sealed envelope which he was examining closely for clues that nobody else in the room – amateurs all – could possibly have seen.

The secretary approached with his youthful volunteer, and the two exchanged a glance. Yes, this was he: the same George Williamson, previously Detective Sergeant Williamson. They arrived at the desk and the ex-policeman looked up with a level stare that said he was being interrupted by the secretary.

'George – may I present Harold Jute. His father is a most generous benefactor and Harold will be joining you for a time. He has just come down from Oxford and has expressed a wish to work with the Society.'

Mr Williamson did not stand, but appraised the young man with a swift, comprehensive glance and nodded a perfunctory assent to the secretary.

'I am so terribly excited to be working with you, sir,' said Harold, standing beside the desk. 'I have been interested for some time in the work of the Detective Force, and when father told me that I might work here with—'

'Sit down. There is work to do. Let us apply your enthusiasm to the case at hand. What do you see here, young man?' said Mr Williamson.

'A letter.'

'You might have the makings of a detective yet.'

'Er, thank you, sir.'

'This is a letter sent to Lord ———. He receives so many importunate letters that he now sends them to the Society that we may examine them first.'

'It is unopened.'

'You are most observant.'

'I . . . I mean, surely you must open the letter to begin your process.'

'On the contrary. One may learn much of a letter before opening it. What do you see?'

'May I touch it? Thank you. Well, it is a pre-paid envelope posted from the General Post Office at St Martin's-le-Grand judging by the stamp. The hand looks like a feminine one and, yes, there is a faint perfume.'

'Good. The markings, writing and odour tell as much. Inside, there are three sheets of thin notepaper with writing on one side only.'

'But . . . but it is yet unopened. How can you be sure?'

'The charge is one penny. That signifies a weight of half an ounce. Half an ounce equates to one and a half sheets of standard quarto notepaper or three sheets of thin notes. Experience tells us that ladies – and this letter at least pretends to be from a lady – are more likely to favour multiple sheets. The thinness of these means that the ink will often be absorbed through, hence the single sides.'

'I see.'

'Open it with this knife. Carefully.'

Harold opened the envelope and extracted three sheets of notepaper just as Mr Williamson had described them. 'I say, Mr Williamson – if these fellows are as dull as this, I understand why so many are exposed!'

'No.'

'Sir?'

'Do you know who I am?'

'You are Mr . . . Mr George . . . I am afraid I am confused.'

'I have been introduced to you as George Williamson. But you have never before seen me. I could be anyone at all, and yet you have accepted me as described because there is nothing to contradict the impression that I am who you believe me to be.'

'*Are* you?'

'Of course I am. I seek only to illustrate that nothing you see and read here is what it first seems. The people who write these letters, these "screevers" or "slums" as they are also termed, are skilled beyond the comprehension or imagination of your average criminal. They might write twenty letters like this a day, keeping logs of their targets and the details of the letters they have sent. There are letter writers like this who have escaped the police and the Mendicity Society for years: intelligent, sometimes formally educated, men who have not managed to make a living writing novels or articles for the papers. Quite frankly, they will never be caught.'

'But we know this letter is from a lady, do we not?'

'No. We know that it is written *as if* from a lady. The feminine hand and the scent are simple enough falsities. These writers may have a dozen different hands to call upon. Believe nothing. Now – let us read the text.'

My Lord,

It is with most pained heart that I presume to address to your benevolent lordship's notice. I lived for time within your lordship's seat with some late relatives and have on occasion caught sight of your benign presence.

I am descended from a respectable family of the parish of St Anne, Limehouse, of which I am the last, and I am the widow of a late respectable schoolmaster who died of fever some five years ago, leaving me with four children under eleven years of age, and obliged to dispose of my premises to settle my husband's few debts, defray funeral expenses, &c.

Of late, my comfortable station in life has been reduced to that of shameful penury through Almighty's unfathomable Grace in wasting my lower extremities with rheumatic gout and preventing me from attending to my duties as governess of a Sunday school, not least the upkeep of my family. It is their plaintive cries that rend verily my heart, not the threats of the debtor's gaol and the distraining of my chattels by my late landlord's brokers.

I have been obliged to quit my late residence to escape arrest and feed my children by whatever means I can. That I have remained free of the workhouse is only through the kindness of an acquaintance, whose damp cellar we occupy.

By the Grace of God, I have been granted the opportunity to reclaim my furniture. And yet even as this hand of aid is extended to me, I live in fear of arrest and incarceration for my outstanding debt. Only charitable assistance to the sum of 10l. 6s. 5d. can

succour my mournful state and return my possessions.
As my children wither under the nourishment of mere
potatoes and water, I offer up my final hope to your
lordship, who all name as a champion of the working
people. Whatever pecuniary charity you could offer
towards helping me to overcome my difficulties will,
I assure your lordship, go with me in gratitude to my
grave.

I beg to subscribe myself, my lord, your lordship's
most humble servant,

Harriet Burgoyne, 2b,
St Mary's-hill.

'A sorry tale,' said Harold.

'Indeed. Most pitiful – but quite clearly a fakement. Consider the weight of fortuitous coincidence within it: the last of her line; late relatives; a late husband; a late landlord . . . such unpunctuality is most suitable, is it not? None of these people are alive to be consulted upon the letter writer's account.'

'I suppose that is true. But we do know she is of the parish of St Anne.'

'Do we? Might not anyone go to the parish records and pluck a name from them?'

'I . . . I imagine so.'

'In fact, the letter is a very fine example of its sort, which is why we know it is not true. Tell me, what do we know of the widow Burgoyne from this letter?'

'Well, she is from a respectable family, the widow of a schoolmaster and something of an educator herself. She is a mother and a Christian with a physical affliction who has fallen into hard times through no fault of her own.'

'Quite. Nothing whatsoever deserving of reproach. It is a perfect case of need. Even the amount is modest and convincingly specific – at least, it would be a perfect case of need if the same letter had not been sent to two dozen other people.'

'What tells you this? Have you seen the same letter before?'

'Not exactly, but I am convinced of it. In part, its very perfection of form and tone is suspicious; only a professional writer would be so thorough. But also look again at that phrase "rend verily my heart". Does that strike a note of recognition with you?'

'It is poetry? I'm afraid I do not know it.'

'It is taken from a song that was quite a phenomenon a few months ago: a sentimental piece entitled "My Foolish Heart".'

'I am afraid I do not follow your logic.'

'I see that your fine Oxford education has taught you little about the common man. He is a garrulous sort because, as a rule, he cannot, or will not, read. His understanding of the world comes from others of his sort. Market gossip is his newspaper. Not for him the morning press – he relies upon the tradesman's rumour, the ballad and witticism of the penny gaff. In one day, the latest song or joke can be across the city faster and more comprehensively than any news, passed like pestilence wherever people hear and speak.'

'I see, but—'

'But the popular taste is fickle and short-lived. Today's phrase of the moment is tomorrow's embarrassed silence or mocking snigger. I would say that the average lifespan of songs such as "My Foolish Heart" is about two or three months.'

'The letter is dated two days ago.'

'It is. But it was written three months ago when the song was popular. It had clearly stuck in the writer's mind like mud to one's sole and he used it without thinking. From this, we may discern that a number of these letters were most likely drafted identically at that time and posted at different times as opportunity and intelligence allowed. Certainly, the real widow Burgoyne – if she existed – would not wait three months to post this letter.'

'Might not the writer have simply remembered the phrase and used it as he wrote?'

'Hmm. Let me explain it in terms that you might understand. Imagine that you have been to see a play, a comedy, and a line particularly takes the fancy of you and your fellows. For weeks, you repeat it to each other until it becomes quite threadbare. Then, two or three months later, you find that you are in conversation with the same fellows and the opportunity arises to once again use this phrase. Do you do so? Would it be as amusing?'

'I expect not. Fashion rather favours the new – unless I was satirizing the original.'

'Is Mrs Burgoyne's letter in a satirical tone?'

'I suppose not.'

'Indeed. For the working man, only the most contemporary phrase or tune will do if he is to remain at the forefront of his peers.'

'Forgive me, Mr Williamson, but is not all of this detection somewhat redundant? We have the woman's address at St Mary's-hill. Why not simply go there and verify the facts ourselves?'

'And have the letter writer or one of his accomplices observe us from an upper or opposite window and flee? Such people expect the Society to come looking for them, and keep a lookout. No – we may be sure that the writer of this letter does not live at the return address itself. He is far too clever for that. In any event, the address is almost certainly a false one – the "b" is highly dubious.'

'You say "he"?'

'He.'

'But . . . What are we to do now?'

'Respond. I will instruct Lord ——— to reply this day to the given address and we will see what happens tomorrow.'

And so it was that the very next morning, Mr Williamson and young Harold Jute waited in the hall of the General Post Office at St Martin's-le-Grand.

There can be few interiors as impressive as that vast and lofty space, its graceful Ionic pillars stretching up to the distant panelled ceiling where pipe smoke swirls lazily looking for egress. Footsteps and muted voices seem to echo about that marble vault as self-animated spirits, and human presence is reduced to entomological proportions as it passes momentarily through.

Mr Williamson watched the people. There, a man walking quickly to the Money Order Office to cash an urgent note; there, a diligent clerk sent to make a collection from the Foreign Letter Office; there, a woman impatiently opening a letter that will break her heart; there, a rural visitor to the city gaping dumbly at this cathedral of communication that is larger and grander than the nave of his home-town church.

For his part, Harold chanced a few looks at the investigator beside him. 'Mr Williamson?' he ventured once he had mustered the courage, 'may I ask you why you left the Detective Force?'

'You may not.'

'Do you think, then, that we could talk a little about your police duties as we wait? I admit, I am quite fascinated with the work. Why, just today I read of a curious case that occurred over on Holywell-street a couple of mornings ago. I was wondering . . .'

'No. I no longer do that work.'

'I see. I am sorry to pry. Then . . . may I ask what drew you to the fine work of the Mendicity Society?'

'I have a skill. The Society is able to use it. Do you have more questions?'

'Well, I do wonder why we are waiting here rather than at St Mary's-hill?'

'You will see. It is about the right time. Let us ascend to the Returned Letter Office.'

Those of an inquisitive nature would do well to pay a visit to this, the most interesting room of the General Post Office. The letters that come here are lost, just as surely as many of the city's inhabitants are lost. They are posted, start their journey, but find no destination, waiting in limbo to be read and made real in another's mind. Who knows what news, what sentiments and what secrets find their way here like scraps whirled by the wind into the dead air of an alley?

'See here,' said Mr Williamson pointing to the board where addresses of undelivered letters are written. 'Number 2b, St Mary's-hill. Evidently, the letter carrier has discovered what I knew to be the case: there is no 2b. The letter has already been left here that so the rightful recipient may come to collect it when he sees the address listed.'

'And the pencilled notes alongside the original addresses?'

'The re-delivery addresses. I was hoping our mysterious letter writer would have come in and added his. Nevertheless, I have an idea that we can solve this mystery.'

Mr Williamson talked to one of the clerks and was handed a bulky ledger: the Daily Packet List.

'In this book, Mr Jute, the details of those same undelivered letters on the board are entered and, where relevant, the re-delivery addresses additionally appended. Let us look over previous weeks and ... yes ... look here: do you see the number of letters sent to the false address on St Mary's-hill?'

'There are many.'

'Quite. And the re-delivery address is identical in each case: 3 Moor-lane.'

'So – we go now to the re-delivery address at Moor-lane.'

'We do.'

It seems unnecessary to state, however, that the two gentlemen did not find the letter writer at Moor-lane. What they found was a rather portly old woman whose name was predictably not Mrs Burgoyne and who admitted, under the onslaught of Mr Williamson's threats of gaol, what the latter had assumed all along.

'I don't write the letters, sir. Truth is, I can't read too prettily – only this name "Burgoyne". I just receives 'em.'

'Then what? Who collects them?' said Mr Williamson, his notebook at the ready.

'O, nobody collects 'em. I takes out the money order and goes to the Post Office to cash it.'

'Without any proof of your identity as Mrs Burgoyne?'

'They knows my face and they never asks. If they did, I could organize a friend to swear it soon enough.'

'Hmm. To whom do you give the money?'

'To nobody, sir. I makes out a new money order – less ten shillings for my own troubles, you understand – and I posts that to a Mr Mann at an address on Milton-street. 'Tis but ten minutes' walk from the Post Office, but I posts it all the same.'

'Who arranged this process with you? "Mr Mann" himself?'

'O, nobody, sir.'

'What nonsense are you speaking now, madam? Who asked you to do this?'

'All the writers, they knows me and what I do. I just receives a letter telling me what to send and where. They all knows I ask for my ten shillings and that is that. No need to meet 'em at all – just how they like it.'

'Milton-street, you say? That does not surprise me at all. Are you familiar with that street's reputation, Mr Jute?'

'I cannot say that I am . . .'

'Hmm. No other street in the metropolis is more closely associated with the ink-fingered endeavour than Milton-street. It is home to poetasters and hacks, penny-a-liners, copyists, plagiarists, petty novelists and fancy-makers of all varieties. They do not stay long, for they are thrown out or imprisoned for debt before they can get properly accommodated. We should go there immediately – he is likely to be home and expecting letters.'

'Am I in trouble?' asked the fraudulent widow.

'Assuredly. You are to save all future letters you receive and a man will come to collect them. Fail to do this and you will find yourself at Newgate.'

Thus leaving the grumbling old woman, the two gentlemen made their way hastily to Milton-street. Unfortunately, even as Mr Williamson rapped at the door, the man they sought, having been forewarned just moments previously by a panting boy sent by the false Mrs Burgoyne, was exiting from a rear window with his few possessions almost spilling from his leathern bag. The reader need wonder not a moment longer, however, about his identity.

It was I.

THREE

What thoroughfare is there in London to compare with Holywell-street? Certainly, there are others grander and more handsome, just as there are those narrower and darker – but none have the distinctive character of this most unusual passage.

From the church of St Clement Danes to the church of St Mary-le-Strand it stretches, a line of sin strung between two pillars of virtue – a parallel shadow and antithesis to its majestic neighbour the Strand. As the broad courses of commerce and progress flow ineluctably around, human flotsam is washed here to eddy and drift at a different pace among the blind alleys and courts. And if there *was* once a spring here, it is now subsumed beneath the Old Dog tavern, all holiness lost.

Untouched by the Great Fire, the overhanging gables sigh with the pressure of history, closing almost together above the cobbles to shut out the light of modernity. No bold stone *façades* for these edifices: it is plaster and lath that peels away and decays over centuries of rain and wind, begrimed multipaned windows that admit only the merest illumination. Some call it charming; others call it rotten – a sewer in place of a well.

The shops are of a dilapidated sort, quite out of the current fashion for plate glass. Rather, they adhere to the style of generations past, wooden signs creaking above doors with tiny dimpled glazing through which to peer into another world. Whether anyone would want to explore this world is another matter: the second-hand clothes shops and masquerade warehouses offer only worn and faded goods; the barber's is a dingy bourn from which few travellers return, and moneylenders lurk in wait up unlit passages for the desperate.

But it is, of course, the booksellers who have made the street their own – and because of whom it has earned its reputation. Covering almost the whole southern side, their sloping trestles are stacked with spines and their windows thick with tomes and prints to snare the passer-by. Boys stop to gaze at maps and pictures of great ships; gentlemen pore over intricate engineering diagrams; ladies on an illicit diversion from the larger thoroughfares chatter about the latest images from Paris – and all are united in their loathing fascination, their fearful hope, their pagan Christian longing for immoral filth.

For it is also in those windows that the proprietor tempts the law with his blasphemous tracts, his lubricious tints, his provocative lithographs and proscribed copper plates. Crowds gather, people point, and outrage is the communal pleasure as all stare upon what must not be seen.

Should a gentleman venture into those shops and ask for something 'warmer' than the common fare, he might – if trusted – be directed into an upper room where the bookseller stores titles and pictures that would make an old soldier blush. Every variety of amatory endeavour is here described and depicted in terms of the basest and most lurid manner. No imagination is required, and none sought, in the works printed, stored and sold upon these premises.

The reader will have no doubt discerned my admiration for the place. There is something of the last century still existent there: the anti-religious liberalism and nonconformist spirit that has kept it a writer's bohemia. By which I mean a sanctuary for the poor, dissolute, oddly attired and tenuously employed; the press-men, publishers, printers and penny-a-liners; the freethinkers, church-haters, plagiarists, garret-dwellers, fantasists and barely sane.

And it was into this world that Inspector Newsome strolled that afternoon. He was accompanied by a tall and burly new recruit to the Detective Force: one John Cullen who, for the time being at least, was still officially a constable until his suitability for the superior department could be properly ascertained.

The indigenous populace of that place seemed to sense that the two were policemen, despite their lack of uniform. It was the same awareness displayed by hens when the fox is close, and Inspector Newsome was aware of the movements of the people ahead as they slunk into shops, closed doors and sent secret warnings to those who had set such mechanisms in place: 'Watch your merchandise! The buzzers are close.'

'This is the place,' said Mr Newsome to his colleague as they stopped outside Colliver's coffee house. 'The proprietress has left word that she will meet us outside and show us to the room. No doubt she does not want us to interact with her customers.'

Faces scowled from the smoky interior at the policemen. From outside, they looked in at a hearty fire and tables populated by boisterous red-faced men who were otherwise engaged in a variety of discursive activities. One group appeared to be having an energetic argument over a newspaper article.

'It is cold today, is it not, sir?' remarked Mr Cullen,

breathing into his hands and glancing out across the rain-slick cobbles.

'You are not on the beat now, Constable. We need not bother with such meteorological banter. Look around you; see what you can see. That is what a detective does.'

'Yes, sir.'

'And you need not call me "sir" while we are in the street. Our presence here has already been telegraphed to every business, but we need not advertise it further.'

Mr Cullen looked across the road and watched the directionless progress of an itinerant umbrella mender. With his back-borne burden of walking canes, broken ribs, flapping scraps and fishing rods, the man seemed an ambulatory human porcupine. Mr Williamson would have been able to say something insightful about the man and his background, mused Mr Cullen, who had once worked with the detective. The constable, however, could only think that this bitter cold portended snow.

Presently, a woman could be seen making her way through her customers to the door. She emerged in a cloud of smoke, heat and the earthy aroma of coffee.

'Mrs Colliver, I presume,' said Mr Newsome.

'I trust you will be letting me have my room back today,' replied Mrs Colliver. 'I am losing money every day with that man of yours standing at the door.'

Her cheeks were red with the heat of the coffee house. Her bonnet was tied so severely beneath her face that the cord vanished between her flabby chins. If she was not guilty of some crime, she exhibited all the signs of being so: eyes shifting about anywhere but on her interlocutor, and her hand nervously pushing stray tendrils of blonde hair back inside the bonnet.

'I can speak with Mr Colliver if you are busy,' said Mr Newsome.

'Dead. Now – let us get this over with.'

'I would also like to speak with you after we have examined the room.'

'I have already told all I know.'

'And you will do so again. You may lead the way.'

The lady hurried them through the coffee house to a wooden stairway that led upstairs to the rooms. There, the uniformed constable lounging at the door to number seven jerked to attention when he saw the detectives and did his best to look assiduous in his duty. Mrs Colliver jangled keys upon a ring.

'Nobody has entered this room since it was sealed – is that correct?' asked Mr Newsome.

'That's right,' replied the constable and the lady simultaneously.

'Good. You may leave us for the moment, Mrs Colliver.'

'Will I be able to rent my room tonight?'

'You will be advised of that momentarily, madam. Let me take the key – I will return it to you shortly.'

She muttered her way back downstairs while jabbing rebellious hair back into her bonnet and Mr Newsome held the eager Mr Cullen's arm: 'Do not touch anything in here, Constable. Use your eyes and let us hope that your brief time in the company of Sergeant Williamson has taught you something of investigation.'

'Yes, s—. Yes, Inspector Newsome.'

The room was cold due to the window still being wide open. The inspector walked over and looked at the ledge outside where the victim must have held on. There were no marks, but the night rain may have obliterated any. A scuff mark on the wall below the window may or may not have been caused by a rapid exit.

'What causes a man to leap from a third-floor window?' said Mr Newsome.

'Perhaps he was thrown,' offered Constable Cullen.

'I think not. Had he been thrown, I fear he would have gone head-first and been unable to grab hold of the ledge. No – something happened here that he wanted to escape from. And the door must have been barred to him.'

'There are four dirty glasses here,' said Mr Cullen pointing to a plain three-legged table. 'Were not only two men present?'

Mr Newsome bent and smelled each glass. 'Sherry. I must speak again to Mrs Colliver about her claim that the men ordered no drink. What else?'

'Neither bed appears to have been slept in. They are barely disturbed.'

'True, but look here by the pillow of the bed nearer the window: a long blonde hair, possibly of the unruly variety. Neither man had such hair.'

'Did the gentlemen have a lady in the room with them, then?'

'That remains to be seen, Constable. If they did, they did not use the beds, and she must have made a hasty exit after the precipitation of Mr Sampson. Or perhaps the hair has been here for weeks. Keep looking; there must be something else.'

In truth, there was little else to be seen. It was a room like any other room of its sort: a hearth with the fire long ago burned to ashes; a generic rustic painting slightly askew on the wall; a few sticks of unimpressive furniture and a smeared looking glass above a table.

'Can you smell something, Inspector?'

Mr Newsome sniffed. 'Nothing unusual. What is it?'

'I don't know . . . just the faintest . . . I don't recognize it.'

'I cannot smell anything. Have the chamber pots been used?'

Mr Cullen gingerly pulled them out from under each bed. He held out the one from the bed where they had found the hair. 'Yes. Look.'

'I have seen the contents of a pot before, Constable.'

'No, sir. It is something else.'

The two peered inside the gleaming white interior at the small brown mass inside.

'The pith and pips of an orange,' said Mr Newsome blankly. 'Perhaps it is that you could smell.'

'But there is no skin. Just this one chewed mouthful spat into the pot.'

'So what are you saying? That our case rests upon a missing fruit? Are we to alert the police constables of the city to keep an eye out for an injured orange?'

'No . . . but Sergeant Williamson—'

'Sergeant Williamson is no longer with us. We will have to do without him and his superhuman detective vision. I will admit, however, that there is a mystery here: the four glasses, the single strand of hair, the reason for Mr Sampson's leap. There are people we must speak to, and we can begin with Mrs Colliver.'

The two investigators ensured that the room was secure and returned downstairs to the private quarters of the land-lady, where the air was close and hot from the fire. No matter what the temperature, Mrs Colliver did not remove her bon-net, nor loosen the cords that held it stubbornly to her head. The two policemen had already removed their coats before sitting at the bare table in the centre of the room.

'Do you want coffee?' asked Mrs Colliver.

'That would be very nice,' said Constable Cullen.

'We will not, thank you,' said Mr Newsome. 'Let us get straight to business. I know, madam, that you have recounted the facts before, but I may understand them differently. I am a member of the Detective Force.'

'What's that, then?'

'It is a lot of trouble for you if you don't moderate your tone. Now – you have said before that you admitted the deceased, Mr Jonathan Sampson, at ten o'clock in the evening.'

'To his room, yes. But he arrived about an hour earlier.'

'Was he alone when he arrived, or with the other gentleman?'

'I cannot be sure. I do not see every customer. My impression is that he arrived alone and was joined shortly after by his friend.'

'What makes you think they were friends?'

'Mr Sampson seemed to know and like the other fellow.'

'I dare say I know and like the Queen, but she might not term us friends.'

'I mean, they had quite a lot to say to each other. They sat close and spent the time in discussion.'

'Discussing what?'

'How could I know, sir? The house is noisy at that time of the evening. There is food to be served.'

'Well, did they frown? Were they serious or jocular? Did they argue? Did they laugh?'

'They seemed contented enough, I suppose. Their heads remained close as they tried to make each other heard.'

'Or not heard by others. And you have said that they did not drink.'

'Only coffee.'

'Tell me about this other man. What was his name? What did he look like?'

'He did not pay for the room so I did not take his name. He was well dressed. A jovial enough sort.'

'Like myself, then.'

'Rather better dressed. And more jovial.'

'How old was he, do you think?'

'Quite young, I suppose. Twenty something.'

'An unusual friend for a man of Mr Sampson's years.'

'A man might have any friend he likes.'

'Indeed. Have you seen him here before or since?'

'No.'

'More, Mrs Colliver. You are withholding information from me.'

'I am not.'

'Then why do you shift in your seat and twitch so? Anybody might think it was you who committed the murder.'

'Murder? What are you saying? I don't want anyone talking about a murder at my coffee house. Can you imagine what they would say? "Go to Colliver's for a coffee and get murdered." He jumped!'

'How do you know? Were you in the room? I thought you were asleep when the incident happened.'

'I was. That is what I have heard. I do not know what happened in the room.'

'More of that in a moment. You told the inquest that the men went to the room at ten o'clock. They were both quite sober, you said. And yet we found four used glasses that smelled of sherry in that room. Can you explain that?'

'Might not they have brought their own drink in a bottle?'

'And four glasses? Nobody reported seeing the young man carrying a bottle.'

'You would be surprised what I have found people bringing to those rooms.'

'I am sure. So the glasses do not belong to you? I could take them and smash them if I wanted to?'

'If you like.' But Mrs Colliver's tone said that she would be happier if he did not.

The inspector scowled and looked at his colleague. 'Mr Cullen – have you any questions, or are you going to just sit there?'

The constable cleared his throat. 'Did either of the gentlemen have an orange with them, or buy one from a girl while here?' he asked, extracting a notebook.

'No. No orange,' replied the lady, forgetting for a moment the hair about to spill from her bonnet.

'And I would like to ask about a long blonde hair that we found on the bed nearest the window. Might it be yours?'

Mrs Colliver's hand went reflexively to her bonnet. 'It could well be. I clean the rooms myself.'

'Would you take off your bonnet for us?' asked Mr Newsome.

'Why?'

'Why not? Have you something to hide?'

'Nothing.'

'Well, then . . .'

Mrs Colliver looked from one man to the other, then at the tabletop as if making up her mind. Finally, with a grimace, she extracted the bonnet cord from between her chins and unleashed a mop of loose blonde hair over her face. But it was not the hair that the policeman noticed – it was the bloody contusion just above her forehead, the hair about it still caked and sticky.

'Who did that to you, madam?'

'Nobody. No one. I fell while cleaning the hearth last evening.'

'How did that happen?'

'Well, I . . . I was bending to rake the ashes and I slipped.'

'Slipped on what?'

'My dress.'

'I see. Because it looks to me like the mark was made by a blunt instrument of some sort being struck upon your head.'

'Wouldn't I have called the local constable if that were the case?'

'Yes, I am quite sure you would. I want you to provide us with a list of the other people who were staying in your rooms the night of the unfortunate event.'

'All gone.'

'That may be true, but I am certain you took their names – genuine or false – before you took their money. If I can locate them, I will speak to them to see what they heard. Have you a girl here cleaning or serving?'

'Only in the coffee house. I alone attend to the rooms.'

'Convenient. I will speak to the girl anyway. Now – you say you were awoken at two o'clock by someone moaning? Not by a man frantically kicking at the wall and trying to hold on to a window ledge?'

'By the moaning.'

'It must have been quite dramatic moaning.'

'Terrible. I thought at first it was the spirit of my dead Harold: Mr Colliver.'

'How do you know it was two o'clock?'

'It was my impression. I did not see a clock.'

'Could it have been three?'

'I suppose so.'

'What did you see when you looked from the window?'

'The poor man lying on the ground. The constable was bending over him.'

'And you recognized the man on the cobbles as your tenant despite having been rudely awoken, despite the darkness and despite the constable bending over him. You must have a very sharp eye, madam.'

'I have.'

'And you saw the incident from these rooms here, is that right?' asked Mr Newsome, standing and walking to the leaded window.

'That is right.'

'It is a sharp angle to see the cobbles below the fateful room.'

'Not if one opens the window.'

'I see that you have been rehearsed well.'

'What do you mean?'

'Never mind. Did you see the jovial, well-dressed young man flee from the place?'

'I did not. As you say, the angle is awkward. I only heard his voice.'

'What did he say?'

'Something like, "O, my friend has jumped from the window. I will fetch his friends."'

'He said "jumped" rather than "fallen" did he?'

'Something of the sort. Is it not all the same?'

'No. What did you do in the immediate aftermath of the incident?'

'Why, I went to the room.'

'And what did you find?'

'It was empty. The door was open. The beds had not been slept in. The window was open.'

'And the four glasses?'

'I must say I did not notice. I was distracted. Some other guests had been awoken and I tried to becalm them. Perhaps one of them put the glasses in the room while the door was open and I was otherwise occupied.'

'A natural enough impulse, I suppose, to put four used glasses in another man's vacated room. How long was the door open?'

'Until a constable came and asked me to lock the room. An hour or so.'

'And did anyone else enter during that time?'

'They may have. But most went back to sleep once the body had been removed. I did too – until the constable woke me about the door.'

'You sleep easily after one of your guests has been tossed from a window.'

'I work hard. I was tired.'

'So it would seem. We will wait here while you bring us that list of tenants. And fetch your girl.'

Mrs Colliver put the bonnet back on and stuffed her hair into it before muttering her way back down to the coffee house. As she did so, she saw the back of a man rapidly turning the corner at the end of the corridor and fleeing out through the alley door.

'*Hoi!* Stop! This is a private area!' she yelled.

'Who was that?' said Mr Newsome, appearing at the doorway.

'A fellow running from the corridor.'

'A thief?'

'There is nothing in this corridor to steal . . . unless he was listening at the door.'

Mr Newsome ran to the alley door and looked out. It was empty. He hurried along its length, looking for recesses as he went, and emerged into the street. Nobody there was conspicuously hurrying away from the alley.

'Pardon me, sir – did you see a man emerge from this place a moment ago?' Mr Newsome asked a passer-by.

'Why, yes – then he asked me if I had seen a man emerge a moment ago, ha ha!' replied the man with powerful gin-scented breath.

The inspector grimaced and fought an urge to violence. He turned back down the alley.

'Describe him to me, Mrs Colliver,' he said on returning.

'I saw only his back. He was wearing a broad-brimmed hat, dark trousers . . . he looked like anyone.'

'Have you seen him before?'

'It is hard to say without seeing his face. I think not.'

'Very well. See to that list, and fetch your girl.'

Mr Newsome returned to the fug of the private quarters and smiled at Mr Cullen. 'What do you make of her testimony, Constable?'

'It is not very helpful.'

'It is lies from beginning to end – that's what it is.'

'It is certainly lacking detail, but how can you be sure it is all lies?'

'Look at what she did *not* say. Her sentences are clipped as if she is frightened of giving too much away. She has an answer to every omission. That ludicrous comment about the ghost of her husband was pure theatre – I am sure someone else has put it in her mind. Then there is her general manner and that wound on her head, no doubt put there by the person who has silenced her. Still, there is little we can do, I suppose. We could arrest her, but no magistrate would gaol her for this.'

'You suspect the other fellow – the one who fled and said he was going for friends?'

51

'I can think of no one else who might benefit. Could it be that he visited her shortly before he fled and warned her not to tell the police anything? Could it be that the fellow who appeared to be listening at the door just now was the very same person? I have no idea.'

'What do we do next?'

'We investigate, Mr Cullen. We investigate further. Did Mr Williamson teach you nothing?'

'Yes, sir.'

'Let us first go out into that alley and see if we find anything that will tell us who else is interested in this case.'

FOUR

Who had been that man listening at the door?

There are many in this city of ours who are criminal: men (yes, and women) who would cheat, lie, steal and beat their way to a living. There are the poor, the ignorant, the godless, the callous, the heartless and the cruel – none of them strangers to the magistrates' court and the gaol cell. They drink, fight, cheat and wear morality loosely as a second-hand coat. It gives little comfort, but it has certain superficial benefits.

But none of these characters are as bad, as reprehensible and parasitical as the Society for the Suppression of Vice spy, whose role it is to prevent or prosecute infidel lectures, immoral congregations, profanity, licentiousness, drunkenness, obscene songs, swearing and – above all – the publication and supply of indecent literature. It is not the opportune pocket that he picks, nor the easy chance he exploits, nor the back-alley brawl that fills his stomach – no, *he* feeds off the desires of his fellow man at Haymarket, at Regents-street, at Fleet-street.

Here is one of the opprobrious race now. He ranges across the entire city, but Holywell-street is his preferred hunting ground, particularly of late. Let us observe him in the manner he observes others: dishonestly, anonymously, secretly.

See how he moves, insinuating himself among the passers-by as they stand before a window or wait for a cab. See how he peers over a shoulder, or at the reflection in a window to catch a questionable transaction. Watch his eyes dart and his ears twitch as he lingers just within range of a whispered exchange. He is waiting, always waiting, for a law to be broken.

And you can be sure he knows all the laws by rote. All that is required is for him to see the briefest glimpse of an indecent image being transacted, or for the street traffic to be held up for the merest instant by unhealthy interest in a shop window, or to overhear an exclamation of distaste at such a window, or to note a comment that might be interpreted as unChristian – and then he can run off to the magistrate or constable like an obsequious schoolboy to report his outrage. The culprit will be arrested and charged while he, the spy, will remain unnamed and free to continue his 'good work'.

We will allow this one to remain anonymous for not a moment longer. His name is Eusebius Bean.

No other Vice Society spy has prompted so many convictions and no other is as omnipresent wherever the scent of vice may lurk. Perhaps his success is due to his remarkable blandness: a face that, beneath his wide-brimmed hat, has nothing whatsoever remarkable about it; clothing that is nothing out of the ordinary; a manner that is unassuming to the point of invisibility – why, the man might well be a tailor's straw-filled model.

Only his tongue, flicking at the corner of his lips occasionally like a serpent, shows his anticipation of the next transgression to be observed. Will it be a plaster medallion showing Leda and the over-familiar Swan? Or an ornamental meerschaum pipe bowl featuring an Oriental scene requiring no imagination? Or perhaps an indecent print slipped briefly from its brown envelope by a hawker so that a gentleman customer might verify his purchase?

To the people strolling and shopping, he is just another of the street's insalubrious characters along with the beggars, the flute-playing fool and the blind knife-sharpener. But the shop-keepers and kerb-dwellers of the street know him for what he is and they are careful to avoid him. No doubt they would like to beat him half to death in a dark yard, but they fear the power behind him.

As well they might, for, as we have already seen, Eusebius Bean has been following Inspector Newsome and Constable Cullen. It is something out of the style of his usual work but he has all of the necessary skills, and – as we will soon see – a particular impetus to act so.

We may be sure that he had heard quite enough before fleeing from the corridor outside Mrs Colliver's rooms. But the reader may be wondering why this man, whose common province was the explicit print and saucy sonnet, was follow-ing the two policemen in the first place.

As a rule, those of Eusebius's ilk exist almost independently of the Society for the Suppression of Vice. Paid weekly, ignor-ant of each other's identities, and kept at a sanitary distance from the respectable people at Lincolns-inn-fields (who might find distaste in their methods), they seldom meet their pay-masters in person – so it was a great surprise to Eusebius when, the day before Inspector Newsome's visit, a gentleman wearing smart livery had approached him wordlessly in the open street and handed him a letter, then loitering as if for a response.

Vocationally fearful of observation, Eusebius had stepped

into the doorway of a closed shop and – after checking the liveried gentleman was not watching him – unfolded the paper.

Dear Eusebius

Your duties as a diligent servant of the Society have come to my attention and I commend you on your many prosecutions. Due to the efforts of men like you, ladies may go about the streets less afraid of encountering debasement of the most horrific and degrading form, and gentlemen may be assured that their sons are not being corrupted.

Indeed, I would like to make use of your talents in a personal matter of extreme delicacy and importance to the Society. I would be grateful if you would accompany the man who handed you this letter to my home address, where I will give further detail and extend my thanks in person.

J.S.

The signature did not mean anything to Eusebius, but then he knew virtually nothing of the Society itself apart from its money in his pocket. The letter-bearer stood discreetly at a distance while he read, then motioned that they should walk a little to a waiting carriage.

Unaccustomed to such travel, Eusebius sat uncomfortably upon the fine leather seat and tried not to touch any of the lacquered wood about him as they headed west along the Strand, along Pall Mall and towards the parks. The sweet-smelling interior of the carriage was a pocket of luxury amidst the noise, smoke and stench of the city passing by the windows.

Was this, he wondered, how a gentleman sees the world? His tongue quivered at his mouth's edge, tasting the air of refinement.

If the carriage had impressed him, the letter writer's abode cowed him. Its stone *façade* towered over him and he felt quite naked once divested of his broad-brimmed hat and damp gloves by an unsmiling male servant. He patted his hair, which, unused to seeing the light, was quite slicked to his head.

The room he was shown into was empty. A healthy fire crackled in the grate and evidence of wealth and taste adorned every surface: oil paintings upon the oak-panelled walls, a rug with Oriental designs in the centre of the room, and furniture with inlays and curlicues that made his own rough chattels look like firewood. There was a smell of flowers or some Oriental scent in the air

Not wanting to sit in any of the beautiful chairs, he remained standing with his hands clutched before him. Nobody came. He began to shuffle. Had his presence not been announced to the master of the house?

Feeling bolder, he walked to a large window and looked out into a garden. Still nobody came. Finally, Eusebius could not resist. His sensitive ears alive for the merest creak of approach, he moved to a sideboard and opened a door to peer within at a selection of bottles. Then, after looking around, he opened a drawer to see some leather gloves and a pile of silk handkerchiefs. Theft was not his aim – only knowledge. Then he walked silently across the rug to a door leading to another room. A sound was coming from within and – being no more able to stop himself than a cheap harlot can resist a glass of gin – he could do nothing else but bend to the keyhole.

A man sitting with his back to the door could be seen from the shoulders up. His head was almost completely bald but for a few wisps of thin pale brown hair clinging to the scalp. The skin itself did not seem quite human – at least, not living. It was yellowish, flaky and encrusted all over with pimples at various stages of either pustulence or desiccation.

As Eusebius crouched at the keyhole, the man slathered some manner of unguent over his naked head with quivering fingers until the whole was anointed with the glistening stuff – a sight that even our observer found curiously repugnant. Then the man took a dark brown peruke from the table before him and positioned it on his head.

At that moment, the door was opened suddenly from the inside and Eusebius was caught leaping to a standing position as the man, in fact the signatory 'J.S.' of the letter, turned around. The servant within who had pulled the door open attempted to suppress a grin as Eusebius reddened dramatically.

'Do not be ashamed, Eusebius,' said the man in the wig, facing him now. His voice was half rasp, half gargle – as if he had not quite swallowed something.

'I am sorry, sir. I . . .'

'I said do not be ashamed. This was a test and you have passed. I need an observer just like you: a man who is inquisitive, a man who will not let a closed door stop him from learning what he must – even when he finds himself in unfamiliar surroundings.'

The man's face was similar in appearance to his scalp, only the skin was more scarred with cicatrices denoting a history of disruption. There was an aromatic air about him, but Eusebius tried to concentrate only on the diluted brown eyes, which were intelligent and amused.

'Come and sit by me, Eusebius. Would you like some tea?'

'Do you have milk?'

'Ah, a milk man, are you? I will get you milk if that is what you wish, but I hope it is not the milk of human kindness that sustains you.' He nodded to the servant by the door, who left without a word.

Eusebius, not discerning the allusion, made no response except to sit close by the man. The room was decorated in the same luxurious manner as the reception room, with the one difference that this one had many freshly cut and aromatic flowers arrayed in vases about the space. They were of exotic, and presumably expensive, types never before seen by the spy on his peregrinations about the city.

'Well, to business. You are apparently a close observer of Holywell-street,' said 'J.S.'.

'I spend much of my day there. There is plenty of vice.'

'So I hear, so I hear. Have you heard of the accident that lately occurred there?'

'The man falling from the window? Everyone on the street is speaking of it.'

'What are they saying, Eusebius? Tell me all you know. You are my eyes and my ears there.'

'An accident, as you say. The man was drunk and fell from the window. Some say he was a sod . . . I mean, he was of an abhorrent persuasion . . .'

'Do not be embarrassed. I have seen all manner of vice. The words of the street do not shock me. Has there been any talk of foul play in this case?'

'Do you mean murder? No, sir.'

'Good. Then let us not use that word outside this room. That is how rumours begin and we would not want to influence any investigations into the case with a false scent.'

The bewigged man smiled and placed a hand over Eusebius's on the carved wooden arm of the seat. Though the back of his hand was blotched and scabrous with the same canker that affected his face, the palm was curiously soft, dry and warm. It remained there, covering the clammy paw of Eusebius, even as the servant entered carrying a porcelain jug of milk and a glass on a silver tray. If the servant noticed the gesture before he left, he did not show it.

'The police are already involved, Eusebius. Soon, I expect the Detective Force will be visiting the premises of Mrs Colliver. It is of the utmost importance to me that their investigation is thorough. We know that there is vice lurking in every crevice of that poisonous alley and I want to see that it is all brought to light.'

'Yes, sir. But what can I do? I am not a detective.' Eusebius looked at the perspiring milk jug and flicked out the point of his tongue. His hand was still imprisoned gently under that of 'J.S.'.

'It is quite simple, Eusebius. I would like you to follow the policemen as they go about their duties. Whenever you are able, listen to what they find; talk to the people they talk to; keep note of where they go – and report all to me personally. Put nothing in writing. You may come here any time you wish – I seldom leave the house.'

'I am not sure I understand, sir. You do not trust the police?'

'It is not that. They are a fine body, but they are a secretive organization and I would like to know that justice is being pursued with all expedience.'

The hand upon Eusebius's gave a squeeze and was finally retracted, allowing him the opportunity to pour himself some milk with a slightly shaking hand. He gulped this down enthusiastically as his benefactor watched with an indulgent smile.

'My, you are a thirsty boy.' And with this, 'J.S.' extracted a silk handkerchief and reached to dab at Eusebius's milk-whitened lips, a gesture that caused the spy a degree of embarrassment.

'I will do as you ask, sir,' he said quickly.

'Of course you will. But remember one thing: this is our little secret. You are not to tell another soul.'

'J.S.' leaned so close that his face was just inches away. Eusebius caught a waft of the man's breath: a hideous miasma reminiscent of both rotten meat and fresh blood. It was as if that foetid air had emanated from a core quite corrupted and decayed – an eruption from an inhumed coffin rather than a living man.

'Not another soul, Eusebius.'

'On my honour, sir. May I go now?'

'Good boy. Here is a sovereign in addition to your remuneration from the Society. I have another for you each time you bring me good information. Will you have more milk?'

'No, thank you. I have business to attend to.'

'Well, be on your way.'

FIVE

———·◆·———

'What d'yer want?'

Misters Williamson and Jute stood at the doorstep on Milton-street and beheld with undisguised distaste the slatternly girl before them. With her hair in disarray, her perpetual grimace of irritation, and with lead-blacking on her fingertips, she was among the worst servants in all of London: in short, a cheap, slovenly trollop. That was my Nelly.

'Is your master or mistress at home?' asked Mr Williamson.

''Pends oo wants 'er, don't it?'

'I am calling on behalf of the Mendicity Society. I believe—'

'We don't give to no charity. Be off with yer.'

'We are not collecting, miss,' interjected Mr Jute. 'We are come to enquire after—'

'I got a list.'

'I'm sorry . . . I don't understand . . .' said Mr Jute, already ruing his attempt.

'I says I *got a list*. I am to clean the silverware – what little 'as not bin stolen; I am to beat the rugs; I am to take a letter to post; I am to buy a chop for Mr P . . . and now I 'ave to answer the door to charity beggars. An early grave for me, ain't it?'

'Listen to me, halfwit girl,' said Mr Williamson in a tone that seemed to slap her face, 'we are here to see your master or mistress – not engage in idiocy upon the steps. Alert them this minute or I will fetch a constable.'

At this, Nelly's face crumpled and she began to sniffle. Then began a high, unbroken whine as the first fat tears started to roll. She wiped a glistening streak from her nose along the back of her hand, and the two gentlemen looked at each other quite at a loss as the whine rose further in volume.

'Who is bullying my Nelly?' shrieked a voice from within.

And the voice was made flesh when a porcine specimen of the feminine race bustled Nelly from the door and beheld her visitors with the sort of huffing belligerence that might have intimidated a bare-knuckle fighter – particularly if he owed her rent. There was a smell of pork fat about her.

'Whoever you are looking for, he is not here,' she said.

'It is a man who very likely receives and sends many letters: a Mr Mann,' said Mr Williamson, perceiving her to be the landlady.

'I know the one. "Mr Mann" indeed! Hasn't paid his rent this last month. I was just about to throw him out this very day. You can aid me – I believe he is in his rooms.'

And she turned to walk back into the dark hallway, whereupon the two gentlemen followed her to a door. The landlady knocked and, leaving no time for a response, rattled the key in the lock and stepped inside.

'The cur. He has fled,' she said in a tone that suggested not the least surprise.

The condition of the room suggested that someone had indeed rapidly grabbed whatever clothes they could carry, probably along with some minor possessions of dubious value.

Drawers were open and a ramshackle wardrobe gaped open – as did the window.

'Please leave us, madam,' said Mr Williamson. 'If we are able to search this room carefully, I may be able to locate the missing rent arrears.'

'See that you do,' she replied, and lumbered out shouting: 'Nelly! *Nelly!* Where is that chop for Mr P, you lazy dolly-mop?'

'The woman did not even ask us who we are,' remarked Mr Jute, somewhat bemused by this excursion into the lower classes.

'She cares only about her rent. Now, let us see what our letter writer has left behind.'

The room was as typical an example of its sort as could be wished – the selfsame room occupied by countless other hopeful scribes across the city. There was the fireplace so small that it would struggle to heat the chimney, the mantel populated with tasteless porcelain knick-knacks, the faded curtains thick with dust, and carpets worn through almost to the wood. It was, in short, a place for ambition to starve and die.

A room can often say much about its inhabitant, but these rented cells at Milton-street offered slim opportunities even for a man of Mr Williamson's perspicacity. The men who stay in them own little and leave less when they flee.

Nevertheless, a mere member of the public could have discerned that a writer had stayed there. Witness, for example, the collection of newspaper columns collected together in a yellowing bunch, the number of words jotted on each so as to verify the earnings for that issue; witness the meagre collection of letters from sundry journals expressing interest in the article on London weather but not deigning to commission it; witness, indeed, the printer's proofs of an article for *the Times* that was cut to make space – of all things – for a piece on London weather by an editor of another journal. Are not these the papers on *every* writer's desk?

What else? A pair of shoes with the sole worn through on the right foot; a leather-bound notepad (unused); a lock of hair (ah, Nelly!) slipped into the folds of an article on brandy imports. Everything else needed to make a living (pens, wit, talent) had gone through the window.

Still, the two investigators found evidence enough. Fleeing precipitously as I had, there had not been the opportunity for me to take *all* of my papers and records.

'See here,' said Mr Jute, leafing through a sheaf of curling pages. 'It looks like part of a novel manuscript. Our letter writer evidently had higher ambitions.'

Mr Williamson peered at the uppermost page and saw the words 'Red Jaw' stand out from the text. He grimaced slightly. 'They all have higher ambitions, but we are not interested in that kind of "writing". Keep looking.'

A warped bookshelf holding a handful of books drew the ex-policeman: second-hand copies of Dante, Virgil, Homer and sundry other classics of their kind. He took each and flicked through the pages, holding them up by the covers and shaking them to see what he could find between the leaves. A fragment of a handwritten list fluttered from the Dante.

'Mr Jute – it seems we have our first piece of damning evidence. What do you make of this?'

Argyle: [Inverary Castle] 2 Hamilton-place

Beaufort: 22 Arlington-street

Bedford [Woburn Abbey], 6 Belgrave-square

Queensbury [Drumlanrig Castle], Montague House,
  Whitehall . . .

'Why, it appears to be a list of dukes and their London residences.'

'It is precisely that. Now – we are looking for a ledger of some kind. It will be hidden somewhere . . .'

And as he spoke, Mr Williamson cast his expert eye around the room, settling finally on the edge of the bed from which the lip of the chamber pot peered out. He bent down on one hand and knee and peered under, catching the sharp vegetal stench of my most recent evacuation. It was a shrewd move, for there he found two further pieces of evidence.

'What do you make of this?' he asked his companion, extracting the items.

'A lady's garter if I'm not mistaken, Mr Williamson.'

'And one with lead-blacking fingermarks on it. I think we must have another conversation with young Nelly. What of this other piece?'

In my haste to leave, I had grabbed my ledger but let half a loose leaf fall. It was this scrap that Mr Williamson took between thumb and forefinger and brought into the light. Though out of date, it would have assuredly put me in gaol if I had not leapt from the window that day:

Dec 4 – Addressee: Lord Wyndford. I am Charles
Peabody, ruined by poor investments but with a chance
to pay my creditors. Asked for a sovereign. Wyndford is
stingy but has paid once before. [Hand two].

Dec 6 – Addressee: Lord Holland. I am Josiah Weston,
a schoolmaster reduced to penury by poor health and

*debt. Four children: Jonathan, Milly, Victoria, Mary (a
cripple). Wife dead. Asked for 5l. Holland a benevolent
fool – send fortnightly. [Hand one].*

*Dec 9 – Addressee: Lord Brougham. I have expired due
to his lack of charity and been buried in a pauper's grave
– written from landlord's point of view. (Perhaps this
will encourage the old miser to pay up on other letters.)
[Hand four] . . .*

'He has been most industrious,' remarked Mr Jute. 'But
what is this notation about "hands" at the end of each entry?'

'It is the style of writing he employs: the written words and
also the tone of voice. Perhaps he writes as a woman, or as a
semi-literate fool. In this way, he can send any number of
requests to the same recipient and be paid numerous times.'

'Quite a skill. That's rather clever.'

'That is a crime, Mr Jute.'

'Of course, of course. So what do we do now? We have
evidence of his records but not the man.'

'We now know what letters he has sent and to whom. We
can intercept those letters, stopping the fraud, and study them
for further clues. We can also arrange for the false widow
Burgoyne to hand over any further letters she receives. Our
writer has been stopped momentarily – that is as much as we
can hope for until we can study more examples of his work.
Where he might be now is quite impossible to guess.'

'So we have done good work. My father will be pleased. I
wonder if young Nelly might make us tea and volunteer some
information about her special friend the letter writer?'

'Let us find out.'

The two gentlemen ventured downstairs to the kitchen,

where they were welcomed at the table by the landlady and served tea by Nelly. The fire crackled somewhat in vain against the chill, and, in the flames' sharp shadows, the landlady had even more of the swine about her: that broad nose of hers wrinkling and snorting bestially beneath an ill-concealed moustache.

'Tell me, madam,' began Mr Williamson as he readied his notebook, 'what else can you tell me of this gentleman lodger?'

'A cur. They all are, those writers. I don't know why I take them in any more. Did you find any rent money?'

'Regrettably not, but we may be able to find him with your help. Can you describe him?'

'A sly-looking sort. I felt he was watching me all the time. Had an odd grin about him, like . . . like the way a cat looks at you. Like he was too good for the likes of us. Sly he was – it comes from thinking too much.'

'I mean, was he tall or short?'

'About medium.'

'The colour of his eyes? His hair? Any marks that might distinguish him from another man?'

'He had brown hair I suppose. Thinning a bit. His eyes I couldn't speak of – I was nervous to look in them. He looked like all of them writers. You know what they look like. All the same.'

'His voice, then?'

'In truth, he wasn't much of a talker.'

Mr Williamson looked to Mr Jute to see if he could gain any sense from the woman, who was quite clearly an imbecile.

'Thank you, madam. You have been most helpful,' said Mr Jute. 'Now – a few questions for your girl here.'

'Nelly Jones,' said Nelly with a coquettish smile for the younger man. 'Will you put my name in your notebook?'

'Would you like us to?'

'Go on then.'

'What can you tell us about the man who stayed here?' continued Mr Jute.

She cast a rapid glance at the landlady. 'Nothing. He was a man. They's all the same . . . present company expected, I mean.'

Mr Williamson caught the glance and spoke to the landlady: 'Madam – I wonder if you would mind going to the butcher's on the corner and bringing I and my colleague a bacon sandwich – we had a terribly early start this morning. Nelly would go, but she must answer some important questions.'

'You will be paying for them, of course? And for my time in walking there?'

'Naturally, madam. Nelly will be safe with us.'

And with much huffing, snorting and wrinkling, the malformed harridan banged up the stairs and out of the house. Her servant relaxed visibly, slouching back in her chair and looking with a renewed lascivious air at the younger man.

'Was he a friendly man to you, Nelly?' asked Mr Jute.

''Pends what yer mean . . .'

'Did you spend time together talking? Did he help you in your duties, perhaps? Did he tell you anything of his writing?'

Nelly exhibited a smile that would have had her thrown out of church, had she ever attended one. 'He were nice enough to me. He told me pretty words from books. I dunno what some of 'em meant, but they was ever so pretty.'

'Do you know if he had friends in the city? People he spoke of who he would visit?'

'Ha! That's a good one! Friends, yer say? He hated *everyone*! Yer should have heard him when he come back from the coffee house: "So-and-So says he is to publish his history of

Sussex, the ———." Or, "That ——— Mr Thingummy is to receive an advance on his volume." Or, "Mr Wotsitsname, the talentless ——— got three pound for his piece in the *Chronicle*." Friends? He had none.'

'Which coffee houses were these?' asked Mr Williamson, his pen poised above the notebook for a salient fact.

'Dunno. Just coffee houses.'

'Tell me, Nelly,' said Mr Jute, 'if you were to go to him now, where would you go?'

'I never saw him outside the house. Truth be told, sir, I am mostly here in this very room, or in the rooms upstairs cleaning out the grates and suchlike.'

'We have reason to believe that his name was not really "Mr Mann",' said Mr Williamson. 'What did *you* call him?'

'I called him "Mr Mann". Missus says I am to call all tenants by their names so.'

'But when you were alone . . . when madam was not listening . . . did you call him something different? You have no need to be ashamed.'

'Well . . . I called him Andrew.'

'Ha! A capital joke,' expostulated Mr Jute.

'Explain yourself,' said Mr Williamson somewhat fractiously.

'Well, it might be a coincidence, but "Andrew" comes from the Greek. It means "manly" or "man-like". That would make him "Manly Mann".'

'Amusing, I am sure. A joke at everyone's expense. May I ask you a delicate question, Nelly, now that your mistress is out of the house? Were you and the gentlemen more than conversational acquaintances? More than friends?'

'Oh sir! What do you take me for?' said Nelly (my Nelly!) with sparkling eyes and a leer that answered the question more honestly. 'I am a *good* girl.' She flashed Mr Jute a look that suggested she was indeed as 'good' as he might expect.

'Hmm. I think we have gathered as much information as we can here,' said Mr Williamson, standing. 'Short of taking Nelly around every coffee house in the city in search of the man – and it might well come to that – I cannot think of anything else at present that will further our case.'

'I could stay and press Nelly further if you think it might be of benefit,' said Mr Jute.

'I think not. I dare say the man has already imagined that we might one day question the girl, which is why he has told her nothing of consequence – including his true name. That is the extent of his foresight and duplicity.'

'Do you think we will ever catch the man, sir?'

'Patience, Mr Jute. Patience and reason. He is somewhere close. These gentlemen are parasites upon the body of the city. They need its journals and publishers to survive. Why, he is most certainly sitting in a coffee house somewhere fewer than two miles from this place.'

SIX

In fact, Mr Williamson was quite correct. After leaping from that window at Milton-street, I had fled to one of my habitual locations: the Cathedral coffee house, just a few steps from the writers' paradise and purgatory of Paternoster-row and in the very shadow of St Paul's. Assuredly, I would not be returning to that lodging house – not least because a constable of the Mendicity Society had been situated nearby (there, and at the false widow Burgoyne's) lest I do so.

I am, as will have been discerned, a writer: of begging letters by necessity, of newspaper copy by inclination, and of novels by destiny. The reader may have been acquainted of late by a work of mine detailing a case in which Mr Williamson, then Detective Sergeant Williamson, was a prominent player. I would like to say the sensation of that work has made me a rich man, but I was obliged to sell my copyright at perilously short notice to save myself from an impending stay at Whitecross-street debtors' gaol. The publisher, I hear, has become a moderately wealthy man.

So, once again, I had been thrown upon the cold and blackened bosom of the city to sustain myself. There, amid the cacophony of traffic, the choking smoke, the faceless crowd and the inhuman masonry, I was once more to chase stories to fill my stomach – at least until the Mendicity Society tired of pursuing 'Mr Mann'.

O, there are bodies I could apply to for charity, but I cannot tolerate plaintive letters to the Literary Fund so that those 'literary' men can sneer at my body of work and deny me ten pounds because I am not a 'writer' in their eyes. I would rather chase the fire engine, loiter at the magistrates' court and gain access to the public inquest than take *their* charity.

Thus, at the windowseats of the house, I ordered a tongue sandwich with plenty of mustard and looked absently through the day's papers. Behind me, the noisy throng smoked and drank: penny-a-liners talking fantastical rubbish about the book of theirs that was sure to be printed by Such-and-Such publishers of Paternoster-row, or the article of theirs that was certain to run uncut in all of the following day's press. At talking they are artists; at writing, they are talented talkers.

Before me, the city was framed within the plate-glass window – an animated canvas containing everything a man could desire to fill his nib: the omnibuses bristling with top-hatted and bonneted passengers; the magdalenes with their insinuating winks; the false beggars preying on tourists; the street boys always one penny away from the grave; the lonely death in the upper room; the fallen horse and the splintered bone; the duke with dung-splashed legs; the thief with the duke's watch in his palm.

And the unnamed, unknown murderer walking there among the crowd – just another face, just another fare, just another man with the power and the intention to take the life of others. It could be any one of them, for any man or woman can kill. One might not think it, or will it, but there is evil in us all. It remains hidden and buried in those of a healthy mind, but if one should uncover even the outermost tip of that darkness within, it will grasp tentacularly and draw one in, deeper and deeper until wrong seems right and the most depraved longings are confused with the higher emotions. Lust, greed, ire, envy . . . these are the tips of the tentacles that lead to the rotting blackness at the core of everyone.

Take, for example, the young fellow sitting beside me. With a yearning and almost desperate gaze, he watched every attractive lady walk past, casting his eyes hungrily at their ankles. He scanned every torso in hope of the momentary movements of clothing against their forms. A bachelor, perhaps, or an unsatiated young husband. Such insensate desires take hold of a young man and, if unmoderated, motivate him to acts that would ultimately affront his morality, deny his religion, shame his family and bring calumny upon his name.

If I was in need of a story, I was to find it there in that index of fallible humanity. It would be some person, some incident, some crime, some phrase picked from an overheard conversation. Indeed, it was less than an hour later when Mr Williamson himself, fresh from his enquiries with Mr Jute, came into that very same coffee house and sat, alone, by the fire. Here was my story.

I watched him read through the newspaper: a man who carried his own dark space with him though surrounded by two dozen chattering others. The house became busier, but the seats either side of him remained empty. Was that a scowl, or a frown, that crossed his face as he read an account of the Holywell-street incident and its open verdict? Was he instinctively weighing the evidence for himself and deciding that he would have solved it soon enough?

Here was a man to whom stories cling as the smuts of the city air cling persistently to one's clothes. Thus, it was only natural, when he finally left the coffee house, that I return his interest in me by following *him*.

He took an omnibus east past St Paul's, and so did I, hiding my scrutinizing eyes behind a late-edition paper left on the seat. I was with him as he alighted at the top of Fish-street-hill, and I watched him, a seemingly diminutive figure inside his black greatcoat, as he stood looking up at the fuliginous finger of the Monument: a sombre digit disappearing into rain-laden grey.

'Not much of a view today, Mr Williamson,' said the attendant Mr Jenkins, taking the entrance fee from his most regular visiter.

'Much the same as always,' answered Mr Williamson. 'Do you have any news for me?'

'I have not seen any of the gentlemen,' said Mr Jenkins, answering the question he had been asked, in many forms, over the last seven years.

'Hmm. One day, Mr Jenkins.'

'I hope so. Not much custom in this weather. It will be bitter cold aloft, if you want my opinion.'

'Thank you, Mr Jenkins, but I think I will make the climb all the same.'

'As you wish, Mr Williamson. I was to close shortly, but I will wait for you.'

And climb he did: two hundred and two feet up those spiralling black marble stairs, his own footsteps echoing back at him within that chill space, round and round, seeming ever more inwards and upwards, towards the dim light of the upper doorway.

On exiting that portal, the wind of the upper aether whispers inimically that you have left the temporal world, teasing your hair with frigid breaths and drawing you fatally towards the edge where you see it: the great city of London.

No glittering spectacle, this – no fascinating canvas, but a limitless tapestry of soot and ash and smoke. There is the Custom House and the Mint; there is the flat, dead river with its steamboat plumes; there is the industry of Southwark pouring forth smoke from its chimneys; there is Westminster-bridge vanishing into the swirling greyness. And there is the void disappearing below.

Of course, there is now a cage around the platform so that the very sky is barred and the urge to oblivion withheld by iron. The metal is cold to the touch, even in summer, but still few can resist approaching the limit to gaze upon emptiness.

Dusk begun to fall. The dying day was edging towards a thin band of light at the horizon and fog could be seen rolling in: one of those suffocating, swirling infestations that would, in a few hours, make the Monument a crow's nest above an uncharted ocean, make church steeples angular peaks and Southwark's chimneys the ribs of half-submerged wracks raking through murky and deceptive shallows. St Paul's would become a leviathan drifting lost.

His breath hung still about him now in wraiths. Who can fathom what went through his head when he visited that place, this man who had seen death and cruelty countless times? As he stood there amid the swirling fumes of the city, did he too think of mortality? Was it eternal sadness that he felt, or was it revenge?

Finally, with the light fading, he descended into darkness.

'Anything of note this evening, Mr Williamson? Any fires? Any collisions on the river?'

'Nothing, Mr Jenkins. Nothing at all.'

The two paused momentarily beneath that broad plaque

of unintelligible Latin on the structure's base and the attendant locked the door. Then they shook hands once more and parted without further comment.

I followed Mr Williamson west.

He went on foot, as sure of the streets as only a policeman, or a criminal, can be. The night held no fear for him and the increasing fog did not disorient him as it cast haloes about the gaslamps. Onward he walked, following a pattern along Upper-Thames-street, to Bridge-street and then up Farringdon towards Skinner-street.

I need hardly tell the Londoner where he was bound, for one can smell the place well enough from a distance. Its noisome gases have shamed the city for years: those mephitic exhalations emerging as steam from the seething mound containing upwards of 80,000 bodies. It was Spa Fields burial ground.

Putrefaction poisons the air about this Golgotha, and morbific matter swells up from the earth – which is no longer earth but coffin upon coffin to the very surface so that the sexton must, under cover of night, rake bones from the surface and apply the long hand-drill to release noxious bubbles of rot that sting the eyes and coat the tongue with their coppery tang.

Such was the case as Mr Williamson entered the ground. The attendant – a being that appeared to be half clothing and half soil – looked up from his exertions with the drill and gave the merest nod of recognition. He could have been the First Man, or the last: a creature coughed from the clay partially formed and still lacking the higher reason of humanity, his feet clogged with the compost of decomposition and his features a loose approximation of his species. Both visiter and sexton were flickeringly illuminated by the sparking chimney of the squat bone house.

Mr Williamson raised the collar of his coat around his nose to mask the stench and walked to the modest gravestone in the 'good part' of the ground. A simple pewter vase containing a single flower had been knocked over at the foot of the stone and he righted it with cold hands. To his right, another attendant was at work heaping soil on to a barrow with a shovel.

'You there – what are you doing?' said Mr Williamson.

The man stopped, apparently startled by a living voice, and stared dumbly.

'Did you hear me? I asked you what you are about.'

The attendant with the drill approached. 'Bert dun tor. 'E clearn groan.'

Mr Williamson blinked and focused on the one who had made the utterance. The man's face was as devoid of sapience as an ox, and almost as hairy. The other sexton with the shovel, if conceivable, seemed still less cogent: a piece of animated skin and sinew with a dull light in his eyes.

'Mus clear owd wud. Mek spes fo' new ded,' continued the ox man.

'You are clearing old graves?'

'Yus'ser.'

'On whose authority are you doing this?'

The ox man shrugged. It was not clear whether he had understood the question or whether he simply did not know the answer.

'You are not to clear this plot. Do you understand? This part of the ground is to remain undisturbed. No digging here.' Mr Williamson looked from one grave-digger to the other. In that dark and enfogging place, he thought he could see a strand of glistening drool hanging from the chin of the shovel wielder.

'Here – I have a shilling for each of you. Now go about your business elsewhere.'

A coin dropped into each filthy palm and the two trudged towards the bone house with the barrow. Presently, a fresh plume of sparks erupted from the chimney, casting a feverish red glare across the vaporous atmosphere of the burial ground. A nauseating pall drifted over the neighbouring properties.

Mr Williamson bowed his head momentarily before the grave and then turned to leave. But as he did so, he was startled by a large black dog barring his path to the gateway. It did not growl or bark, but sat looking at him with an uninterpretable gaze. He stepped boldly towards the animal, yet it did not move. Rather, it maintained its unnerving stare as if trying to communicate some canine intelligence.

'Bruce!' yelled a voice from the bone house, and the dog stood to trot over to his master without another glance at the departing interloper.

Still, I followed: south now towards the river and over Blackfriars-bridge. He arrived home just as the fog was reaching its impenetrable limit: a moist, almost viscous opacity wrapping all in its choking cloak. Bricks wept with it; timbers absorbed it; horses snorted at it; gaslight disappeared in it, and it clung in droplets to his coat as he stepped over the threshold to see the envelope waiting for him.

There was no stamp or postmark; evidently it had been hand-delivered. He took off his coat and started a fire in the cold grate, postponing the opening of what was likely to be a message of little consequence from the Society – perhaps something from the enthusiastic Mr Jute, or a bulletin from one of the ongoing investigations.

Only after he had made a pot of tea and eaten a supper of the previous day's beef and potatoes did he sit in one of the two empty chairs before the fire to examine the letter. Following the rituals of experience, and to fill the hollow, silent time before he slept, he turned the envelope in his hands, smelled it, held it before the light and attempted to discern what he could.

There was no writing at all on the envelope, which was curious enough and suggested that it was not from the Society or, indeed, anyone who knew him. The quality of the paper was exceptionally fine. It was scentless and there was no trace of hair, fabric or other matter caught anywhere in the folds – in fact, it was quite pristine but for some minor marks where it had been slipped under the door.

He carefully opened the envelope with his pocket knife and folded out the letter, which was but a few lines written in a simple script. Brief it may have been, but the contents were to prove cataclysmic, leaving him sitting there, immobile, long after the fire had burned out and the chill of the night had crept into the house to sit beside him.

Detective Sergeant Williamson

You do not know me, nor is it necessary that you do so, but you may take it on the highest authority that what I have to tell you is the truth. You will soon learn as much.

The death of your wife Katherine seven years ago was not suicide. She was murdered.

No doubt you have read of the Holywell-street case of Jonathan Sampson. Follow this murder to its conclusion and you will have the solution to both crimes.

Sincerely
Persephone

SEVEN

We may be assured that Mr Williamson's bed remained unslept-in the night he received that letter.

Is it possible to conceive what thoughts entered his head when he saw those words stark and unequivocal: '*She was murdered*'? His instinct and logic had always told him that this must have been the case – had not the details of that inquest seven years previously provided evidence enough of it? But to see it written thus must have made the outrage as fresh and painful as if it had happened the previous day.

Did those words cause him to imagine her there, atop the platform seeing all and being seen by the murderers – those three gentlemen – standing there with her? Did he imagine her face turning to meet the eyes of the others? Despite all she had heard from her husband about the evil of men, she would no doubt have exchanged pleasantries with her co-viewers. When had her smiles turned to a mask of horror?

Murder. The act – even the word itself – was an abhorrence.

Of course, he had done everything he could in those weeks and months following her death, including re-questioning all those appearing at the inquest (in his own time), and haunting the base of the Monument itself for a glimpse of those three men. But hard proof had been lacking, regardless of his certainty.

He had not wept that evening he received the letter. His lachrymal facility had withered years ago and been replaced with a stoical carapace nothing could penetrate. Rather – as the night had stretched out slowly towards the dawn – he had called upon his cool analytical powers and applied himself to the letter with more focused precision than he had ever used with the begging fakements he saw day to day. It was, as yet, his only significant clue in Katherine's murder.

The letter had been addressed to his previous rank of 'Detective Sergeant', denoting that whoever had written it knew of him from his days with the Metropolitan Police. Since his official position was barely known to the newspapers (the Detective Force being necessarily subtle in its operations, and keen to protect its anonymity), this person must have garnered the information from another source – but one infrequent enough to be unapprised of his recent change in fortune. That is, unless the letter was intended for, and accordingly addressed to, a man who was known as an illustrious investigator.

This thought immediately prompted the logical next: the writer's reason for sending the letter in the first place. If simply an act of good faith, the mysterious delivery and origins would seem unwarranted. What else was being hidden along with the sender's identity? Could it be that they had a personal interest in the case which might be served by Mr Williamson solving it?

Following the argument through, the initial insistence that 'You do not know me' was rendered quite unnecessary by the unfamiliar signature and the lack of originating address. Why mention that Mr Williamson did not know the writer when this was self-evident? One assumption was that he did indeed know (or know of) them, and that they had stumbled over their own earnest attempts to disguise this.

An alternative, of course, was that the writer wished simply to disassociate themselves from the case, a supposition reinforced by the phrase *'nor is it necessary that you do so'* – a curious addition. If true, it suggested that the writer had no personal involvement and that any investigation would not need to touch upon their identity. What, then, was their interest in, and connection to, the two cases?

Admittedly, the whole thing could have been a tasteless hoax. If this were the case, however, it was the most convincing Mr Williamson had ever seen: one full of nuance, and credible because of its complex seeming simplicity. Its insistence on the *'highest authority'* was intriguing. The high authority of the writer? Or of the source of information? Or of the murderer's identity?

Mystery then piled upon mystery: *'You will soon learn as much'* said the letter. Mr Williamson's first thought was naturally that the writer was assuming he would re-start the investigation and discover the claims to be true. But was a further reading that something would happen shortly to confirm the letter's veracity? He considered possibly related cases he had worked on recently at the Mendicity Society and could think only of the particularly clever begging-letter writer he had so lately pursued. A connection seemed unlikely.

Whatever else in the letter was dubious, it had indeed been almost exactly seven years since Katherine Williamson had died. True, the incident had caught the attention of the whole city at the time, but how many remembered with such precision one date among many once the newspapers had been thrown away and the next scandal had trodden over the last?

Perhaps the letter writer had personally made time to check the date – or perhaps they, too, had some more personal reason to remember it.

A grammatical conundrum next presented itself. Where the letter said '*this murder* . . .', was it referring to the murder of Katherine, or, as correct grammar suggested, to the case of Mr Sampson? If the latter were true, this was a stupendous piece of news! What few newspapers that had reported the Holywell-street case had presented it as nothing more than a curious accident. Even so, Mr Williamson, who had spent years considering the facts of his wife's death, could not immediately discern any conceivable link between the two cases other than the lack of key witnesses and a death by falling.

What, furthermore, was Mr Williamson to make of the odd construction: '*Follow this murder to its conclusion*'. One might normally speak of a 'solution' to a crime, as the writer subsequently did. A 'conclusion', on the other hand, almost suggested that the end point had already been arrived at by its perpetrators, or that it was part of a story with a pre-defined ending. Some knowledge clearly stood behind the choice of words, which, in such a carefully evasive letter, were likely not to be purely accidental.

And finally, perhaps the most infuriating mystery of all: who, or what, was '*Persephone*'? The name meant nothing at all to Mr Williamson. In truth, he did not even feel sure how to pronounce it. Its singularity suggested to him a theatrical *soubriquet*, but he could not recall ever having heard it or read about it in the theatrical sections of the papers. Indeed, he could not have said whether it was male or female, though the hand seemed feminine in his extensive experience. If it *was* the false hand of a skilled forger, it was the best he had ever seen.

In spite of his best efforts, and as dawn cast its weak light through his curtains, Mr Williamson seemed no closer to finally proving the murder of his wife. Infuriated and frustrated by the letter and all it signified, his mind seemed close to exhaustion. Within his hands lay the answer to the mystery of his life – his one unsolved crime – and he was determined to do everything to find the solution. If that meant taking some time off from the Mendicity Society, then so be it; they valued him highly enough to allow him that.

Three avenues of investigation seemed clear. There was the true identity of Persephone, there was the Holywell-street case, and there were the original facts surrounding the death of his wife. He would pursue all three, even if it led him to the very abyss.

At that moment, though, surrounded by his jottings and his memories, sleep mercifully overcame him and he slumped, as he often did, in that chair before the cold ashes of the fire.

His rest was brief enough. He had awoken shortly before lunch, sent a letter to the Secretary of the Mendicity Society requesting a brief leave of absence, and had set about gathering together various editions of the last few days' newspapers. Saved from their future as kindling, these sheets allowed him to collate the few facts of the Holywell-street case. Naturally, the police would have kept back some key facts for themselves, but there was enough detail in the inquest reports for his keen mind to work upon.

Clearly, the young man who had run away from the scene was the key suspect. The landlady also had many questions to answer. Regarding the latter, there was one colossal barrier to Mr Williamson's further investigation: he was no longer a policeman.

There was nothing to stop him, as an interested citizen,

from questioning anyone he wished, but none had any obligation to answer if they wished otherwise. A less honest man might have pretended to be from the Detective Force, or at least capitalized on the name of the Mendicity Society to extract answers, but Mr Williamson was not that man. If he was caught doing the former, he could find himself fined or in gaol; if the latter, he might lose his one source of income and heap further shame upon his name. Criminality – but for one notable lapse – had always been anathema to his very being.

As he had feared, this state of affairs was proved to be exactly the case as he arrived at Colliver's coffee house later that evening and sought out the woman herself, who seemed emboldened after her temporary escape from the questioning of Inspector Newsome.

'Excuse me, madam,' he had begun, extracting his notebook, 'I wonder if you would mind me asking you a few questions about the recent incident here.'

'Who are you?'

'I am merely an interested party. Now – on the night of the incident . . .'

'I have spoken to the police already. I have nothing else to say to them.'

'You admitted two gentlemen to the room, the victim and—'

'Are you from the papers? I have talked to them, too. A load of animals, they were.'

'Madam, if you would just spare me a moment.'

'Are you something to do with the law? I am answering no questions to legal sorts.'

'Please, madam – I will take only a few moments of your time. The matter is a personal one; I am not a journalist, lawyer or policeman.'

'No. Be off with you unless you are ordering food. I am busy.'

Mrs Colliver turned her back on him and walked towards the kitchen. Mr Williamson fought the urge to strike the woman insensible with a nearby coffee pot.

There were certain clues here if only he could track them down – and if people would only speak to him. Unfortunately, Holywell-street did have the reputation of harbouring a recalcitrant sort. He turned to the nearest table where two cabmen were enthusiastically interacting with their beef and vegetables. Very likely they ate here at the same time each evening.

'Gentlemen – may I ask you a brief question or two? Were either of you on duty on the night of the late incident at this address?'

The cabman with a shining beard of gravy took in Mr Williamson's smart attire, the lack of numbers or other official insignia, and the non-police-issue stovepipe hat. This man who had interrupted his feeding had the vague air of policeman, but was clearly not one.

'—— off,' opined the cabman without malice, returning his attention to the plate as if his interlocutor had simply vanished from sight.

Indignation burned Mr Williamson's face and he found his hand moving instinctively to his hip, where he no longer kept a truncheon. He looked about the place to see who had observed the interchange and observed its inhabitants studiously avoiding his gaze. Clearly, they took him for some powerless official, or, worse, an eccentric. He knew well enough that every man has his place, his time and his uniform. And to them, he was a nobody.

Mrs Colliver was approaching once again, this time with a constable behind her. 'This is the man. He came in here asking me questions. Now he is bothering my customers. He says he is not a penny-a-liner or a policeman.'

The constable made to speak, but stopped short when he saw who the 'nuisance' was. There were not many constables in the city who did not know of Mr Williamson, either by appearance or reputation.

Mr Williamson did not speak. He merely nodded to the constable and accompanied him without struggle or fuss into the cold of the street, where a persistent drizzle had polished the cobbles to glistening dirt.

'I am sorry, sir,' said the policeman after the door had closed behind them.

'You are doing your job. You need not apologize to me.'

'Is it the Sampson case you were asking about?'

'Yes. Can you tell me anything of it?'

'I cannot.'

'O, come now, Constable. I know how you fellows talk. I was a beat policeman myself for many years. You must know all the facts.'

'It is not that. I am not permitted to speak of it.'

'Yes, I understand that. It is common to keep certain details from the populace, but—'

'No, sir – I am not permitted to speak with you in particular.'

'What? That cannot be. On whose orders?'

'Inspector Newsome, sir. He made it clear some months ago that we are not to talk to George Williamson about any case touching upon the Metropolitan Police. He said that you are no longer a policeman and must not be privy to our affairs.'

Mr Williamson could not respond for a moment as commingled emotions of anger, incredulity and humiliation raged beneath his impassive exterior. It was fear, however, that was the dominant sensation – fear that this impassable impediment might forever prevent him from the solution he had sought for so long.

'I am sorry I cannot help you, sir,' offered the constable.

'Hmm. Hmm. I understand . . .'

'I do know that Constable Cullen is working on the case with the inspector.'

'Constable John Cullen of Division L?'

'Yes, sir. Only he has moved to Division A now. He might become a detective.'

'Hmm. Indeed he might. Thank you for your kindness, Constable.'

'Please do not let anyone know I spoke to you, sir!' he shouted to Mr Williamson's departing back.

But the ex-detective sergeant was no longer listening as he strode on towards the Strand and headed west, undistracted by the clattering chaos of traffic, the steaming ordure of the horses, the yells of hawkers and omnibus drivers, and the ever-churning crowd. On these immense thoroughfares, he was just another passing face exhaling steam, just another hat and coat, just another ephemeral existence flowing through the city that would outlive them all.

He walked with purpose towards Charing Cross, the rhythm of his feet on the streets a soothing influence upon his mind. By the time he passed the swirling torrents of carriages around Trafalgar-square, his thoughts had ordered themselves once again and he was following another, far quieter and more ordered route through his own reasoning. Night might have fallen upon the city, but the inner illumination of his thoughts was bright.

The name. The name seemed theatrical to Mr Williamson. If not the actual identity of a performer, it could well be that of a character. But how to say it? 'Purse phone'? 'Percy phone'? He did not want to mispronounce it and find ridicule or, worse, a lack of recognition. So he had written the word on a page of his notebook and would show it when he reached his destination.

That destination was the Haymarket Theatre, and more particularly the private rooms of its manager Mr Buckle. If there was such a performer, or such a role as Persephone, Mr Buckle would surely know of it – provided Mr Williamson could find him in a temperate state.

He may not be known to the public at large, but there can be few writers who have not heard of Mr Buckle. Any aspiring comedian, tragedian or melodramatist with ambitions of seeing his words in the mouths of actors had first to aim his text beneath the eyes of this theatre manager. Never mind that he preferred to work only with a select list of accredited playwrights – there was always the slimmest, most fantastical, chance that a striking scene might take his fancy and bring the unknown literary starveling to fame and fortune.

Indeed, his study within the secret unseen warrens of the theatre was a graveyard of discarded, disgraced and disreputable manuscripts. Upon his desk, upon the floor around it, upon a sagging leather chair was a veritable snowfall of sheets: here a lady compromised by her decision; there a young man facing a choice that might ruin or make him; here a scene of bloody murder heard from the wings; there an imitation of Master Shakespeare that might well have been titled 'Hamlet's Return'. And there, ignominiously buried beneath a tower of other rejected imaginings, was one of my own: a poignant tale of a writer making his way in the city.

'Ah, Mr Williamson!' said Mr Buckle upon opening the door. 'Come in, come in. What brings you to my rooms?'

Mr Williamson reflected that his host was a man who seemed always hurriedly midway between his origin and his end, his hat askew, his clothes half-fastened and his attention momentary. This evening, he was relatively cogent, clutching a woefully unamusing comedy he had already paid thirty pounds for.

'I am pursuing an investigation, Mr Buckle, and I hoped to utilize your expertise.'

'But I have heard you are no longer with the Force. Is that right?'

'You hear everything, Mr Buckle.'

'The benefit of having half of London through the doors each night – or rather less than half these days. The cold weather perhaps; it is keeping them away. Our current production does not help matters, either. Have you seen it?'

'I do not go to the theatre.'

'Quite right. A loathsome business. So what prompted you to leave the Force? Did you finally have your stomach-full of crime?'

'It concerned elements beyond my control. This investigation is purely a personal matter.'

'Personal, eh? A juicy story, I'll bet. If I know George Williamson, it will be something dangerous. Murder is it?'

'Very likely.'

'How can I help? Will you be wanting to arrange another covert observation of my auditorium? That was an exciting episode, was it not?'

'Hmm. Not this time, Mr Buckle. It is only information I require. I remember that you once boasted to me that you knew every actor who had performed in the city over the last twenty years.'

'It sounds like something I might say. And quite true into the bargain. Won't you take a seat? I can clear away some of this scribacious manure and we can have a civil exchange.'

'Alas, I do not have time. Have you seen this name before? It could be an actor or a character.'

Mr Buckle stopped collecting the scripts from his chair and took the notebook, his memory flicking through a library of plays, scripts, shows, rehearsals, auditions and sundry narratives.

'No. It means nothing to me, Mr W.'

'Are you sure? You have never heard it?'

'I have not. It could be one of those foreign performers one sees at Vauxhall or at the minor theatres once in a decade. You know the sort: they come here from America or the Orient and do a show with serpents or fire or some such. I know nothing of that sort. They are not professionals. Where did you hear of this one?'

'It is something I am looking into. I thought it might be a performer, though I have reason to believe it is not a foreigner.'

'Well, you could ask at the other theatres or at the theatrical coffee houses, but if I don't know the person I dare say nobody will. I know every actor who has performed in this city—'

'For the last twenty years. Hmm. Well, would you mind asking your theatrical fellows about this name if you have the opportunity?'

'Of course. Of course. And do visit again! Are you sure I cannot interest you in tickets to the current drama?'

Mr Williamson closed the door behind him, reflecting grimly that Mr Buckle had likely already forgotten both the name and the request to ask about it. As he exited the theatre, he saw that the streets had become more populous. He pulled his coat collar up against the chill and stood beneath a gas-lamp as people moved around him.

In London, there are those who walk and those who stand. There are those who stride with purpose and those who dawdle. A man of the streets – a man like Mr Williamson – knows these rhythms and reads them as Mr Buckle reads a new script: searching for the subtext, the heroes, the villains and the next incident. One might know a man almost by his pace alone: the worker hurrying home, the idler waiting for the theatres to open, the thief waiting for his next victim, the mendicant with no destination but the grave.

Or the prostitute looking for her next payment. In Haymarket, even those with the sharpest eye would find difficulty telling the magdalene from the respectable women, for their dress is often of equal quality. Only the pace is different. The street girl walks with a meandering air, stopping to brush mud from her boot so that her ankles show, or tilting her face up to the gaslight so that her beauty may be better admired from across the street. She seems to be purposeful enough in her direction, and indeed she is, but that destination is vice. When she perceives that she is observed, or when another falls into the same pace, recognition occurs. Sometimes it is accidental, as when a lady is unduly and scandalously propositioned while waiting for a carriage, but for the main part the messages are correctly read.

'Aren't you a handsome one?'

Thus was Mr Williamson interrupted in his cogitations by the girl at his elbow: a whore.

'Be gone, girl. I am not looking,' he replied with pursed lips of distaste.

'I perceive you *are*, sir. Perhaps you don't know what you want?'

He turned to look at her face. She was a pretty girl of about eighteen, her large eyes dark beneath the light and a black woollen shawl making her skin seem paler. An investigator he may have been, but her smile and her untarnished beauty were weapons against even his ossified heart. 'Be gone, I tell you. I am not interested.'

Her teasing smile remained undiminished. 'Tell me what you're looking for, sir. I may be able to help.'

He was about to take a sterner line with her when an idea occurred to him. Did not many of these girls know each other and recommend each other when a customer's tastes extended to something different? For a small share of the charge, they might pass business among their sisterhood. It was a wild supposition, but the girl might at least have heard of the mysterious letter writer as one of her own trade. He took out his notebook and showed her the name. 'I am looking for this woman. Do you know her?'

The girl cocked her head to see the name in the gaslight, brushing against Mr Williamson so that he was forced to smell the cheap but affecting perfume rising from her naked throat. 'Perhaps I do know her. Could you tell me more about her?'

'She is older than you – perhaps as old as thirty. She will be educated and most likely has gentleman customers, some of them very powerful. She is probably interested in the newspapers and can read and write well.'

'What might she look like? Have you had relations with her before, sir?'

'Hmm. Hmm. I . . . She is refined, intelligent . . .'

'The colour of her hair? Her eyes?'

'I do not know. I know only her name and some other details.'

'I see.' The girl gave a knowing smile. 'So what would you *imagine* her to look like, this woman you seek?'

'Er . . . She is likely attractive. A slim frame. Her eyes are green or blue. I . . . don't know. I cannot say. Do you know the name or not?'

'I believe I may know the lady. A very refined sort to be sure. She doesn't walk the streets as I do; the gentlemen come to *her*.'

'Where will I find her?'

'I'll show you. She won't admit just anyone, but if she knows it's I come to collect a shilling for the service, she may see you. And if you'll pay me a shilling also . . .'

'Fine. Is it far?'

'Sir, I believe you would cross our island to find this lady. Am I correct?'

'Hmm. Proceed. But I warn you: there will be trouble if you are cheating me.'

The girl smiled, unconcerned, and rested a hand on his forearm. The contact seemed to burn through the dense wool of his coat to the sensitive skin beneath. He felt his face suffusing with a blush. 'You will not be disappointed, sir. I promise you,' she said, squeezing his arm to magnify the effect. 'My name is Charlotte, by the way.'

Mr Williamson glanced around and then allowed himself to be led by Charlotte into the flow of people. It had seemed to him during that brief glance that nobody had noticed their conversation.

But his usual observational acuity had failed him.

EIGHT

Who was the lurking observer watching Mr Williamson lured into the eyes of pretty Charlotte beneath that gaslamp on Haymarket? All in good time – let us instead begin with a necessary preamble.

There is, as we have seen, a commodity in this great city of trade that is listed in no newspaper: a commodity sought by every man (and, yes, by women also) as ardently as daily sustenance; a commodity so precious that it has found a thriving market since the dawn of history; a commodity that is advertised and sold at competitive rates in almost every street of London. And yet it is an all but invisible trade.

The satiation of the carnal impulse.

The need is as powerful as hunger, as consuming as opiates, as ruinous as gin – and as thriving as the population of rats beneath our streets. The Christian charities vociferate that there are 80,000 magdalenes in London, and it may well be true. One thing is certain: for every life, there is also a secret life of dreams and desires that cannot not be fulfilled by one's money, one's work, one's religion, one's marriage. And it is a life that must be fed, that feeds upon the ravening soul, even as it leads to disease and ruin.

Inspector Newsome was a close student of such matters. His years on the street had taught him more than any Oxford degree or medical book about the nature of humanity. In crime, as in love and desire, there were patterns to be observed and locations to be mapped. Information, as ever, was the arbiter in the battle between good and evil.

To this end, Mr Newsome had taken steps that – if Sir Richard Mayne knew of them – might have seen the inspector before the magistrate and his career in the Detective Force in peril.

Every constable knows where vice resides on his beat. He knows which house is a brothel; he knows which girls charge what to whom and where they lodge; he knows where 'special' services may be obtained, where illicit prints are sold and which servants have additional sources of income. How does he know such things? Because he is out at all hours watching the day and the night unfold. He talks to everyone and becomes a repository of rumour to rival even the infallible telegraph of the scullery maid. And if he occasionally takes a shilling to look away from the odd transaction, would he not be aiding the commercial progress of the city's valuable trade in satiation?

Imagine if all of that information could be collected together. Would not the secret lives of many become an open book to the man who had sole access to them? Would not such a man discern invisible threads of crime interweaving throughout the whole of society itself? Inspector Newsome thought so.

Within his office at 4, Whitehall-place – known also as the headquarters of Division A, or Scotland Yard – there was a locked oaken cabinet. Inside that cabinet was a heavy ledger in which the lascivious secrets of London were kept, restocked

daily by reports collected from across the city by those constables – particularly of Division C, Haymarket – who wanted
to protect both their jobs and the illicit payments they took.
Their notes and messages came directly to that office and were
entered meticulously into the ledger by the inspector's personal
clerk.

As well as introduction houses, brothels, supper rooms
and the abodes of London's finest courtesans, all manner of
perversion and peculiarity was catalogued there. A little
whipping? Go to Mrs ——— at that unassuming address on
Regents-street, or to Mrs ——— at Margaret-place. If of the
sodomitical taste, the brothel of Vere-street attracted an
elevated sort (though unfortunately prone to the occasional
blackmail case), whereas ladies seeking extra-marital services
found the curious male brothel of Bond-street highly recom-
mended. For flagellation of a more varied and aesthetic nature,
one might choose from Tavistock-court or Russell-square –
and many did.

As for the common brothel frequented by costermongers,
sailors and soldiers, they were too numerous to monitor, and
the people visiting them were of sufficiently little consequence
to bother with. If, perchance, a notable man should visit them,
the beat constable would soon know and report it.

Five days had now passed since the Holywell-street incident and, having locked his office door, Inspector Newsome
was scanning the most recent entries in this most valuable
resource. Contained in it was information that might have
shocked the entire city and caused scandals to besmirch the
very structures of power, but he had become accustomed to
what he saw there. True, he could scarcely use the knowledge
he had, its nature and origins being too sensitive – but that
didn't mean it wasn't, or wouldn't be, useful.

Here was Lord —— out for another thrashing at Russell-square; it was becoming almost a weekly thing for the man. And there was Mr ——, that venerable lawyer whose colleagues would have been more than intrigued to know than he was wont to dress as a lady twice a week at Mrs ——'s. Ah, and Bishop ——, whose love of his fellow man took a more literal than exegetical form at his weekly visits to Vere-street. Such upstanding gentlemen – all with ready rhetoric on sin – were themselves all wallowing in the sewers of vice.

For reasons of his own, the inspector was looking particularly for those names connected with the Society for the Suppression of Vice, whose members were frequently well represented in this book of shame. Were the truth about those particular men and women to be revealed, St Paul's itself might crumble upon its foundations in ignominy.

Greater revelations were yet to come – not least those concerning a certain ex-detective – but at that moment his clerk had entered from the side office and advised him that Sir Richard was waiting. The inspector locked the ledger away, dropping the key into his pocket, and picked up a pile of books as he left. There was much to discuss.

'So the woman is quite clearly lying,' said Sir Richard, having listened to the inspector's summary of the interview at Holywell-street two days previously.

'Doubtless she is. But there is little we can do. A force more threatening than the police is keeping her silent, which is interesting in itself.'

'Quite. But which force is that? What else have you discerned?'

'We spoke to the woman's girl: a rather stupid sort who I believe knows nothing of value.'

'I see. How *is* Constable Cullen faring in the Detective Force? Has he learned anything from Sergeant Williamson as we had hoped?'

'Rather not. The man is slow-witted. I will allow him to stay until a replacement can be found, and then I fear it will be back into uniform for him.'

'It is your decision, of course. A pity – I thought we might make something of him. Now tell me about the other residents at the time of the incident. One of them must have heard something.'

'It seems that the majority of them – all men – gave false names and addresses as is common in these places. I regret now that I did not earlier secure all of the rooms to be searched – it is too late now to find evidence. Nevertheless, I have been able to locate one of the guests, one of whom Mrs Colliver happened to know by sight: a Mr Jessop, a bookbinder of King-street who claims he took a room there because he was too drunk to walk home. Fortunately, his was the room opposite the one where the incident occurred: number seven.'

'I fear you are going to tell me that he was so intoxicated that he remembers nothing.'

'Much more intriguing than that, sir.' Inspector Newsome paused, delighting in its effect upon his superior.

'Well, out with it, Inspector! I do believe you have missed a career in the theatre.'

'Yes, sir. Mr Jessop retired around the same time as the two gentlemen: at ten o'clock. By that stage, Mr Jessop was virtually insensible, but shortly after closing his door he claims he heard the door opposite being opened and closed, and voices including that of a woman.'

'Mr Colliver showing them to the room.'

'Presumably. Thereafter, and here he could not be sure of

the time, he heard footsteps in the corridor that he assumed to be other guests going to their rooms. He says he saw their shadows moving through the crack at the foot of his door.'

'Did he hear their doors opening or closing?'

'He did not.'

'What do you make of that, Inspector?'

'That the other guests closed their doors quietly? That he was too drunk to notice? He says he heard no voices this time – only footsteps.'

'Very considerate guests at Colliver's coffee house. Is that all?'

'No. He was awoken again in the early hours by a door banging. He had no idea of the time but it was still dark. Again, he heard a number of footsteps but no voices. Then somebody entered his room.'

Sir Richard sat upright in his chair, as Inspector Newsome must have known he would. 'Somebody *entered his room*? Was the door not locked?'

'Mr Jessop said he thought it had been, but he couldn't be sure due to his state. The door was locked when he awoke the next morning and his own key was on the floor inside. In fact, when I checked with Mrs Colliver, she found that the spare key to the room was missing.'

'Who was the intruder?'

'A man. He pushed Mr Jessop in his bed as if trying to wake him, or see if he was sleeping. When Mr Jessop finally stirred, the man said to him that he should forget anything he had heard that night or he would be murdered.'

'Are you sure this was not all just a gin phantasy? What do we know of this mysterious man?'

'Mr Jessop said that the man's voice was calm and well spoken like a gentleman. He said he knew he was not dreaming because he saw the silhouette of the intruder against the open door.'

'Is that all? He is threatened with murder in his own room and that is the extent of his memory?'

'It was early in the morning. Mr Jessop was still crapulous. Indeed, he went back to sleep and awoke late enough that our constable was already stationed outside number seven when Mr Jessop left. The constable did not think to question him, but I have verified the fact with our man.'

'Why was this not heard at the inquest or reported to his nearest police station?'

'Alas, Sir Richard, not every Londoner has the high public-spiritedness we expect.'

'I certainly expect less of that tone, Inspector. There *must* be something more than simply the words spoken. Is there no description?'

'The intruder was not wearing a hat. He was most likely clean-shaven. There is nothing more that can be of help.'

'The more I hear of this case, Inspector, the more convinced I am that there is something fearfully complex behind its seeming inconsequence.'

'May I ask, sir – have you heard anything more from the Vice Society?'

'A pertinent question, and one I should answer. I am being asked questions from the highest quarters of that Society about this case. The newspapers may have lost interest, but those with influence continue to harass me for a solution to the crime. Your revelations today suggest that there is indeed a secret to be unearthed.'

'Does this change my investigation?'

'Only that we must continue with the greatest alacrity until it is solved. I am uncomfortable being under the scrutiny of these people. Tell me of the other drunken witness to the accident, the mariner Ned Coffin.'

'I have been unable to locate the man. Our constables know of him, but he is not where he habitually resides. If he is alive, he will surface shortly and we will talk to him.'

'I see. Let us hope so. The family then – we have spoken of Mr Sampson's brother and sister who attended the inquest.'

'The sister is still inconsolable and, I fear, has in any case an unrealistic conception of the deceased. His brother, how-ever, provides a clearer picture of a bachelor who spent much of his time at his club, at the supper rooms and in the company of ladies.'

'By ladies, you mean prostitutes.'

'Yes, sir. It seems he spent much of his money on ladies somewhat beyond his pocket. He was in debt to a few of his fellows, but in no danger of being gaoled for it.'

'Did his brother know of any reason why he would have gone to the coffee house, or with whom?'

'He said it was probably just a place to take a girl he had met.'

'Does that seem likely? He was with another man.'

'Yes, sir.'

'But . . . O, I see. Do we have anything new on who the other man might have been?'

'Perhaps from Mr Sampson's club. The brother said he had never met any of Jonathan's friends. It was almost, he said, as if his brother wanted to keep his family and friends separate. Understandable enough for a single man with that style of life, one might say.'

'I suspect you are correct. Have you been to the deceased's home at Hoxton?'

'Indeed. The brother took me there. It was all quite normal

for a single man living alone. No evidence to help our case, except perhaps a rather impressive library.'

'What manner of books? One might know much about a man from his reading.'

'That is what interests me, sir. I have brought a few examples. The titles are on the spines. I have the other books under lock and key.'

'Ah, I was wondering at those volumes you brought in with you. Let me see. Pass them over.'

'I should warn you, sir—'

'Give them here. I do not recognize the titles: *The Cult of Ganymede*; *Eispenelas and Aitas*; *The Corinthian Rites*; *The Art of Astyanassa* . . . a historical interest, then.'

Sir Richard opened the slimmest of the volumes, *The Art of Astyanassa*, and was met immediately with an image demonstrating the adaptability and flexibility of a lady so inclined to please a number of gentlemen at one moment. The police commissioner flushed, cleared his throat, and rapidly turned the page to see two ladies and two gentlemen engaged in a tangle of limbs that would have been improper even if they had not all been quite naked. His jaw clenched, and, with his eyes refusing to meet those of Inspector Newsome, he closed the covers and picked up *The Corinthian Rites*, opening it at random to read a line. Whatever was written there blanched his blush into pallor.

'There were dozens of these books, sir. Many of them illustrated so – some of them in French, Latin or Greek. They are not cheap – perhaps ten shillings for the larger leather-bound ones. I note that the publisher and vendor of most of them is one Henry Poppleton of Holywell-street. I also found a recent bill from that publisher concerning a delivery of books.'

'Yes, yes. I know of the man; he has spent a few periods in gaol for his outrages upon public morality. Tell me, Inspector – have any of our men seen these books?'

'Only I and Constable Cullen, sir.'

'Good. I do not want this . . . this unspeakable filth polluting the Metropolitan Police as it has infected certain minds in our society. I trust that you will keep the books locked away until the moment we can dispense with them. Then they should be burned.'

'Yes, sir. I have made plans to visit the publisher as soon as possible to question him about Jonathan Sampson and anything else he might know.'

'Good. Good. So – is there anything further?'

'One thing only. I went to the deceased's place of work to speak with his fellows there. They all described him as something of a solitary figure: an intelligent man, a diligent worker, a civil enough sort, but not one to mix freely with work colleagues. Everything as one would expect bearing in mind what we know.'

'Indeed. And his club?'

'That is proving more difficult. Naturally, I would like to gain access to the club to speak with those who spent time with Mr Sampson in his "secret" life, but obstacles are being put in my way: such-and-such a time is inconvenient; the secretary is unavailable on this day; visiters are not allowed on such a day . . . I wonder if your sources at the Vice Society might help me gain access.'

'Which club is it?'

'The Continental.'

'I know of it. It has something of a reputation. Perhaps I can contact some of its more respectable members. I will see what I can do.'

Inspector Newsome collected the indecent books from Sir Richard's desk and put them under his arm in preparation to leave. 'Well – if that will be all . . .'

'Wait, Inspector. You told me two days ago that you thought this was an accident. Do you still believe so?'

'Sir – if this is not a murder, I will retire.'

As those two senior figures spoke, perhaps the reader has been wondering about the whereabouts of Constable Cullen, who was not of a sufficient rank to appear alongside Inspector Newsome in Sir Richard's office. He did not have his own desk at Scotland Yard and instead was waiting in an anteroom for his superior to return for further investigation.

Life as a detective was not as he had imagined. It involved long hours and a lot of brainwork of the sort that Sergeant Williamson had made look so simple when they had worked together just a few months previously. When that great investigator had left the Force, there had been much rumour and gossip among the men about the reasons for it, and many had come to John Cullen for his opinion. In truth, he could offer nothing but the physical abuse his erstwhile superior had sustained on the case. That, and the small matter of aiding a prisoner's escape from gaol.

Mr Williamson would have had the better of this Holywell-street case by now, mused Constable Cullen, who found it a fabric of lies and mysteries that simply could not be teased apart. How to prove that Mrs Colliver was lying? How to interpret the bleary-eyed and drunken testimony of Mr Jessop? There must be *something* – a clue – that was staring them in the face. If only he, John Cullen, could discern what that was, he might be accepted into the Force permanently and, one day, himself become a great detective.

Needless to say, that was never going to happen. Had he been able to look just a few days into the future, he would have seen something far more interesting – and he would have realized that he would be working once more with Mr Williamson sooner than he could have expected.

NINE

⸻

Mr Williamson was most uncomfortable. As he walked stiffly arm in arm with Charlotte up Windmill-street, he felt that everyone was watching and judging him. Surely everyone could see that the girl was a magdalene and that he was her client?

In his mind, he stopped her a dozen times and told her that this was a ridiculous idea – that she was clearly lying, that she should leave him and return home rather than walk the streets. But if there was the slightest chance that she did indeed know a woman called Persephone, this might be his best opportunity thus far of moving closer to a solution.

He walked rigidly upright, as if the gentle pressure of her arm in his were a mortal threat to be resisted at all costs. He tried not to look at her.

'If you talk to me, people will think we are friends rather than lovers,' said Charlotte, discerning his discomfort.

'We are *not* lovers!' said Mr Williamson, rather too loudly.

'Still, you might at least speak to me as we walk. What is your name?'

'A fine time to ask. But I would prefer not to tell you.'

'Then make one up. "Charlotte" isn't mine.'

He looked sidelong at her and beheld again her youthful beauty. She smiled as if she had known him for the whole of her short life. How could she smile so and yet be mired in depravity, selling her body to sin every night? How could she be so pure of complexion and yet be rotten to the core?

'Why do you call yourself Charlotte?'

'It's a pretty name, isn't it? Prettier than my real one anyway. Aren't I pretty?'

'I . . . well . . . I suppose so.'

'My, you're a flatterer!'

Mr Williamson blushed deeply and returned to his stiff demeanour. 'Are we almost at our destination?'

They were walking west along Brewer-street, and Charlotte steered them right into Golden-square, whereupon she approached a grandiose-looking house and produced a key. The door banged shut behind them and Mr Williamson had entered that pulchritude-baited trap . . .

We will see presently what he experienced there, but perhaps it would first be beneficial for us to take a brief digression (or transgression) into Charlotte's world that we might understand it better.

I have had much cause (for one reason or another) to investigate *Venus vulgaris*, and she is a curious species. Oftentimes, she begins her career at a tender age: sold into her trade by poor parents, or tricked into it by a procuress and trained in the arts of pleasure, or attracted to it by the sums to be made with a pretty face. Charlotte was of the latter variety: a milliner's girl who found she could make much more money by 'being kind to gentlemen'.

Stroll across London from West to East and you will see their varying habitats. At St James-square, the prettiest girls vie for the attentions of gentlemen who, for a short time, might maintain them in rooms of their own – at least until a younger and more attractive girl catches the eye. At Regents-street, the girls are still among the finest of their type, and if they occasionally stroll out, it is to visit the supper rooms before they retire home with a new friend (though it is easier in winter to rely upon the services of an introduction house, where she can meet a suitable fellow chosen for her, for a small consideration, by the discerning mistress). Even at Soho and Leicester-square might one find a pretty specimen, though her dress does not have quite the style or newness of her westerly neighbours, nor her face the same light of youth.

Head further east from here, however, and one enters the realm of the true street girl. Yes, she has a certain charm, but it is of a vulgar and degraded sort. These are the girls we see entering the coffee houses late at night and flirting shamelessly with the customers, or loitering about the shopping streets to snare a gent wearing fine gloves. Or she might hang out of a lower-floor window on Waterloo-road to attract her prey with an indecent show of bosom and a saucy invitation. Or perhaps she occupies a brothel, from which she rarely ventures into the light of day. These women are no victims; it is the men who are *their* victims.

Alas, beauty fades and tastes remain with the fresh and the young. The bright young thing of St James's or Mayfair is, twenty years hence, the carrion crow of Ratcliff-highway, St Giles's and the docks: so lined and withered that only sailors and soldiers will pay. What they once did for a sovereign then, later, for a pound, they will finally do for three shillings. And if not for money, for a handkerchief or a glass of gin. One must survive one way or another, and the sisterhood of Venus always survives.

Charlotte, it need hardly be said, was of the finer sort. Her rooms were paid for by a gentleman who was not her father (though assumed to be such by her neighbours) and she had the wit to be firmly established in the west. Like the most successful of her kind, she was a shrewd enough judge of character, having learned some time past that it is the older man, the married man, who is the reliable and grateful customer. Perhaps that is what she saw in Mr Williamson as she walked down Haymarket that evening – for, assuredly, she chose her clients more than they chose her.

'May I make you a cup of tea? A glass of sherry to warm you up? It's bitter these days, isn't it?' she said as she took off her shawl and bent to start a fire in the grate.

He looked around at her lodgings, brightly lit now in the gaslight. The *décor* was not lavish, but it suggested the kind of income that he could not himself boast of: good furniture, a new rug, clean curtains of damask and a number of paintings. Above all, the room had a lady's touch that he had not experienced for some years – an atmosphere that seemed warm and light in contrast to the bleakness of his own home.

'No thank you,' he answered. 'Is this the home of the woman we talked about?'

'It is. She lends me her key for when I have visitors. I expect her home shortly.'

'You told me on Haymarket that she will not admit just anyone, and yet I am admitted already.'

'My, what a memory you have! She lives in the flat upstairs – we will hear when she arrives. Tell me: what profession are you in? My first guess was policeman from the way you looked around the street, but there is something else in your manner that I cannot place. And are you going to take off your hat and coat and take a seat, or will you stand there like that until the lady arrives?'

'I would prefer to stand.'

'As you wish. I am going to sit here by the fire and warm my legs.' And at this Charlotte sat and raised her skirt fractionally so that her ankles were exposed. If she had done it for Mr Williamson's benefit, she did not show it.

'Hmm. What time does the lady typically arrive home?'

'Perhaps nine o'clock.'

'Is she in the same line . . . in the same . . . What is her profession?'

'You may speak to her and ask her all you like, sir. But in the meantime perhaps you will speak to me. You have a kind face. Won't you tell me what you do?'

'I work for a charity.'

'O Lord! Don't talk to me of charities, sir!'

'Why not? They do much fine work about the city.'

'I'm sure they do, but they are forever meddling in my business: those from the Magdalene Hospital at St George's-fields, or the Guardian Society at Bethnal Green or the Society for the Protection of Young Females. So many invitations I have to save myself! And spend the rest of my days in Chapel or in service? That is not the life for me, sir.'

'Do you not regret your life of sinful wickedness? Are you not ashamed at having sold your virtue?'

At this, Charlotte reacted in quite the opposite way he might have expected. She laughed. It was a throaty and unabashed laugh that made her slap her thighs, arch her back and put her head back, showing off the shape of her body and her delicate throat in the process.

'Regret, sir? O, not a bit of it! And you need not shake your head sadly so at my laughter – I am no poor waif of the streets. Better this life than that of a *wife*.'

'What do you mean? A wife has a home and her honour. She has a man who cares for her, and she has love.'

'O, sir, I am sure you are a good man, but you have not spoken with women as I have. Marriage is nothing but bondage for most. They give up their freedom, their youth and their life for a man. You speak of love, but what of desire?'

'A woman, I mean a respectable woman, does not feel desire. Her duty and her pleasure is to produce and raise a family . . .'

And here, once again, Charlotte began her laughing, animating her frame with such a carefree and sensuous manner that Mr Williamson was made quite uncomfortable at her lack of decorum. He had never seen a woman so unrestricted in the way she inhabited her own body.

'"Does not feel desire", sir?' said Charlotte when she had regained her power of speech. 'What woman does not feel desire? She might not show it for fear of bringing shame upon herself, but a woman feels desire just as a man does. Perhaps even more so. Have you never been among the working districts after dark in the summer months?'

'I have.'

'Then you will know what sounds emanate from every dark alley and every bush when the public houses close. It is not only men who make those sounds, though I might add that when they do it's the women who cause them.'

'Hmm. Hmm. It is almost nine.' Mr Williamson looked at his pocket watch to avoid looking at the heat- and laughter-flushed complexion of Charlotte.

'I have made you blush. I am sorry. Let us return to the subject of charity. Why don't you sit? At least take off your hat and coat. It is lovely and warm here by the fire.'

'You are no supporter of charities,' said Mr Williamson, still standing and behatted.

'And with good reason. I knew two or three girls who agreed to be taken in by those charities and now they are dead.'

'What do you mean?'

'They were killed. That's God's truth.'

'Absurd. They may have been killed, but there is no connection to a charity. That is just street talk.'

'Really? Did you hear about the girl on Holywell-street the other night?'

Mr Williamson was about to respond with another rebuttal when the street name struck him. 'Are you sure? There was nothing in the newspapers about a dead girl, and I have read all of them. There was, however, another incident on that street recently – five days ago.'

'That's when it happened. I don't read the newspapers so I don't know about any other incident. But Lou didn't kill herself, I can tell you that.'

Despite himself, Mr Williamson ventured to take off his hat and finally sit beside Charlotte at the fireside. The heat almost immediately began to warm through his coat, and he extracted his notebook. 'Charlotte – I would like you to tell me everything you know about this girl Lou.'

'What is this? Why do you need that notebook? I was right – you *are* a policeman!'

'No. I used to be a policeman – a detective. I am one no longer, but I believe the case of your friend might be part of a greater mystery.'

'I see. This changes the situation a little. I wonder if you might pay me now, sir, before we begin to talk.'

'Hmm. I see that you are a clever girl. I will gladly pay you a pound if what you tell me is of use. And you can have your shilling now in recompense for bringing me here. I must warn you, however: I pay for the truth only.'

Charlotte gave a theatrical pout at the suggestion she might be any kind of artificer. It was a most attractive expression. 'I agree. For a pound and a shilling, I will tell all.'

'Then begin with her death,' he said, handing her the money.

'They say it was suicide, with prussic acid if you please, and they found her in an alley off Holywell in the early hours. None of it makes sense, though. First, Lou had no reason to kill herself. She was happy. A beautiful girl she was: tall and slim with lovely blonde hair. She had just found an older gentleman to keep her and she knew she would have a good income from him. Secondly, Holywell was not her pitch – she was a west-end girl as I am, and used to a better sort. Somebody must have taken her there.'

'How can you be sure she did not take her own life? Perhaps she was with child.'

'Ha! When did you ever hear of a working girl who got in trouble, sir? That is only servant girls and milliners' assistants. We skilled girls know how to control our courses by—'

'Please – I need not know the details of your trade. Is there anything else that would make you think it was not suicide? Anything other than her seeming happiness and her being away from her pitch?'

'Perhaps I could not prove it to a magistrate, but I *know*. Would you yourself not know the truth if a close friend or loved one was said falsely to have committed suicide? You just know. And prussic acid? What a horrible way to do it!'

'Hmm. Do you know any more about this older gentleman she had found?'

'Only that he was well off and had a good position in

society. She would not tell me his name, of course. I might have stolen him for myself!'

'Where did she meet him?'

'He saw her from his carriage and invited her to his house. She returned a few more times after that. More than that I don't know. I didn't see her for a few days before her murder.'

'You insist that it was murder, but what motive could there be? And why use prussic acid when a cudgel or razor would do just as well? It is a curious murder weapon.'

'Why, to make it look like a suicide of course!'

'To what advantage? I cannot see any reason. The very fact that her death was not reported shows that the death of a pr . . . of one of your kind is considered to be of little conse-quence. Why go to the trouble?'

'I don't know *why*! I just know she was killed.'

'You said this was connected to those charities for fallen women. What was Lou's connection?'

'She had applied to the Magdalene Hospital a few weeks previously. It was after a man beat her and she got afraid. But they were forever pushing scripture at her and she couldn't stand it, so she went back to the game.'

'I still fail to see any connection.'

'There were others. Kate who lived on Dover-street: she was at the Guardian Society for a while. They found *her* in the Thames in May. And Mary of Clifford-street: another prussic acid job after she applied to the Magdalene Hospital. That one *was* in the papers, I'm sure. In July, it was. You will never find me going to those people – not even if I end up a toothless hag selling my a— at the docks.'

Mr Williamson frowned at her language and made a note of the names and places. 'Hmm. These charities take in many girls. Many more leave, and I am sure some subsequently kill themselves.'

'You don't believe me, do you?' said Charlotte.

'I am dubious.'

'But you wrote it in your notebook, so you must be interested.'

'I am always interested in justice.'

'I see that you are. What else are you interested in, I wonder?'

It seemed, as they had been sitting by the fire, that Charlotte's clothing had somehow become looser and less decorous, as if she had been surreptitiously revealing more of herself. Mr Williamson saw that one of her legs was exposed almost to the knee and that the graceful curve of her calf was quite as pale as her face.

She smiled in full knowledge of the effect upon her guest, who in his woollen coat was now feeling quite uncomfortable from the fire's heat.

He fumbled for his watch. 'Where is this lady? If you are—'

'She does not abide by any rules of mine, sir. When she returns, she returns. You may read if you like. Here, have a look at this one.'

Charlotte reached to a side table and took the first book from a pile. And as she leaned forward to hand it to him, he could not help but see inside the loose neck of her blouse – a sight whose effect upon him was profound.

'Hmm. Hmm. Hmm.'

For want of a more cogent response, he took the book.

'This is a new one of mine. Many visiters say it is my best,' said Charlotte.

Without looking at the spine, Mr Williamson opened the

cover and saw the publisher's name: Henry Poppleton, Holywell-street. The title page read *Levantine Mysteries*.

'I fear it is not the sort of thing I would enjoy,' he said.

'Read to me, sir. If we must wait here for the lady, we might as well spend the time in an improving manner. You should be in favour of that, taking the opinion you do of my life. Please – read to me. Just begin at chapter three.'

'I . . . I do not think it is appropriate.'

Charlotte could not know, of course, that Mr Williamson had once, many years ago, read to his wife thus, beside the fire. The memory of it, particularly under these circumstances, proved difficult.

'Please, sir. It soothes me so to hear another voice in this lonely room.'

He turned to the first page and scanned the first sentences. They seemed inoffensive enough. He looked around, as if expecting someone to be observing him engaged in such oddness. He looked at Charlotte, who seemed to have changed in an instant from the leg-brandishing temptress to an eager student, albeit one with a plaintively pretty face.

'Very well. Very well. A few lines only,' he said, with a look of extreme awkwardness. He placed a finger beside the first line to mark his place and began to read, at first with a faltering voice that seemed not to be his own in the silence of that unfamiliar room.

It was on the third day that finally I met the Sultan: a man of a mahogany hue in brilliant robes of scarlet silk and midnight velvet, bejewelled all o'er with the largest rubies and emeralds I had ever beheld. However, it was the sparkle in his eyes that was brightest.

He beckoned me closer to him and addressed me in a

tongue that I did not understand. When I expressed my incomprehension, his eyes flashed with anger and he rang a tiny brass bell beside him. Upon a moment, three burly Negro attendants dressed in golden sashes entered the room and grasped my arms with iron strength.

I screamed, but this only seemed to enrage the Sultan more. He stood and, in a single motion grasped the thin cloth of my dress and ripped it from me so that I stood there quivering quite naked before his . . .

Mr Williamson's eyes automatically scanned what followed, and heat rushed into his face. He looked at Charlotte, whose countenance had taken on an expression he had never before seen in a woman.

Her eyes were shining and her face was flushed. She had reclined into a position of such indulgent languor that her legs were positioned in a way no respectable woman would allow. The emotion she exhibited, though utterly alien to him, was fearful to behold – as if she had transformed during those brief moments into one whose moral and intellectual restraint had been replaced by something unashamedly animal.

He hurriedly reached for his hat and stood, letting the book fall to the floor.

'Hmm. Hmm. You have lied to me, Charlotte. You have brought me here dishonestly. There is no woman living upstairs – admit it.'

'Sir – you knew that all along. And yet you came.'

'I did *not* know it!'

'You did. I knew what you wanted from the moment I saw you on Haymarket. I am never wrong about a man. She, this woman, was simply your excuse.'

Quite apoplectic now with unvoiced emotion, and certainly

too vexed to speak, Mr Williamson walked to the door and exited the building without a further word.

Even as he walked and allowed the night chill to bleed the heat of Charlotte's fire from his clothes, it seemed that the scent of her seemed to cling persistently about him. His face burned with indignation and his fists clenched within the pockets of his coat as his mind worked at the next step – perhaps his only chance.

He did not go directly home. Rather, he went back the way he had come, along the Strand, up Fleet-street and on to Ludgate-hill, where he turned at the scarf shop to enter a small courtyard where the offices of *the Times* can be found. There, he managed to place an entry for the following day's edition:

Vauxhall Judge seeks Achilles from
Manchester and his Moor.

TEN

I wonder what the reader made of that excerpt from *Levantine Mysteries*. Truncated as it was, no doubt it was a little too 'warm' for many of our finer ladies and gentlemen, who look upon such texts as indecent corruptors of the innocent mind.

The truth, of course, is that no man (or woman) can resist these narratives. Were one to hide such a book in their private libraries, and were they to find this book while alone and unobserved, they would devour its every word and phrase in a phrenzy of hunger, reading until they had explored every scandalous term, every sordid tableau, every flouting of what they call morality. O yes, they would feel guilty about it later, and they would burn with hidden shame the next Sunday in chapel – but they would go back to that book, now hidden, to read again those words that appal and enthral.

I admit it: I have myself written such books and I am not ashamed. You will not perhaps be familiar with *The Bachelor's Almanack* or *A History of the Rod* or *The Youthful Adventures of Harry Grope*—— (the latter title – I concede – is indeed one of which I am not proud, but the fee kept me from gaol and so I am grateful for it). There is a skill in these works that your writer for the grander newspapers could not approach, nor your common playwright mimic. One must understand the secret desires of one's fellow man and see that bestial, blood-raging soul within even the purest heart. For are we not all animals despite our graces?

Do not think me aberrant; I write not of flagellation (the English vice), sodomy, or tribadism. You will find no equine or canine relations in my work, nor those tales of violent intercourse to which the Frenchman is prone. No, I restrict myself to the natural machinations of man and woman, and, when I am lucky, I manage to sell them to none other than that character of whom we have twice already heard: the book purveyor Mr Henry Poppleton Esq.

He is a legend among our publishers: a champion of the free word, a pioneer of the print, and a producer of songs, poems, translations, histories, radical irreligious tracts (for which he has spent a stretch in gaol) and, yes, obscene texts of the widest diversity and richness.

Watch him now through the window of his principal shop on Holywell-street, around which there is the usual gaggle of observers looking in at the latest prints exhibited alongside the serried spines and stacks. He is quite an unmistakable man, is he not?

Amusement quivers perpetually at the corners of his mouth, rather as if he is party to a secret of which his inter-locutor is unaware. Indeed, it seems that he is about to reveal at any moment that whatever he is discussing is a colossal joke at our expense. His whole demeanour, in short, is something akin to a wink, but a wink expressed by his entire body – a wink that descends like a gaudy curtain separating us from the inner machinations of his mind and leading us to wonder which side is the audience and which side the show.

He is often drunk, that is true, and he has an appetite out

of proportion to his height, but there is no man in London to match his encyclopaedic knowledge of the erotic library, and few to rival his way with an arch word or pithy deflation of a tiresome conversation partner. Both the former and latter qualities would be called upon at that very moment, as Inspector Newsome and Constable Cullen entered the shop with a chime of the bell.

It need hardly be said that Mr Poppleton knew immedidiately that he had policemen in his midst. In plain clothes, and virtually reeking of authority, they also had the look of men quite unused to the bibliophilic environment as they stared blindly upon spines that might well have been potatoes in a barrow rather than man's highest endeavour. The shelves of volumes stretching from floor to ceiling and forming a labyrinthine world of musty learning created an environment as foreign to them as the forests of the Orient.

'Yes, gentlemen? Can I help you with your selections,' asked Mr Poppleton to his latest customers, his lips twitching with a seething subcutaneous mirth.

Both policemen looked towards the counter where he stood. The taller one seemed to lack confidence – clearly he was of the lower rank. The shorter man with the curly red hair peeping from his top hat was obviously more astute. It was the former, however, who spoke (but only after a small nod of permission from the latter that suggested they had decided beforehand who would speak).

'Yes. We are looking for information.'

'You are in the right place; these shelves are stocked with it.'

'I mean information from you, sir, if you are willing to answer some questions.'

'What manner of questions might you have?'

'It is regarding . . . regarding the "warmer" sort of writing.'

'"Warmer" you say? I have books on Africa, on certain elements of Vulcanic geology . . .'

'I think you wilfully misunderstand me. I am referring to books of a corrupting sort.'

'Corruption is it? Then politics is the section for you.'

'Is this a bookshop or a penny theatre, sir?' interjected a now irritated Mr Newsome. 'My colleague asks questions and receives insults masquerading as wit.'

'I apologize, sir. I did not mean to imply that your colleague is an idiot. I suggest Dr Schiller's volume on the heating of liquids – that is positively full of information on warmth. In fact, I have a copy here – the last one – for ten shillings.'

'That is enough!' ejaculated Mr Newsome. 'As you are no doubt aware, we are detectives investigating a case. I would like to speak with you about your other stock: the more "curious" books that are not on display here.'

'I fear I do not know what you are speaking of, sir. What do you mean by "curious"?'

'You know very well what I mean: indecent and obscene publications. Affronts to public decency and corruptors of innocent minds.'

'Ah, you refer to the Bible! I have one just here . . .' Mr Poppleton's smirk was now threatening to take over his entire upper body.

'Blasphemy does not shock me, sir.'

'Blasphemy? Have you perused the Old Testament, sir? Have you read the Song of Solomon? Have you read of Onan? Have you read the Book of Leviticus? There are indecencies enough there to corrupt the young!'

'You know very well what I refer to.'

'To Shakespeare perhaps? We have incest, adultery and

wantonness in those pages to satisfy the most dissipated degenerate.'

'I am losing my patience.'

'Or are you thinking of something more classical in tone? Aristophanes and his women of Athens? Suetonius's tales of Emperor Tiberius and his little boys. Strato? Tacitus? Or a little Boccaccio perhaps? All recognized pillars of literature, and all with veins of the obscene.'

'Mr Poppleton – if you prefer, I could have policemen battering down your doors and searching this place for every page of filth. Or you could give me a few moments of your time.'

'Don't I give your men enough to leave me alone, Inspector Newsome? You *are* Inspector Newsome, I presume?'

'So you know who I am. Congratulations. The fact is that you are breaking the law at this very moment and I could arrest you.'

'Breaking the law how?'

'That crowd at your window is causing a nuisance, and I am certain there is material displayed there that is of an objectionable nature.'

'I believe that the Metropolitan Police Act of 1839 specifies that any such nuisance should take place in a public thorough-fare. The materials you refer to are on my private property.'

'Yes, I recall that you have some acquaintance with the law. Two years in Newgate was it not?'

'Man was made to read. I read what is of value to me and I know the law.'

'I would like to banter with you all day, Mr Poppleton, but you disgust me so I will resist the temptation. The fact is that a quantity of books published by you have been found in the possession of a man recently murdered on this street.'

'I know of no murder.'

'I refer to Mr Jonathan Sampson.'

'The fellow who jumped out of the window at Colliver's? That was not murder.'

'What makes you so sure?'

'What kind of a murder would that be, throwing one's victim out of a window?'

'The kind of murder designed not to look like a murder, perhaps.'

'You are the detective. I am sure I know nothing about it.'

'On the contrary – you knew the man. Your books were at his home.'

'I do not know everyone who walks through this shop, sir.'

'That may be, but I am certain you know each customer who buys a copy of *The Corinthian Rites* or *The Art of Astyanassa*. I am certain of that because you sell such titles personally to ensure that they are not being bought by a policeman in disguise. And you deliver them with a handwritten bill so that your customers might not be caught in public with the books. Therefore, you have met Mr Sampson on numerous occasions.'

Mr Poppleton's irrepressible humour appeared somewhat pressed as he glared at the inspector. PC Cullen, who had been standing beside Mr Newsome, looked on with some measure of grudging awe as the detective sprang his trap.

'Lost for a witticism, Mr Poppleton?' said the inspector. 'I note that you are not denying what I say.'

'All right – I met him. I sold him some books.'

'And yet you denied knowing the man. Why would you do that if you had nothing to hide?'

'There are aspects of my trade I might wish to hide, as you know.'

'Where were you on the night of the incident at Colliver's?'

'At my club. All night. I stayed there in a saloon room after rather too many sherries.'

'You will not mind telling me which club so I may verify this.'

'The Continental.'

'Ah, so you also knew Mr Sampson socially! That was his club also, was it not? What – no reply? You were quite garrulous when we entered and now you have become mute.'

'I knew of him by sight.'

'So perhaps now we can start with some truth. What can you tell us about your relationship with Mr Sampson?'

'He was a customer, nothing more. Yes, I saw him at the club, but one need not associate with customers outside of work. I believe he was happier not to have it widely known that he purchased books from me.'

'Understandable. Why do you think he was at Colliver's that night?'

'How would I know?'

'There was a man with him, as you may know. A jovial, well-dressed man. Does that sound like a fellow from your club?'

'Any number of them.'

'One that you might have seen talking to Mr Sampson?'

'I . . . cannot think of one. No.'

'You seem very uncomfortable, Mr Poppleton. Quite a pallor has come over you. Are you unwell?'

'I feel . . .'

'. . . as you did after drinking too many sherries on the night of the incident, yes?'

Mr Poppleton now looked most faded. His characteristic smirk was utterly deflated and he seemed a smaller man behind the counter. Inspector Newsome cast a covert look at Constable Cullen as if to say '*This* is how one questions a suspect'.

'I would like to see your order books, Mr Poppleton,' continued the inspector.

'Impossible. They are confidential. I could not possibly . . .'

'I am not asking. This is a police investigation and you will provide me with the evidence I seek.'

'I keep those ledgers at my printing shop.'

'Then let us go there now together.'

'I cannot leave the shop. There is nobody to relieve me, and I will not lose custom for this.'

'Constable Cullen here will stay and we will go to get the ledgers. It will not take longer than an hour.'

'I fear your constable would not be able to satisfy the needs of my customers and . . . and as far as I am aware, you would need to see a magistrate before taking property from any of my premises.'

'So be it. I will see a magistrate this very hour and then I will see those order books, wherever they may be. And do not think you can erase them in the meantime – I have receipts you have issued and we will be seeking to corroborate those sales.'

The door closed behind the policemen with a chime that seemed less cheery than the one that had hailed their appearance, leaving Mr Poppleton quite without his usual good humour. Indeed, after checking that the gentlemen had passed out of vision, he closed the shop and hurried upstairs, where few customers ever ventured.

Had the publisher been more observant in his hurried glance at the street outside, however, he would have seen that one of the faces peering in through a patch of pane-condensed breath was none other than Eusebius Bean.

The Vice Society spy had watched the whole interview.

Unwilling to expose his role by entering the shop, he was nevertheless sufficiently suited to his employment to make capital from what he saw. From his position there before the glass, he had watched it all unfold as if he had been an audience member at one of those dumb-shows of which the artistically inclined are fond, where each *moue*, each pointed finger, each blink and each minor alteration in the silent choreography of the *tableaux* becomes a script of the piece. To Eusebius's unblinking eyes, it had been a story of accusation, guilt, triumph, anger, evasion, threat and fear.

And what kind of spy would he have been if he had not been able to focus on their lips whenever possible, so that the words 'Sampson' and 'Colliver' – among others – made the drama even clearer? By the time the policemen had passed hurriedly by him, Eusebius might well have been handed a transcript of what had occurred there.

He had much to report to his sponsor 'J.S.', though the thought of seeing the man again was one that perturbed him somewhat. Indeed, he was thinking just of that purulent breath when a carriage stopped outside the shop and the liveried driver beckoned to him. It was the same fellow who had delivered the earlier letter. Eusebius nodded to him in acknowledgement and ascended into the carriage, which was empty.

But it was not to the gentleman's house that they travelled. Rather, it was to the address of a physician at Berkley-square. A sombre-suited gentleman was waiting for him at the door and, with wordless deference, showed Eusebius through a corridor smelling of unfamiliar medicaments to a treatment room, where his senses were further assaulted.

Lying on his back upon a table in the centre of the room was 'J.S.'. He was covered in a white sheet, under which he seemed to be naked – 'seemed' because, although the shape of his body beneath showed the familiar contours of an un-clothed male form, it also exhibited a multitude of small bulges in places where none should be. As Eusebius stared transfixed, it appeared almost as if these bulges were animated with the slightest pulse of their own.

'Do not be afraid, Eusebius,' said 'J.S.', turning his head to face the visiter. His wig was not in place today and his scaly, ruined scalp glistened with soothing oils. 'Today is a day when I must undergo a rather tiresome procedure that need not interrupt our business. I know you are a broad-minded fellow.'

'Yes, sir.' His eyes would not detach from those aberrant bulges.

'Tell me everything, Eusebius. What have our detectives been detecting?'

'Sir. They visited a man called Jessop, a bookbinder of King-street. I spoke to the man afterwards and he was quite open about it: he had been at Colliver's the night of the incident and had been rudely awoken in his sleep by an unknown assailant who threatened to murder him if he spoke of anything he had heard. I led him to believe I was a member of the press.'

'Fine work, my boy. Let us hope the policemen will be aided by that information.'

'They also visited the brother and sister of Mr Sampson, but they both declined to speak to me, whatever lies I manufactured.'

'People can be impolite. I suspect they have their reasons.'

'Yes, sir. The detectives also visited the deceased's home and place of work. I am afraid I do not know what they saw or heard there.'

'You are a good boy. Is there more?'

'Inspector Newsome has, alone, made enquiries at Mr

Sampson's club, the Continental, though he has not so far gained admittance.'

'And will very likely not succeed in doing so.'

'Sir?'

'Never mind. Tell me, Eusebius – you have seen much: what do you make of the two detectives on this case?'

'The older of the two, Mr Newsome, is a shrewd investigator. He is not like many senior policemen; I mean, he does not seem much like a gentleman. I believe there is more of the street than the library in his character. I would not underestimate him. The other man, Cullen, is a lower policeman. I cannot understand why he is in the Detective Force at all.'

'Has either man noticed your presence?'

'I am sure they have not.'

'Good. How you would feel if *you* were to have the opportunity to work alongside Inspector Newsome on this case, Eusebius?'

'I do not believe that would happen, sir.'

'Do not tell me what could happen or not happen. Would you like to work with the police on this case? To attend each interview, hear each word, follow each new development, and be my eyes as the story unfolds?'

'I think I would enjoy that.'

'As I thought. You are a good boy.'

A door opened and a man entered: the physician. He looked at Eusebius and then at the recumbent form of 'J.S.', who nodded in approbation. Whatever was to take place, the spy would be a witness to it.

'I have an unfortunate condition, Eusebius. I come here twice a month to see the doctor and he attempts to purge me of the poison in my blood. Do not be embarrassed – I feel no shame.'

The doctor lifted the sheet from the legs and Eusebius beheld the fat, black leeches feasting upon the pimply flesh. Each one was glistening and gorged on blood.

'It is not a fashionable treatment, but it is one with a long and illustrious history,' said 'J.S.' as the doctor applied a dull edge to detach each one.

With each audible de-suction, Eusebius felt hot bile rise in his throat.

'I understand that you were collected by my carriage on Holywell-street near Poppleton's bookshop, Eusebius. Perhaps you will tell me all that you witnessed there,' said 'J.S.'.

Half mesmerized and half nauseated by the procedure taking place before him, Eusebius Bean narrated all he had seen in a tone that wavered only when the sheet was raised above the waist, revealing things for which not even *my* pen would deign to find vocabulary.

ELEVEN

— • ◆ • —

. . . Thinning of the blood is followed by a progressive softening of the brain and the attrition of the mental faculties so that the intelligent man becomes simple, and the simple man little more than bestial. In all cases of persistent and prolonged cases, the result is incarceration in the lunatic asylum, usually combined with the necessary restraint of a strait waistcoat to prevent what has become a reflexive, obsessive disorder. Even periodic self-abuse can lead to impaired eyesight, cranial pressure, anaemia and facial disfigurement, by which the guilty may be known. (See figures 1, 2, 3).

Mr Williamson looked at the figures printed in Dr Mullond's *Diseases of Venery* and beheld a series of faces deformed horribly by self-inflicted sinfulness. Eyes stared madly and mouths flapped open like those of idiots. He crossed his legs, rubbed his eyes in the dim light of his fireside chair, and placed the book on the table beside him. He had not slept. Each time he closed his eyes, he saw images of Charlotte that enraged his blood.

Distractedly, he looked again at the letters he had received that morning after his affecting Golden-square experience. One was from the Secretary of the Mendicity Society asking, in subtly urgent tones, when he might expect Mr Williamson back at his desk in Red Lion-square to address the accumulating cases of letter fraud. The other was from his erstwhile colleague Harold Jute, who was highly enthusiastic about pursuing 'Mr Mann' and who had been thinking of ways they might, together, pursue the fakement writer. Neither letter could distract him from the other thoughts that occupied the investigative part of his brain.

One singular fact of that otherwise disastrous meeting with the young magdalene would not leave him: her mention of the curious deaths by prussic acid. As a policeman, and later as a detective, he had smelled the bitter-almond smell often enough to recognize it. And he had smelled it on the mouth of his dead wife.

Now it seemed there were other notable cases of the poison being cited as the cause of death in suspicious suicides. There had, of course, been hundreds of straightforward prussic acid suicides in the intervening years – wasn't the substance available in every apothecary? – but these were not just any deaths. One had occurred on the same street and on the same morning of the murder that was supposed to be linked to his wife's, while the other was also connected to a prostitute.

For at least a year after Katherine's death, Mr Williamson had excised columns of the *Police Gazette* and *the Times* relating to poisoning suicides, though no pattern or hint had emerged from his private enquiries. That evening after returning from Charlotte's room, he had spent further hours going through his collection of past editions of the *Gazette*, hoping to find something – anything – to verify what the girl had told him.

And Charlotte had been telling the truth. At least, he had

found mention of the women she had described, Kate and Mary, but the detail had been perfunctory, as it often was when prostitutes died. The logical next step would be to pursue the link and talk to all of those unfortunate women (and perhaps the men) who had known the dead prostitutes. Perhaps they would also know the elderly benefactor of Lou, or the final days before her false suicide.

And yet, though this might have been his only opportunity to prove or disprove 'Persephone's' letter, it was a line of investigation he would rather not have pursued. These women were treacherous, and he knew he lacked the skills to defend himself against them. His rigid moral architecture found itself on foundations of sand in their presence, especially when, like Charlotte, they were such expert manipulators of men.

A woman – any woman, he reflected – could dissimulate with a greater facility than the most accomplished male criminal. A woman could keep a secret so securely that the greatest detective would never discern that it was hidden – at least, not a man like Mr Williamson, to whom virtuous women were idealized creatures seldom found in reality.

Further thought on the subject was interrupted by a knock at the door, which he attended only to find the step outside empty. A folded piece of paper at the foot of the door, however, was quite clear in its instructions:

Temple Bar at twelve noon today. Alone.

Mr Williamson looked at his pocket watch and immediately reached for his coat and hat.

Is there another monument in our city as illustrious as Temple Bar? No doubt some will point to St Paul's, which indubitably has the advantage of height and grandeur. Others might put

Somerset House in the pre-eminent position, while those of an architectural tendency may argue for the new Parliament buildings. They are all fine structures in their way, but none has the historic romance of Temple Bar.

'Romance?' I hear the reader challenge. 'Where is the romance in severed heads displayed on poles from the apex of that Portland stone edifice? Where is the romance of almost two centuries of thunderous traffic, both human and equine, passing ceaselessly through its three arches? Where is the romance in a mere city *gate*?'

I reply that the romance lies exactly in those things. There is not another monument in this, the largest and greatest city in the world, that so many have passed *through*. Like the slender neck of the hourglass, it has channelled multitudinous grains of existence. It is the needle eye through which innumerable threads of destiny have slipped. Who has *not* walked or driven beneath it? Kings, queens, poets, playwrights, beggars, murderers and saints – all have come this way on their individual paths to fame, posterity, notoriety or oblivion.

And yet . . . and yet is it not also in some way invisible in the way that a doorway can be invisible among the walls around it? We move from one side to another without pausing to stop in that central nowhere – for why would we? Our origin lies behind and our destination beyond – in the middle is a limbo: not east, not west. There is only movement here.

It was at Temple Bar, then, that Mr Williamson was waiting at twelve that same day. Only, it made for a highly imprecise *rendezvous* as an actual address. 'Temple Bar' commonly referred to all of the businesses and thoroughfares thereabouts, so the only solution was stand conspicuously beneath one or other of the pedestrian arches under the gate itself. This might have been easy at two o'clock in the morning, but the flood of humanity at midday was such that Mr Williamson was jostled and tossed like driftwood upon the spume.

By ten past twelve, his composure had quite fractured and there was no sign of anyone else waiting. He decided to visit a coffee house on the Strand (from where to observe the gate) and walked through the arch to the west side . . . whereupon he noticed the door built into the wall left of the arch. Here, the masonry of Temple Bar continued into the adjoining building, but the door seemed to be part of the arch itself. No doubt he had seen this door on uncountable occasions, yet only now did he think of it as a possible access to the mysterious upper room above the arches.

He looked around and saw that he might well have been invisible to the rushing crowds entering and exiting the arches in a blur of urban purposefulness. It was as if that door and the small space before it were little more than shadows to the human flow. Suddenly he understood, and he knocked.

The door was opened immediately with a rattle of the lock. He could see nobody in the relative dimness within, but he stepped in regardless. The door closed. And a figure behind the now closing door caused him to take a sharp intake of breath.

The man was an unnaturally tall Negro with a face to frighten anyone who did not know him. Even in the poor light, Mr Williamson was able to discern the flat nose and scarred temples that spoke of the prize ring, and a terrible left eye that was covered entirely with a milky membrane. In that musty vestibule echoing with the reverberating throb of the traffic all around, Mr Williamson could not quite see the hideous scar about the Negro's neck, although he knew of its existence.

'Benjamin – you startled me. I am glad to meet you again,'

said Mr Williamson, watching his own palm disappear into the meaty paw and smiling, despite himself, at the other man's broad white grin. 'Is he here?'

Benjamin nodded, pointing upwards, and the two men ascended past a grimy circular window and then outside onto a leaded shoulder of the edifice so that they were standing atop the pedestrian arch of Temple Bar itself. Mr Williamson paused for a moment to look on the torrent of London passing beneath his feet: hundreds of faces and dozens of carriages charging along, but with not a single face upturned to see his gaze. It was a curious and beguiling perspective that captivated even this most austere of men.

Benjamin pointed to the door ahead of them, which was ajar, and Mr Williamson was first to enter a close, murky room lined entirely with shelves of ledgers and books of assorted sizes. There was a dusty reek of antiquity about the place and it occurred immediately to the investigator that he must have been one of just a handful of men ever to have entered in almost two centuries – this room that a million people looked up at each year.

'Welcome, Mr Williamson. Will you take a seat?'

The speaker was sitting at the table in the centre of the room. Before him was that day's edition of *the Times*, a front-page notice circled boldly in pencil. To one unacquainted with him, he seemed an unusual specimen indeed. Though attired as a gentleman, his face seemed to be that of a wily street character, its crooked nose evidence of at least one violent encounter, and his intelligent smoke-grey eyes suggesting a good education – whether at the university of the London gutter or at Cambridge, one might not have said. His grin was sardonic but friendly as he stood and held out a hand.

Mr Williamson shook it warmly and took the offered seat.

'Mr Dyson. I am glad to meet you again, though I believed I never would. This is a most curious location.'

'Is it not? Mr Cornwell of Child & Co. bank holds the only key to this room and he was kind enough to lend it to me for this meeting. Think of it: there are two sets of leaded windows each side of us – one facing east and the other west. There are two circular windows above us – one facing north and the other south. Where are *we*? We are nowhere – neither of the land nor of the air. We see all and nothing sees us. It is a Divine seat, is it not?'

'I will thank you not to blaspheme, Mr Dyson.'

'Ah, Sergeant! Your rigid moral backbone has not relaxed a bit. And I believe you could call me Noah after all we have been through together.'

'I am no longer a sergeant – nor a policeman, as I am sure you know.'

'Yes, yes, I had heard as much. Was it Inspector New-some's doing?'

'Hmm.'

'A pity. You were the better detective.'

'I am surprised that *you* have not heard more from the inspector.'

'He knows that my invisibility is something he should not seek to expose.'

'I gather you had to leave your house in Manchester-square as a result of that business. Are you still resident in the city?'

'It was indeed a regrettable, and expensive, course of action – but necessary for me to escape the observation of the Metropolitan Police. You will forgive me if I do not reveal my current address to you at this moment.'

'Of course. I understand.'

'Now, George – what is this notice in *the Times* all about?

I congratulate you on your witty conceit: referring to the costumes – or rather, the disguises – we wore at that Vauxhall Gardens masquerade when last we collaborated.'

'I thank you for responding . . . for trusting me sufficiently to do so.'

'Trust has nothing to do with it – we can see everything up here and we observed your approach with half a mind that it might be a trap of the inspector. In truth, I replied to your message in *the Times* partly out of fancy and partly out of the knowledge that you are no longer a detective. In fact, Benjamin and I were highly curious as to why George Williamson might want to see *us* once again.'

Benjamin had not joined them at the table, but was reclining upon a lower rung of a library ladder and reading a cobwebby volume on his knees. He smiled and said nothing, primarily because his tongue had been violently extracted some years before.

'Mr Dyson – I will be frank: I need your assistance.'

'You recall, of course, that the Metropolitan Police have "asked" for my assistance once before? That ended badly for a number of people, including me. I lost my house at Manchester-square in the name of anonymity.'

'I have told you that I am no longer a policeman. This is not a police matter. It is personal.'

'Then I am intrigued, albeit still uncommitted. Tell me the story.'

'My wife was murdered seven years ago, though the inquest called it a suicide from the Monument. Two days ago, I received a letter informing me that it was indeed murder and that the solution lies in the solution to another crime: that of Jonathan Sampson who fell from a window in Holywell-street five days ago.'

'I have heard about your wife and I am sorry for your loss. I am also aware of the ambiguity surrounding that inquest. As for the incident on Holywell-street, it was certainly most unusual. Do you have the letter with you now?'

Mr Williamson took it from his breast pocket and pushed it across the table to Noah.

'Ah, an amusing classical allusion,' said Noah after scanning the text.

'What do you mean?'

'Persephone: the queen of the Underworld, the bride of Pluto.'

Mr Williamson noted the curious pronunciation: *Per-SE-phone-ee*. 'You know the woman?'

'I forget that you have no Greek. She is a figure from mythology, tricked into spending a season in Hell, during which winter reigns on Earth.'

'Why would somebody choose such a name?'

'Who can guess? I doubt that it is the writer's real name, but the choice of it here is interesting for a number of reasons. It seems she claims to be a voice from beyond this world (but below it rather than above): the same world where the truth of your wife's death resides – and evidently Mr Sampson's also. It is a mere metaphor, but a telling one if we expand upon it in the context of the letter. The writer is in a position of possessing privileged and possibly secret knowledge. She (for it is certainly a she) is a woman of grace and power, as well as one of considerable erudition. And – if we are to follow the allusion still further – one in thrall to a power greater than her own: a power of evil. Fascinating, Mr Williamson. It is truly a mystery for a man of your talents.'

'Hmm. I spoke to Mr Blunt at the Haymarket Theatre and he had never heard the name. Why do you know it and not he?'

'That is what I mean. "Persephone" is from the Greek. We are accustomed to using the Latin deities: Pluto for Hades, Vulcan for Hephaestus, Proserpine for Persephone. Only a true classical scholar – very likely one who has knowledge of the ancient language – might recognize the Greek deity.'

'I have heard of "Proserpine".'

'And so would Mr Blunt. The question is, Mr Williamson, whether we believe this letter to be a hoax.'

'I have had some experience with false letters. I believe this one is real.'

'But then you *want* to believe it. I can see little in it that convinces me.'

'Hmm. Will you help me?'

'I am not sure I understand the challenge. You are a greater investigator than I – and I am certain you have already pursued every clue available to you. What could I do that you have not already done? I have no more power and influence than you.'

'That is a significant point, Mr Dyson. I have no authority to question people, and Inspector Newsome has seen to it – since I left the Force – that the constables of the city will offer me no help.'

'As I say: I have no advantage over you in this respect. But there is something else, is there not . . . ?'

'Mr Dyson . . . Noah – it is a delicate matter. My investigations have led me into the world of the street girl. It is one I am not familiar with, except as an enforcer of the law. They . . . do not respond as other people do. They . . . I am afraid I do not know what to do with them.'

'I am sure they could demonstrate readily enough.'

Benjamin let out a deep, rolling laugh from his position by the shelves, and Mr Williamson turned a crippling shade of crimson.

'I am sorry, Mr Williamson. Forgive my humour. I understand,' said Noah. 'The truth is that there is no finer liar in the whole world than the street girl, especially if she is a young and pretty one. In a moment, she knows exactly what you want of her – even if *you* do not – and she becomes that person. She will tell you anything, promise you anything, make you pay anything you have because she knows she can. Her power over men is quite limitless.'

'Hmm.'

'I see you have already experienced the effect.'

'This is part of my inability to investigate fully, as your joke at my expense reveals. But there is more to it. Noah – you know this city better than any policeman . . .'

'Stop. I have heard this speech before from Inspector Newsome – inside a gaol cell.'

'Please – at least listen to me. You know parts of this city better than I do. I know nothing of Greek and Latin and mythology; I know nothing of . . . of women's wiles; I cannot speak to a gentleman and seem like one. These are the places that my investigation may be taking me. I am one man – one who is cursed with an honest heart. And this is not a mere case, Noah – this is the truth of Katherine's murder.'

'I pity you, George. But I have no connection to these events. I have my own life and concerns, my own business affairs to attend to and my own issues with the police. Yes, we worked together recently – but both of us under duress from a higher power. I will be frank – why should I help you?'

'I am surprised that I must remind you. You were in gaol and it was *I* who enabled your escape – an act that caused me, ultimately, to be ejected from the Detective Force even as I made it possible for you to locate the object of your lifelong vengeance. Is that not worth a gesture of good faith?'

Noah Dyson looked over to his friend Benjamin, who had now closed his book and was listening closely. He nodded solemnly.

'I agree to nothing yet,' said Noah. 'I am afraid that your lack of detective privileges is going to be an insurmountable barrier to gathering information.'

'That is where I have some good news. You will no doubt remember Constable Cullen. He is working with the inspector and has accompanied him on the interrogations so far. I believe he may be persuaded to talk to us and reveal much important information.'

'PC Cullen is working in the Detective Force? I find that difficult to believe.'

'I, too, have my doubts. I can think only that Mr Newsome wants to keep him under close observation after the constable's aid in our previous escapade. Or perhaps the Force admired his bold actions in that case and is willing to test him.'

'Do you think he could be under the influence of the inspector?'

'Inspector Newsome is certainly not to be underestimated, but the constable always admired me rather than my superior.'

'Well, you at least have some clues from the newspapers to follow: the young man, the absent Ned Coffin . . . and I believe there may be something Inspector Newsome has overlooked in his investigations so far – something that has not been mentioned in the newspaper reports or at the inquest.'

'What is that?'

'There is a cab stand on Holywell-street, is there not?'

'Yes – but there were no cabs there at the time of the incident. There were only two witnesses to the fall.'

'Is not Tiresias proof enough that a man need not see in order to know?'

'Is this another Greek you are referring to?'

'Perhaps. Perhaps. I have an idea. What else do you have that Inspector Newsome does not?'

'There is the Persephone letter itself, what little it offers. And my questioning of a street girl called Charlotte—'

'Not her real name, of course . . .'

'Hmm. My questioning of her has suggested a series of murders masquerading as suicides – all involving prussic acid and, seemingly, a connection with those charities aiding fallen women. She mentioned that the dead girls had attended or applied to the Magdalene Hospital, the Guardian Society, and the Society for the Protection of Young Females. One of these deaths took place on the same evening and on the same street as Mr Sampson's. There may be a connection, and there may be more people to speak to. I feel I cannot do all of the work alone when the criminals are so close at hand.'

'Interesting.'

'Quite. There is also the Holywell-street publisher Henry Poppleton; I understand that many street girls possess certain books of his and he may know something about such a girl dying on his doorstep, so to speak. At the very least, he might have some ideas, and it is possible that he also knows of our Persephone if he is a bookish man. That is all I have, but I believe there is enough to solve both crimes – if only I can chase all of the clues. Noah – will you help me to do so?'

'It does sound intriguing. But as I have said: I have my own life and affairs. Do not think me ungrateful for what you did for me – I must think carefully before I entangle myself once more in any affair concerning Inspector Newsome. He has had a deleterious impact upon my own life, to be sure. I will give you my final decision tomorrow.'

'When and where?'

'Well, Holywell-street seems to be the centre of our mystery; let it be there. We will meet at the Old Dog tavern at noon.'

'Noah – I thank you for meeting me today. You did not need to do so.'

'George – I told you once that I considered you a good man, an honest man. I believe it still – but I am slow to trust anyone. Benjamin will show you out.'

The giant Negro escorted Mr Williamson back into the rush of Temple Bar and returned to the room.

'What do you think, Ben?' said Noah Dyson.

Benjamin replied with a prolonged series of complicated hand movements: a language of sorts that the two of them had created to compensate for Benjamin's aglossal state. He 'spoke' thus for some time, his fleshy palms describing shapes, words and occurrences in a splendid dumb-show that had Noah variously nodding and cogitating upon the dexterous monologue.

No doubt, as dusk crept over the city, pedestrians looked up at those usually dark windows and wondered at the flickering candlelight within, creating their own tales to populate the unknown realm. Was it the bankers at work over their ledgers? Was it conspirators plotting the downfall of the capital? Or was it a murderer at work, going about his grisly task in full view of the world?

The truth about Noah Dyson, however, was stranger than any story that might have been created to explain him. We will find out more in good time, but perchance the reader would like to know that not so very long ago he had been a prisoner of the Detective Force: suspected of being (but not proven to be) a cracksman – a master thief. Compelled under threat of trial and possible hanging to work with Mr Williamson in the pursuit of a dangerous incendiary, he had contributed towards a case that veritably set the city alight with scandal. That, however, is quite a different story.

TWELVE

Six days had passed since Mr Sampson had fallen from that Holywell-street window. Today two more would be killed.

It was still dark when Mrs Colliver left her house at five o'clock that morning. The streets were crisp with frost and the city as darkly silent as a cemetery. There was a cab at the stand outside her premises and she had travelled east through Temple Bar, along Fleet-street, up Ludgate-hill, past the cathedral, down Watling-street and south to Upper-Thames-street. No doubt the London reader will have already guessed the rest of her route: further east until she was beneath the blackened column of the Monument, then south to the shore of the river and Billingsgate fish market.

As ever, it was a striking place on that dark winter morning: the leaping gas flares animating all beneath their pale and sickly light; the roaring, ruddy-cheeked vendors; the thicket of masts by the wharf; the scores of servants seeking the best prices; and the fish itself – a silvery slick-slithering array of turbot, sole, plaice, mackerel, eels, salmon and sundry monstrosities of the deep.

With her basket in hand and her woollen shawl pulled tightly around her shoulders, Mrs Colliver had entered the market with some trepidation. She was not there to buy fish, but to meet someone.

'Best 'Olland eels, get 'em fresh!'

'Scots salmon just harrived from the 'Ighlands!'

''Astings mackerel caught this very mornin'.'

Our lady paid no heed to these shouts. She was looking for the same man who had hit her head with his truncheon that morning six days before when Mr Sampson had fallen – the same man who had rushed from the premises and apparently not been seen again. In her basket, tightly folded, was the note he had sent her the previous evening:

Mrs Colliver

Touch your forehead and you will know who I am. You will meet me at five-thirty tomorrow morning on the Thames shore at Billingsgate market. If you are not there alone, I will return to you one night when you are not expecting me. Do not be followed.

Naturally, she was afraid. Certainly, she had more reason to be afraid of him than of being investigated by the Detective Force, whose worst threat was gaol and whose power was nothing compared to this man and his friends: the power of murder.

She spent a few minutes perfunctorily examining the scaly wares, casting looks around her for anyone who might have followed. Only when she felt that was making a spectacle of herself did she walk from the stalls to the edge of the wharf, where the reek of the boats and the foetid water was at its greatest. Porters hurried to and fro along gangplanks and she had to step aside to avoid being knocked into the river.

Where was he? She cast a glance along to where the throng

of vessels petered out into almost impenetrable blackness. All was shadow there: just the suck of the water against pilings and the creak of hulls . . . then a figure, loitering. The silhouette of a workman's cap was just discernible against the water's surface.

'I thought for a moment that you would not come,' said the gentleman as she crunched over frozen puddles towards him. It was not only the chill that set her limbs a-quiver.

The voice was too cultured to be any common river man. As her eyes adjusted, she saw that the attire – a rough pea coat and heavy boots – was also quite at odds with the voice.

'No, sir. I am here.'

He took her arm and led her further away from the wharf to an even deeper night, where the river slapped unseen against steps.

'I said nothing to anyone,' said Mrs Colliver, her breath steaming about her.

'The police have spoken to you, have they not?'

'Yes, but I said nothing.'

'Did they see your head?'

'No . . . yes. I said I fell. They believed me.'

'I see. What else did they ask you?'

'About that night. I said I was asleep. I saw nothing. I heard nothing.'

'They asked you about glasses that had been used for sherry.'

'Yes . . . but how did you know?'

'No matter how. What did you answer?'

'I said the glasses were not mine. I said nothing to cause you trouble, sir.'

They were standing in almost total darkness next to a muddy bank. The river was an expanse of dark, swirling glass.

'Watch your step there, Mrs Colliver. The ground is littered hereabouts with rope and chain.'

'I swear I said nothing. They could never find you. I would die before I would give you up. I just want to run my coffee house and rooms. I don't want any trouble. Won't you say that you will leave me alone now? The matter is over now . . .'

'You are blathering, Mrs Colliver.'

'Why did you ask me here? What have you to tell me? What do you want with me? My shoes will be ruined.'

He did not answer. Rather, he brought down the truncheon on the top of her head. She grunted and fell to her knees, supporting herself upon one hand in the dirt.

He struck again, directed more by sound than by sight, and imagined the blood blossom black upon her bonnet. She fell face down into the riverside mire and was still. He looked around, saw nobody, and wrapped a length of heavy chain around her middle, cursing as the cold mud seeped into his gloves. Then, checking once more that he had not been seen, he rolled the body down the stairs with his foot so that it toppled head-first into the river and disappeared below the surface – just another soul swallowed by that ceaseless Styx.

Later the same day, Inspector Newsome was in his office at Scotland Yard with his secret vice ledger before him on the desk. The foregoing days' bulletins from constables around the city had been entered by his clerk and he was scanning the entries for anything of particular interest.

Apart from a noisy squabble at a place in Holborn, where gentlemen of a curious letch were encouraged to dress as ladies, there seemed little of note. Indeed, he was about to close the book with a sorry shake of the head when the most recent entry caught his eye. At first, he thought he was mistaken, but the name was quite clear. So unexpected was the revelation that an involuntary laugh escaped him:

Haymarket, seven o'clock: George Williamson, previously Sergeant of the Detective Force, seen standing on Haymarket in front of the theatre. He was approached by a local girl called Mary (or Madeline or Charlotte) and then accompanied her to her rooms on Golden-square. He stayed there until after nine o'clock and left alone . . .

Curious indeed. There could be no question of the constable mistaking the client in this case. Such street encounters were not generally reported unless the gentleman was of note – and many of the constables knew the ex-detective by sight or by description. The mystery of the matter was that it was utterly inconceivable to Mr Newsome that his old colleague would ever engage in such an act. Unless . . .

One possible conclusion immediately suggested itself: Mr Williamson was investigating a case. It seemed unlikely to be anything concerning the Mendicity Society, for there was little reason to accompany the girl to her rooms when she could have been questioned just as easily in the street (or during daylight hours by two men to avoid accusation of impropriety). Besides, the latest rumour was that Mr Williamson had been absent from the Society for some days with an unspecified illness.

Despite cogitating upon the matter for some minutes, the inspector was unable to think of any reason for the odd behaviour of that most moral of men. And the lack of an explanation was a potent irritant to him – such an irritant, indeed, that he decided to send a man to that address at Golden-square and question the girl Mary (or Madeline or Charlotte) on what had been discussed. Wherever Mr Williamson was involved, there was very likely a crime – one to be claimed and solved by the Metropolitan Police.

A discreet cough from the clerk's office interrupted such musings and told the inspector that Sir Richard was now in his office to receive his regular bulletin. Mr Newsome closed the ledger and handed it to the clerk before heading two doors down the corridor to the office of his superior.

He was about to knock when he heard voices inside: Sir Richard's, and another he did not recognize. Debating for a moment whether he should enter, he leaned closer to the door to catch a detail . . . and the conversation inside stopped.

'Enter!' called Sir Richard.

Inspector Newsome entered, rather embarrassed at the idea that his eavesdropping had been detected. 'Sir – I was just about to enter.'

'So I gather. Our guest here alerted me to your presence, though I admit I heard nothing. He has the keenest hearing of any man I have met. May I introduce you to Mr Eusebius Bean, a representative of the Society for the Suppression of Vice.'

The inspector took Eusebius's lifeless hand in his own and could not hide an expression of distaste at the quality of the greeting. 'Pleased to meet you, sir.'

'Be seated, Inspector. Eusebius has joined us on the recommendation of . . . of a senior member of the Society. He will be aiding you in your investigation.'

'Sir?'

'Now, I want none of your insolence, Inspector.'

'The Detective Force is quite able to investigate the case on—'

'I said that the gentleman will be aiding you.'

'Could you tell me, sir, on what basis the "gentleman" will be aiding me? I am sure, as you say, that he has hearing to challenge a dog, but does he have any police experience? Any investigative experience?'

'Eusebius is an agent of the Society. He is quite used to an investigative role.'

'Ah. A spy.'

'Inspector – this is not a request. I am taking Constable Cullen off the case – he has proved to be quite inadequate to the task, as you know well enough. In his place, Eusebius Bean will work with you. He knows the streets of London as well as any beat constable – perhaps better – and he is acquainted with many of the chief suspects in cases of vice.'

'I am certain he is.'

'He may see patterns in your investigation that you have not seen. He may be able to provide aid from the generous benefactors of that Society.'

'The law and its application is the only pattern I follow.'

'Eusebius – I am so very sorry for the inspector's behaviour. Would you mind leaving us alone for a moment? You may have a cup of tea in the room there.'

Sir Richard rang a small brass hand bell on his desk and a clerk appeared at a connecting door. Eusebius rose without expression and accompanied the clerk into the room beyond. The door closed.

'Do you not think that I am thinking exactly what you are thinking?' said Sir Richard with whispered urgency. 'Do you think I am content to allow this stranger into our ranks in this way? His Society, and, yes, the Mendicity Society also, are becoming a menace with their private constables and spies. Soon, every charity in the city will have its own private force and the Metropolitan Police will be just one of many. I will never allow that!'

'Have we really no choice, sir?'

'None – and keep your voice down. This temporary appointment comes from a high authority. Legally, I need not comply – but politically it is advisable to do so. My only recourse is to see that the case is solved and this man Bean is taken away from us as soon as possible. You must aid me in this. You *will* aid me.'

'Who is this Eusebius Bean? I have never heard of the man.'

'He is, as you say, one of their spies. A very successful one, by informed accounts.'

'There is something about him . . . something I cannot place. I do not trust him.'

'Inspector – you have only just met the man.'

'I have met men like him – many of them now in gaol.'

'Enough. Constable Cullen will be returned to his divisional duties – see that you explain it to him – and you will take Eusebius Bean with you on all future inquiries.'

'Yes, sir.'

'And I do not want to hear from the Vice Society that you have left him in St Giles's some evening at the mercy of the Irish.'

'As you wish. May I ask if any progress has been made on my access to the Continental Club?'

'I will meet somebody this very day, though it seems they are loath to admit even an investigating detective. Naturally, we could insist, but that is not the prudent way. Now – let us start afresh with Eusebius Bean.'

Sir Richard rang the bell once more and Eusebius appeared at the connecting door with a glass of milk in his hand. Inspector Newsome wondered whether there was a slight smirk to the man's features, as if he had heard everything discussed in his absence.

'I apologize, Eusebius,' said Sir Richard. 'As you may realize, your appointment is rather unorthodox. Perhaps we can try once more to create a civil atmosphere. Inspector?'

'What do you know of this case?' asked Mr Newsome somewhat uncivilly.

'I know what Sir Richard has told me, what I have heard on the streets and what I have read in the newspapers – not necessarily the same things.'

'Quite. Do any ideas occur to you? Any paths of inquiry we might follow?'

'Mr Jessop seems like an important witness. Speaking to him again may prove fruitful.'

'Yes, but he was quite insensible at the time. Perhaps, instead, you have an idea how we might get more truth out of Mrs Colliver? She is harbouring important truths.'

'Follow her wherever she goes.'

'That is not how we do things in—'

'Wait – that is a reasonable suggestion,' said Sir Richard. 'We may have been watching the premises for the return of the mysterious young man, but have we been following the lady? Who knows where she goes? Perhaps she is reporting to the same person who struck that blow to her head, informing them of our investigation. Look into this.'

'Yes, sir,' said the inspector, knowing that this kind of espionage would be anathema to Sir Richard on any other case.

The smirk on Eusebius's face seemed now quite unmistakable, his galactic lips attending to the glass with cool impassivity.

*

The day of his murder began much as every working day did for Mr Jessop, the bookbinder who had been rudely awoken on the night of the Holywell-street incident.

In his dim little room above a bookshop on Paternoster-row, he sat at his large table surrounded by the materials of his trade: boards, twine, knives, aromatic sheaves of Bermondsey leather, and pungent vats of glue from the Smithfield lanes. A large book press stood empty by his right hand. If he had a small bottle of gin beside him, it was only because the fireplace was rather inadequate and because the day was a particularly cold one.

Few people see these upstairs rooms. Indeed, few see anything on this narrow alley whose tall houses lean towards each other as they rise, banishing the light. And yet this is the Promised Land for writers with manuscripts beneath their arms, who approach publishers' premises hopefully and run their fingers reverentially over the modest brass plaques on the doorposts.

Never mind that rejection, humiliation and penury await them here; never mind that the windows are full of weighty volumes that have – unsold – outlived the aspirations of writer and publisher alike; never mind that there are countless other writers 'waiting to hear' whether this time their novel/play/biography/encyclopaedia will find favour with the publisher's reader. For the writer, if nothing else, has imagination to succour the hungry years of failure.

No such creativity was necessary for Mr Jessop. With his gin and his fireplace and his steady flow of work, he was content enough. Had he reflected that he was perhaps the only man who had spoken to – and might be able to identify – the mystery young man of the Holywell-street case? Had he given any credence to the threat of that night: that he would be murdered if he did not forget all he had heard? Evidently not.

The door opened. A well-dressed young man stood framed there.

'Mr Jessop?'

'Yes, but the shop is downstairs. Customers are not permitted entry here.'

'I am not a customer. It is you I seek.'

'Do I know you? There is something familiar . . .'

'We have met briefly.'

Mr Jessop looked at the young man, who was dressed in a fine overcoat, a silk top hat and tan kid gloves. The face, an impassive, ruddy-cheeked aristocratic sort, was not at all familiar.

'No, sir, I cannot place you . . .'

The young man smiled and calmly opened his overcoat button by button. Mr Jessop saw that there was a policeman's truncheon fastened to the man's belt with a leather strap.

'Are you a detective? I have already spoken with an inspector.'

'No, Mr Jessop. I am not. And you may recall that you were warned not to speak to anyone about that night at Colliver's coffee house.'

'You . . . are you the gentleman that awoke me? I believe I recognize your voice.' Mr Jessop glanced at the crescent-shaped leather knife on his desktop.

The young man saw the glance and smiled indulgently. 'Evidently you did not seriously heed my warning. What have you told the police?'

'Nothing. Only that I was awoken by a man I did not see or recognize and that he threatened me. That I heard some voices. Nothing, really.'

'And yet more than enough.'

The young man shook his head as if his presence there were

an inconvenience in the usual pattern of his day. He extracted the truncheon almost apologetically, stepping towards Mr Jessop so benignly that the latter did not even expect a blow. Thus, the tremendous blow upon his forehead quite stunned him and he toppled from the chair virtually insensible.

As he lay on the floor with blackness and bursts of light playing wildly behind his closed eyelids, he heard the scrape of the sash window being hoisted open. Cold air poured across the floor and tightened the skin where his shirt had come untucked. He heard the small table beneath the window being pulled away and footsteps approaching.

'Here – let me help you up,' said the young man, taking an arm. 'Let us get some cold air to clear your head. I hope you have learned your lesson and will keep your tongue if those policeman return with questions.'

'Ass . . . assuredly,' said Mr Jessop, whose tongue was thick and whose legs were without strength.

He allowed the young man to take his weight. But as they approached the open window, they accelerated and a hand was placed on the back of Mr Jessop's head, pushing it down. And suddenly it seemed they were rushing towards that gaping aperture.

He didn't have time to scream as his knees hit the window ledge. Shock took his voice as he tipped head-first towards the street. Nor was there opportunity for any kind of cogent thought as the cobbles rushed to impact his scull and snap his spine with a smothered crunch.

Mr Jessop was dead.

THIRTEEN

Number 24 Holywell-street is an address familiar to many of those of London's lesser writing fraternity, though they know it better as the Old Dog tavern. It has been host to generations of boastful failures for almost two centuries, and its timbers sag like the shoulders of a depleted hack: ink-stained and ruined with brain fatigue.

I was sitting there by the fire on that day, oblivious as the police to the two murders that had occurred earlier that morning. Fleeing the chill, I was making some amends to a manuscript and enjoying the warmth of the flames. Around me, more minor talents talked loudly with their fellows about literary matters of which they knew nothing but the sounds of the words in their mouths. Perhaps one or two had experienced the lifetime pinnacle of an article in the *Chronicle* or *Illustrated News*. Another might have had his pages taken by a publisher's reader some months previously. *All* were 'novelists', moving from coffee house to library to bookshop in their endless journey towards the final chapter.

I had not seen Noah enter the place, but I knew he must have been there when I saw Benjamin. The tall Negro was an unmistakable figure who, as soon as he entered the taproom, caused a number of the writers to reach for notebooks. Synonyms began to flow and commas were spilled as their eyes followed him to a table in the corner, where he joined a man wearing a cabman's overcoat: Noah Dyson.

Had those scribblers of the Old Dog known the true story of this pair – as I do – they might have soiled their very britches at the thought of the novels available to them at that corner table: tales of slavery, of transportation, of treasure, of murder, of robbery . . . Here were two men who had travelled the world together and lived a dozen lives. But that is a different story – one that I might share later. They were waiting for the arrival of another.

Mr Williamson entered from the street, bringing a breath of cold air into the hot fug of pipe smoke, beer and male conversation. He looked quickly around the room and walked directly to the corner table where he had seen Benjamin. Only on sitting did he realize that the other man was Noah. Though the man's face was undisguised, his clothes and posture made him seem a different person from the one who had sat in the secret room above Temple Bar.

'Mr Williamson – it is a cold one today, is it not?' said Noah.

'I have known worse. I am surprised to see you attired so. Are you seeking to avoid someone?'

'Call it prudence. Eyes follow you, and now they may follow me. Will you have something to eat before we begin our investigations?'

'Does this mean you agree to help me?'

'I have given it some thought. There is a debt to be repaid, then I am free.'

'I understand, and I thank you.'

'Careful, Mr Williamson; let us not be reduced to emotion

in a public place. What would people say about you then? Here is the waiter . . .'

A dour man with the mien of an undertaker appeared at the table and, without looking directly at any of the three men, reeled off his list in a disinterested monotone: 'Roast beef, boiled beef, beef pie, haunch of mutton, boiled pork, roast veal and ham, salmon and shrimp, pigeon pie, and sheep's trotter special.'

They ordered (Noah speaking for Benjamin), and began to speak again only when the waiter had retired.

'You said something at Temple Bar about a man not needing to see in order to know,' said Mr Williamson. 'Will you tell me now what you were thinking?'

'Tiresias: the blind seer.'

'If you say so. What of him?'

'You know of course that there is a cab station on this street. You may also have noticed old Joseph, the waterman.'

'Perhaps.'

'He is there at all hours: feeding and watering the horses, putting fresh hay in the foot wells, opening doors for a coin or two, holding the horses as cabmen come in here or to Colliver's for a quick pie. The man must be ninety years old and he has been the waterman on Holywell-street for most of that time.'

'I have read nothing of him in the accounts of that fateful morning. The police have not questioned him. He cannot have been at his station.'

'Since we do not yet know, we will not assume as much. Let us remember that he is blind and has been so since birth. Who questions a blind old man as a witness – particularly when he seems to many to be deranged?'

'And this is your "seer"?'

'We will see. Or rather, you will see. You are to question him closely on the events of that night. I will be visiting Mr Poppleton in his shop.'

'What do you expect to get from *him*?'

'Mr Poppleton – whatever his other faults – is a man of divers intelligence and will likely respond more favourably to intelligence than to a policeman's questions. I have an idea to dangle before him and see what reaction I get. Now – let us eat before we venture out into the cold once more.'

The food arrived with a clatter of pewter plates on the rough wooden tabletop and the three gentlemen set about their meals with good appetite. Despite himself, Mr Williamson could not help watching the peculiar ritual of the tongueless Benjamin, who chopped his beef pie into the smallest possible pieces, forked a quantity into his mouth and then appeared to suck upon the *bolus* quite contentedly before swallowing it whole with an immense gulp. After watching a few mouthfuls thus consumed, Mr Williamson realized he was staring rather than eating.

'He tells me that he derives far more satisfaction from his food this way,' said Noah. 'Though his sensitivity to taste is unfortunately impaired by the lack of a tongue.'

Benjamin smiled that broad ivory grin and made a complicated gesture with his right hand.

'He suggests that you try it yourself – just as you have seen it done.'

'I . . . it hardly seems . . .'

'It is a suggestion. That is all. You may ignore it.'

Mr Williamson looked at the pigeon pie on the plate before him and then at his dining partners, who seemed thoroughly intent on their meals. He chopped up some of the pie, took a large mouthful, began to suck on it . . . and immediately began to cough.

Benjamin's great bass laugh rolled across the taproom and a huge black hand came down on Mr Williamson's back to clear the blockage. They ate in silence thereafter.

When they emerged once more into the street, they took three directions: Noah towards that illustrious shop, Benjamin to a rag-seller further along, and Mr Williamson to see the elderly cabman.

Joseph the waterman might well have been an ancient civic statue of pitted stone and spreading lichen, worn away a little more each passing decade by the rain and wind. His bent form was hoary with age, and frost seemed to cling to his tattered overcoat as he shovelled a pile of steaming manure from the road into the gutter. Blind he might have been, but that tiny domain of his – the water trough and bucket, the kerb stone, the line of cabs and canvas sacks of hay – was so familiar that he moved within its sphere without hindrance or hesitation.

Mr Williamson approached from the opposite side of the street, his notebook at the ready, and was about to speak when Joseph turned to him. Where one might expect to see eyes, there were only narrow, empty slits in a face lined with age and dirt.

'A cab, sir?' said Joseph. 'There will be a driver along presently – one has just popped off to Fleet-street. Forgive me for asking, but you are a policeman are you not?'

'What would make you say such a thing?'

'The sound of your walk. A policeman always walks a particular pace. It is unmistakable. Habit, I suppose, from walking the city streets. Doesn't much matter what boots he is wearing, I can always tell.'

'I was a policeman once.'

'But you still walk like one, eh?'

'Evidently. I would like to ask you about the events of six nights ago.'

'The incident at Colliver's? I was here at my station when he fell.'

'There was nothing about that in the newspapers. There were only two witnesses: the constable and a drunken sailor.'

'So says Cribb, the constable. He is not the sharpest knife, that man – though he sometimes brings me a cup of coffee. Let me ask you, sir: how many times have you passed beneath Temple Bar?'

'Too many to count, but what . . .'

'Could you describe the statuary of that gate to me?'

'Why, I . . . there are four figures. They are . . . I cannot recall the exact . . .'

'We don't always see what we look at every day, do we? I am here all weathers and most hours, sir. But I might as well be carved in stone for all people see me. I see not, and am seen not.'

'Hmm. What can you tell me about that night?'

'I heard the shouts. In the upper room there.' Joseph pointed unerringly to the window with scuff marks still etched blackly beneath it.

'What manner of shouts?'

'I did not hear the words at first; the window was closed, you see. I am sure I heard three distinct voices. After the window was opened, I heard one phrase repeated: "I cannot!" That was Mr Sampson. I know because it was also his voice that yelled as he held on to the window ledge.'

Mr Williamson added all to his notebook. 'What three voices did you hear? Can you tell me more?'

'One of them was the same gentleman who emerged

shortly thereafter and made the comment about going for Mr Sampson's friends. And one was a woman's voice.'

'A woman? Are you sure?'

'I may not have eyes, but I have ears. It was a young woman. Not Mrs Colliver – I know *her* voice.'

'What did she say, this young woman?'

'I could not discern any words. I heard only noises. She may have been drunk.'

'And you heard all of this through an upper-storey window at some distance?'

'You doubt me, sir. Don't you know the silence of the city at that time in the morning? When all are sleeping and the air is dead cold, one might hear the pigeons roosting and the very rats scuttling in the walls.'

'Hmm. What of the fall itself?'

'I heard the body drop and the bones crack. There was nobody in the street but I at that time.'

'Not even Constable Cribb?'

'Not yet. Immediately after the fall, I heard a most unusual laugh from inside that room. In fact, it was more like a yelping: a kind of high-pitched "*yip-yip-yip*".'

'Have you heard that laugh before?'

'Not before or since, sir. I wouldn't like to, either. It sounded like someone who had lost their mind.'

'What then? What did you do?'

'I started to walk over to where I could hear Mr Sampson groaning, and that's when some people came out of Colliver's in a hurry.'

'People? I understood it was one man only.'

'You are not listening – that was later. I heard them pause on seeing me. One of them approached rapidly as if he was to address or attack me, but I suppose he saw my eyes. In fact, he waved his hand before my face to reassure himself – I heard the material of his cuff – but he said nothing.'

'Tell me about these people.'

'They did not speak, but I could hear they were keen to get away. I believe – from the sound of her shoes – that the young woman was among them. Another man was with her, perhaps holding on to her because her footfalls were irregular.'

'What else? You identified me as a policeman – what can you tell me about *their* footfalls?'

'Only what I have told you. Not every person has a distinctive step. After pausing momentarily, perhaps to satisfy themselves I had seen nothing, the three of them walked rapidly further down the street to the carriage that was waiting there. The woman's footsteps seemed to be dragging somewhat. No doubt you will ask me how I knew there was a carriage . . . Well, I could hear the horses breathing and the rattle of their brasses.'

'You have a prodigious ear. What of the man who approached you?'

'As I say: he said nothing. A curious thing, though – he smelled of perfume: not a strong scent, but something upon his clothes perhaps. It was lavender and something else – some kind of flower that I couldn't place. And coal tar – I smelled coal tar.'

'What manner of perfume is that – coal tar and lavender?'

'I tell you what I smelled, not what it means.'

Mr Williamson looked dubiously at Joseph and noted down his words. The waterman's face showed no guile or deception, though the lack of eyes made it difficult to read any emotion in that weathered countenance. 'Has nobody questioned you about this incident? Not the police?'

'Only you, sir. As I say, who questions a blind old man?'

'Hmm. When did PC Cribb appear?'

'The man is quite punctual on his rounds – it was a few moments after the other three had fled to the carriage.'

'Did he see *you*?'

'I believe not. There was something about the incident that struck me with a horror I could not quite fathom. I sensed that something . . . something evil had occurred and I was afraid . . . so I retired to the doorway over yonder at Levi's shop. I sometimes rest there during the slow times. I was crouched there when Cribb arrived and I must have been in shadow.'

'Why did you not announce your presence and give him your testimony? You were safe with a policeman in the vicinity.'

'Truth be told, sir, I do not like to be mixed up with the police. Questions take time; then one must stand before the magistrate or judge and repeat oneself. My horses need me here always.'

'You speak as one who has experience of legal pro-ceedings.'

'I am old. My memory fails me.'

'Hmm. What of the mariner Ned Coffin?'

'Aye, he came a-singing down the road shortly after. I could smell him even from my doorway.'

'This is hardly a street for a sailor to be walking drunk, is it? He should have been over Wapping way or at the Minories.'

'A man may drink wherever he likes. He, too, saw the body – presumably with the constable bent over it – and he shouted "murder". He must have misinterpreted what he saw and thought the policeman had knocked Mr Sampson down.'

'Is this when the young man emerged and made his comment about going for friends?'

'That's right. He ran towards that waiting carriage and it set off with a lash of the whip.'

'What can you tell me of the young man? This is important.'

'It is as you said. I have nothing more to add. Perhaps the strange laugh was his. It is possible.'

'Hmm. Why were you not at the inquest into this case, Joseph? Your testimony is important to see justice done.'

'Nobody asked me. And, besides, my duty is here with the horses. They must eat and drink as we do. I have no time to be going to inquests.'

At that moment, a cab rounded the corner from St Clement Danes and rattled towards them. Joseph jerked at the sound and stepped into his habitual space from where he could open the door.

'I must work now, sir. I believe I have told you all there is to tell.'

Mr Williamson looked at his copious notes and nodded to himself. 'Thank you, Joseph. I may return with more questions.'

'Whatever you wish, sir. Keep warm, won't you? I feel that we're going to get snow – and plenty of it.'

The cab arrived with a clatter of hooves and wheels. Joseph began his eyeless ritual as if the conversation had been no more than birdsong interrupting one cab's departure and the arrival of the next.

Noah no longer appeared to be a cabman. With the aid of a reversible coat and some minor adjustments to his dress, along with a smart top hat he had brought with him in a bag, he was now a gentleman about town. He paused briefly at the window of Henry Poppleton's shop, affecting an interest in its contents, then entered.

Inside, he made a show of looking at some titles on animal husbandry while occasionally looking around in a self-conscious manner. He sensed rather than saw Mr Poppleton watching the new customer from his position at the counter.

'May I help you, sir?' said the publisher.

'Why, yes. I . . . I am looking for a book for a friend: a university friend of mine. He is fond of certain . . . exotic literature.'

'Exotic, you say? Drama, is it? Poetry?'

'No, no . . .' and here Noah looked around to check what he already knew: that the shop was otherwise empty. He whispered nevertheless: 'He has a taste for something "warmer".'

'"Warmer" you say? Would your "friend" be acquainted with *The Adventures of Sir Henry Loveall*? Or perhaps *The Lustful Turk*?'

'They are rather old titles. My friend wanted something newer.'

'Well, sir – it rather depends how "warm" your "friend's" tastes are. Would they extend to algolagnia or klismaphilia? Nymphomania perhaps?'

'I . . . that is, *he* is partial to depucelative literature.'

Mr Poppleton nodded approvingly. 'Has your "friend" read *The Seven Sins of Sarah*?'

'He is more appreciative of the Aretine style.'

'I see. He likes his descriptions bluntly to the point . . . so to speak.'

'Rather so. And illustrated accordingly.'

The publisher smiled and reached behind him to where a rope dangled beside a tall wooden bookcase. He pulled on it without sound, but a few moments later a door opened above and a young man walked down the stairs to where they stood.

'John will watch the shop while I accompany you to the alternative shelves,' said Mr Poppleton.

The two ascended and passed into a tiny room in which the books were laid out flat on tables so that the lover of such works might take a seat and appreciate the contents at their ease. The door closed behind them and Mr Poppleton eased a bolt into the jamb.

'I speak with all modesty when I say that I both sell and print the finest stock in all of Britain,' said the publisher. 'Only in Paris or Brussels will you find a greater selection.'

'I see you have images by Raimondi,' said Noah with suitable deference, opening the cover of a large leather-bound edition.

'Not original, of course – but true to the master.'

'And is this a copy of *Venus Mirabilis*? Quite rare.'

'Indeed it is. Permit me to say, sir, that you certainly know the literature well.'

'I have travelled a little on the continent and have a small library of my own. Of late, however, I have found myself wanting something new. I feel I have read all there is to read.'

'What you say is a profound truth, sir. A man's appreciation of the carnal arts feeds upon itself and is never satiated. What fulfilled us a year ago is now but a preliminary course, and what seemed to us thrilling three months past is today a commonplace.'

'I have come to the right man, I see. Would you recommend something?'

'Every man is different. It is difficult to know.'

'An acquaintance of mine told me that he had recently discovered something of interest at your shop, but he unfortunately passed away before he could tell me what it was. Perhaps you knew him: Mr Jonathan Sampson.'

Mr Poppleton's retail demeanour hardened into something less amenable. 'I do not discuss my customers.'

'Of course. Quite understandable – although this one is no longer among us. Do you know, when I read of his death on this street, my first thought was that the man was most likely engaged in some kind of lurid endeavour! He was always one for the more *outré* activities was old Sampson.'

'As I say, I do not speak of customers. Will you be making a purchase?'

'There is a book I have heard spoken of, but I am not sure of the complete title.'

'What have you heard?'

'Maddeningly little, I am afraid. I have heard it mentioned, but in tones suggesting it is something rather special. It would appear to be a book with a classical theme, or at least I assume so from a word in the title: "Persephone". Do you know it?'

Outside on the wintry cobbles of Holywell-street, Mr Williamson looked at his watch and at the shopfront of Henry Poppleton. Noah was inside for around twenty minutes. Benjamin – who was clearly of limited use for interrogative purposes – continued to loiter outside the rag-sellers further up the street towards St Clement Danes, ready to come for help if needed.

As Mr Williamson watched the activity on the street, he slowly became aware of a character not following the typical rhythm of the human traffic. The man had walked past two or three times without showing any particular inclination to reach a destination – and he was clearly neither a beggar nor a vendor. His attire gave little away as to his profession, but he seemed curious rather than suspicious to Mr Williamson, who soon disregarded the oddity as a common element of this most unusual street.

That man, inevitably, was Eusebius Bean. He, too, had taken careful note of two unusual characters – a lofty Negro, and a top-hatted man with a pocked face waiting near Poppleton's bookshop. The latter had previously been speaking to the waterman Joseph, and Eusebius now perceived, with his vulpine intuition, that both the interrogator and Negro were somehow working in collaboration. Perhaps it was the darting glances between the two, or the positions of their bodies . . . whatever the evidence, he sensed a connection.

Benjamin was the first to understand what was about to happen when he heard a distant chatter of boots upon the road – many boots. A whistle sounded three shrill blows from a remote upper storey and was followed at close intervals by the same signal all along the street so that the message could be unmistakable:

The police were coming. There was going to be a raid.

A phrenzy of activity gripped certain bookshops along the street. Shopkeepers ran outside with assistants and began to affix boards over their windows. Iron grilles were dropped on to hinges and a rattle of chains echoed along that narrow thoroughfare as if it were a transport ship. And those habitants of Holywell-street who had witnessed the spectacle before made themselves secure behind closed doors and curtained windows.

By now, the terrible onrush of feet was audible to all. The Negro made a series of urgent gesticulations that meant nothing to Mr Williamson. Should he rush into the shop – which at this moment was being battened against the impending onslaught by Mr Poppleton's assistants – or should he flee and leave Noah to make his own escape?

He rushed towards Mr Poppleton's doorway, the sound of boots coming ever closer.

'Closed for today!' said a youth about to drop an iron gate into place across the doorway.

Mr Williamson pushed past him and entered the shop just as the metalwork clashed into position.

Inside was almost dark, the windows now being barricaded. Henry Poppleton himself paced animatedly shouting orders to his boys.

'John – pile the special books in the yard, but keep them clean and dry. If these brutes break through, you are to set light to all of the volumes. Yes, all of them. Peter – have you checked the window on the upper floor? Those ——— will bring ladders if I know them . . . O! Who are you?' said the publisher, noticing Mr Williamson for the first time.

'I am a customer.'

'We are closed.'

'So it would seem, but I am locked within the shop.'

'No matter. It is the fault of the police. We will endeavour to weather this storm and hope they do not get through. Keep away from the windows . . . and, please, take the opportunity to browse.'

With this, Mr Poppleton banged up the stairs to that upper-storey room, where he began to help young John carry armfuls of books down and through a corridor to what must have been an enclosed court at the rear.

Mr Williamson looked quickly around and could not see Noah. There was an uneasy silence in the shop, all sound muffled by the books and by the boards outside. The rattle of boots had now become an ominous shuffling outside the window. Daylight came only dimly through the slats of the boards. Numerous shadows shifted.

Then a truncheon rapped three times on the iron gate outside and a man spoke: the unmistakable voice of Inspector Newsome.

'Henry Poppleton – I have a warrant signed by the magistrate entitling me to enter on suspicion of finding indecent books and prints sold to the general public from these premises. If you do not admit us, we will be forced to gain entrance. I will give you exactly one minute to open this door.'

The publisher paused halfway down the stairs, his arms full of books. He remained there as if frozen. The silence of that anticipatory tableau was such that a man of fancy might have thought to hear the very ticks of the inspector's watch outside.

'You there!' said Mr Poppleton to Mr Williamson, 'come and help us get these books to safety. Quickly, while there is a hope.'

Knowing exactly what the books contained, and that destroying them would aid the criminal, he was reluctant to participate – particularly because a senior member of the Detective Force was about to come through the door at any moment. But that room upstairs might be the place where Noah had gone. He nodded his acquiescence.

The room was as last we saw it, albeit somewhat depleted of stock. There was also one other notable difference.

'Sir, there is an unconscious man on the floor here,' said Mr Williamson with unfeigned surprise as he saw the prostrate form of Noah.

'Pay no mind to him,' said Mr Poppleton. 'He had an accident. Now – take this pile of books and follow John out to the yard. He will direct you what to do.'

'But this man has a bloody wound to his head! What manner of accident did he have in a mere reading room?'

'We have not the time to discuss this matter. Take these books to the yard before the police burst in upon us!'

But it was too late.

A tremendous crash marked the beginning of the assault on that fortress of words. There came the sound of breaking glass as the barricades bowed under the massed onslaught, and the very building seemed to rock with the violence visited upon it by boots and clubs and pry bars.

Mr Poppleton dismissed his customer and the unconscious man with a contemptuous backhanded gesture and set off down the stairs with his incriminating texts.

Mr Williamson knelt to the insensible form beside him, slapping the face. 'Noah! Noah! Wake up!'

No response.

More windowpanes shattered. Light began to appear in the shop once more as boards were ripped away. The batter and rattle of attack was relentless.

Resorting to an old trick from his days on the beat, Mr Williamson pinched Noah's nostrils and held his jaw closed so that no breath could enter his inert form. Either he would asphyxiate, or his body would wake itself with urgency to avoid extinction.

Noah snuffled and his eyes darted open. His hand went to the wound on his head and he looked at the blood on his palm.

'George? Why—?'

'We have no time. Inspector Newsome is smashing down the shopfront, as you can hear. I would prefer him to catch neither of us here. I believe there is a yard at the rear – can you walk?'

'We will try.'

'What happened to you? Who struck you?'

'Later. We must try to escape.'

With much assistance, and amidst the terrible cacophony of the raid, Noah managed to descend the stairs and out into that enclosed yard, a grimy brick enclosure where most of the indecent stock of the shop had been piled upon a platform of wooden slats.

Mr Poppleton was in a state of extreme agitation, made worse now by coming face to face once more with Noah. Then, as the first policemen began to pour into the shop through door and splintered windows, the publisher closed his eyes in resignation and shook his head. He looked to John.

'Burn them. Burn them all.'

The boy made to light a lucifer match, but at that exact moment Inspector Newsome entered the yard at a run, his face crimson with effort and his truncheon raised.

He was immediately robbed of the power of speech, however, by the scene before him. For in addition to the expected pile of corrupting filth, he saw there in that piteous quadrangle the wanted publisher Henry Poppleton, the disgraced former-detective George Williamson, and the escaped transportee Noah Dyson, who had not so very long ago threatened the inspector's life. If the latter looked around suddenly, it was perhaps because he also expected to see Benjamin.

Surprise or no surprise, his words were decisive: 'Gentlemen – you are all under arrest.'

FOURTEEN

It was difficult for Inspector Newsome to define precisely what it was about Eusebius Bean that he disliked so much. The spy was so quotidian in appearance, so banal in manner, that he barely existed. Yet exist he did, and he had been following the inspector since Sir Richard had ordered it.

They were sitting in Mr Newsome's office at Scotland Yard the morning following the bookshop raid and Eusebius was giving his report on what he had witnessed prior to the raid (the second time, incidentally, that he had given such a report – though not to the police). The inspector was only half listening. Instead, he was shuffling the disparate pieces of the case in his mind. These latest developments were quite astounding and had left him at a loss to explain the seemingly endless ramifications of that simple fall from a window seven days before. He certainly dare not go to Sir Richard with these latest developments without first attempting to make sense of them.

'Must you do that with your tongue?' he interrupted Eusebius.

'Do what, Inspector?'

'That constant licking at the corner of your mouth. It is quite distracting and gives you an air of the insane.'

'A harmless habit.'

'Well, see if you can stop it. To summarize what you have rather long-windedly said thus far: Mr Williamson questioned the waterman while Noah Dyson went into the bookshop. Benjamin waited up the street.'

'Benjamin?'

'The Negro. He is with Dyson.'

'Yes. I saw the waterman (Joseph is his name) pointing at the window above Colliver's and I deduced—'

'Leave the deducing to the detectives, sir. Besides, we have the gentlemen in custody and we can speak to them at our leisure about what was said.'

'On that subject, Inspector: I do not see how you can hold Mr Williamson, Mr Dyson and the Negro. The former two cannot be convicted of any crime save being in a shop, and the latter was merely waiting on the street.'

'You are quite the lawyer, Eusebius – but incidental evidence points to Mr Williamson being involved in the investigation of this case. That may not be a crime, but I want to know why and what he has discovered – as well as his reasons for involving Dyson. There is something highly suspicious going on here, and if a period in gaol for these gentlemen is my only means of leverage, I will use it.'

'Who is this Noah Dyson and why do you speak of him with such dislike?'

'The man, and his dusky colleague, is a menace – but one I have underestimated before. Gaol is the best place for him.'

'He is a criminal, then?'

'He was a transportee and escaped his captivity in Australia. If it were that simple, he would be back there now. But he has also been a cracksman and has worked for the

Detective Force in . . . in an unofficial capacity. The situation is complex.'

'From what little I have heard about these men, I fear they are unlikely to be cooperative, whatever you threaten them with. Is it not possible to speak with them frankly and discuss the case? If they have a stake in it, they may be happy to have the assistance of the Detective Force.'

'Unlikely. And more complicated than you imagine. My relationship with each of the parties has not been without difficulty; there is a certain degree of . . . of animosity.'

'May I suggest a solution, Inspector? The Vice Society has many wealthy benefactors, as you may know. Perhaps I could enquire whether one of them might provide a venue where we and the gaoled men might converse in an atmosphere of neutrality, away from the threat of prison and the force of the law. I know that there is much enthusiasm among my employers for this case to be solved.'

Inspector Newsome looked at Eusebius sceptically. The very reasonableness of the suggestion made the spy seem even more objectionable – but it *was* an intriguing idea. He affected to give it some thought.

'I could most likely organize somewhere this very day,' offered Eusebius.

'All right, all right – see to it. But do not let Sir Richard hear of it. Digressions from procedure disturb him. And let me know as soon as possible where and when we will meet. I will be here waiting.'

Mr Newsome watched the back of the departing spy with distaste, and some distrust. There was something about the man – something indefinable that made one reticent in his presence. It was as if he were mentally recording everything in order to use later, probably against one. It was a concern that perhaps he should have gone to Sir Richard about, but, alas, the inspector thought he had the better of Eusebius Bean.

That thought was fleeting, however, and gave way to the more pressing information on the desk before him: the news of Mr Jessop's brutal end, the report that Mrs Colliver had gone missing, and the apparent murder of someone who the inspector would very much have liked to speak with – someone with whom Mr Williamson *had* spoken just the previous day. The sooner he could talk to that wayward ex-detective, the better. Fortunately, the opportunity was conveniently at hand.

A profusion of fresh flowers in vases adorned the opulent reception room in St James's, filling it with an almost nauseating sweetness. The gentlemen seated there in incongruous comfort, however, did not appreciate the finery of its furniture and *décor*, for Mr Williamson and Noah wore irons about their ankles and handcuffs on their wrists.

Though alone in the room, they knew that the constables who had accompanied them from their separate gaol cells were close by in adjoining quarters. Both men were dishevelled and ill-tempered after a sleepless night on a cold stone floor, but their senses were keen and they remained observant. Noah had glimpsed a fine library and a liveried servant through a briefly opened door, while Mr Williamson was reading the room for clues as to whether the residence was that of single or a married man.

'What is this about, George?' said Noah under his breath.

'I have no idea,' replied Mr Williamson in equally hushed tones, 'but I sense Inspector Newsome's hand in it.'

'Where are we? I could not see clearly from the carriage but I am certain we are close to the park. Is this house part of the Force's assets?'

'I have never been here before and do not know of it. Did anyone question you at the prison?'

'No. You?'

'No. Evidently that is the purpose of this curious development. I imagine that the inspector knows he cannot repeat his previous tactics with us.'

'What tactics might he have? He has no case and no reason for suspicion – we were merely customers in a locked shop . . . or does he know about your investigation of the Holywell-street case?'

'I have no reason to believe so, but we will see. We must be careful what we reveal.'

'The Persephone letter?'

'Perhaps. Let us wait to see what this episode is about. Follow my lead. Have you had any communication from Benjamin?'

'No. I am sure he managed to make his escape. Very likely he knows where we are . . .'

Noah paused as a handle rattled. The door opened and Inspector Newsome entered with Eusebius Bean following silently behind.

'Mr Williamson, Mr Dyson – welcome,' said Mr Newsome, not quite making eye contact with Noah. 'I trust you both slept well . . . No answer? Well, I suppose you have reason enough to be discontented.'

'Why are we here, Inspector Newsome? And what is this place?' said Mr Williamson.

The inspector and Eusebius took seats opposite their captives before the fire. 'This is a private residence kindly offered to the Detective Force so that we may speak together in an . . . unofficial manner.'

'Offered by whom, and to whose benefit?'

'That is unimportant, Mr Williamson. What is important to me is your interest in the Holywell-street case and why you should be found together with the elusive Mr Dyson on the premises of a major suspect in that case.'

'I have expressed no interest in the case you speak of, though I have read of it in *the Times*. As for being in a shop, might not a man visit a bookshop without suspicion?'

'Let us not be childish. You have attempted to question Mrs Colliver on the matter at her coffee house; you were also seen and heard yesterday discussing it with the waterman on Holywell-street – and you have recently questioned a prostitute of Haymarket. What is your interest, Mr Williamson – and how is Mr Dyson here involved?'

Mr Williamson hoped that the rush of blood from his features was not visible. The thought of policemen observing him with Charlotte at Haymarket was an outrage, a humiliation that left him momentarily speechless.

Noah perceived the shock of his co-captive and, pointing to Eusebius, addressed Mr Newsome with his customary lack of fear. 'Who is this fellow sitting beside you like a faithful dog, Inspector? I see from his stature that he is not a policeman.'

'Who he might be is of no consequence to you, Mr Dyson. I am asking the questions. Among them is why you were found in the courtyard of Mr Poppleton's shop amidst a pile of indecent literature and with a fresh injury upon your head?'

'I entered to purchase a book and was struck on the head when a number of policemen battered in the storefront. On regaining consciousness, I was quite amazed to see that a fellow customer was George Williamson, previously of the Detective Force. I understand you were instrumental in his dismissal.'

'Nonsense!'

'My story is nonsense? Or my comment about Mr Williamson?'

'Both.'

'Prove it.'

Colour rose in the inspector's face and he seemed ready to explode. Eusebius leaned closer to him as if to offer a whispered comment, but was waved vigorously away as if an insect. Mr Newsome breathed deeply and turned once more to Mr Williamson.

'I have no interest in prosecuting either of you. I simply want to know of your interest in this case. If you are seeking a solution, there is no reason why we cannot share what we know to our mutual benefit.'

'That would require reciprocal trust,' interjected Noah, 'and I have seen no reason that you can be trusted.'

'*You* are an escaped convict and could be shipped back to the Antipodes any time I see fit!'

'I believe we have an agreement on that subject, Inspector.'

'An agreement, you say? Do you mean that you have threatened my life if I pursue the matter? That is neither legal nor an agreement, Mr Dyson.'

Noah gave a lupine smile. 'I have no idea what you mean.'

'So it was a different Noah Dyson who entered my private address a few months past and left a dagger under my pillow?'

'It must have been.'

'What made you seek out this man, George?' said the inspector, turning to Mr Williamson. 'I am sure you do not need his help as an investigator.'

'You have seen fit not to tell me about your colleague sitting beside you there,' said Mr Williamson. 'In return, I feel no obligation to explain why I am reacquainted with Mr

Dyson. And if we are talking about trust, I think a measure of it might be achieved if we were not sitting here in irons.' Mr Williamson held up his wrists with a rattle.

Inspector Newsome nodded and took a ring of keys from his waistcoat pocket. He handed them to Eusebius. 'If you will be kind enough.'

'I know you,' said Mr Williamson as he offered his bonds to be unlocked. 'You were patrolling Holywell-street just prior to the raid. If you are not a detective – and I am sure you are not – you are certainly a habitual observer of some variety. Indeed, I will venture that you take your usual payment from the Society for the Suppression of Vice. Am I right?'

Eusebius's face remained as blank as if he had heard nothing.

'Astute as always,' answered Mr Newsome with a forced smile.

'I am curious what causes that Society to work so closely with the Detective Force, Inspector. I would have thought that Sir Richard was against their spies. Indeed, I wonder if he knows of your methods of prying into my business as a private citizen?'

'In turn, I am curious about your interest in my case, Mr Williamson. Are we going to speak about it, finally – or merely chat around the subject as ladies do?'

'Before we offer any comment at all,' said Noah, 'I would be interested to know under what terms we participate in this discussion. As prisoners? As suspects?'

'Ah yes – Mr Dyson and his terms. You give nothing for nothing, isn't that so? In fact, you are both free to go. I apologize for my precipitate incarceration of you both. But it seems quite evident that we may be of help to each other. I accept that our dealings before have been . . . well, have been not ideal. On this occasion, however, there is no threat – just an exchange of information. Do those terms seem acceptable to you, Mr Dyson?'

Noah looked to Mr Williamson, who nodded slightly and addressed the inspector: 'I would say that our treatment so far is evidence enough of your trustworthiness . . . but perhaps we might tentatively agree to those terms.'

'Then speak. What is your interest in my case?'

'Hmm. The story is a complex one.'

'I would expect nothing less.'

'You know, of course, about Katherine's death.'

'Naturally. A tragic occurrence, but years ago and part of your past.'

'And you know that I was never convinced of the verdict of suicide.'

'Mr Williamson . . . George, you know that there was insufficient evidence—'

'No. Regardless of what beliefs I have held these passing years, the fact of the matter is that, shortly after the Holywell-street incident, I received information that Katherine's death was indeed murder and that the solution to that crime was the same as that behind Mr Sampson's accident . . . if an accident it was.'

'Preposterous! How could there possibly be any connection? There is no similarity whatsoever, apart from a fall from height. How did you receive this information? From whom?'

'It was an anonymous, hand-delivered letter. No return address.'

'And you believed it? George, your judgement has been clouded by your personal feelings. Where is this letter? I am sure it is a hoax.'

'It has been my business of late to know a false letter from a true one, and I believe this one is true. I have it in a secure place.'

'May I see it? If there is information relating to my case—'

'There is no other detail. The contents are exactly as I have told you, but it suggests the Holywell case is no accident. Is that right?'

'I am not at liberty—'

'Wait,' said Noah. 'That is not in the spirit of our terms, is it, Inspector? Do you suspect murder or not?'

Mr Newsome pursed his lips and gripped the arms of his chair. 'All right. The evidence points to murder, but we have no ideas about suspects or motives. There are multiple clues and mysteries, but no clear conclusions. The investigation is ongoing.'

'So what *do* you know?' asked Mr Williamson.

'Ah – now we get to the heart of the matter. What do *you* know?'

'Hmm. We know what we have read in the newspapers and heard on the street: the fall, PC Cribb, Mr Sampson's incoherent words, the drunken mariner Ned Coffin, the unknown young man and his carriage – as you say: many clues but few conclusions.'

'What else?'

'How could I know more? Did you not instruct all constables that they were not to cooperate with me under any circumstances and on any case? I am no longer a detective – I have no authority to question people. Mr Dyson here has offered merely to offer advice.'

'Do not take me for a fool, Mr Williamson. You have been pursuing your own case and interrogating people, that aged waterman on Holywell-street included. Who, for example, is Persephone?'

Noah and Mr Williamson managed by an effort of will not to turn to each other, but the weight of the silence that followed the name was enough to tell Inspector Newsome of its significance. Eusebius, who until this point had been sitting quite placidly, flicked a tongue at the corner of his mouth and shifted position.

'Come now,' said Inspector Newsome, 'I told you we have spoken to that street girl you visited at Golden-square. You may assume we have learned all that was discussed, so let us not pretend otherwise.'

'You have been following me,' said Mr Williamson with barely suppressed emotion. 'On what authority? Am I a suspect? Who do you have watching me and why?'

'It was purely coincidental. As I said before, you were seen by a constable at Haymarket. He overheard your conversation. You know how the men gossip, and so I heard the news.'

'I think not. You said earlier that I met the girl at Haymarket. Now you say Golden-square. Do you think I would not have noticed a uniformed constable near me at Haymarket? There was none. I was clearly followed.'

'All right. I will be frank. This is an unusual case: a difficult case. We have men watching the coffee house to see if that young man returns and they saw you attempting to question Mrs Colliver. It seemed an odd coincidence that a previous member of this force would be asking questions, so, yes, you were followed – but with good reason, for you asked the girl about Holywell-street.'

'She told me about another incident on that street the very same morning: the suicide of a prostitute. I have not read of it in the papers.'

'Yes, there was a death, a suicide – no doubt one of many

in the city that day. But there is no indication that the two incidents are connected in any way. I am afraid the girl Charlotte was merely creating a story to extort money from a gullible client. They will tell you anything, these girls. Nevertheless, I am interested in this "Persephone" you were so eager to locate.'

'The writer of the letter I received was "Persephone". I thought perhaps it was a professional name so I asked the girl. As you have found – she duped me.'

'I do not recognize the name. Is it foreign? What have you discovered about it?'

'Nothing. Most likely it *is* a foreign name. Or perhaps the name is just nonsense to disguise the identity of the writer.'

'That is all? You receive a letter telling you that Katherine's death was a murder and this is the most you can discover about the mysterious Persephone?'

'My investigations are ongoing, but I feel the most propitious avenue is the Holywell-street case itself.'

'But you must have extracted some further suppositions from that letter, or you are not the George Williamson I know.'

'The writer is intelligent and very likely has access to privileged information. However, the letter is so brief that there is little more I can say.'

'Or *will* not say. What else? What did Joseph the waterman tell you yesterday?'

'He heard the incident and was the only man on the street at the time of the actual fall – before PC Cribb and Mr Coffin arrived on the scene. He heard Mr Sampson repeating "I cannot" before he fell. The constable arrived shortly after the fall but did not see Joseph, who was resting in a doorway.'

'"I cannot"? Cannot what?'

'I do not know. This is the extent of my discoveries, Inspector.'

'You have barely told me anything.'

'I have told you more than I would normally wish. Now – I would like to know what *you* know. What did you find in that room, Inspector? What did Mrs Colliver tell you? What other people have you questioned? What of the other guests at the coffee house?'

'These details are highly confidential, you understand.'

'As is my private life, which you have invaded.'

'All right. I reveal this information purely with the intention that you may be able to offer your combined insights and help to solve the case:

'The room contained four empty glasses that had held sherry; Mrs Colliver denies all knowledge of these glasses. The woman herself has a nasty wound high on her forehead that she claims was accidental but which she was at some pains to conceal. And the one guest that we have been able to locate, a Mr Jessop, says that he was woken in the early morning by a man who threatened his life if he spoke of anything he might have heard. He heard little, however, because he was quite drunk. We have no useful description of the man who woke him. As for our only other witness, the mariner Ned Coffin, the man has vanished. Perhaps he is at sea; perhaps he is dead and at the bottom of the river. What do you make of all of that?'

'Evidently Mr Sampson's death was no simple fall.'

'So it would seem.'

'I would like to see any notes you made on examining the room, and I would like to speak with both Mrs Colliver and Mr Jessop with the authority of the Detective Force behind me.'

'That will not be possible.'

'I must insist. The solution to the crime may very well be—'

'I do not make notes as you do – I simply remember. And it is not possible to speak to those people because Mr Jessop died shortly before midday yesterday. He seemingly fell head-first from a window at his place of work. As for Mrs Colliver, she has gone missing, having left her premises before dawn on the same day.'

'Hmm. Hmm. Murder, of course.'

'It would appear so, though we have no evidence as yet, and no body.'

'You must have ideas, Inspector,' offered Noah, who had been reclining comfortably with his hands clasped in his lap as the conversation progressed. 'The empty glasses, the warning to Mr Jessop, and now the apparent murder of an important witness: it all points to the perpetrator nullifying any clues that may lead back to him – a perpetrator, moreover, who is keeping a close eye on the police as they investigate his trail. What do you *think* is going on here? Let us dispense with proof for a moment.'

'Well, Noah – I would be intrigued to know what *you* think,' said Mr Newsome. 'You are something of an investigator yourself, are you not?'

'One need not be a detective to suggest a credible story, Inspector. Anyone of mild intelligence could do so. Let us say a couple of men agree to rent a room together for purposes either immoral or criminal. They are joined by two (or more) others with a bottle of sherry and some manner of disagreement occurs, the cause of which is Mr Sampson's fall or murder. The men flee immediately and are lost in the city.'

'That is rather an elementary story, Mr Dyson. For what purposes did they meet? Who were these other men you speak of and where were they when PC Cribb arrived? What was the argument about and why is it of such significance that witnesses have been silenced? Your story does not answer these questions, does it?'

'You are the detective, Inspector. I asked you for your ideas.'

'One aspect of your story is accurate: Mr Jessop did say that he heard many footsteps in the corridor that night and morning, suggesting a number of others. Who they are, where they came from and where they went are questions I currently have no means of answering.'

'Evasive as always,' said Noah. 'What have you discerned about the victim himself? May I make a guess that your investigations of his lifestyle led you to Mr Poppleton?'

'Why would you suggest such a thing?'

'I deduce from your expression that this is so. Nevertheless, a single man of his age . . . his interests would no doubt have extended in that direction. Did he belong to a club?'

'The Continental.'

'That seems fitting; the place does rather have the reputation of being a nest of vice. Have you questioned anyone there?'

'Not yet. Gaining access to the place has been more difficult than expected.'

'I know a member. I feel sure I will be able to gain access.'

'That could prove very useful. What could also prove useful is what you learned from your conversation with Mr Poppleton yesterday. Can we at least agree that you were there to interrogate him?'

'I questioned him about Mr Sampson and asked whether the victim had been a customer. He became agitated, but I could proceed no further, however, because I was struck from behind and knocked unconscious. Whether it was my particular questions that caused the attack, or something else, I cannot say. I did not see or hear my assailant.'

'Another useless piece of testimony. If nothing else, it suggests more time should be spent talking to Mr Poppleton. We have him in custody, although it is not his first time in gaol and I fear he would rather serve his customary two years than speak to me about this case. Nevertheless, I will try.'

Noah cast an almost imperceptible glance at Mr Williamson, who, although seemingly deep in thought, appeared to acknowledge it with an affirmative blink.

'It seems we are in a position to begin negotiations,' said Noah with a smile that caused the inspector to once more grip the arms of his chair.

'What negotiations?'

'I will be able to gain access to that club and question its familiars on the lifestyle and acquaintances of the late Mr Sampson, one of whom might know our mysterious young man. I might also add that I am likely to be more successful in this endeavour for not being an investigating policeman. They do not like authority much at the Continental. No doubt this would help both of our cases. You, on the other hand, have access, via the Metropolitan Police, to the whole city – if you cannot locate a Persephone, then she must not exist. Do we have an agreement?'

Mr Newsome looked from Noah to Mr Williamson as if he were being tricked in some way. Neither could be trusted in his experience.

'There is one more piece of information I should share with you, gentlemen. If I did not know for certain that you were both incarcerated last night, I would be highly suspicious. As it is, this latest occurrence further inclines me to agree to the terms and participate as you describe.'

'What occurrence are you referring to?' said Mr Williamson.

'The body of Joseph the waterman was washed out of the mouth of the Fleet River just after dawn this morning. His throat had been cut. Whoever is behind this Holywell-street murder, they are standing invisibly at our very shoulders and seeing to it that the solution cannot be found. And I will not be prevented from solving this crime.'

'Nor I,' said Mr Williamson, his eyes focused inward upon a different time and place.

'Well then – if Mr Dyson is to investigate the club and I the name, where will you focus your attention, Mr Williamson?'

'I will look into this murder of Joseph.'

'Look into what? The river? All we have is a corpse.'

'I may no longer be a sergeant of your Force, Inspector, but I have lost none of my sense. If the unfortunate Joseph was indeed washed from the mouth of the Fleet, he must have been dropped into it at Clerkenwell.'

'What makes you think so? That disgusting sewer is entirely covered over within the city as far I know.'

'Almost entirely. There is much demolition work proceeding east of Field-lane, and a stretch of the river has been temporarily uncovered as they clear the houses. It was in yesterday's *Times*. I will go there and see what I can find; it is the only place where a man's body may have been introduced to the river and washed to the Thames ... provided your information is correct about the body emerging just at that point.'

'It is correct.'

'Then I will begin there.'

'That is no area to be venturing alone, unless one is

a professional criminal,' said Noah. 'I suspect even the inspector's men do not venture there after dark. You will take Benjamin to protect you.'

'Let us waste no more time chatting, then,' said the inspector. 'The sooner we can solve this case (whatever our reasons), the sooner we can dispense with each other's company. I suggest that we meet again next Friday to compare what we have found and see if we are any closer to a solution. We can meet at the house of Mr Allan – Mr Williamson knows it.'

'What about this gentleman here?' said Noah, indicating Eusebius Bean. 'What role does he play, Inspector?'

Eusebius, who had been sitting quite placidly absorbing the conversation, showed no sign that his name had been spoken. He did not react or reply.

'He is merely an observer. You need not concern yourself with him.'

'See that he does not observe us,' said Noah. 'London is a dangerous city, especially after dark. A loitering figure might be a friend or a foe.'

'Is that a threat, Mr Dyson?'

'You may decide, Inspector.'

Mr Newsome looked to Eusebius, whose expression said nothing at all.

FIFTEEN

———◆———

Noah stepped down from the cab on Pall Mall and beheld the Continental Club before him. And what an aspect it presented in the winter twilight: gaudier (if that can be imagined) than the Hellenic Club, and as lacking in gravitas as the Oxford and Cambridge Clubs were distinguished. Its profusion of columns and capitals, its porphyry, Portland stone and pediment made it an architect's crazed dream of clashing styles. The members did not seem to mind. Rather, the *façade*, like the singular reputation of the place, drew a certain sort.

Other clubs might attract those of a military background, or perhaps those with a taste for exotic travel. Other clubs prided themselves on their exclusivity, or upon the unique accomplishments of their limited membership. But the Continental existed purely for pleasure. Here could be found the finest food, the choicest wines and liqueurs, the best Havanah cigars, and the most dissipated fellows with the bawdiest approach to a life that was not worth living except under the constant influence of a surfeit of indulgence.

Noah had said to Inspector Newsome earlier that same day that he was not himself a member but knew one. That was a lie of sorts. He was, however, known to its committee and welcomed (regardless of the membership rules) on the rare occasions when he visited. To understand why this was the case, it will be necessary to learn a little more about this man who first materialized in our story in that musty room at Temple Bar. And it will therefore be necessary to turn back our story momentarily, like thread on a spool, and have him climb backwards into the cab from which he has just exited.

Let us imagine, if we can, those horses trotting in reverse back along the Strand, led by their carriage through Temple Bar (a smile playing upon Noah's face inside), along Fleet-street and up Ludgate-hill, past St Paul's and onwards east until the roads narrow and become less straight. Now we are passing – still in retrograde manner, the horses inhaling their own steaming breath through flared nostrils – the Tower and St Katharine's Dock, the lofty warehouse walls of London Dock and the seething miasma of those mariner-haunted rookeries.

Perhaps one might not expect it, but the young Noah had once called streets like these his home and roamed them with his gang of diminutive thieves. Poorly shod and often cold, he had nevertheless been a king among his kind until the police had caught him at the scene of a brewery fire and sent him off to the hulks of Woolwich to wait for the next transport ship and his ticket to a fugitive life of adventure.

A street boy he might have been, but he could read. For every watch or handkerchief he stole, he purloined two books also – and read them. Not just in English, but in Latin and Greek, too. On occasion, and if the attire came into his hands, he could quite easily pass himself off as the spoiled son of a gentleman, lost in the busy streets while collecting books for his father. Many an 'omnibus fare' he made that way, charming well-to-do ladies with poetry and scripture recited from memory.

Yes, a curious man, this Noah Dyson, still moving

backwards in time through our narrative, no doubt watching people reversing out of shops, the hands of clocks moving against nature and the unintelligible cries of omnibus men's '!thgir llA'. Finally, the cab reverses to a halt outside a small storehouse near Broad-street, Stepney, whose single chimney sucks an endless column of steam from the frigid air into its narrow aperture. Noah descends, walking unerringly without looking behind him, and the door opens unbidden so he can enter.

In forward motion now, we will become invisible witnesses to the inside of that manufactory. The first thing we notice (after the urine-like scent of the place) is that every man within is of the Chinese race: emaciated fellows in baggy white linen suits who go unsmilingly about their work like automatons. The air is thick with the hot closeness of steam, and the origin of the work appears to be a number of hide-covered chests that (we might know if we were botanists) are fashioned from mango wood.

Peering inside each chest, we see rows of rough spheres, about the size of two balled fists, wrapped tightly in moist leaves. They have recently arrived from Malwa, via Calcutta, and represent the finest raw material of their kind anywhere on the globe.

In short, Noah is one of the most prized refiners and suppliers in London of Benares opium, both to chymists and those members of the aristocracy who enjoy the pipe. We need not concern ourselves here with those tiresome debates about China and the members of that race who use the drug to their own destruction – our interest is founded upon Noah's trade, which allows him privileged access to many of the clubs and elite chambers of pleasure in this city. True, laudanum is readily available, but it is a pale substitute and the spirit content impairs the experience. Only the finest raw opium will do for the man of taste, and if it is not exactly a crime to smoke it once in a while, a certain discretion is required in its supply and usage to avoid a slur upon one's good name.

Prone as they are to lackadaisy, these Chinese had to be monitored closely and so we find Noah paying close attention to the vats of opium solution that, by a repetitive cycle of straining, boiling, evaporating and soaking, fill the air with their acrid steam until they are reduced and perfected into that sacred elixir of unmistakable sticky perfection.

One might legitimately ask how a man becomes a trader in opium. Perhaps when he has escaped from penal Sydney aboard a sandalwood boat and seen for himself the serried ships anchored off the coast of Macao, the enormous quantities of cash changing hands, the chests hoisted on creaking tackle from deck to deck and the masts marking time against the Oriental sky. Perhaps when he has already himself been a thief and a prisoner. Perhaps when anonymity is his most highly prized possession and ready capital his perpetual key to freedom. A man must make a living somehow, and he might as well sell pleasure of a physical kind if he is not blessed with the talent of writing.

But I digress. Having briefly glimpsed a fragment of the man's secret life, it is time for us to quickly unspool our way back across London – rushing back through the streets in a terrifying blur to make the railways seem tardy – and arriving once again at the Continental Club, which Noah was about to enter.

'Good evening, Mr Norman,' said the porter, who knew every one of the three hundred members by name, and this particular non-member by a necessary pseudonym. 'We have not had the pleasure of your company for a while.'

'Indeed, Jackson, but tonight I feel the need of a fine meal and a good smoke.'

'Ha ha! You are in the right establishment, sir!'

'Could you perhaps see that this package finds its way to the secretary?'

Mr Jackson sniffed at the parcel and winked conspiratorially before putting it under his desk. 'Yes, I will, sir. A number of the members will be most gratified.'

'Thank you, Jackson.'

And Noah passed where Inspector Newsome had previously found it impossible to enter: into the Continental's lofty hall, whose chequered marble floor, graceful Ionic columns and vaulted ceiling (injudiciously thick with gilt *and* fresco) were a foretaste of the place's glorious lack of restraint. A sound of murmured conviviality echoed down the broad sweep of Carrara marble staircase, inviting the visiter to ascend towards it.

No doubt the common reader has little conception of a club's drawing room, but one might begin by picturing a crackling fire in a huge hearth; the leathery scent of numerous wing-back chairs; a womb-like comfort instilled by the burgundy carpets and curtains – and, of course, that singular atmosphere created when men group together without the refining influence of women. The fifty or so gentlemen gathered there that evening were red of face, garrulous of nature and as coarse in tone as one might expect of a 'Continental man'.

Noah took a seat away from the mass of people and ordered a port from the liveried waiter. Then he reclined into the arms of his chair to observe the erstwhile associates of Mr Jonathan Sampson.

The Continental was as renowned for its eclecticism as

for its eccentricity. Whereas other clubs might attract a pre-dominantly legal, or medical, or military *clientèle*, the Contin-ental drew men from across the professions – albeit the sort of men who placed pleasure marginally above reputation.

Who amongst them might have known Mr Sampson well? The gamblers must certainly have taken his money; the drin-kers would have shared port and sherry with him; the lechers would no doubt have discussed their bawdy book collections with him – but were any of these men his friends?

Can one truly know a man? One might speak with him, eat with him, joke with him . . . but his secret thoughts, dreams and fears remain hidden within. A man who would reveal his vulnerabilities in a place like this might just as well stay at home with his wife. For all his vigour and brashness, the club man is an actor in a drama that he plays in place of his life: bellowing his lines to cover the whispers of his hollow soul . . .

Noah's musings were disturbed by the noise being made by a man holding court by the fireplace: a man wearing a flamboyant sandy-coloured moustache and an enormous, spirit-swollen red nose. The tarnished medals on his breast boasted a military past, and his raucous topic was one of great fondness to the soldiering fraternity: brothels.

'Ah, now . . . ah, if it's a Negro girl you're after, you want to visit Mrs Todd of Half Moon-yard at Whitechapel. She has the best ones – direct from Paris, I hear. Can't speak a word of English, but, ah, one doesn't want to talk, does one!'

An eruption of lecherous mirth went off from that seated group . . . and Noah's glass paused abruptly on its way to his lips.

One of the laughs was a high-pitched *yip-yip-yip* like a curious hiccough or an animal's cry.

Noah looked sharply and caught the laugh again, this time

seeing the man as he leaned forward to slap his leg. Anywhere else, it would be a thing of amusement in itself, but evidently these fellows were familiar enough with it to make no comment or reaction, suggesting that its possessor was a regular visitor.

The gentleman in question was young – perhaps twenty-three – and bore all the distinguishing traits of insouciant wealth. His suit was of the finest cloth and his boots a work of art in polished leather. His face was flushed, even at this early hour, with an excess of wine, and he exhibited those delicate features of an aristocratic line no doubt stretching back to the Conqueror: a broad, pale forehead; thin lips dyed red by his drink; and a slim, fragile nose that had never suffered a greater assault than snuff. His black hair, in odd contrast to the perfection of his dress, was quite unkempt.

Noah knew the kind: most likely the son of a duke. The young man could not afford a house befitting his tastes on the 300 pounds annual allowance his father gave him, so he resided here at the club's saloon rooms where everything he could desire – library, baths, fine dining, fresh periodicals and servants – within reach of his unworked fingertips. If he left the place at all, it would only be for hunting, shopping and women.

Was this the man who had fled Colliver's coffee house the night of Jonathan Sampson's fall? Was this man a murderer? Here, in this sanctuary of pleasure and privilege, a world apart from the cold and filth of the other London, did this yelping dandy have blood on his slender hands? His was a life of ceaseless indulgence. His countenance would not show signs of age or care for many years yet. Only his eyes provided a clue to the inner man, for, despite his frequent laughter, they seemed to remain hard, black and cold like the eyes of a serpent.

Lost in his own reflections, Noah did not notice at first that his stares had been noticed and that muttered comments were being exchanged among that group. He drained the remnants of his glass and was about to summon the waiter when the dinner bell sounded.

And what a table they laid forth at the Continental. Only the finest Staffordshire china, Sheffield silver and Italian crystal graced that expanse of pure white linen. Throughout the meal, Noah was careful to note whether the group he had observed were observing him, and was glad to see that they were. By the final course, he was quite dizzy with satiation after a well-cooked steak with oyster sauce, wonderfully fresh peas, crisp asparagus, Dublin stout and a glutinous pudding that quite finished him off.

Much as he would have liked to sample the further array of sauces by Burgess and Lazenby, he simply could not spoon another mouthful into a taut stomach. Instead, he leaned back in his chair and looked around a table that was depopulating as members retired singly and in groups to their card games and post-prandial drinks. As Noah had hoped, the military man from the living room was preparing to address him.

'I say! Are you, ah, a new member, sir?'

'I attend very rarely . . . Mr . . . ?'

'Major. Major Archibald Tunnock, retired. I, ah, have not seen you before and, ah, I am here most evenings.'

'I am Norman – Adam Norman. I should come more often, if only to enjoy the table and the cellar.'

'Yes! A fine repast, what! I say – would you, ah, like to join me and some of my fellows in the cigar room? They have some, ah, rather fine Havanahs.'

'I believe I would like that very much.'

And thus it was that Noah found himself, precisely as he

had hoped, with the group he had observed in the drawing room, reclining together in the infernal semi-darkness of the cigar room, where blue-grey skeins of smoke twisted lazily in an atmosphere of whisky-scented languor. Major Tunnock had introduced each fellow by Christian name only (a Peter, a Harold and a John) and all of them seemed to be fresh-faced graduates greatly impressed by the bluster of the old fighter. The young man with the unusual laugh – identified merely as James – was among them, but now seemed somewhat reticent in front of this stranger. As they all spoke together, James had evaded every direct address of Noah's with a non-committal response, those black eyes searching his interrogator with cool speculation.

'And what do *you* do for pleasure, sir?' Noah had asked him.

'O, I go about the city with my fellows.'

'Do you have use of a carriage here at the club?'

'There is one, I believe, but I generally take a cab.'

'Do you enjoy the library here? I understand it has a fine collection in Greek.'

'So I hear, but I rather tired of the ancients at university.'

'What of girls? I suppose a young man like you has the pick of them.'

'I visit the supper rooms from time to time, or the parks in the summer.'

Only that final answer had elicited any kind of expression from James: a thin and secret smile that flickered briefly across his face like a shadow.

Noah had been more assiduously pressed on his background by the group, presenting himself as an importer of Oriental foodstuffs, and suggesting with consummate vagueness that his was a privileged but not especially illustrious background. By this, he meant them to understand that he was the illegitimate offspring of some nameless notable whose identity none of them would be so tactless to enquire after.

'Are you, ah, a married man?' the major asked Noah.

'I am not. I am afraid I cannot find one woman I can settle on.'

'I find that I like to, ah, settle on a different one each evening!'

The group laughed dutifully, albeit without as much abandon as they had when they were surer of their company.

'O, I see: the major is a romantic!' said Noah.

'Romance has little to do with it, my boy! But it is, ah, difficult to find a good woman, don't you find?'

'I visit a regular girl. She has a place in Golden-square.'

The major nodded and thoughtfully twirled an end of his moustache. 'Golden-square you say? There are some French girls thereabouts. That is good. A regular girl, ah, learns what one likes and can be depended upon. Though I do tend to become, ah, bored.'

'Bored, Major? I could never become bored of a good girl.'

'Ah, yes – but don't you find that you get, ah, accustomed to a certain, ah, practice and yearn for something, ah, different?'

'It is interesting you should mention that, Major. I was discussing the same thing with a fellow just the other day. We were talking about books.'

'Books you say? I trust you are referring to, ah, a special kind of book?'

'It is true, I am a collector of . . . of particular varieties of literature, shall we say.'

'You are indeed a "Continental man", sir, even if you, ah, rarely attend. What have you read recently?'

'I enjoyed *The Venusian Acolytes*, though I admit it was a

little too genteel for my tastes. Before that I was pleased to acquire a series of images under the title of *The Scullery Maid's Education* – a fine and detailed study that I have shared with my Golden-square girl, if you understand my meaning . . .'

There was a murmur of recognition and approval around the group, unfathomable glances being exchanged between them all. If this gathering was an assessment of their new smoking fellow, it seemed he was performing suitably.

'Indeed! Indeed! I know both titles and the latter is, ah, very fine. Very fine. Tell me, Mr Norman, what was the nature of your, ah, discussion with your fellow the other day? About becoming, ah, accustomed.'

'We were of the opinion that a man's tastes do not remain static but develop and progress. What seems exciting today is *passé* in a month or two. Novelty is critical, and so is . . . how should I put it? . . . An element of the forbidden.'

The major looked meaningfully around the group as if an earlier point of his had been proved by Noah's words. The end of his cigar crackled and flared red. He ejected a cloud of smoke from the corners of his mouth. 'What you say is, ah, quite right, sir. It is something that I and my fellows have discussed on many occasions. And is it not like any, ah, pleasure? I may drink this whisky for a year or so, but then my fancy is taken by Barbadoes rum, or something stronger still.'

'You are quite right, Major. I am fortunate, however, that my regular girl is open to new ideas.'

'She sounds like a good girl, but every girl has her, ah, limits. Does she like a whipping? A sharp spanking?'

'Well, I . . .'

'Forgive me, sir! I have made you, ah, blush. I am an old soldier and I have travelled further down that, ah, road than many men.'

'It is quite all right, Major.'

'We speak frankly here at the club. We men of the, ah, city need not be genteel about such things.'

'Well, quite.'

The major again stroked his moustache and looked pointedly at James, who had been examining Noah with unnerving attention throughout the entire conversation. At the major's look, James nodded in wordless acquiescence, excused himself and walked towards the library.

Noah applied himself to his cigar for a moment and accepted another glass of whisky from the waiter. James's momentary absence seemed like an opportunity.

'Jackson the porter tells me that one of the members has recently passed. I am afraid I miss that kind of news being absent so frequently. Did any of you fellows know him?'

'Sampson was his name – Jonathan Sampson.' The major's tone was flat.

'The name is unfamiliar.'

'He was, ah, a quiet one.'

'Sampson, you say? Wait – was he the same who fell from the window in Holywell-street?'

'The same.'

'That was a curious case, was it not? There was much discussion among my fellows about it.'

'Curious indeed. But as I say, he was not among our, ah, group.'

'Even so – there must have been a good amount of speculation in the smoking room about his fall. Was it merely an accident? Was he with a girl, do you think – or a man?'

The end of the major's cigar again glowed red and he surveyed 'Mr Norman' with eyes that suggested the exterior of the windy old soldier was, like his medals, something he might choose to wear according to his mood. There was another twirl of the moustache.

'You are right, Mr Norman. It was a most unusual incident. Speaking for myself, I think the man was a sod and was caught at it.'

'Perhaps. Perhaps. Certainly he was up to some mischief there. We will never know.'

'Quite.'

At that moment, Major Tunnock looked across the room to see James returning with a paper in his hand. And the convivial smile returned like a gas flame springing into life.

'Mr Norman – James has something for you. It is, ah, something from the "confidential" section of our library that you might like to read – but not here at the club if you please.'

'Really? What is it?' Noah took the pamphlet from James and glimpsed the title: *The Gentleman's Poetics of Transgression*. There was no author, but the publisher was Henry Poppleton of Holywell-street.

'It is an, ah, idea. It touches on what we were discussing just a few moments ago and it might be of, ah, interest to you.'

'I will read it with interest, Major. Thank you.'

'And here is my card. If you find the contents to your, ah, taste, you may contact me either at the club or at the address on the card. We can meet again. I like to make the acquaintance of fellows such as you who have such, ah, refined tastes.'

'You are all too kind. I am having a most pleasant evening. I regret now that I do not attend the club more often.'

Noah did not proceed directly home from the club later that evening. He first made a short visit to the office of the secretary to receive his payment for the earlier delivery of opium.

'It is a pleasure to see you in person, Mr Norman,' said

the secretary. 'Is your usual man, the Negro, unavailable this evening?'

'No – I felt the need of some company tonight. Indeed, I made the acquaintance of your Major Tunnock.'

'Ah, yes.'

'You disapprove of the major?'

'Between you and me, he does rather lend certain associations to the club. You know how these old soldiers can be.'

'Quite. I was speaking with one of his young acolytes: James . . . I did not manage to learn his surname. A sartorial sort.'

'I suppose you mean James Tattershall – one of our residents.'

'A pleasant fellow: intelligent, lively . . .'

'And quite a distinctive laugh!'

'Indeed. Do you know much about him?'

'He is, as you say, a pleasant fellow. I believe that he is waiting for an inheritance and is spending his bachelorhood enjoying London before he retires to the family seat.'

'Does he share the major's interests, do you think?'

'He is a young man. It is not my business to know what he does away from the club as long as he is more discreet than the major. Nor is it your business, Mr Norman.'

'You are right. Forgive me. I am naturally curious.'

'Quite permissible, but you understand that I must maintain my secretarial duties with honour.'

'I thank you for that. Good evening to you, sir.'

It was much later that evening, after the visiting members had returned home and the boarding guests had retired to their rooms, that young James gained access to the secretary's office and discovered that the infrequent member calling himself Mr Norman was not – as suspected – a member at all.

Nevertheless, there was an Adam Norman listed as a supplier to the club under the category of 'Oriental materials'. Whoever he was, the man seemed to be neither a policeman, nor a gentleman, nor a tradesman. And he asked the most inappropriate sort of questions.

SIXTEEN

As we have heard, Mr Williamson had determined to visit Clerkenwell, or rather that disgusting, Irish-infested rookery bordered by Field-lane at its west and Smithfield at its east – a part of our modern city that would likely be recognized today by the lowest Londoners of two hundred years ago.

Naturally, no man but an inhabitant would venture there at night unless he wanted to be knocked on the head and robbed of his very shoes, so Mr Williamson had made the sensible decision to set out shortly before dawn and arrive just after first light. Much against his initial protestations, the estimable Benjamin walked at his side, quite dwarfing him in comparison.

The Negro was truly an impressive specimen. Well over six feet tall (but seeming taller in a fine black overcoat and a top hat worn at a quirky angle), he seemed as lithe and muscular as some exotic beast. That milky eyeball of his attracted almost as much attention as his build, but few dared to stare – even when they became aware of the scaffold scars about his neck. A scarf covered those today, and Benjamin strolled as if the excursion were merely a morning errand to purchase bread.

The city was eerily silent as the first streaks of light appeared in a cloudy sky. No omnibuses were running at that time, and the cabs were absent. The shutters of shops were still down; upper windows looked out blackly upon the world; the gaslamps hissed impatiently to be extinguished; and frost crunched under their boots. Here and there, they caught the scent of charcoal and coffee from a corner vendor or the yeasty-moist aroma of new bread. Occasionally, they would see some wretched figure swaddled in shawl or blanket harvesting rags, ash or bones from the street. In short, it was one of those winter mornings when it feels as if the light will never come – that this city of sin will remain forever in night.

'It is bitter, is it not?' said Mr Williamson as they turned north on to Bridge-street at Blackfriars.

Benjamin made an affirmative response.

'Hmm. I admit, Benjamin, that I feel awkward when talking to you. I see that you prefer to use your language of hand movements with Noah rather than articulate your thoughts verbally.'

Again, the affirmative response.

'I am curious, however. I have met men without tongues before and they speak. True – it is a mangled and inelegant noise they make, but they can be understood. Is it, perhaps, the case that you simply prefer not to do so? I suppose there is a certain pleasure in retiring from the world in that way. It is, after all, a dirty and hateful place not worthy of our finer thoughts or actions.'

A vast hand settled on Mr Williamson's shoulder and remained there as they walked. It was, perhaps, another affirmative.

Dawn began to settle weakly over the chimneys as they progressed up Farringdon-street – and soon they began to smell their destination. It was the stench of poverty, of the cesspit, the pigsty and the stopped gutter, the slaughterhouse and the rat-ridden ragman's yard. Within this warren of lanes and yards were practised the unspeakable trades of the gut-spinner, the bone boiler, the tripe dresser, the tallow-melter, the paunch cooker, the glue reducer and the trotter scraper.

'I would cover your nose and mouth as we venture forth,' said Mr Williamson, doing so with his scarf.

Benjamin's nostrils twitched at the scent of death and decay, and he followed the advice.

They took Cow-lane and passed eastwards around the rookery, cutting across the lower corner of Smithfield's bleak expanse before venturing down West-street into the rotten core of that place. The street itself, its very buildings as black and decayed as if they had been submerged in the Thames for decades, was all but deserted. Only a slovenly street girl leaned against a wall, either too drunk or cold to lift her head to the strangers. Mud splashed about their feet.

'We proceed to where the demolitions continue,' said Mr Williamson, his voice sounding oddly unfamiliar to him in the dank air.

And soon they were among the devastation: timbers askew, masonry littering the ground, and a great gaping hole where a row of buildings had once stood. It was as if, Mr Williamson reflected, a giant beast had taken the fabric of the city in its maw and ripped out a jagged mouthful. Was this the unholy place – not even to be found on maps hereafter – where poor Joseph had taken his final faltering steps?

Benjamin pointed and made a noise.

There among the truncated walls and puddle-filled pits was a figure making his way awkwardly through the ruins. Even from some distance, the man seemed huge – not as tall as

Benjamin to be sure, but as squat, square and solid as if he had sprung from the massy stonework about him. Mr Williamson and Benjamin exchanged looks; the man did not appear to be a threat.

'I will speak to this Hercules,' said Mr Williamson, again his voice seeming an alien presence there. 'You! Yes, you there!'

The giant fellow paused and looked towards them. There seemed no expression on his face, nor, indeed, any capacity for emotion. He approached without haste through the scattered bricks and cast dead eyes over them, revealing nothing in his gaze. Close up, he seemed a barrel of muscle and bone dressed in rags.

'Sir, do you live hereabouts?' asked Mr Williamson.

The man looked at his questioner as if the words had been mere noise. Were it not for his occasional blinking, he might well have been a figure of wax.

'Hmm. There were people here two evenings ago. An old blind man with white hair. Did you see them perchance, or hear about the strangers from your, er, neighbours?'

No response. The man was like some beast of burden that had wandered here from the market and become lost in these relics of a community.

'His body was thrown in the Fleet among these fallen houses, where the buildings have been knocked down.'

At the word 'Fleet', a flicker of recognition seemed to pass across that broad face.

'Yes, the river – the Fleet. Where might the body have been thrown in? Is there access to the water hereabouts?'

The man turned, gestured in the direction he had come from, and bade them follow. They did so, stepping over lumber and the detritus of destruction as the ground fell away into a natural depression. And soon they could smell it: a ferric scent suggestive of blood and viscera commingled with the evacuations of countless beasts, both animal and human.

'Fleet,' said their guide in a voice so deep it seemed to come from beneath their feet: so devoid of feeling that it might be a ruminant's moan. He pointed at the ditch where that hideous course had been exposed to the sky. Then he began to walk away.

'Wait! Did you see an old man with white hair? It would have been two evenings ago . . .'

But the large fellow simply continued on as if the two others did not exist and the encounter had never occurred. They did not attempt to stop him.

'This is no place for humankind,' said Mr Williamson, as much to himself as to his companion.

The Fleet passed before them: a glistening black ribbon about ten feet across that steamed in the early-morning chill. Its banks were steep and obstructed with the mess of the demolitions, but a rudimentary 'bridge' had been fashioned from a large timber and thrown across the gulf. Muddy footprints went across it.

'Look around, Benjamin. Look on the ground and see if you can see anything – anything at all that might help us, even a hair.'

They separated and went poking around the damp rubble, all the while uncomfortably aware of the river's putrid proximity. Soon their boots and gloves were saturated with an admixture of water and substances that were worth not questioning too closely.

No more than two minutes had passed before Benjamin signalled that he had found something.

Mr Williamson came to where he stood pointing at the

ground. Despite the night's rain, it was obvious that a quantity of blood had been spilled at that spot. It had spattered across some blocks of stone and stained the water held in the fissures. Mr Williamson made sure by sniffing at the stains.

'Blood. And . . . look here, Benjamin. Are those white hairs stuck on the corner of that block? He must have fallen after . . .'

A strange laugh punctuated the silence: a child's laugh.

Both men looked up.

The laugh came again and Mr Williamson searched the opposite bank until he saw where it had come from. A boy was sitting on a crumbling wall and observing them. At least, it was the figure of a boy, albeit with the appearance of a filth-caked imp.

'Boy! Do you live hereabouts?'

'What yer lookin' for?' answered the child, who appeared quite amused by the *charade* occurring there by the river.

'I asked if you live here. There was an old man here two evenings past – a blind man with white hair. He would have been with others. Did you see anything like that?'

'Might of . . .'

'I have a coin for you if you can tell me more.'

'You'll 'ave to come over this side. I don't cross on account me old man'll 'it me 'til I'm blue.'

Mr Williamson looked uncertainly at the weighty plank spanning the seething blackness. Benjamin put a warning hand on his forearm.

'It's safe!' shouted the boy.

Mr Williamson approached the bridge and put down an exploratory boot. It seemed solid enough. He took a step, then another until he was above the water that rushed with surprising speed beneath. The bloated corpse of a dog bobbed obscenely in an eddy between rubble and the bank.

'Come on!' yelled the boy, almost making Mr Williamson stumble.

But he crossed safely, and was followed by Benjamin, whose weight made that single beam flex alarmingly in the centre.

'Are yer a devil?' the boy asked Benjamin as the two men approached him. 'Father sez they's devils the other side.'

'Quiet, boy!' said Mr Williamson, beholding that diminutive figure in detail. His hair was so matted that it stood from his head in stiff peaks, and his face was a mask of dark smears that abated only where the back of his hand had wiped frequently at nose or mouth. The eyes, however, were small and lively points of inquisitiveness.

'Do you live here?' repeated Mr Williamson.

'Over this wall 'ere. On Black Boy-lane.'

'How apt. Do you sit here often looking at the river? Did you see any strange men here as I described just now?'

'Me name's Roger.'

'Very well, Roger – will you answer my question?'

''Ave yer got that coin yer was talkin' about?'

Mr Williamson impatiently fumbled for a shilling and laid it in a palm that had seldom seen water. Either the boy was shrewd, or an idiot. He closed his fist around the coin as if it were a diamond.

'An old 'un oo 'ad no eyes – I saw 'im. He was 'ere with another feller, young feller. Just the two of 'em.'

'Describe the young man.'

'Wearin' a topper. Quite tall. Black coat like your mate chimney chops.'

217

Mr Williamson exchanged a glance with Benjamin, who was evidently the 'chimney chops' referred to.

'And what did you see?'

'Cut 'is throat, din't 'e?'

'The young man cut the old man's throat?'

'Jus' like when father does the calves – sprayin' every-where!'

Young Roger's eyes glistened with the thrill of it and he fidgeted excitedly on his mural perch as a civilized child might if passing a toyshop window.

'This was murder, Roger. A very serious crime.'

'Father lets me watch sometimes. I like to break the calves' tails – it makes 'em moan so terrible! Once, when father was away, I 'it a lamb with the poleaxe an' its 'ead—'

'Roger! I want you to tell me about what you saw. Did the men speak before the murder? Did you hear any words?'

'They spoke. The old 'un asked where 'e was, said 'e could smell a river.'

'Are you sure? Could you hear the words clearly?'

'Course. I 'eard *you*, din't I?'

'Hmm. Is that all you heard? Perhaps I should have my dusky friend here see how well you float?'

'I ain't finished! The old 'un said somethin' what I missed, an' I 'eard the young feller say somethin' somethin' . . . Free-pass somethin'.'

'"Freepass" – are you sure that was the word?'

'I 'eard it with this very lug,' said Roger, indicating a fungal-like growth on the side of his head that might well have been a human ear. 'Then the young 'un took out the razor real slow so the old 'un wouldn't 'ear, an' . . . he slashed it like *this* . . . an' the old man opened his mouth . . . an' there was no words . . . and 'e fell . . . but the blood, the blood . . .'

'Roger!'

'An' when 'e was bled dry, the young feller pushed 'im to the river – *splash!* 'E was away off to the Thames.'

Mr Williamson could not help but picture that woeful corpse washing through the mephitic darkness beneath King's Cross, Holborn, and Ludgate Circus; beneath houses where people were talking or eating; beneath the busy streets where life proceeded with its usual dust and racket; beneath a city that itself was built upon the bodies of countless forgotten souls – then into daylight and the Thames.

'Why did not you report this immediately to a constable or to your father, Roger?'

'What's a "con-stable"?'

'Hmm. Where did the young man go after committing this crime?'

'Back the way 'e come from, easy as yer like.'

'Did anybody else see the incident? Were there any other people in the vicinity?'

'Was jus' me. No, wait – there was a prossie an' her feller across the bridge there jus' before, but they went afore the other two gents come.'

'A prostitute was here with her client?'

'Did it standin' on account of the wet. She saw me 'ere an' winked at me over 'is shoulder. Lucy is 'er name. When I am old enough, father sez—'

'But they did not see the young man and the old man?'

'Dunno. P'raps. Don't think so. They left before.'

'If you are lying to me, I will ask my companion Benjamin to come and turn you black when you are sleeping.'

'I 'ave a knife.'

Mr Williamson smiled. 'Benjamin – would you show young Roger your neck for a moment?'

Perceiving the ruse, Benjamin maintained a stony expression and slowly unwrapped his scarf so that the scars about his neck became visible, the skin striated and stretched from its horrifying trauma.

'Can you see that, Roger? Do you know what happened there? Benjamin's head was once cut completely off. But he just picked it up and replaced it as calmly as he liked . . . then he ate the man who did it.'

Roger's eyes goggled at the injury and he licked at dry lips, finally lost for words. Benjamin's monocular glare was quite terrifying.

'Now – are you telling us the truth, Roger?'

'On my father's knives.'

'Well, I suppose that will do.'

A voice was heard from behind the wall: 'Roger! Where are you?'

'That is father. I 'ave to go or 'e will beat me.' And young Roger disappeared over the wall with a flash of grimy leg.

Mr Williamson looked lugubriously to Benjamin, who was rewrapping his neck against the chill. 'Let us return over the bridge to West-street and see if that slattern we saw is the Lucy referred to by Roger.'

Benjamin nodded, smiling to himself at the story of his beheading, despite Mr Williamson's solemn mood.

'Have you heard that word before, Benjamin? "Freepass"?'

The answer was negative.

'Neither have I. Let us hope that Noah has – or that he knows somebody who can tell us.'

The two men descended to cross the Fleet once more, unaware that another had observed the whole episode with Roger.

*

Over on Black Boy-lane, young Roger was quite giddy with excitement as he stood before the gentleman who was assuredly not his father. The man was old enough to be a grandfather, and his face appeared damaged by some manner of illness, perhaps the pox.

'Did you tell them everything, Roger?'

'I did. 'Ave you got me prize?'

'Wait a moment. What did you tell them?'

'What yer said: about the old 'un, about the razor, that "Freepass" word . . . all like yer said. 'Ave yer got my prize?'

'You are a good boy. Your prize is just there.'

A canvas bag wriggled of its own accord by a wall. Roger skipped over to it and delicately opened the cord at its neck. A lamb's head emerged bleating into the light, and the expression of the boy's face was further from tenderness than one could possibly imagine.

'Enjoy it, Roger.'

'I will. And . . . mister – might a man lose 'is head and still be alive?'

'Anything is possible, Roger. Anything. The devil has many guises.'

SEVENTEEN

And while Benjamin and Mr Williamson were over in Clerken-well, the body of a young female was found slumped against a wall in a grubby court just off Moor-lane, north of Fore-street. It seemed as if the girl had simply sat for a rest in the night and expired there in the frost. Her head had slumped forward suggesting sleep, but she was cold to the touch and would never again wake. A broken gin glass lay about five yards away from her.

Inspector Newsome tilted the head back to look upon her face. She was young and not entirely unattractive, her features showing none of the anguish or pain one might associate with dying at night in a freezing metropolitan alley. Spittle glistened icily on her chin.

'A whore,' said the police surgeon. A corpulent fellow in a too-small top hat and with his coat buttons straining to res-train his stomach, he was clearly not suited to the early hour.

'I think not. She was a dollymop,' said Mr Newsome, refer-ring to that class of girl who resorts casually to the streets for occasional income as their whim takes them.

'What makes you say so, Inspector?'

'Her clothes. Were she a prostitute, a girl of this age and

relative good looks would be making enough money to dress better than this. Look: her stockings are cheap, her shoes are heavily worn and the dress has been washed and repaired so often that it should be in pieces. And look at her fingers – she spent most of her last day blacking boots or the fireplace for the residents of whatever low-rent abode she worked in. No doubt it is close – they seldom venture further than they have to.'

'A servant?'

'I would say so. Yes – look at the calluses on her hands from the scrubbing brush.'

'Indeed. I see why you are a detective. But I fail to see why I have been abruptly woken to attend to the body of a mere servant, dollymop or otherwise.'

'Because, doctor, my observations go only so far. I need you to discern the cause of death and discover anything else about this girl that is of physiological interest.'

'The cause of death is simple. She emerged from a gin palace of some description, slumped here to gather her wits and most likely froze to death. There are no visible wounds. I need not have got out of bed for this.'

'No. That is an assumption unworthy of your position, doctor. You see her class and the broken gin glass in the court and you automatically decide that she must have dropped it. Have you smelled it to see if it contained gin – or smelled her mouth?'

'Inspector Newsome – this is quite preposterous. The girl is a nothing. There will not even be a headline about her. Perhaps people will gossip for a day or two, and then an upturn in the weather will give them something better to speak of. Why should I spend my time seeing to this?'

'Firstly, because it is your job. Secondly, because I have

told you to do so. And thirdly, perhaps you would like to examine something a little more closely.' The inspector took out his handkerchief and picked up a fragment of the broken gin glass, which he held out for the surgeon. 'Smell this . . . not too closely.'

'Bitter almonds . . . prussic acid!'

The doctor stepped back as rapidly as his portly frame would allow.

'Quite. And also a scent of gin. No doubt the two were mixed.'

'So, we have a suicide.'

'Not your initial diagnosis, doctor.'

'Nevertheless, we now have the cause of death. My work here is done.'

'Forgive me – I am not a medical man – but is there something in this girl's posture that tells you she has drunk the poison? Because the existence of the glass here is no evidence at all that she took it. Perhaps it has been here for some days before she arrived. Perhaps there is a colossal wound in the girl's back that we cannot see.'

'Prussic acid will kill whether in a small dose or a strong one – only the period between ingestion and death varies. She drank the gin, slumped against the wall here and it was over. There – may I go home now?'

'Wait. Let us say the poison was mixed with gin to disguise the taste – that is credible. But then, with a matter of seconds to live, she throws the glass from her body to land nine yards away. Why?'

'How should I know? Because she was angry at the world?'

'Doctor – I want you to take this body back with you and examine it closely. I want to know of any other wounds. I want to know if she did indeed ingest the poison. I want to know if that black substance on her fingers is indeed boot-blacking, or whether it is something other.'

'All of this for a whore?'

'All of this for justice.'

'Forgive me – I will do it, of course. But we have had occasion to work together before and I believed I knew your methods. Why do you now care about this inconsequential death?'

'Consequence, doctor, is my business to decide. Come to my office this afternoon with your full report. And mention this to nobody else.'

It was strange indeed for the inspector to have been at the scene of such a minor death. Stranger still had been his request to all stations and watch houses the day before that the suicide of any street girls in London should be reported directly to him as soon as they were discovered and that no one was to investigate the scene before he arrived.

The reader will no doubt have guessed the reason why.

That meeting at the opulent house on the previous day had seemed to the inspector to have been a particularly difficult game in which everyone was lying – or least telling a version of the truth that was most beneficial to him – and that any advantage to be gained was in the slips or suppositions of the opponent. Mr Williamson had apparently made such a slip when he had asked about the death of the prostitute in Holywell-street that fateful night.

The question itself was telling enough, but far more so was the way he had immediately dropped the matter. Here was a man who could make a statue speak with his relentless questions and counter-questions, but he had left this conversational avenue for dead. Why?

Mr Newsome had looked further into the case of the dead girl found on the morning of Mr Sampson's death. It had seemed superficially straightforward: a body found slumped in an alley, a gin glass nearby – just another melancholy metropolitan incident. Of course, that glass and the position of the girl no longer seemed so straightforward. And when local constables had questioned other girls of the neighbourhood, none of them seemed to know the victim or her name. Perhaps friends of the girl had remarked on her absence to constables wherever she did hail from – an eventuality covered by the inspector's request for all stations to heed such reports.

Unfortunately, the body had now been disposed of in unconsecrated ground so no further information was available. Only one other piece of potentially useful information had proved useful: the girl had had long blonde hair like Mrs Colliver's, and like the strand found in that room.

Remembering Mr Williamson's longstanding obsession with the role of prussic acid in the death of his wife, Mr Newsome's next task was to ask his clerk to look through past issues of the *Police Gazette* for cases involving prostitute suicides with that poison. They were few enough, but at least one – a certain Mary – had been found with a glass near her body. It was then that he had asked for any subsequent such deaths to be reported to him. And he had despatched a man to speak once more with the girl Charlotte at Golden-square lest she had mentioned something about it to Mr Williamson. Assuredly, she had not previously told everything she knew.

Neither man – Noah or Mr Williamson – could be trusted in the inspector's estimation. At least George had a reason for this quest after truth, but Noah's involvement was pure mystery – he and that phantasmal Negro with whom he went about. Evidently, the only way to cooperate with either would be in that subtle, ludic form of negotiation in which they had previously engaged.

Which left the question of 'Persephone'.

This, to Mr Newsome's mind, could be the key to the whole case – if the letter was genuine. Who could possibly know of a connection between the two cases? And why say so little if they had an interest in seeing them solved? Naturally, he had put the word out among his special constables to ask about the name, and he had asked his eye-weary clerk to read through the entire secret ledger of vice for a mention of it. Shortly, he would himself venture out to some of the city's least-known attractions in search of 'Persephone', but first there was the matter of Mr Henry Poppleton, currently resident in a solitary cell at Giltspur-street gaol.

In fact, that is where we see the inspector now, smiling to himself at the memory of Noah Dyson once occupying this very cell as the (rather unhelpful) subject of interrogation. There is a smell of cold stone and the chamber pot in that cramped and chilly place. The sound of traffic comes in through the barred street-facing window and the two men speak with steaming breath, though only one wears a coat.

'In the name of C——, will you not get me another blanket, Inspector? A man could freeze to death in this cell,' said Mr Poppleton, who was sitting on his horsehair mattress wrapped in his single woollen blanket. His pinched face peering from inside that cocoon of warmth might have been amusing under other circumstances.

'You are in gaol; a certain degree of discomfort is your due,' said Mr Newsome, who was seated on a chair brought in especially for his ease. 'Indeed, you might look forward to two more years of this if you are again charged with supplying indecent literature. A man of your age . . . would you survive?'

'Do I not pay your men enough? You had no cause to attack my shop like that. We have an agreement: I pay your constables to leave me alone and you leave me alone.'

'Alas, this is a case like no other. I have been under pressure to find the solution and you are a part of it.'

'I have no idea what you are talking about.'

'All right – I will see you in two years . . .'

'Wait!'

'Yes?'

'What do you want to know?'

'I have already asked all the questions. Were you at Mrs Colliver's rooms the night Jonathan Sampson fell from the window?'

'I was not.'

'Do you know who was, or what happened?'

'I know only that he was a customer. His death draws attention upon my trade, even in an oblique manner. It makes me nervous, Inspector.'

'You are lying. What is it that you hide? Or whom? I do not believe that you are the murderer—'

'What murder?'

'Let us dismiss this *charade* of ignorance, Henry. Is the truth of this case so injurious to you that you would go to gaol for two years and most likely die of consumption or over-work?'

'Perhaps.' The publisher's voice was a mere murmur.

'I located your order books, Henry. The list of customers is quite startling, even to me.'

Mr Poppleton wilted inside his blanket.

'However, there are a number of customers who remain mysterious. I do wonder at fourteen John Bulls living at different addresses. And who are the men behind the initials

"J.T.", "H.J." and "J.S."? They certainly seem to buy many of your special stock. I note that there was a John Bull living at Mr Sampson's address, so I assume he is not the afore-mentioned "J.S.".'

'I . . . my customers are confidential . . .'

'Very well – who is Persephone?'

A shiver passed through Mr Poppleton's frame at the mention of the name. His already sickly face appeared to drain entirely of blood. Words would not come.

'I see that the name is of some significance to you. Save yourself needless suffering and tell me what you know.'

'I cannot . . . I . . . cannot.'

'An interesting response. Are those not the words Mr Sampson uttered shortly before he passed through the window at Colliver's coffee house?'

If the publisher had seemed vanquished by the name, he now seemed quite slain at this piece of intelligence.

'Tell me, Henry! Is she a girl? Is she a prostitute? Were you there when it happened? I know that you were, that you drank sherry with the others, that you had a girl with you there – that you know the young man who emerged into the street. When did *you* emerge, and why weren't you seen? Save your-self, man! Speak to me!'

'I . . . I am lost. They will kill me.'

'*Who* will kill you? I will protect you – just tell me.'

'Ha! *Protect* me, you say! They are even now among you! I am a dead man merely because you know her name – you and the other fellows.'

'Which other fellows? Henry! Look at me – which other fellows?'

'In the shop. Before the raid.'

'Noah Dyson? Mr Williamson?'

'I am dead. I am a dead man.'

'Save yourself, Henry. Why should you die that they might enjoy their freedom? I can have you sent to Australia where you will not be found.'

'Dead. Dead. I am dead. Speak to me no more. I have nothing more to say.'

'If you are to die anyway, just tell me what you know.'

But Mr Poppleton had passed into another realm entirely, rocking slightly now with his eyes focused upon no definable point. He began to mumble incoherently to himself about death and oblivion.

Mr Newsome was taken with the urge to slap sense into his interrogatee. Past experience had taught him, however, that people in such a condition were beyond coherence or threat of violence. Perhaps it would be possible to converse again in a day or two.

So, cogitating deeply on what he had heard, Mr Newsome rapped on the cell door for the turnkey and made his way out of the gaol to the waiting carriage. The reins clanked, the whip cracked and they were off west to his next appointment.

Down Skinner-street they went, then up Holborn-hill to Holborn itself, heading towards Oxford-street and the world of the illuminated shop window. And as they proceeded inch by slow inch through the traffic there, the inspector gazed absently out of the window and pondered the crowds.

All of London was there: in top hat and corduroy cap, in silk and canvas, in fine woollen coats and in wretched shawls that barely covered starving bones. Through those gaslit windows were the dreams of all, exhibited with such grace and charm that, bewitched by their magic, one might sell one's very honour to touch and own them. But taken from the window, from their velvet cushions and their empyreal illumination, those same things would ultimately prove as fulfilling as a handsome stone above one's rotten corpse.

The carriage came to a halt in the environs of Hanover-square and Mr Newsome shook such uncharacteristically dark thoughts from his mind, reflecting quizzically that something about this case inclined him to a curious saturninity. There was business to attend to.

The property before him could have been a residential one like many in the area, but the closed curtains on the ground floor provided a clue to the contrary. In fact, this was one of those addresses that featured so prominently in that secret ledger of his.

Mrs Percival's house was something of a legend among the lascivious of London. Not only were her girls of the greatest beauty and the most refined manners, but one could experience things here that were not available anywhere else in the city, many of them administered by the strict Mrs Percival herself. Whether or not there was a Mr Percival was not a question she was ever asked – anyone could take the role for a sum.

The door was opened by a liveried servant in a state of extreme old age.

'I am here to see Mrs Percival,' said Mr Newsome.

'Yes, sir. May I tell her who is calling?'

'Inspector Newsome of the Detective Force.'

This was clearly not the cryptic phrase the servant expected, but he nodded gravely and asked the inspector to enter, showing him to a reception room that might have made the finest club proud. Paintings of women in various stages of undress suggested that this was not a respectable residence, and, indeed, it was highly probable that there were about a dozen attractive young ladies in the rooms above at that very

moment engaging in acts that would render Sir Richard
Mayne speechless for a month.

'Good afternoon to you, Inspector.' The lady herself
appeared at the doorway.

Her voice was cool and formal. She was certainly not the
siren one might have expected. Rather, she had the look of a
prosperous and morally vigorous widow with her greying hair
drawn tightly into a bun atop her head. Her rouged lips were
thin, but amused. Not for her the lace and silk of many in her
profession – she was dressed almost entirely in black and
presented an austere aspect to the world. It was, of course, all
a masterfully subtle illusion demanded by the clients of her
particular speciality.

'Ah, Mrs Percival. We have not met, but—'

'But I have heard your name, Inspector. Who in my profession has not? Do not remove your hat on my account.'

Mr Newsome removed his hat without embarrassment,
placing it on a table beside him.

'I did not expect to see you in person here, Inspector –
I thought that your constables did your work for you. Nevertheless, what might I offer you? A little fustigation? Some
scourging or flagellation? Some phlebotomy perhaps?'

'I fear I have not come for the treatments of the house. It
is information I seek.'

'Do I not send you all that I have? You must have every
aristocrat in Britain in your little book by now.'

'I do indeed appreciate the information you supply, but this
is a different matter, hence my visit.'

'Then let us move from the reception room. I believe my
customers would receive a most unwelcome shock to see a
detective on entering the reception room.'

Mr Newsome followed the grand abbess to another lavish

room across the corridor – one that offered further insight into the nature of her trade. A variety of implements were artfully arrayed on a low table: a short wooden shaft with twelve leather thongs; a 'cat' with needles woven into its ends; a brush of shiny holly; a vase full of nettles; and a variety of restraints, including some Metropolitan Police-issue handcuffs. A large container of water in one corner of the room contained strips of green birch that gave off a fresh, woody scent.

'Do you see anything here that suits your letch?' asked Mrs Percival with a slight arch of the eyebrows.

'The cuffs – and those only on a criminal.'

'So, to business. What may I do for you if not make you bleed?'

'Have you ever, in your illustrious career, heard of a girl called Persephone?'

'I have not.'

'You answer precipitously.'

'It is a strange name. I have known and employed many, many girls, but they choose more mundane names. Even the French girls have rather predictable names. What makes you think she is one of Venus's handmaidens?'

'It is a mere idea. I do not think she is a performer, and, as you say, the name is odd enough to be theatrical. Could it be that she is a prostitute and that you do not know of her?'

'Of course. The name suggests an imagination beyond that of the normal street girl, so perhaps it is the *nom de lit* of that highest class of girl: a courtesan with her own apartment on Park-lane. I admit I do not know such women or what they call themselves. I am paid in pounds; they are paid in diamonds.'

'But those women must rise to that position from *somewhere*? Surely they do not simply go from childhood into the arms of a duke. Might not this girl have passed through a number of roles and houses such as this before reaching those heights?'

'She may have, but not with that name. A whore's name is like a dress, Inspector: one wears it according to one's mood and one's liaison.'

'I see. It seems there is no chance of me locating this girl, if indeed she exists.'

'Perhaps. Do you know anything at all about her?'

'She is intelligent and has access to privileged information.'

'That describes almost every woman *I* know, Inspector.'

'If she had passed through this house or any other house you have known to better things, how might it have happened?'

'If a girl has beauty, grace, a shrewd sense and an ability to learn, she need set no limit on her dreams – provided she is willing to sell her body and her soul. I have known at least one such girl. I saw her walking by the river – a perfect rose growing amid the manure of this pestilential city. She had already begun by dollymopping around as a milliner's girl. But she knew her power over men. Like laudanum to their senses, she was: men falling in love with her all about the place.'

'What happened to her?'

'The usual. One gentleman could no longer bear to share her and set her up with her own place. Naturally, she kept seeing other men when her benefactor was absent and, by degrees, she worked her way beyond the world we know. The last I heard, she was with an Italian prince who visited her but twice a year despite supporting her like a princess in London.'

'What was her name?'

'She was Joanne while she lived here. Then she was Katie. Now, I have no idea.'

'Might any of your girls know her, or where she lives?'

'I am certain not. A girl like her does not acknowledge where she came from. Like Venus herself, she was born from the very waves. I heard that she had a sister in the same profession, but I know nothing more about that, apart from a rumour that the sister died some years ago.'

'Died how?'

'I believe it was suicide.'

'Do you know what year, or the girl's name?'

'No. As I say, it was just a rumour. The girls talk, as do your constables. Now – I cannot talk to you all afternoon. I have Mr —— coming for a thrashing.'

'The magistrate?'

'The same. There is another entry for your book, Inspector.'

'Thank you for your time, Mrs Percival. If you remember anything else, please let one of the constables know.'

'I will. And perhaps one day you will allow me to flay you?'

Mr Newsome smiled. It was the politest offer of violence he had ever received.

Back in his office, the inspector did something he had not done before: he took a piece of paper and began to make notes about what he knew of the case, drawing a circle around each piece of information and attempting to add lines of connection between each.

There was Mr Poppleton's bookshop and his cryptic comments. There was the evidence of Mr Jessop. Then there was the Continental Club, the mysterious Persephone, the words of the dying Mr Sampson, the murder (or disappearance) of Mrs Colliver . . .

The circles remained stubbornly isolated. The solution had to be there among those comments and characters and clues, but it seemed the only way to connect them was with a leap of imagination that he did not possess and could not contrive. Had he been a writer, he would have recognized the process.

He leaned back in his chair, frustrated, and ruminated on the absence of Eusebius Bean. When the spy had not arrived at Scotland Yard that morning as arranged, the inspector had been unconcerned and had not reported it to Sir Richard. Indeed, the day's activities had been all the more pleasant without the perpetual presence of the man at his side. Certainly, the visit to Mrs Percival would have been quite impossible with the over-observant fellow in attendance.

A momentary thought occurred: could it be that Eusebius had himself fallen victim to the Holywell-street curse? He, too, had been on the street when Mr Williamson had questioned the waterman. Perhaps he had been observed and linked to the police investigation. If this was the case, Mr Newsome found himself unmoved at the possibility.

There was no time, however, for further thought on the subject because he was about to receive information that would give him some lines to connect his circles.

A knock on the door signalled the arrival of the police surgeon.

'Inspector Newsome – I trust you are well,' said the doctor, wheezing from the short walk between street and office.

'As well as I was this morning, doctor. What do you have for me?'

'It seems there was some truth in the prussic acid idea after all. Her stomach reeked of it – quite dangerous.'

'Any other injuries to her person?'

'None. The stain on her fingers was lead blacking. And she had had knowledge of a man, most likely on the evening of her death.'

'By "knowledge" I assume you mean intercourse.'

'Quite. But there was no sponge to be found, not as are sometimes found in the more professional girls. So your dolly-mop theory may be correct also.'

'I see. Is that all?'

'One more thing: she had apparently eaten an orange or some other fruit prior to her death. I found evidence of pith and seeds in her teeth and stomach – only a little, though. Evidently she did not like it.'

'Do you have those seeds?'

'Not with me, but I have them still. I am afraid they are masticated almost beyond recognition.'

'I would like you to send them to me, whatever the condition of the remains.'

'As you wish. Will that be all?'

'You have a done a thorough job despite yourself, but there is one more thing – do you corporeal doctors also study illnesses of the mind? I am thinking of the urge to suicide and what causes it.'

'It is something of a specialism, Inspector. Not one of mine, I am afraid.'

'Who of your acquaintance would know more on the subject?'

'Well, there are those physicians at the asylums, of course. And I believe that Mr Herbert takes an interest in the matter of suicide. He has even published on the subject.'

'Mr Herbert the surgeon?'

'The same. It is a sort of hobbyhorse of his.'

'Thank you, doctor. You may go now.'

The door had barely closed when a knock came from the other door leading to the clerk's office. It was the clerk.

'Inspector Newsome, sir? I have some information.'

'Good. What did you find in the *Police Gazette*?'

'Alas, little more than you did. Magdalene deaths are little reported, as you know. There were a few, but no more in the last five years with prussic acid.'

'So what information *do* you have?'

'I took the liberty, sir, of looking through the ledger for the other thing. But I did not find any reference at all to a Persephone.'

'Must I repeat my previous question?'

'Er, no, sir. This letter arrived today for you. It was delivered this morning by post.'

Mr Newsome opened the letter and folded out the single page. There was no signature:

Inspector Newsome

The girl you found dead this morning was one Nelly Jones, a maid in the service of Mrs Scarrock of 12 Milton-street. Just six days ago, Nelly was visited by a certain Mr George Williamson, who spent time alone with her while Mrs Scarrock was out.

It is my duty as a citizen to offer assistance in this way.

'Well, well – Mr Williamson has few friends in this city,' said the inspector.

'Sir?'

'Never mind. Go back to that ledger – contact the special

constables if need be – and find me everything you can on the haughty girls of Park-lane.'

'Park-lane.'

'Is there an echo in this room?'

'No, sir. Thank you, sir.'

And as we leave Mr Newsome there at his desk rubbing his chin and pondering the news he had been given, let us spare a thought for my Nelly – poor Nelly – who was killed in a cold alley, her delicate rump left to settle on hard cobbles and her hair dirtied by Night's damp fingers.

True, she was coarse, common and corrupt. But she was a being fuller of life than many – and often fuller of gin. I never loved you, Nelly. Giving such an emotion to you would have been like giving a fine gold watch to a monkey as a plaything. We enjoyed each other as men and women do. You listened to my words and found music in them. I pursue my story hence for your sake (as well as for my own glory and riches).

EIGHTEEN

We have accounted for the movements of our three principal players – Noah, Mr Williamson and the inspector – in the two days following their meeting at that house at St James's, but the perspicacious reader will have noted the curious absence of two others.

First among these is the plain-faced Eusebius Bean, whom we last saw sitting silently like a well-behaved child beside Inspector Newsome as the Holywell-street discussion progressed. When those other three gentlemen left, however, the spy remained behind to communicate his thanks to the Vice Society luminary who had so generously offered his house for the *rendezvous*.

It will perhaps be of little surprise for the reader to hear that the procurer of that property (though not its owner) was none other than 'J.S.', who appeared to Eusebius from a connecting door shortly after the investigators had left in their separate carriages. Together, they retired to the just-vacated room and sat in the seats still warm from the visiters.

'J.S.' appeared to be in rude health, his pale-brown eyes as solicitous as those of a kindly grandparent, and his complexion glistening with the salubrious sheen of some fragrant emollient. One might never have guessed that the scalp beneath the wig was utterly corrupted or that the mouth was virulent with decay.

'Could I offer you a glass of milk, Eusebius?' said 'J.S.'.

'No thank you, sir.'

'You are good boy. It was a capital idea to bring those men here, and to contact me directly. We must provide our investigative colleagues with every opportunity to pursue this case, even if it means working with civilians.'

'Yes, sir. I have remembered everything that was said.'

'Of course you have, but it is unnecessary. I heard and saw everything.'

'But . . . when?'

'Look there, Eusebius, at the painting of the hunting scene on the east wall. A fine rendering, is it not? But if you were to look closer at the undergrowth where the hounds forage for a fallen bird, you would see a small aperture with a larger one in the wall behind it. From that small room, I was able to observe all. It is why I suggested this property. The man who owns it likes to . . . well, never mind about that.'

'Ingenious, sir.'

'I knew that a man of your temperament would appreciate such a ruse. It is important, you see, that we at the Society know everything about this case.'

'Could you not simply ask the policemen?'

'Ah, you are too innocent! Men like Inspector Newsome dislike men such as we "intruding" in his work. He likes to keep the details to himself so that he may take all the glory when the case is solved. It is pure arrogance. Fortunately – thanks to you, Eusebius – we are now able to pursue the case ourselves. A solution is certain with more people investigating the case.'

'I suppose so.'

'It is a curious case, is it not? You have heard all of the evidence – what do you make of it?'

'I, sir? I am sure I have no idea.'

'Come, now! That is not the Eusebius I know. I see your eyes and I know that all the information is being absorbed into that pretty head of yours. Tell me: what do *you* think happened in that room at Colliver's coffee house?'

'Well, it seems Mr Sampson embarked upon an adventure he was not prepared for. Too late, he decided he would like to change his mind, hence his "I cannot". His fellows were angered and he was either pushed or jumped from the window. They subsequently fled.'

'You are a clever boy. What of the girl?'

'Which girl? She of Golden-square, or the one found dead that morning?'

'My, you were listening very carefully! I refer to the one found dead.'

'I cannot see any connection.'

'Good. That is good. I believe the policemen are chasing a phantasm there.'

'Sir . . . I admit that I am a little afraid . . .'

'Afraid, my boy? Why ever is that?'

'It seems that many people are dying who have a connection to this case. Mr Jessop, Mrs Colliver, Joseph the waterman . . .'

'But you have no connection to the case, Eusebius. You did not hear or see the incident. Who do you think is killing these people?'

'The men who were in the room with Mr Sampson.'

'Who do you think those men might be?'

'I . . . I really cannot guess.'

'Working men, perhaps?'

'Rather not. I believe the carriage they escaped in was their own. And the working man prefers gin to sherry.'

'You are right, of course. What a young detective you are! I was right to choose you as my special observer. I do not want you to be afraid. We must endeavour to do everything in our power to bring these men to justice so that you need be afraid no longer. You will be instrumental in that.'

'How so?'

'You are to cease your partnership with Inspector New-some for the time being and pursue Mr Williamson. I sense that he is the finer investigator, and I think we both know that he knows more than he has told.'

'Yes, sir. And Mr Dyson?'

'He is no concern of yours. No – you should keep your hawk-like eyes upon Mr Williamson. Report to me all that he does.'

'I will.'

'Your place in Heaven is secure, Eusebius. You are truly an angel of righteousness in this wicked city of ours.'

The second of our temporarily absent characters is, of course, Constable Cullen. It had been three days since he had once again reluctantly adopted the uniform of his rank and been ignominiously returned to L Division as a common beat policeman. At that moment where we left Inspector Newsome cogitating in his office, the constable was out alone upon the familiar streets. But where?

Let us indulge ourselves and, in fancy, fly as a spirit over the city in search of him. It is dark and chilly. London is a tapestry of charcoal and ashes far below us, its larger streets illuminated with gas and a blanket of smoke lying over all as

invisible millions gather round fires in their homes, or freeze
to death on the open road. The river is a black serpent slither-
ing inexorably through the desolation, countless ships' masts
harrowing the sky at the Thames Pool. But for the hopeless
sigh of the upper air, there is silence on our flight.

We descend through smoke and fly low along the frigid
river, beneath the bridges – London, Southwark and Blackfriars – until the nine graceful arches of Waterloo-bridge
approach . . . and there he is, standing alone at its mid-point,
looking east at the chimneys and spires against the sky.

Within that top hat, and within that stately scull, Constable
Cullen is perhaps recalling the interview that brought him
to this point: that final briefing in the office of Inspector
Newsome.

'As you know, Constable, your time with the Detective
Force has been a trial period. How do you think you have
performed during this time?'

'I have learned much, sir. We have searched the scene of a
murder and questioned witnesses. I feel that I have begun to
learn many of the skills of a detective.'

'Your questioning of Mr Poppleton was not especially
effective.'

'The man was quite rude and obstructive, sir. He was
mocking me.'

'Indeed he was. But I'm sure you would find a drunken
Irishman considerably ruder and more obstructive if you had
to interrogate one. A detective must exhibit an unquestioned
authority.'

'Does this mean that I am not to remain with the Detective
Force, sir?'

'I'm afraid so, Constable Cullen. You are a fine policeman,
but not for the Detective Force. I thought that perhaps you

had learned from Mr Williamson, but I see now that it was your loyalty rather than your brain that he prized.'

'Sir . . . I believe that with further experience I will—'

'Well – that is all I have time for, Constable. You will return to L Division with my commendation on good work done. And you will speak to no one – absolutely no one at all – on the subject of this case. I am quite serious on this point. If I find that you have passed any information to Mr Williamson or his cohorts, I will see to it that you are thrown out of the police. Do you understand?'

'Yes, sir.'

So now the forlorn constable stood leaning on the parapet above the cold water, his breath steaming about him in the stillness. It would soon be dawn and time for him to return home to sleep. But not before his life had been changed irrevocably.

A man was approaching from the north on the same side of the bridge that Constable Cullen stood. Even from a distance the shadowy, top-hatted figure was tall and solidly built – a column of blackness even in the lamplight. The policeman assumed his full height and touched the truncheon at his side.

And as the figure came nearer, it became clear that he was indeed a walking shadow: a Negro.

'Hello, Ben!' Constable Cullen immediately recognized Noah's dark friend by his ghostly eye. The two formidable gentlemen exchanged a handshake that might have crushed the bones of lesser men. 'How long is it since we worked on that case together with Mr Williamson?'

Benjamin shrugged good-naturedly.

'I will tell you, Ben: I miss those times. What I would not give for some real investigation. What brings you to . . . ? O, what is this?'

Benjamin was holding out a letter to the policeman. Mr Cullen felt an anticipatory prickle of excitement across his neck and moved closer under a lamp that he might read more clearly.

Dear Mr Cullen

I understand that you have been working with Inspector Newsome on the Holywell-street case and that he has now returned you to the streets. That is his way. You may or may not know that I am also pursuing a solution to that case for my own personal reasons.

I wonder if, on the strength of our former association, you might like to leave your tedious post there on the bridge and accompany Benjamin to a place where more details will be given and where you will be invited to contribute what you know as we pursue justice together once more.

No doubt you are apprehensive about leaving your post, not least the consequences of doing so. All I can tell you in consolation is that if we find the solution, you need no longer worry about Inspector Newsome.

George Williamson

Constable Cullen was taken with rush of giddiness that he tried his best to conceal in front of Benjamin. It hardly seemed possible: Mr Williamson wanted *his* help on a case!

'I am to go with you, Ben?'

Benjamin nodded.

'Just leave my post this moment and not return? Just walk away and forget about my duty to the Metropolitan Police that I have served for three years?'

Benjamin nodded.

'I see . . . Then let us not waste another moment!'

And the two men headed north across the bridge, a muscled Negro arm around the shoulders of the constable, who blathered on with sufficient effusion that Benjamin need do nothing but smile.

NINETEEN

It was just after dawn on that same day as Mr Williamson and Noah Dyson sat in a fireside nook within the smoky confines of Dick's coffee house on Fleet-street, just a short distance from that eminent arch where they had so recently been reacquainted. The former was in a state of some agitation.

'We must go immediately to the Continental Club – with the inspector if necessary – and arrest this man James Tattershall: he with the distinctive laugh.'

'Wait, George – do not be so ready to put on your coat. Let us consider everything that we know before acting precipitously.'

'There is nothing precipitous about it – our murderer is a member of that club. Or at least he knows who it is – perhaps this Major Tunnock.'

'We know nothing of the sort. There is a young man with a strange laugh. Perhaps he is our man – perhaps not. The prudent path is for me to arrange another meeting once I have made a more thorough study of this tract they gave me. I have been invited to do so by Major Tunnock. That is the occasion when we might learn more and strike.'

'You ask me to wait as a murderer walks free?'

'The deaths of Mr Jessop and Joseph tell us that they already know of our investigation, and yet they do not hide. Evidently, they do not fear us. They are not running.'

'Hmm. What of this tract?'

'I have read it through once. It is poor sort of amateur philosophy on the nature of erotic transgression. What is of more pertinence is that the gentlemen at the club clearly have something to hide – something that, as we have suspected, is of a morally dubious nature and may connect a number of crimes. I believe they might tell me more in a private place – particularly if they thought they could lure me there with the promise of information.'

'A trap, then.'

'No doubt, but we will be ready for it. If these are the men who were in the room with Mr Sampson, they have already demonstrated they will stop at nothing to preserve their freedom. We must proceed with all caution.'

'I would like to take this fellow James from the street and question him. Arrest him if necessary.'

'With what effect, George? Now you are thinking like Inspector Newsome. James is rich and knows powerful men. He will tell us nothing and will obtain a powerful legal counsel. But perhaps if I can talk to him in his own environment, among his fellows, he will give something more away, even inadvertently.'

'Our murderer is frustratingly close.'

'Indeed, but there is still no connection with your wife in sight. Tell me more about your excursion to Clerkenwell. Benjamin has told me about "Freepass". What is it?'

'I have no idea. A person? A place? I have never heard the name in any context. Is it two words or one?'

'Can you be sure that the boy was not coached to tell you

the word? It seems odd for him to identify, or even know, such a term so precisely.'

'Of course, I have considered the possibility. But a distraction is of equal importance to a truth if seen from the correct perspective.'

'Quite. Perhaps your Constable Cullen will be able to tell us more if Benjamin has been able to lure him away from his duties.'

'I hope so. I would prefer to solve the case without meeting Mr Newsome again.'

The coffee house was now filling with men on their way to work. Chill air flooded in across the floor each time the door opened, and trade was brisk as they hurriedly drank their steaming beverages before rushing to their futile labour. One hundred years hence, all their efforts would be ash – vanished and insignificant, unless they were writers.

A familiar Negro figure appeared at the window, accompanied by an almost equally burly police constable – Mr Cullen. They entered the coffee house and made their way through the throng to where Mr Williamson and Noah sat.

'Constable Cullen – welcome and thank you for coming,' said Mr Williamson, standing and shaking the policeman's hand.

'Sir – it is an honour to be invited to work with you and Mr Dyson once again. And Ben, of course.'

'You need not call me "sir". And please sit down – you are attracting attention.'

'Yes, sir . . . I mean Mr Williamson.'

'Constable – I also extend my thanks,' said Noah. 'You have done a brave thing leaving your position. You may be confident that I will cover whatever wages you lose.'

'Thank you, Mr Dyson. But I would gladly work with you gentlemen for no money at all.'

'Hmm. As you may know, the case at hand is the Holywell-street murder of Mr Jonathan Sampson,' said Mr Williamson. 'We have spoken with Inspector Newsome about what he has learned, but this information has taken us no closer to a solution.'

'Are you working with the inspector, sir?'

'Certainly not. Our conversation was not voluntary; it was more a crossing of paths.'

'Why this Holywell-street case? Are you in competition with the Detective Force?'

'We will come to that in a moment. First, we need to know what he did *not* tell us. I understand you accompanied him in his initial investigations. Did that include a search of the room Mr Sampson fell from?'

'It did. There was little to find: some glasses, the open window, a blonde hair on one of the beds. The inspector seemed rather at a loss.'

'A blonde hair you say?'

'Yes . . . did he not mention it?'

'He did not. I suspect there are many other things he did not deign to mention. Constable – I want you to cast your mind back to that room and see it once more in your mind. Close your eyes if need be. What is there that a detective might notice especially? What is amiss? What evidence is left there by the departing criminals? What do you see?'

'Let me think . . . it is cold on account of the window . . . I see the four glasses . . . the looking glass is smeared as if a hand or face has touched it . . . O, and there is that strange smell: sweet like a flower or something else . . . perhaps it is the orange . . .'

'What orange?' said Noah.

'The orange I found in the chamber pot beneath the bed

in the room – or at least the seeds and pith of one. No peel. Inspector Newsome seemed to think it unimportant so I did not pursue the matter.'

'Are you sure it was an orange?' said Noah with a curious look.

'I suppose so. But the seeds were all chewed up and almost dry.'

'And was that the smell identified on entering?' said Mr Williamson.

'Perhaps. Though I suppose those few seeds would not leave such a strong scent on their own. It could have been . . . well, it could almost have been sweet almond. I have smelled candles scented thus as I pass certain shops.'

'Constable . . . Mr Cullen – do you think that you were able to smell lavender also in that room, or some other floral scent?' said Noah.

'Lavender? Perhaps . . . it was very faint, but there was a floweriness to it.'

'You are critical to our case,' said Noah. 'You are perhaps the only living person who has smelled the killer or killers. We must identify these scents and in some way use that knowledge to take us closer. You are to remain alive at all costs.'

Mr Cullen could barely restrain his smile. He was 'critical' to a criminal case of George Williamson.

'There is one more thing . . . I do not know if it is important . . .'

'Speak up, Mr Cullen,' said Mr Williamson. 'Everything is important in its way.'

'Well, when we visited the shop of Mr Poppleton, the publisher said to the inspector: "Don't I give your men enough to leave me alone . . . ?" I wondered what he meant by that, but I did not dare ask Mr Newsome.'

'That is most interesting,' said Noah. 'We will have to look into it.'

'So what is next? Where do we go now?' said the delighted ex-constable.

'I have an idea,' said Noah. 'There is a man I have heard of who might be able to help.'

The four gentlemen left the coffee house shortly thereafter, heading west. In their enthusiasm, they must not have noticed the rather plain-faced fellow who had been watching them across the smoky room the whole time. Indeed, he seemed so bland and unobtrusive that he might well have been a coat stand. But shortly after they exited, he was not far behind.

As they make their way west, let us fill the interim in a thoughtful and soon-to-be relevant manner. Let us consider insanity.

What is it that renders a man mad? Could it be some chymical imbalance in his brain – a cerebral shifting of ballast? Is it a cataclysmic assault of fate like the loss of a child? Or is it passed from parent to child along with similarities of appearance? Perhaps the city itself – with its relentless, maddening din and inescapable press of crowding humanity – is enough to push a man to the limit of his patience and reduce him year by year to a broken vessel. Certainly, there are those among us who, downtrodden by debt, hunger, despair and the nagging duty of a novel, have stood at the edge of a bridge and looked into the black waters as the only salve to a hopeless life.

Some take their lives; others break. And for those of means, there is the private asylum, where one may be hidden from society by solicitous parents and coaxed gradually back to a semblance of normality. No mere hospitals these, but islands of calm and care where the sensitive sons of the wealthy may be nursed and attended to by physicians who apply the very latest medical thought to rebalancing the mind.

The particularly handsome villa on Albert-road in the environs of Primrose-hill could well have been a private residence. Its large rear garden was hidden discreetly from view by a tall hedge, although the views from the ten bedrooms looked out magnificently over Regents-park and the adjacent countryside. There was a spacious dining room and a number of drawing rooms, but this was not a family home – it was Doctor Norwood's Private Asylum for Gentlemen.

As Noah, Mr Williamson, Benjamin and Mr Cullen approached the door, there was no brass plaque to announce the property's function, nor indeed any outward clue whatsoever. Noah knew of the place only because he had recently started to deliver small quantities of his fine opium to the surgery. The stories told about the inhabitants by the staff had intrigued him greatly, as well they might.

For their part, Mr Williamson and Mr Cullen did their best to mask any apprehension they felt, for let us remember that lunacy is often looked upon with the same kind of fear afforded to cholera or consumption – as if proximity to it might cause infection. At the very least, it is humbling to see the fragility of one's fellow man: his body sound, but his mind broken and jagged in pieces before one.

'Welcome, welcome!' said Doctor Norwood, the bespectacled, grey-haired gentleman who opened the door and beckoned them into the airy hallway.

'I thank you greatly for allowing us admittance,' said Noah. 'I know that you do not normally accept visiters.'

'Quite, quite. It would upset the gentlemen greatly to see strangers too often. Routine is their greatest ally on the path back to health. But I am happy to make a rare allowance for one of our favoured suppliers.'

Mr Williamson frowned at the 'suppliers' comment, but did not pursue it. 'You surprise me, doctor. Is not routine in itself sometimes a kind of obsessive behaviour?'

'Ah, very perceptive, sir! You are quite right. We discourage our gentlemen from pursuing that which plagues them and instead direct their attentions to a fresh endeavour that the diseased part of the mind might be relaxed. Thus, a man who compulsively sings might be encouraged instead to write poetry or make wooden models. In time, the mind might forget that it was ill and the man might one day sing without fixation.'

'Is it true that a man may believe himself to be Jesus Christ?' asked Mr Cullen.

'Well, that is rather the common view promoted in certain newspapers. I believe they do have a Christ at Bethlem, and I think I am correct in saying that there are three Dukes of Wellington in London alone. It is rather an undistinguished form of lunacy that does not trouble my gentlemen. The educated mind is, in many ways, more prone to inexplicable madness. It feeds upon itself and becomes quite lost . . . but wait – here is one of the men now.'

A tall and immaculately attired man walked down the stairs towards them. He had the lofty forehead and thin features of the high born. As he arrived at the bottom, he made a little bow to the visitors. 'Good afternoon, gentlemen. A wonderful day today, is it not?'

'It certainly is,' replied Doctor Norwood. 'Are you going to the garden for recreation?'

'Yes, doctor. I am painting the oak tree. In watercolours this time.'

'Excellent. Do not let us keep you, and remember to wear your coat – it is quite cold.'

Mr Williamson watched the man take a coat from a stand and exit a door to the garden. 'He seems completely normal to me, doctor.'

'That is the mystery of the mind, sir. A man might function entirely normally in every other sphere of his life but become a maniac at the tone of a bell or the sight of a clock. Indeed, that very man came to us with a morbid fear of losing time – he carried as many as fourteen pocket watches and checked them perhaps two hundred times a day. Now we must not let him see a single clock or think about time at all. He has his lunch at four in the afternoon if it pleases him. He has celebrated his twenty-seventh birthday for the last three years.'

'Are your patients not dangerous?' asked Mr Cullen.

'If you mean violent – no, not at all. Though they can be passionate in their speech. The only danger we face is that all of the gentlemen are highly intelligent and skilled at dissimulation. In many cases, they spent years hiding their infirmity from those around them. Only last month, one of our gentlemen almost escaped by pretending to a visiter that he was me. All doors are locked in the evenings.'

'Do they receive Christian learning?' said Mr Williamson.

'There is a sermon morning and evening for those of the inclination, but we have found that a number of our gentlemen find the notion of the Resurrection a greater insanity than anything affecting their own brains. The Lord to them is just a quaint lunacy.'

'Does not the fool sometimes speak a profounder truth than a king?' said Noah, as much to himself as the others.

Mr Williamson scowled and Doctor Norwood concealed a smile.

'What can you tell us of Aubrey Alsthom, doctor?' said the former.

'Yes, yes – the reason for your visit. Let us go to my office for a moment.'

The doctor led them to a small study with a solid wooden desk by the window and an array of comfortable seats. A fire blazed comfortingly in the grate. The gentlemen sat, Doctor Norwood at his desk.

'Aubrey is a highly unusual case. His parents brought him to us a few months ago with a chronic case of monomania that manifested itself in astonishing feats of memory. Aubrey had managed to absorb around ten years of *the Times* newspaper and could recall a single word at a moment's notice, even if that word occurred on relatively few occasions. If one were to ask him a more common word such as "street", he would go into a state of paralysis as he attempted to recall every instance. Laudanum was the only way calm him.'

'So I presume he is now permitted no access to a newspaper,' said Mr Williamson.

'Quite right, quite right. He is not even permitted a book. Rather, he has taken to working wood with small knives. Quite a beautiful chess set he has made. Of course, we take the knives from him each evening so they cannot fall into the wrong hands.'

'Doctor Norwood – you have my received my letter on this subject and you know what we propose to do. You have kindly acceded to the request, but I must ask once again: will it harm Aubrey or hinder his treatment?' said Noah.

'I fear it will agitate him, but if we limit the session to less than thirty minutes, I hope he will be unaffected. I understand that his help in this case might lead to the capture of a murderer, and I am keen to lend any assistance I can. In addition, this may be a useful opportunity for me to see how much he has healed in these past weeks. However, and I must be firm on this point – if I see that Aubrey is in danger of a paralytic episode, I will call everything to a halt and give him the laudanum.'

'Of course, doctor,' said Mr Williamson. 'How should we question him? Is there a particular method?'

'Indeed. Indeed. The process is highly specific. You must say to him "Search for . . ." and add the word or phrase you wish to locate in the volumes of his memory. But a warning: it must be a word that is likely to be relatively uncommon. Consider carefully what context you are seeking within and avoid generalities. Wherever possible, provide another word that might appear in juxtaposition with the one you seek. Thus "Victoria" will raise numerous occurrences, but "Victoria-street, Lambeth" will limit the search. He will think for a moment and then begin to reel off a list of matches in chronological order.'

'May we interrupt?' said Noah.

'Yes – indeed, it is advised. His responses tend to be breathless effusions, so say "Stop!" quite firmly and he may be able to provide more detail on the most recent utterances. Miss your cue, however, and you will have to begin again.'

'How accurate is he?' said Mr Williamson.

'Unerringly so. Once, at the start of his stay, we obtained an old edition of *the Times* and chose a suitably unique phrase. He identified the day and the month and the passage within moments. Shall we go to meet him?'

Doctor Norwood led his visiters towards the door where the chronologically fixated young man had earlier exited and they proceeded to the garden, which, though quite chilly, was populated with half a dozen young men engaged in a variety of improving pastimes. The aforementioned gentleman was indeed painting the oak tree from his position on the lawn; another was carefully attending to an area of shrubs; still another was engaged in drawing birds that settled in the naked branches above the garden.

Sitting apart from the others on a wooden bench was Mr Aubrey Alsthom, a prematurely balding young man with the intense expression of the intellectual. In his long, slender fingers was a miniature wooden figure of indistinct features that he held up to the light and twirled for closer inspection. The approach of the strangers drew his attention and he looked at them coolly.

'What have you made there, Aubrey?' asked the doctor.

'It is a figure of Plato, Doctor Norwood.' The voice was but a cadence.

'I think you need to give him another chin,' offered Noah with a smile.

'Do you think so? I did wonder about that. I may have to start again.'

'Aubrey – these gentlemen have come from the city especially to see you. They would like to ask you about *the Times*.'

'Is . . . is that not forbidden? I mean . . . I should not . . .'

'Becalm yourself, Aubrey. Let us consider it a brief clinical experiment, then we will let you return to Plato.'

A wooden bench was carried over by Benjamin and Mr Cullen, then all sat around Aubrey, whose eyes had begun to glisten either through trepidation or glee. There was a sense of commingled anticipation and fear among the four investigators. Mr Williamson had his notebook at the ready. At a nod from Doctor Norwood, Noah began:

'Aubrey, I would like you to search for . . . "Freepass" – as a single word if you please.'

Aubrey's eyes lost focus and rolled upwards, becoming mere flickering whites. His left eyelid twitched briefly. His mouth sagged open slightly ... then he returned with a strange, unearthly monotone:

'"... a collision between a collier and a cutter just off Freepass-stairs in the Thames Pool ... Mr Arbuthnot's Murder'd Moor alehouse in Freepass-alley ... the horse fell at the corner of Cock-lane and Freepass-alley ..."'

There was no need to shout 'stop'. Aubrey had finished. There had been only three mentions of that place in the last ten years or so.

'Excellent work, Aubrey,' said Doctor Norwood, patting the young man's knee.

Aubrey smiled uneasily as if unsure whether he should be enjoying himself quite so much.

'Search for ... "coal tar",' said Noah.

Again, the eyes took that ghastly turn and there was the twitch.

'"... Johnson's patent coal tar is the finest such product for preserving wood ... a manufactory refining coal tar and other such products ... Dr Parkinson's Coal Tar Remedy for vomiting of blood ... the timbers had been treated by numerous applications of coal tar ..."'

'Stop! I think we have discerned the pattern there,' said Noah. 'I fear the term was too generic.'

Mr Williamson made a note and seemed to be deep in thought, no doubt cogitating upon how best to use this preternatural mental resource. 'Aubrey – please search for ... "lavender".'

'"... Mr Nelson of Lavender-hill ... Viners' new Motto scents, including lavender, myrrh and cedar ... a necklace lost in the environs of Lavender-terrace ... Thomas Lavender

Esq. presented himself to her Majesty . . . Hendrie's Perfumed Spirit of Lavender . . . Drury's lavender water for handker-chiefs . . . Mr William Lavender said that . . ."'

'Stop! Hmm. I do not think that is a helpful avenue of investigation. I am beginning to understand the need for greater specificity. Perhaps we should try a name. Search for . . . "James Tattershall".'

'". . . the attendees were James Smith, John Tattershall and George Plothers . . . Tattershall's Throat Lozenges against coughs . . . shooting at Glenfiddich were Charles Booth, Henry Athers, James Brookes, James Tattershall and Sir John Smythe . . ."'

Aubrey stopped. 'That is all. I apologize for the initial match – the proximity of the two names tricked me.'

'You have no need to apologize, Aubrey,' said Mr William-son. 'We greatly value your prodigious talent. Perhaps you could search for . . . "Major Archibald Tunnock".'

'". . . the court martial of Major Archibald Tunnock on grounds of gross indecency and conduct unbecoming an officer . . . the unsuccessful Tory candidate Major A. Tunnock had to be escorted from the room . . . *My India* by Major Archibald Tunnock, an unvarnished soldier's tale . . . a meet-ing to be held at Friar's Hall by Major A. Tunnock on the question: 'Vice and its Ends' . . ."'

'Stop! That is as concise a biography as we could wish for on that person,' said Noah.

'Hmm. Let us attempt something more detailed,' said Mr Williamson. 'Aubrey – could you search for "suicide" and "prussic acid" in juxtaposition?'

Noah nodded his approval.

The young man was paler now than when the questioning had begun. Perhaps it was the cold, but there was a slight shivering in his form. Nevertheless, he raced through the volumes of his mind and returned:

'". . . the lady was found lying in the street having taken a phial of prussic acid . . . the girl Juliet, a mere seventeen, took the poison because she was *enceinte* . . . in addition to taking prussic acid Mrs Cotton had strangled herself with a cord . . . the woman was seen drinking from a phial of what was believed to be prussic acid before she jumped and was dashed against the buttress of the bridge . . ."'

'Stop!' said Noah. 'I am afraid, George, that this avenue will yield hundreds of such matches. By all means return to it and elicit some dates from Aubrey for further research, or refine the search, but I fear we will exhaust him thus.'

'Hmm. Perhaps you are right.'

'I believe Aubrey is becoming fatigued,' said Doctor Norwood. 'Perhaps we should stop and recommence another time if need be.'

The young man did indeed now look quite deflated and pale.

'Just one more, if we may,' said Noah, glancing at Mr Williamson. 'Aubrey – search for . . . "Persephone".'

A pause. The eyes flickered. The mouth opened and the lips moved as if he were speaking silently. Then . . .

'Nothing. I am sorry,' said Aubrey.

'What do you mean, "nothing"?' said Mr Williamson as politely as he could.

'It means there is no occurrence of that word in the last ten years' editions, sir. Not in headlines, advertisements or features.'

'Hmm. Should we spell it differently?'

'I have searched for the possible phonetic variations, hence the slight delay.'

'Are you sure?'

'There is, I am afraid, only one way to be sure: one must read all of the last ten years' editions.'

'Hmm. Hmm.'

'I think we should now leave Aubrey to his whittling,' said the doctor, standing.

The others followed suit, albeit reluctantly, and thanked the young man in turn before making their way back to the house.

'Did you manage to elicit the information you wanted?' asked Doctor Norwood as they strolled.

'I fear that we would need much more time with Aubrey to fully exploit his knowledge,' said Mr Williamson. 'I was only just beginning to fathom how the questioning could work.'

'Alas, we are playing with the delicate sanity of a young man. We may already have asked more of him than he can bear. Perhaps you can return again later, in a week or so.'

'We do not have a week—'

'Thank you, Doctor Norwood, for the generosity you have shown,' interjected Noah. 'In truth, we had so little information before that this has helped to some degree.'

'Hmm,' said Mr Williamson. 'I apologize for my tone, doctor. We are frustratingly close to justice. Thanks to Aubrey, I will now be able to locate this Freepass-alley and venture there.'

'I, too, have had further thoughts on the case as a result of this meeting,' said Noah. 'I think my next port of call will be the British Museum reading room.'

TWENTY

Is there any other place in London that has such resonance to the writer as the reading room of the British Museum? Not in a dozen lifetimes could one read its half-a-million volumes, and yet those endless shelves are a multitudinous reminder of one's own failure to achieve posterity in a leathern spine.

If we lean on the balustrade of the gallery and look down upon the hushed readers below, what do we see? It is a veritable human encyclopaedia of hacks, scribes, copyists, journalists, novelists, diarists, biographers, historians, cataloguers and plagiarists – monomaniacs all, surviving on a meagre diet of thin hope and sugared dreams.

There is a musty scent of books and damp clothing, for most are here to escape the bitter cold of their lodgings. If they are currently reading their way through the newspapers on offer, it is merely a preliminary to the colossal *opus* they will begin later that day, or tomorrow, or next year. See the copyist, almost as blind as a mole, squinting at the tome he is reproducing for a publisher; see the student of University College debating whether he should copy that page of Greek or simply tear it out; see the aged author glancing around to see if anyone has recognized him as the progenitor of that shoddy novel that sank in a mire of indifference last year.

And, of course, I. I have had a productive morning researching a new list of likely benefactors for the begging letters I am to start writing once more. I will try the Literary Fund again, I suppose, and target the Royal Society – those old gentlemen of science have not the wit to see through a piece of masterful prose unless it has an erroneous equation in it.

But let us not lose track of the story. It is the day after that strange episode at Doctor Norwood's place, and immediately below us is Mr Noah Dyson, his desk stacked with an interesting array of books. There is one on medicine and another on herbal remedies; there is an edition of *the Times* from seven years past; there are a number in indecipherable Greek, and a directory of London charities. He has already written a number of letters that are safely in envelopes inside his jacket: one to Major Tunnock accepting the invitation to converse further, and three others . . . of which we will hear more in good time.

Is he not a curious fellow, this Noah Dyson? One day we see him in the east of the city at his opium manufactory; another day we see him at the library desk as comfortable among books as if he had always been a university man. There must be few who can inhabit such different worlds with equal ease, but then he is a man who has seen the world as few have.

Those hands that turn the page so delicately have hoisted rope in the uncharted frozen wastes of Lancaster Sound, have clung to the splintered wreckage of a whaler sunk by behemoths, have been tanned almost black on Antipodean decks, and wielded weapons against pirates off Cape Matapan and Jamaica. Those eyes that scan the page with such application have seen vistas and horizons we could never conceive:

the Morea, Pernambuco, Honduras, Buenos Ayres, Exuma, Tortola, Demerara, Bahaia, Madras . . .

Now, however, he is looking again at that tract given to him by Major Tunnock – a particularly nasty and radical piece of writing:

THE GENTLEMAN'S POETICS OF TRANSGRESSION
Being a study of the advanced erotic appetite

Man is an inexhaustible seeker of pleasure unlike any other beast. His curiosity, as demonstrated in his very Fall, is his driving impulse towards satiation whatever artifices of so-called morality stand in the way of his primordial desire.

And thus it is that every carnal pleasure is a serpent-lured transgression against the diaphanous veil of decorum that we drape over these animal bodies. Is not the de-pucelative act itself the first such rending of that sanitary membrane? Is it not true that we each – Christian and heathen alike – owe our existence to an act of destruction – of transgression?

Look at the children of the common classes: these people to whom Faith and education are as unknown as a foreign tongue. In their simplicity, in the low lodging houses of our rookeries, they rut and breed without shame or guilt BECAUSE IT IS AN INSEPARABLE PART OF THEIR BESTIAL NATURE!

In short, Man's inexorable urge is towards the carnal, towards transgression, towards the abyss, as the immortal Bard has put it:

. . . *there's no bottom, none,*
In my voluptuousness. Your wives, your daughters,
Your matrons, and your maids, could not fill up

The cistern of my lust: and my desire
All continent impediments would o'erbear

Once one has begun on that path, once one has torn away that veil of mystery and passed to the other side without divine censure, without guilt or shame, there can be no pause or hindrance. One transgression leads to the next as satiation requires another and another step towards the abyss.

Sailors of the southern oceans have brought us a word, 'tabu', used by those primitive peoples untouched by our parody of civilization. Even they, in their ignorant nakedness, recognize that some things are forbidden because they are 'holy' and 'unclean' – holy AND unclean! Is that not a lesson to our pious clerics from the black-skinned savage?

Only by breaking the tabu of the forbidden does one see the truth of our religion – that it is a hollow charade, itself saturated in the transgressive urge towards the abyss?

Consider the martyr: does not his body, torn and broken by his tormentors, seek the consummatory ecstasy of oblivion? Is not his pain a threshold he must cross to achieve the perfection of satiation? Is not the very Christ figure – humiliated, whipped, penetrated by nails and stripped almost naked – a representation of sensual attainment? Towards death lies the path of the seeker after fulfilment.

In death we find the horror and the ecstasy – the final transgression. And in the sexual act do we come closest to it physically and metaphysically, Man's spending of his seed being consequent with the fleeting transport from this world to the next. Through the carnal act do we approach that End by degrees of transgression – until we arrive at the unspeakable horror and stare it in the eye, triumphant

in our attainment of the ultimate. In Thanatos do we find
the purest embodiment of Eros . . .

Noah folded the tract away and pursed his lips. It was the
kind of thing written by earnest graduates, a barely logical mix
of literature, religion and mythology in a show of seeming
profundity. But as an insight into the thinking of the group
from the Continental Club, it was useful enough, and suggested a number of ideas in relation to the case at hand.

He was about to return to his studies when one of the
silent-moving attendants of that venerable place approached
carrying a volume and spoke with a well-practised whisper.

'Your book, sir.'

Noah looked up. 'What book? I did not request another
book.'

'I am sorry, sir. I will return it to—'

'Wait.'

Noah looked at the people seated at his table, all of whom
were engaged in their own thoughts. He looked around the
reading room, but if he had expected to catch someone looking at him, he was disappointed. There did not seem to be
anyone present he had not seen before.

'Sir . . . ?'

'I will take the book. Thank you.'

It was a relatively new volume: volume five of Mr Charles
Knight's magisterial encyclopaedia *London*. The hard cover
was finished in an attractive marbled design, its brown leather
spine still aromatic and its gilt glinting dully. There was a slip
of paper tucked between the pages towards the end and Noah
opened the book at that place.

'The Reading Room of the British Museum' proclaimed
the title on that page – and there was an etching showing the

very space where Noah was sitting to read about it. He might well have been one of the fellows sitting in the picture – being observed.

He looked around again. Nobody seemed to be watching. Was this an innocent mistake, or some message being delivered to him so subtly that he could not fathom its meaning? He looked once more at the book and began to turn the pages of the chapter hoping to find some further clue ... and there on page 390, circled in dark pencil, was the suggestion of one.

Amid a list of illustrious names, that of Ptolemy was the one that had been picked out. An absent reminder scribbled by a hurried geographer? Another coincidence? Or a signpost to another clue?

Noah left his seat and ventured to request a Ptolemy from the attendants. A ladder was procured and soon the heavy volume was on the table before him. He turned the large, thick pages looking for something, for *anything* that might tell him what was happening.

And there, beside an archaic map, was a folded sheet of notepaper addressed: 'For your interest'. Again he cast a furtive glance at the people around him on the table: a couple of dishevelled characters reading the newspapers, and an elderly gentleman engrossed in his Latin. He looked up at the gallery and saw nobody observing him from there. He turned to look at the doorway into the vestibule between the two reading rooms ... and glimpsed a body rapidly disappearing.

Immediately, he was up and running down the space between tables, his shoes hammering across the wooden floor. Faces looked up in alarm and a murmur of excitement rushed through that space so accustomed to bated breath.

Down the stairs and out towards Montague-place Noah

ran, but there was no sign of that quickly vanishing figure. He looked up and down the street and saw no one hurrying.

'He was out of here like a rabbit,' said the young man sitting in the sentry box at the entrance to the library. 'Like his coat-tails were on fire and no mistake.'

'Did you see his face?' said Noah.

'A blur – that's all I saw, sir.'

'Was there a carriage waiting? Where did he go?'

'A carriage? That is possible – I did hear horses, but I was reading the latest on the financials, see?' The sentry helpfully held up his copy of *the Times*.

Noah scowled. In his mind, he went over that briefest of glances he'd caught and tried to recall something that might identify the fleeing figure. Had there been the merest hint of scarlet in their attire? An epaulette, or a scarf perhaps? He felt in his pocket to reassure himself that the note was still there, and returned to the reading room to collect his things.

Back inside the library, Noah's books and notes lay on the table for all to see. An inquisitive sort might have been tempted to look over them to ascertain what the gentleman had been studying . . .

We will leave Noah in Montague-place for the time being and transport ourselves across the city to the civilized environs of Berkeley-square, where we find the now familiar face of Mr Cullen. No longer in his habitual uniform, he cannot quite accustom himself to walking the streets without the rhythmical gait of the long-serving constable – something that certain classes of the metropolis can see at a great distance. Though Noah has warned him against this, the habit is as close to him as his skin.

He is looking for prostitutes. Or rather, he is looking for

prostitutes who may have known those girls mentioned by Charlotte to Mr Williamson: Lou, Kate and Mary who had met grisly ends. Such women are easy enough to see, even in the west. They dawdle lackadaisically on the pretext of waiting for a carriage and dress finer than the morally upright ladies of the neighbourhood (much to the *chagrin* of the latter).

Unfortunately, our investigator has had an unproductive morning. Such girls do not pass their time chatting with strangers on the streets, and certainly not to men who are clearly constables in civilian clothes. As he strolled past a tea vendor into Grafton-street from Old Bond-street, he mused upon how Noah or Mr Williamson might have approached the task. Perhaps he should merely attempt to be himself, accepting finally that the power of the law no longer stood at his shoulder.

And there before him was another representative of the sisterhood he sought: a quite remarkably attractive young lady checking her appearance in the window of a jewellery shop, perhaps imagining which of the diamonds there she would choose when she met the benefactor of her dreams.

'Good day to you, miss,' began Mr Cullen.

She turned with her professional smile in place and made a lightning appraisal of her interlocutor: hat, coat, cuffs, gloves, shoes. Her judgement was not favourable. Her smile dropped: 'You're a policeman.'

'No, miss—'

'Yes. It's senseless to deny it. Every thread of your appearance shouts it.'

'I used to be a constable; that is true. But I am no longer one.'

'So what do you want from me?'

'Do you know a girl called Lou? She works around this area: a blonde girl. Pretty, like yourself.'

'You know how to flatter, sir. Perhaps I do know Lou and can take you to her.'

'Let us not waste time. I know that Lou is dead – found ten days ago in Holywell-street: a suicide with prussic acid. I would be grateful if you could answer some questions if you knew her.'

'What – the police are actually investigating the death of one of our kind? Now I've seen everything!'

'I am not with the police. Speak honestly: did you know her?'

'Will you buy me a cup of tea and a cake? It's bitter cold today,' she said, nodding to the vendor on the corner who was wrapped in the curling steam of his trade.

Mr Cullen saw it immediately as a test. A serving policeman would not have purchased a drink for a street girl and chatted to her thus. 'It would be a pleasure, miss.'

She smiled and they walked to the corner to take cups of tea, standing there next to the wheeled urn so the vendor could keep an eye on his cups.

'I don't know what your game is, or why you ask, but I will tell you this for nothing: Lou didn't kill herself. I know that much,' said the girl, her pale hands clasped around the mug.

'I hear she had found herself a fine old gentleman . . .'

'Where did you hear that? Did you know her?'

'I have heard it from one of your sisterhood: a girl calling herself Charlotte at Golden-square.'

'Ah, I know Charlotte, the sly little b——!'

'Do you not like this Charlotte?'

'O, she's very successful, that girl. No doubt you've seen where she lives. We like to say that she's better with her tongue than any of us.'

'Well, I . . .'

'O, look at you all flushed and red – a big man like you! I meant that she's a better talker and liar. She could persuade a clergyman back to that room of hers . . . in fact, I believe she has. Anyway, she is right: Lou had caught a gent.'

'Did you ever see him? Do you know anything about him? He might be implicated in her death, perhaps.'

'Do you think so? I know only that he was old and rich. Lou said he wasn't much to look at: a bit ugly . . . and he had some problems with his health, with his skin. But he paid well and lived in a *lovely* place.'

'So she went to his house?'

'O yes! He sent a carriage for her, if you please. And another trip to bring her back when he'd finished with her.'

'Did she ever mention his name or where he lived?'

'Course not! She might have expected one of us to try for him. We girls keep such secrets to ourselves. Why, if I had such a gent, I wouldn't be standing here today with my feet numb from the cold.'

'Did she say any more about him?'

'He liked a good beating, and liked to whip her, too. A few times she had to rest for a couple of days, but he paid her well enough to do that. O, and sometimes he had some of his fellows there, too. Just watching, though – nothing immoral.'

'Nothing *immoral*?'

'You're blushing again, sir! I believe you are new to this.'

'I am an investigator.'

'What're you going to do about Lou?'

'That depends on what else you can tell me. I have heard also from Charlotte that there have been other girls of this area who have killed themselves under suspicious circumstances.'

'You mean Kate and Mary.'

'That's right. Do you maintain that these girls also did not kill themselves?'

'Sir – we are killed often enough (not that you police would care) but when have you known us girls to kill *ourselves*? We're thrown on the streets from a young age and we know how to survive. We look out for each other. There's nothing we cannot overcome with our natural advantages of beauty and good sense. Suicide is for pregnant servant girls and unfaithful wives. We don't kill ourselves.'

'So how do you explain these deaths? Who is responsible?'

'I'm sure I don't know. There is talk of the charities, of course.'

'What talk?'

'They are funny places, those homes and hospitals for "fallen women". Never trust a Christian – that's what I say. They have a strange look in their eyes, those gents: looking down on us even as they hide their lechery behind their scripture. I went to them once. I never will again.'

'Why would they kill you girls? They want to help you.'

'So *you* say. Does the rat-catcher help the rat? They will not be happy until we are all gone. And what happens then, when men cannot release what it is natural to release? That's when the world will end – just remember I said that.'

'Will you do something for me, miss?'

'I have the use of rooms just round the corner . . .'

'No . . . no . . . I . . .'

'I am teasing you, sir.'

'Of course. If you hear more about this old man of Lou's, tell nobody what you know. I may visit this area again in a few days to see what you have heard.'

'Do you think I am in danger?'

'I hope not. And, miss – if that carriage comes for you any

time, do not get in it, no matter how much money you are offered. Can you promise me that?'

'You are a sweet man . . .'

'I am serious. Whoever this man is, he is evil and a murderer.'

The look of seriousness on Mr Cullen's face dissuaded another witty remark.

'Thank you for the tea and the kindness, sir. Unfortunately, I do not get paid for talking.'

'I know. I thank you for speaking with me.'

The girl strolled back to her place at the jeweller's shop window with a coquettish glance back at Mr Cullen. A bachelor himself, he could not help but be affected by her, but he turned away to wipe the rapidly forming images from his mind. When *he* married, it would be to a fine girl: a virgin who would bear him fine, strong boys.

And as he stamped his feet and looked into the gritty sky, he was warmed by the realization of what he had said to the girl: 'I am an investigator.' He looked at himself in the reflection of an adjacent shop window: broad shoulders, barrel chest, his top hat making him seem even huger. There were no numbers on his collar, no insignia on his buttons, no truncheon at his belt . . . no organization at his back giving him authority to act.

Was this what freedom felt like?

'I am an investigator.'

'What was that, sir?' asked the tea vendor.

'I am an investigator.'

'Very nice for you, sir. How is the money?'

TWENTY-ONE

The fire crackling in the grate seemed to intensify the already ominous silence. The clock on the mantel ticked maddeningly. Inspector Newsome stood with his hands clasped behind his back before Sir Richard's desk while the commissioner busied himself with some papers. As a reprimand, it was far more effective than a raised voice.

Finally, it was time for Mr Newsome to be acknowledged:

'Well? What have you got for me, Inspector?'

'Questions, clues, mysteries and lies, sir.'

'That is not the answer I wanted. Is it not enough that you have the entire apparatus of the Metropolitan Police at your hands? Is it not enough that you have a suspect in gaol and the aid of Mr Williamson . . . yes, you need not be so surprised. The men talk and, naturally, I hear it.'

'The man is not helping me, sir. I merely spoke to him because I heard he was investigating—'

'I asked you what you have. Be kind enough to tell me.'

'Sir – you will recall that a street girl was found dead on Holywell-street the night of the Sampson incident. It now seems that there may be some connection with a number of other prostitute deaths by prussic acid.'

'What connection?'

'I cannot say.'

'Well, there is a connection or there is not. What has she to do with Mr Sampson?'

'A blonde hair was found in the room, and the girl was blonde. My researches have turned up some other related deaths—'

'These other deaths – what have they to do with the Sampson case?'

'As yet, I do not know. I am pursuing that avenue.'

'I hope you have something better than this. The Force is being made to look like a fool. How long is it since the incident on Holywell-street?'

'I questioned Mr Poppleton and, though he told me little, he did make one very intriguing comment in defence of his stubborn silence. He said: "They will kill me . . ."'

'"They"? Who are "they"?'

'I have absolutely no idea. I can conjecture only that "they" are a group of exceptionally dangerous men responsible for the murder – a group so powerful that he feared them more than a two-year stay at Newgate.'

'So we can be almost certain it was a murder. Is there any sign of a motive?'

'None. But the victim was heard to shout "I cannot" before he went through the window – which would seem to suggest he was compelled to perform some activity he did not want to.'

'What else? You must have unearthed further clues than this in the last few days.'

'Seeds, sir. The chamber pot in the room contained some masticated seeds, and the prostitute deaths I have been investigating also involve seeds.'

'Must I ask what significance this has?'

'I do not know.'

'Good G—, man! Seeds? Prostitutes? A silent suspect? Tell me you are not utterly incompetent!'

'I am to liaise with Mr Williamson shortly to discuss the case. He has been pursuing a related matter for . . . for the Mendicity Society and may be able to aid me in my enquiries.'

'Good. Good. He was a credit to the Force. It is a pity about his health. I hear he is still absent from his duties at Red Lion-square. Tell him your clues and see what he thinks.'

'Yes, sir.'

'And where is Eusebius Bean? Did I not tell you that he was to be at your right hand during this case?'

'Indeed, but the man has not arrived for work the last two days. I thought perhaps the Vice Society had recalled him.'

'That is not the case. I will make enquiries.'

'May I ask, sir – is the Society still applying pressure?'

'I am asked almost daily for a report on our progress, hence my agitation at having so little to tell them. I certainly do not want to return to them with tales of even more sin and filth in the city.'

'May I ask who represents the Society in these reports?'

'That is a question too far, Inspector. Be satisfied that I am maintaining cordial relations with them. I allowed them to raid a manufactory of obscene alabaster figurines at Smithfield yesterday. Such things placate them, and thus a number of very influential people are placated.'

'I understand.'

'Well – do not let me keep you. There is a murder to solve.'

The inspector returned to his office with indignation burning in his cheeks.

As the reader will have perceived, he had not told the entire truth to Sir Richard. Clearly, he could hardly mention any-thing touching on his secret files. Likewise, his collaboration with Mr Williamson (and particularly Noah's involvement) was one that needed to be delicately managed. So what had he *really* discovered?

In truth: very little. His special constables had turned up nothing coherent on the name 'Persephone' – as he had ex-pected. The girl Charlotte had given no additional information – no doubt because there was no financial or punitive incentive to do so. Nor had that illicit ledger of his offered any insight into the mysterious name. He drummed his fingers upon his desk as he thought, and unfolded that piece of paper upon which he had begun to jot his ideas. Little more had been added, but it was all he had:

Suicides: prostitutes/dollymops (outside their common pitch?) killed by prussic acid/gin glass. Why? By whom? Connection to Mr Sampson?

Murder of 'Nelly': any significant connection with Williamson? Who wants to cause trouble for him and why?

Victim: shouted 'I cannot!' Why? To whom?

Suspects: the young man; 'they' who will kill Mr Poppleton: wealthy (have their own carriage) and intelligent (associates of Mr Poppleton and probable club members). Powerful and highly placed?

Persephone: is this a real person or an aspect of Williamson's relentless pursuit of his dead wife? Could she be a Park-lane courtesan? If so, why would she write to Williamson?

Answers were not forthcoming. If there was any conclusion at all from this profusion of clues, it was that the perpetrators were not (with one recent notable exception) what Mr Newsome was used to. No ignorant drunks or dim-witted robbers *these* killers. They were intelligent, organized, influential . . . and clearly observing every step of the dual investigations pursuing them.

Why else had Mr Jessop, Joseph the waterman and (most likely) Mrs Colliver been killed shortly after being questioned? And why had the inspector himself received a letter implicating Mr Williamson in a crime that he almost certainly had no connection with? The faceless villains seemed to know everything, see everything, anticipate everything.

Eusebius Bean. The Society for the Suppression of Vice. The inspector rolled these two entities around his policeman's brain like two marbles and asked that question common to all of the great detectives.

What if . . . ?

What if the pressure exerted upon Sir Richard by the Society was not merely to urge an investigation but to monitor and sabotage it? What if the parasite Bean was watching every aspect of the case and feeding back all of his observations to his paymasters? What if they knew the perpetrators and were trying to protect them? What if they themselves were the perpetrators? Had not Mr Newsome seen for himself that the earnest scripture quoting of many so-called Christian gentlemen was a *charade* made comical by their hypocritical use of brothels and prostitutes across the city?

But what to do? He was just a policeman, albeit a high-ranking one. Sir Richard had made it quite clear that there was a political element to the whole case – that promotion might depend on acquiescence. There was little other choice: he would simply have to catch them and prove their guilt beyond all doubt. Not even Sir Richard would baulk at clear evidence of murder, whatever the perpetrators' standing. And in this endeavour, he would have to start immediately lest the next corpse be his own. He left a message for his clerk to have that information on the Park-lane girls waiting for him when he returned, then he took his coat and went out into the cold.

Whitehall was a drear spectacle indeed: grey and dark in a thickening sleet. He stamped his feet as he waited for the carriage to be brought round and watched the dogged progress of a coster lad pushing his barrow of fruit up the street. The boy was a ruddy-faced example of his breed: all brawn and no brains, but with an indomitable spirit that kept him alive in this urban wilderness. As the barrow passed by, Mr Newsome looked upon the sleet-flecked produce and an idea occurred:

'Halt there, boy!'

'I got p'mission to be 'ere so don't be gimme no lashin',' offered the lad.

'I am not trying to arrest you. I merely have a challenge for you.'

'What challenge?'

'How well do you know your fruit, boy?'

'I'm the ——— lord of fruit, ain't I! There's not a barrow-boy in the city knows 'is fruit like I does. Tasted it all, sold it all – I seen fruit as you wouldn't dream of.'

'Good. There is a shilling in it for you if you can identify the fruit from its seeds alone.'

'Deal.'

The boy spat into his filthy hand and offered to shake – an invitation Mr Newsome declined, despite wearing gloves. Instead, he extracted the jar from his pocket that contained the seeds extracted from poor Nelly's mouth and stomach. He handed the jar to the boy, who was unimpressed:

'It's all chewed an' rotten, the pith an' all!'

'So we have no deal then.'

'Wait! Lemme look . . .'

'Is it an orange?'

'Wait! I is thinkin'. There's a libr'y of fruit in me 'ead – I must look through it, see?'

'Continue at your leisure. I am happy to stand here in this freezing rain . . .'

The lad's face contorted in the pain of cogitation and he squinted at the contents of the jar, turning it critically to achieve different perspectives. Once his expertise had been proved beyond question by this performance, he was ready.

'Got it!'

'Well?'

'I don't see no shillin' . . .'

'Very well. Here it is. But if you are not correct in your judgement, you had better not venture along Whitehall for the rest of your life.'

'S'not an orange. Seeds are too small. Nor a clementine or any of the orange's kin. Wrong shape. And the pith ain't as stringy.'

'I see that you are also a poet of fruit to speak so prolonged upon the subject. What is my answer?'

'It's a pom'granit.'

'A what?'

'Exotic fruit, ain't it? Don't see 'em much. Expensive. Of course, I 'ave eaten one. They's sweet enough, but 'as too many seeds. Too much fuss. Give me an apple any day.'

'Are you sure? I had a doctor tell me these were orange seeds.'

'Did 'e sell fruit for a livin'?'

Inspector Newsome smiled despite himself and nodded his thanks to the coster lad, who ambled on his way. The carriage pulled up with a clatter of hooves and he was grateful to climb into its relative warmth.

Up St Martin's-lane and along Long Acre, he thought upon the question of the seeds. If the lad had been correct in his judgement, did it add anything else to what he knew? Only in that it reinforced his assumption of wealthy men – men who had given the girls a kind of fruit they would otherwise not have bought or even recognized. Was it a bribe to lure the girls – a novelty item? Was one of the perpetrators partial to that particular fruit? The clues multiplied, and with them the questions. Perhaps his next appointment would provide illumination.

As he approached the main entrance of the Royal College of Surgeons, an eruption of young gentlemen flooded out: the doctors and surgeons of tomorrow, all a-chatter about the erudition they had no doubt just received. They flowed around him as if he were a mere lamp post, jostling and talking over him because – without even realizing it – they had taken in his clothes and manner at a glance and perceived him as one lower than they: some manner of tradesman or minor professional.

He pushed his way through the *mêlée* into the entrance hall and made for the entrance to the lecture theatre, from which the last remnants of the audience were trickling. The heat and smell of the absent audience was still there inside that curious wooden accordion of banked seating, and the skylight far above cast a pale light as dusk came on. The timber seating, now relieved of the weight of humanity, ticked and creaked in repose.

'Ah, Inspector Newsome! Punctual as ever. How long is it since we last met?'

The speaker was that eminent surgeon Mr Herbert, who was wiping his chalked lecture notes off the board. A man of around fifty years, his face was flushed from the heat of the room and the exertion of his teaching.

Mr Newsome looked sidelong at the preparation table and was relieved to see no body there – just a number of jars filled with horrors suspended in chymicals.

'Mr Herbert – I admit I cannot exactly recall the last time, but, as ever, I am grateful for your time.'

'Nonsense! I always have time for the police. Do you mind if I continue with my work at the board? I would like to write my notes for tomorrow's session before we lose the light. I do not want to call the man in to light the gas just on my account.'

'By all means. As I said in my letter, I am interested in a number of matters – first among them the matter of suicide and what causes it. I would rather hear it from you than read your work on the subject.'

'Quite sensible. Well, the first thing to say is that self-murder is a sin – there can be no equivocation on that matter. The Bible is quite clear, so we can discount others of my profession who chatter to the contrary.'

'A sin, yes. But what is its cause?'

'Ah, that is the interesting part, Inspector. I, and others also, believe that it is caused by a momentary lapse in sanity: a loss of the logical and emotional faculties that control us under normal circumstances. The suicide – either through pain, loss, sadness or a cumulative aggregation of suffering – becomes mentally unbalanced and takes his life.'

'Can one be guilty of sin when one is insane?'

'Sin is sin, Inspector. There is no dispensation.'

'I see. What of the method? Are there any conclusions to

be drawn on the choice of death: any patterns dividable by class or sex?'

'A fascinating question, Inspector. One would expect that a suicide would seek the fastest and least painful route to Damnation, but, as I have said, rationality has no part of it. Indeed, many such deaths are quite hideously brutal. A man will cut his throat with a razor (a very common choice, this); a woman will leap from height or take prussic acid. Why, there was a case in the newspapers just the other day of a man who, while returning home from the public house, wrapped a length of heavy chain about his neck and jumped into the Thames. Can you imagine?'

'I cannot. Those examples you gave – are they typical? Will a woman jump from height where a man will cut his throat?'

'I have made no study into the subject, but I believe that is broadly accurate, yes. A man's suicide is often more violent – he will leap in front of a train, cut his throat, shoot himself . . . whereas a woman will seek to ingest her end or take a leap. I need hardly remind you of the reputation Waterloo-bridge has for female suicides.'

'Quite. How does one explain these choices based on sex?'

'Frankly, I have no conception, Inspector.'

'As for method – what is the nature of prussic acid as a tool of death? What is its effect?'

'It is quite lethal of course. Even the brands sold by a chymist are utterly fatal, and they are typically only a six per cent solution. Continental brands can be as high as twenty-five per cent. Just inhaling the former dilution can cause dizziness, whereas the latter would cause death without ingestion. You know, of course, that the smell is of bitter almonds.'

'Indeed. What does such a death look like?'

'A strong dose would lead to rapid unconsciousness and

death within seconds. A reduced dose might give the victim up to two minutes, during which time they would manifest glistening eyes, a weak pulse and lifeless limbs. There may be a few moments of lucidity, some foaming at the mouth perhaps. A lucky victim might reflexively vomit, but would, I fear, die all the same.'

'What of the taste?'

'Ha! I have not spoken to anyone who has lived to describe it. I have heard of a Frenchman who drank a diluted version that he might document the sensation – but he died almost immediately. That is French medicine for you! I imagine it is very bitter, perhaps even a scalding sensation.'

'Might it be adequately disguised with an admixture of gin so that the drinker was insensible to the taste and smell?'

'Gin? I suppose so. If the victim was already a little drunk, and if the drink were taken quickly . . . yes, it could be. Does this pertain to a case you are working on?'

'Perhaps. Another question if I may: if a woman were to take a draught of prussic acid and then attempt to leap from height, would she have time to move her limbs to jump after ingesting the poison?'

'An interesting problem, albeit somewhat gruesome. If the dilution were sufficiently weak, she might have time to vault over a parapet before she lost the power of motion. Indeed, it would be quite ideal: she would fall without fear and land without pain, provided the dose were tailored to the height of the drop. A highly effective death.'

'But a sin all the same.'

'Well, quite. I am afraid it is becoming quite dim in here, Inspector. If you would like to talk further, I suggest we move to the museum, which is illuminated.'

The lecture theatre had indeed become quite stygian, its

banks of seats creating a well of darkness from where hundreds of unseen eyes might stare down upon that space containing the two gentlemen. They closed the door behind them and ventured back across the entrance hall to the museum – that lofty and unnerving exhibition of death prolonged in life.

Mr Newsome cast his eyes about the innumerable specimen jars glinting on shelves in the powerful glare of the gas. Sickly, pale things glistened within: bloated tissues, filmy membranes, knotty veins, gelatinous organs and mottled masses lined the walls amid the faintest scent of formaldehyde. It was a hideous shop window of biological preservation to rival any collection in the world – and it shrank the inspector's stomach.

'Splendid, isn't it?' said Mr Herbert, gesturing with an expansive arm towards the larger room with its countless re-assembled skeletons of birds and mammals. A colossal megatherium on a podium stalked towards them, frozen in time and bereft of flesh. In another case, the formidable skeleton of a man stood perhaps seven or eight feet tall, its huge chin jutting out like the prow of a boat.

'I suppose it is,' said Mr Newsome, grimacing at a shrunken *membrum virile* lying forlornly at the bottom of its imprisoning jar.

'What else can I help you with, Inspector?'

'Seeds. Would the ingestion of seeds also act as a poison if need be?'

'Well, no doubt there are numerous plants whose seeds are toxic to mankind – but they are usually processed to access the compounds within. I suspect it would take thousands of seeds to produce a useful drop of poison.'

'I see. I suppose that is why we eat apples, say, without risking our lives.'

'Quite – though the bitterness of the seed is a reminder of the killer within.'

'Would you happen to know if some fruits are more dangerous than others?'

'I hardly think that any we buy are *dangerous*. What are you thinking of?'

'A pomegranate.'

'Well, that is your fruit for seeds, certainly. It must have more than most. In fact, I do believe the etymology alludes to the seeds: the "grainy apple".'

'Mr Herbert – I am working on a case in which the victim has very likely eaten pomegranate seeds. I cannot understand why this particular fruit has been chosen, though I assume some importance owing to the rarity.'

'Interesting . . . I presume you have not had the benefit of a classical education.'

'You assume correctly.'

'But you have heard of Proserpine, of course: the mythological lady who was the bride of Pluto, king of the Underworld? *She* was forced to eat a number of pomegranate seeds so that she would be unable to remain away from him, returning for a season each year: winter in the living world.'

'Continue . . . why the pomegranate?'

'I cannot say. It is a highly symbolic fruit if one wants to venture into it. In the Bible, it represents both birth and death – perhaps the transition between them. The Jews say it was the forbidden fruit growing on the Tree of Knowledge – a symbol simultaneously of carnal intercourse and death. Just look at one: in health, it has the blush of youth (or of shame) – but its skin is quick to corrupt into decay. Cut it and it seems to bleed . . . yes, a fascinating symbol. I would wager it is for this reason that you have found it upon victims rather than any toxic quality it may possess.'

'This is most interesting. Thank you, Mr Herbert.'

'Happy to help, Inspector. It must be something out-of-the-ordinary for you, what? Not just the usual theft and stabbing.'

'Yes – though the "usual" is easier to solve. I will look into this Proserpine element further.'

'Well, do let me know how the case proceeds ... and perhaps it will help you to know that the name Proserpine is a later version: the Latin. Not many people realize that it derives from the Greek.'

'Which is ... ?'

'Why, "Persephone" of course! Inspector ... ? Are you all right? You have become quite pale ...'

TWENTY-TWO

If one were an adventurous soul not afraid of filth, depravity and the ever-present threat of violent robbery and death,
one might take a stroll past St Katharine's Dock to Wapping.
There, by the muddy shore, the wooden houses of centuries
past absorb the dank atmosphere and bow under their own
weight. No police walked these cobbles.

Nevertheless, on that same evening that Mr Newsome was
quizzing the surgeon, one would have found Mr Williamson
stepping through the stinking mire accompanied by his dusky
shadow Benjamin. They were looking for the Murder'd Moor,
the alehouse and sailors' inn run by the Mr Arbuthnot mentioned in Aubrey Alsthom's other-worldly recollection from
the Times.

'No doubt the name comes from some actual incident,'
mused Mr Williamson as they walked. 'Though that apos-
trophe suggests it is of some antiquity. I would not be surprised if the buildings hereabouts pre-date the Great Fire.'

Benjamin held his counsel. If he was perturbed about
visiting an inn so named, he did not show it. Indeed, there
were perhaps more black faces in this locale than any other
in London, though they seemed rather abject specimens in

comparison with his animal health and sartorial elegance. They looked at him in awe and seemed to nod slightly as he passed, whether in deference or in some unfathomable communion of the ebony-skinned, Mr Williamson could not say. It was almost as if he were a king come among them, but risen from among their ranks.

'Do they respect you, or fear you, Ben? Do you feel a kinship with them?'

Wordless, Benjamin stopped and lifted his trouser leg slightly so that Mr Williamson could see the iron ring that he wore perpetually about his ankle – a grim memento of a past when he spoke and sang, of a past still further back beyond history itself when he and his kind were perhaps the first among men.

'Hmm.'

They turned down towards the river and saw the sign of the inn hanging askew from the wooden building. Only the word 'Moor' was legible on its board, which was faded and rotted by untold years of damp. The guttural grunts of a rutting couple or a man being strangled to death came to them from somewhere close.

'Let us enter. I will ask about the young man with the curious laugh and we will see what we can see. I have no intention of spending much time here. And, Ben – be prepared for anything. These places are utterly lawless.'

Benjamin grinned and Mr Williamson took confidence in his companion's apparent lack of fear. Benjamin had, in fact, spent more time among this kind than the investigator could ever have guessed.

It will surprise few to learn that the interior of that place was a seething den of sodden mariners. There was a sour reek of beer, gin, oakum and bodies unwashed for months at a time. Foreign eyes assayed the strangers. Smoke hung thickly about the low beams.

'Opium,' muttered Mr Williamson to himself as they approached the bar.

'Yes, gents! What can I get yer?'

Mr Arbuthnot had the look of a man so corrupt that one would count one's fingers after shaking hands with him. His carious leer was all yellowed teeth and arched-eyebrow suggestion. His dented top hat shone with an accumulation of grease around its brim.

'Two gins and water,' said Mr Williamson.

'Right yer are! Not locals, are yer?'

'No.'

'I guessed it right off. Yer don't 'ave the look of the alley – Freepass-alley, that is. 'Ere yer go – two gins and water.'

The drinks had been adulterated with water drawn directly from the river and were a greenish-brown in colour.

'Do you have many visiters – I mean people who are not locals?' asked Mr Williamson, following the cue given to him.

'Not as a rule. 'Tis a particular sort comes to the Murder'd Moor.'

'Have you had any strangers here recently, or heard of them?'

'A policeman are yer?'

'I am not.'

'Lookin' for yer daughter?'

'I beg your pardon? What do you mean?'

''Ad a feller in here once looking for his daughter. She 'ad turned whore and was living upstairs with No-Legs Jack.'

'No – I have no children. I am doing a tour of the shipping districts with my friend here . . . he has no tongue so I am afraid he has little to add. I am a writer.'

'A writer, eh? Will yer put the Moor in yer book?'

'Perhaps. I believe an acquaintance of mine was here recently: a young man by the name of James, perhaps with his friend Major Tunnock – a fellow with a moustache.'

'If 'e's yer acquaintance, why don't yer ask 'im yerself 'stead of coming down 'ere to ask me?'

'He has gone missing. Have you seen him?'

'I 'ave not seen 'im, but I 'ave a message from 'im.'

Mr Williamson perceived a door opening at the end of the bar and had a sudden sensation of danger. Benjamin, too, tensed in alertness.

'Aye – 'e said if some copper-type feller came 'ere asking questions, we should see to it that he left in a coffin.'

A figure emerged from the opened door: the same immense fellow they had encountered in the ruins by the Fleet River, his taurine shoulders flexed for an onslaught and his face a mask of impassive threat.

In a flash, Benjamin had shrugged off his coat and stepped in front of Mr Williamson. Tables and chairs were scraped back over the wooden floor to create a gladiatorial arena. A great hubbub had begun to animate the room.

'There is no need to fight, Benjamin . . .' began Mr Williamson with the faintest tremor in his voice, but it was clear that a battle was inevitable. He looked towards the street door, which was now blocked by a couple of bearded mariners.

Benjamin was the taller of the two combatants, but the Hercules facing him seemed a human wall. Both raised their fists in a practised gesture and moved around each other, their eyes reading for possible weakness and error. To Mr Williamson, it had the look of ritual, almost of dance. Was it too much to hope that they would find in their opposite an equal match and deign not to fight?

Benjamin darted forward, his arm a blur, and landed a colossal blow upon the face of Hercules. The latter blinked dumbly, dropped his guard and seemed to wobble momentarily on his legs. A rivulet of blood emerged from his nose and ran down over his lips and chin. He shook his head like a dog. Then he raised his guard again and there was the merest trace of a smile.

A tremendous roar of approval erupted from the massed drinkers – this would be a match to talk about for years to come.

Benjamin nodded as if say: 'Right – now I know what I am faced with.' He rolled up his sleeves and set his jaw.

Hercules let forth a bellow and rushed at Benjamin swinging a fist that would have floored a rhinoceros. Benjamin dodged the blow and swung a locomotive uppercut under the chin of his assailant.

The crunch of jaw could be heard even over the din of the audience. Hercules spat out the shattered teeth with a spray of blood and wiped his chin on the back of his arm. Anger blazed in his eyes. He reached for the neck of a bottle on the bar and smashed it on the edge.

'Ben!' shouted Mr Williamson . . . but even as the word died between his lips, a handkerchief soaked in chloroform had been pressed over his mouth and he had been taken under the arms. As they dragged him from that room, his last sensation was the raucous crescendo of the barroom and the sound of toppling furniture.

He awoke later – whether minutes or hours, he could not have said. The cacophony of the fight reverberated distantly through the building and he deduced that he was in a lower-floor room, perhaps at the back of the building. His eyes were blindfolded and his arms and legs were tied to a long, reclined sofa. Footsteps shuffled behind him and he heard indistinct voices muttering.

'Well – Mr Williamson. It is time that we made each other's acquaintance. You have been remarkably persistent in your endeavours.'

The voice was an educated one, but corrupted in some way as if the speaker's throat were damaged. He sounded older than the 'young man' being sought as the main suspect.

'Who are you?' said Mr Williamson, attempting to keep a level tone.

'Who indeed? You are looking for a young man. I am not he.'

'Hmm. Then you are his accomplice in the murder of Mr Sampson, and one of the men engaged in the apparent suicide of prostitutes with prussic acid.'

There was a hurried muttering. Mr Williamson guessed from the sounds of this and their footfalls that there were perhaps four people standing behind him.

'Your reputation as a detective is well deserved, sir. Unfortunately, you have concerned yourself with matters that have nothing to do with you. You are no longer a policeman – and thus your death is of less consequence.'

'You murdered my wife Katherine.'

Silence.

'What are you talking about, Mr Williamson?'

'Seven years ago at the Monument. She was pushed from the top. The verdict was suicide, but I smelled prussic acid on her lips. She did not kill herself.'

Silence. More urgent whispering.

'I . . . I have no idea what you are talking about.'

'What manner of cowards are you to hide there behind me?

Why does only one of you speak? Are you afraid that I will identify your voices? Which one of you would I recognize if you spoke?'

'I do admire your relentless search for a solution even as you face your end.'

'Then show yourselves if I am to die. Allow me the courtesy of telling me the truth about Katherine before I rest with her in eternity.'

'No – it is you who will be doing the talking, Mr Williamson. You are going to tell us everything you have discovered: every clue, every idea, every discussion with your colleague Mr Dyson – yes, we know of him also.'

'He will kill you. He is bound by no moral or legal code.'

'What a fanciful thought – and quite misplaced. Mr Dyson is no concern of ours.'

'I will tell you nothing.'

'We will see.'

Mr Williamson was aware of footsteps at his side. He braced himself for a blow, but none came.

Had he been able to see, he would have seen an emaciated Chinaman extracting a blob of tarry-looking matter from a brass box with a steel probe before holding it in a naked flame to soften. He could, however, smell it.

'Opium.'

'Indeed. Perhaps your tongue will be loosened by this sweet intoxication. Our Oriental host Hoo Chang will administer it as skilfully as any man can.'

'I will tell you nothing.'

The Chinaman worked methodically to apply the melted matter to the small aperture inside a pipe bowl. Then he positioned the long, elegant ebony mouthpiece near to Mr

Williamson's mouth and applied the bowl directly to the flame. When he was satisfied, he nodded to his masters.

A burly bully in a fish-scented cap stepped alongside Mr Williamson and delivered a punch under his ribs that emptied all of the breath from the investigator. As he gasped, the pipe's mouthpiece was forced between his teeth and that bully's hand clasped the jaw shut, covering the nose, too, with a single meaty palm.

Mr Williamson struggled for breath – struggled not to breathe. His face flushed red and a sweat broke out on his face, but he could withhold no longer. He inhaled deeply and the intoxicating smoke rushed into his lungs unhindered.

He coughed. He spat. He writhed against his bonds. But the onslaught began again, and again, until three times thus he had breathed the sweet, oily taste into his lungs and into his blood.

'It is a curious substance, is it not?' spoke the damaged voice. 'It must be treated with respect and taken in the right way. Smoking it is far preferable to eating it in my experience – the effect is stronger, and inhaling it is kinder on the stomach. Yes, I think you will appreciate the experience. You will recall elements of your past in the finest detail – things that had seemingly vanished forever. And you will tell us all we ask.'

Mr Williamson coughed and coughed, straining wrists and ankles against the straps.

'It is no use – you will not expunge it from your organism now. It is coursing around your body and will soon reach your brain. But do not worry – the dose is not fatal: just three grains. That should give you about five hours of delirium, I should expect. Now we will wait for the effect to take.'

'What kind of man are you that would force a fellow human to absorb this poison?' said Mr Williamson. 'To what depth must one descend to become a monster such as you: a murderer, a sadist . . . ?'

'You misunderstand. You should ask what *heights* must be attained to reach the perfection of knowledge that I have. One must pass beyond these mortal realms which chain us with false gods and hollow morality. Beyond those human bonds lies true immortality, Mr Williamson. You fear death, tied to that sofa there. You fear the blackness of the end, but you should approach it with ecstasy. It is the profoundest experience. To peer into that abyss, especially when . . . well, I will not waste my philosophy on you.'

'Your death will be no ecstasy, sir. It will be on the end of a rope outside Newgate Gaol.'

'How comical a thought! It is you who are tied down. The police are dancing to my tune and your Mr Dyson has an appointment with death mere hours hence . . . and you say it is *I* who will hang! Very good!'

Mr Williamson fancied that his breathing had become more laboured and that he was hotter. Was it the drug, or was it his anger? Certainly he seemed to be preternaturally alert, his senses as acute as a dog. Doorways in his mind opened. Thoughts moved at an accelerated speed. The solution to the entire case appeared to flash in and out of his inner vision too quickly for him to see it. The names of Sampson, Colliver, Jessop, Joseph, James and Tunnock tumbled and coalesced.

And for the first time, he seemed to smell lavender; he smelled creosote; he smelled almonds and some other sweet scent. He heard the fight continuing in the barroom, which meant Ben must still be alive. And he heard the muttering of those unseen witnesses to his ordeal. Was it a stretch of fancy to expect that he who murdered Mr Jessop and Mrs Colliver was also present . . . ?

'Ah, I think you are feeling the effect, Mr Williamson. I see your nose sniffing and your ears twitching. Delicious is it not? Do you not feel more alive? You are no use to us in this condition, however. We will wait until you enter a more stuporous state before we make any enquiries.'

'James Tattershall! Is it *you* standing there behind me? You are implicated in these crimes and you will hang. It was you leaving Colliver's coffee house the night of Mr Sampson's murder. You are the murderer of Mr Sampson, Mr Jessop, Mrs Colliver and old Joseph.'

Silence.

Black, gaping silence.

In his hyperaware state, Mr Williamson fancied he could hear the very pocket watches in the room ticking and each individual's breathing. Another door opened in his mind and another vision came to him *apropos* of no discernible stimulus. Was it a guess, or was it a foreknowledge born of intuition?

'Eusebius Bean – are *you* the third man standing there? I see it all now . . . I see it all despite this blindfold . . . Now – who is the fourth?'

'I *told* you this was a bad idea!' expostulated a new voice – in fact, not that of James, Eusebius or their master in the proceedings. This voice made no attempt at whispering. 'I *told* you it could open his mind. I *told* you that he was no normal . . .'

'Quiet!' exploded the broken voice. 'Congratulations Mr Williamson. You are everything people say of you, but whatever you think you know will leave this world tonight – all wasted. All I need to know is how many of these thoughts you have communicated to others, including Inspector Newsome.'

'I . . . will . . . tell . . . you nothing . . . nothing.'

What had been alertness just a matter of seconds ago was now becoming languor in the mind of Mr Williamson. His limbs took on a weight and warmth akin to being immersed in a deep bath, and the rapid flashes of thought within his fevered scull melted into pure sensation.

He was there by Charlotte's fireside in Golden-square, warmth permeating his coat . . . she was speaking but no sound came from her mouth . . . she was standing and moving over to where he sat, a smile on her pretty face . . . she was stroking his hair with cool fingers . . .

'What have you told Inspector Newsome? What has Mr Dyson told you? Do you all know about James, about Eusebius?'

. . . Charlotte became Katherine, his wife, sitting beside him at the fire and talking about her walks around the city. He saw her kindly face as he read to her . . . he saw her walking beside him in the park . . .

'Mr Williamson – tell us about the case. I believe that the inspector does not yet know about James. We are your friends . . .'

. . . he saw her atop the Monument amid the city smoke, her hair straggling from her bonnet in the breeze . . . he saw three gentlemen with her there, their faces a blur, and a hand holding out a flask that she might take a tipple on that cold day . . . he saw rough hands about her and saw the sky wheeling through her eyes as she went over the edge, the bitter taste of poison burning her tongue . . .

'Mr Williamson! Mr Williamson? Can you hear me? . . . Hoo Chang – how much did you give him? He seems utterly insensible!'

The Chinaman flinched and gazed at his feet.

. . . he saw himself a young policeman walking the streets, looking to the sky for the first trace of dawn and bridling at every unseen sound up every alley . . . he saw bodies pulled sodden, pale and bloated from the river . . . he saw a gaping throat opened by a razor . . . he saw a fellow constable set upon by a group of drunken Irish and beaten to death with clubs . . . he saw a two-headed girl wearing a dress soaked black with her own blood . . .

'Look at his face,' said that fourth, unidentified voice. 'He is reliving some dark nightmares from his past.'

'I told *you* to hush!' shouted the fractured voice, sounding even hoarser now in its passion. 'Mr Williamson! Mr Williamson? . . . O, it is useless! The man's pure heart has become quite stupefied at this chymical corruption. We will find our answers from the other one on Sunday. Let us leave this place with all haste. By the back entrance.'

The three gentlemen made to leave. Their leader, the man with the damaged voice, merely nodded to the bully still standing beside the sofa. It was Mr Williamson's death sentence.

. . . he saw himself in a balloon high over the city, his hands gripping the edge of the basket and peering down . . . he jumped, falling through the freezing air, falling without fear towards the gas lit streets . . .

The bully indicated with a jerk of his head that Hoo Chang should vacate the room, which he did, hurriedly, via the same door used by the three gentlemen. Then the be-capped ruffian extracted a razor from his inside jacket pocket and, without a trace of emotion, rested the blade's edge against the fevered neck of Mr Williamson, whose veins throbbed conveniently at the surface in readiness for the slash . . .

Then the interior connecting door crashed from its hinges with a shower of splinters.

The bully's razor fell to the ground with a clink.

And the would-be murderer beheld a demon before him: an immense Negro glistening with sweat and blood, his hands and face lacerated, his clothing almost entirely ripped from his formidable torso, and his single functioning eye burning with a rage so terrifying that it set the bully's legs a-quiver.

As he bent to retrieve his razor, the bully was lifted off his feet by a punch that audibly cracked his scull and sent him almost through the wall.

Benjamin picked up the razor and cut the bonds around Mr Williamson's feet and hands. He ripped off the blindfold and picked up the investigator as if he had been no more than a toy, hoisting him over a shoulder and carrying him.

. . . upside-down now – and through viscous haze – he saw the sofa where he had lain, the opium-smoking apparatus and the inert body next to it . . . he saw the trail of destruction that Benjamin had wrought on his rampage through the building . . . he saw the barroom littered with groaning and unconscious bodies, blood splattered across walls and smeared in great arcs over the glass-strewn wooden floor . . . he saw the body of that huge Hercules lying by the door . . .

. . . he smelled the night air: smoky, cold and putrid . . . and he knew he was home.

TWENTY-THREE

⸺ ◆ ⸺

The funeral obsequies of the late George Williamson, previously Detective Sergeant in the Metropolitan Police, took place at eight o'clock this morning. His remains were interred beside those of his departed wife Katherine at the Spa Fields burial ground, attended by Inspector Albert Newsome and constables who had known him. He leaves no family.

Noah Dyson folded the newspaper and smiled. He looked across at Mr Williamson, who was quite alive, albeit still somewhat fragile after the events of two nights ago. The scene was the reception room of Mr Allan's residence, Mr Allan being a retired policeman and guardian of a house that was used by the Detective Force for covert meetings, for housing vulnerable witnesses and for divers other purposes that should not be known to anyone outside that investigative fraternity. Also present were Inspector Newsome, Mr Cullen and a heavily bandaged Benjamin.

After the briefest – and most sparingly honest – of summaries about their respective activities over the previous days, an uneasy silence had settled as the gathered gentlemen waited for Mr Allan to bring the tea up from the kitchen.

Mr Newsome was glaring at Mr Cullen, who was studiously avoiding the gaze by looking into the healthy fire in the grate. Mr Williamson, who had been suffering from a greater than usual thirst, was sipping water from a glass and cogitating upon his own death, looking occasionally at his previous superior for any clues to what he might have learned. Benjamin picked at the coverings of his multiple wounds and awaited the confabulatory fireworks.

A knock at the street door interrupted the silence: three raps of the brass knocker. All of the men registered the sound, but none stood.

'I believe it is the letter carrier,' said Mr Cullen to break the awkward hiatus.

'No – the letter carrier knocks only twice. That is their habit and it does not vary,' said Mr Newsome. 'It will be a tradesman of some kind.'

'I think not,' said Mr Williamson. 'The tradesman goes first to the kitchen and rings the bell. This is likely some irregular tradesman: an upholsterer or glazier – or a delivery boy, perhaps.'

'An interesting assumption,' said Noah, 'but the delivery boy tends to bang clumsily a number of times at the knocker in his enthusiasm about being away from the shop. This has the sound of a practised hand – someone used to knocking on doors. An older person.'

'Well, now,' said Mr Newsome, 'I disagree. The knocking was brief, but not particularly loud, which would suggest a timidity associated with someone not used to knocking on doors.'

'Unless, of course, the person on the step is a short person, a boy, perhaps, who has to reach up to the knocker and cannot therefore exert the force of a taller person,' said Mr Williamson.

Mr Cullen struggled in vain for something to add and looked over at Benjamin, who was grinning at the game.

'Might it not be a woman in that case?' said Noah. 'The female hand does not like to rap loudly but has a gentle touch. Perhaps she is here to interview for a position.'

'In which case, she would call at the kitchen,' said Mr Newsome.

'Unless she knew Mr Allan employs no cook and that she would have to use the street door to gain his attention,' said Mr Williamson.

'It could be an entirely mistaken call . . .' ventured Mr Cullen, aware now that he was entering a highly skilled arena.

'Interesting,' said Noah. 'We must always consider the arbitrary and random. Perhaps the caller has confused the house with one on the opposite side of the street and knocks so lightly because he is unsure of the address – especially this particular address.'

'The chance callers to this address are few,' said Mr Newsome. 'Indeed, you will have noticed there is no number appended to the door.'

'Let us settle this once and for all,' said Noah. 'Ben – will you go and answer the door?'

Benjamin stood with a grimace and walked to the corridor. They heard him open the street door then close it. He appeared again in the reception room and made a brief hand signal to Noah.

'Whoever it was, they evidently tired of our procrastination,' said Noah. 'There was nobody on the step.'

'Hmm,' said Mr Williamson.

There was a rattle of crockery and Mr Allan entered carrying a tray. The ex-policeman was about fifty years old with prematurely greying hair and a slight limp from an injury gained while on duty.

'Was that someone knocking at the street door?' he asked, laying the tray on a low table in the centre of the room.

'It was nobody,' said Inspector Newsome. 'Thank you for the tea, Mr Allan, but I must now ask you to leave us to speak in private.'

The venerable host, who was accustomed to such meetings, left the room without comment and the four gentlemen again began their mutual examinations.

'Well, then – I will begin if nobody else will venture to do so,' said Inspector Newsome. 'Are we to believe for a moment that this spurious funeral Mr Dyson had me arrange is going to convince anyone of Mr Williamson's death?'

'They left him with a razor at his throat and had no reason to believe his death sentence was not carried out,' said Noah. 'I had the body of the bully removed that same evening and I suspect he will not be missed for a day or two. Besides, the notice has appeared in *the Times*. Nobody knows the truth but the people in this room, and people believe what they like to think is true, especially if it is corroborated.'

'What was in the coffin?' said the inspector.

'Earth approximating my weight,' said Mr Williamson. 'They would have to exhume the box to know for sure that I am not in it.'

'Well, it seems rather an elaborate hoax for very little discernible benefit.'

'The merest advantage is still an advantage, Inspector,' said

Noah. 'The illusion need last only two more days. In that time, we will have our solution . . . or be dead.'

'Let us hope it is the former. Now – we have all been following paths towards the solution of this infernal mystery and I have no doubt that we have all made discoveries. I wonder if we can all fully share these discoveries on the understanding that together we may hold the answer. This puzzle needs every single piece before it will show the final image.'

'Very well,' said Noah. 'But you will earn our trust by beginning with yourself.'

'Earn *your* trust, Mr Dyson? I do not aspire to those lofty heights. Nevertheless, I will begin with something that may pertain particularly to Mr Williamson here. You may not have read of it in the newspapers, but another girl has been found – apparently a suicide with prussic acid. She was a dollymop.'

'Why would that "pertain" particularly to me?' asked Mr Williamson.

'Because her name was Nelly Jones. You interviewed her at Milton-street ten days ago.'

'I did indeed, and make no attempt to deny it. It was Mendicity Society business. Are you implying a connection of some kind? I see none.'

'Only the anonymous note I received advising me that you had spoken to the girl. Evidently somebody wants me to make a connection. Could you think who?'

'I cannot. Frankly, I am more and more convinced that there is a crowd of people behind this case who are observing our every move. That is something that you, more than any of us, should know.'

'What do you mean by that, George?'

'Come now, Inspector – will you have us believe that Mr Eusebius Bean has not been spying on almost every development in the investigation? From the moment I saw him in that opulent house at St James's, I knew him as a spy. And I have the feeling that he has been near to me for some days past – a curious sense of being observed.'

'All right, Mr Williamson – I will admit that I, too, have come to that conclusion in recent days. It explains almost all that has happened: how they have been able to follow movements so closely. Eusebius was imposed upon me, but now he has vanished.'

'Who are "they" – the people who follow?' said Noah.

'That is the question, is it not? I questioned Mr Poppleton in his gaol cell – the same one at Giltspur-street, incidentally, that once held you, Mr Dyson – and he said that "they" would kill him. He preferred internment to divulging their identities.'

'I repeat: who are "they"?'

'It seems they are wealthy. I would guess that Mr Dyson is going to tell us that they are connected to the Continental Club.'

'Let me say what everyone is thinking,' said Mr Williamson. 'The Society for the Suppression of Vice.'

'It would seem so,' said Inspector Newsome with a sigh. 'Proving that, however, will be problematic. Eusebius, as I say, has vanished. He is no doubt watching one or all of us on behalf of his paymasters. Who knows what he has told them?'

'Well, his observation will cease if I observe him first,' said Noah.

'We are getting away from my original point,' said the inspector. 'What do the death of Nelly and that letter contribute to our investigation? Who else knew that you visited her, George?'

'The Secretary of the Mendicity Society, of course. And anyone who had my notes on the case. And Harold Jute, of course – a young man who was spending time at the Society to please his father.'

'"Harold", you say?' said Noah. 'Describe him.'

'Tall, slim, sandy hair, a prominent Adam's apple . . .'

'Then I have most likely met the man. I was introduced to a Harold at the Continental Club. He appeared as you have described – and he was clearly part of that group surrounding a certain Major Tunnock: a lecherous old soldier.'

'My G—!' said Mr Cullen, seeing his chance. 'Do you think that "they" put him alongside you at that early stage because they thought you would investigate?'

'Why would Mr Williamson investigate if he was not even part of the Detective Force?' said Mr Newsome with derision. 'And while we are about it, why is Constable Cullen at this meeting? I know he has chosen to throw away his long years of service for some phantasy as a detective, but I see no benefit in having him here.'

'Mr Cullen has provided important information on the case that you saw fit not to mention last time we met,' said Noah. 'We can trust *him*.'

'I see. I see. Well, perhaps it *was* this Mr Jute who sent the note to me, though I cannot see why . . . Mr Williamson – you look as if you are about to have a thought . . .'

'When I was constrained at the Murder'd Moor, I heard two distinct voices. One of them was a gargled, broken noise I did not recognize. The other . . . the other now seems familiar to me. I was perhaps not listening attentively at that point, but it seems clear now. I believe it was . . . Harold Jute.'

'So we have tentatively identified one of who "they" are,' said Mr Newsome. 'The rest are likely to be of that group around the major. We must act quickly.'

'Wait. Let us not be too precipitous in our actions,' said

Noah. 'I have made arrangements to meet the major and his friends at a private residence on Sunday. That will be an opportunity to see who is part of the group and present our case to them.'

'It is a trap, of course – as obviously as Freepass-alley was to Mr Williamson. They will try to kill you as surely as they tried with him. Did they not make that clear?'

'Ah, but they *did* kill Mr Williamson, Inspector – or so they should think after our excellent ruse. No – I will go to my *rendezvous* and you will be waiting to swoop upon the party. We already know that these men are too well protected to be arrested in their conventional lives. Perhaps if can catch them *in flagrante delicto*, we will have a case from which even they cannot escape.'

'You walk willingly into danger, Mr Dyson.'

'On the contrary. Once you have them in custody, they will be reluctant to tell you anything you cannot prove. If they think they have me in their trap, they may tell me what I need to know.'

'All right – we can talk about that later. Now I want to hear more about Mr Williamson's narcotic flight of fancy and who the owner of that damaged voice was.'

'There is nothing remotely amusing about it, I can assure you, Inspector. I might have been killed but for Benjamin's intervention.'

Benjamin nodded in acknowledgement.

'Yes, yes – but who was the older man? Was it this Major Tunnock?'

'No,' said Noah. 'We have discussed it and the two men have quite different voices and turns of phrase. I have an entirely different theory . . . but I see from Mr Cullen's agitation that he has something to say. Yes, Mr Cullen?'

'Sirs, I went out west as we agreed and attempted to find girls who knew of Lou: the murdered prostitute with a newly acquired benefactor. One girl – whose testimony I believed – told me that the gentleman in question was old, ugly and had health problems that affected his skin. What if those health problems also affected his voice—?'

'What nonsense! It could be anyone at all!' scoffed Mr Newsome.

'In fact, Mr Cullen's report is actually rather interesting,' said Noah, 'as it has been since he began cooperating with us. Let me suggest some words to you, Inspector, and see what you make of them: lavender, almond, and creosote or coal tar.'

'Am I a lady to know about such things? Make your point, Mr Dyson.'

'Joseph the waterman told us he smelled lavender and coal tar when he encountered the murderers face to face. Both he and Mr Cullen have alluded to other scents they could not immediately place.'

'What? There were others at the scene of the crime? You told me nothing of this at our last meeting!'

'And you withheld facts of your own. If we had told you, Eusebius Bean would also have found out. Fortunately, Mr Cullen was able to tell us that he smelled lavender in the room Mr Sampson fell from. It was our strongest clue, and our recent researches have led us to believe that these scents – as scents often do – cover something far more unsavoury.'

'You have centre stage, Mr Dyson. I await your soliloquy. But I expect to hear everything.'

'In my time at the library, I did a little medical research. I found that sores of the mouth are often treated with tincture of myrrh and scented with jasmine. Lavender is used as an emollient in treatments to soothe the skin – as is creosote and almond oil, particularly on the scalp. Together, these scents account for those alluded to by our witnesses, along with the unidentified ones: jasmine and myrrh are relatively uncommon and not generally known.'

'So what are you telling me – that our "broken-voiced man" is unhealthy? I think we might have guessed that.'

'More than that, Inspector. Certainly, Mr Cullen's tale of a man with skin problems is pertinent (especially coming from acquaintances of Lou), but I believe there is more to infer from this particular combination of medicaments. Are you familiar with the mercury cure, Inspector?'

'Not personally, if that is what you mean.'

'I am glad for you. The man who ingests large quantities of mercury develops mouth sores. His condition, when advanced, will cause his hair to fall out and his skin to be covered in sores. There is also a strong likelihood that his face will be scarred with cicatrices if he has had the condition for long.'

'Syphilis.'

'Indeed – all of the evidence points to our man having an advanced stage of the disease. If he is someone of note as we suspect, this might explain his relative invisibility and why I did not see anyone of this appearance at the club. Nobody likes to advertise that their very organism is rotting from the inside. Without those perfumed oils and soothing balms, his breath would be a blast from the grave and his skin a permanently suppurating sheath to a rotting body.'

'You paint a graphic picture, Mr Dyson. But are we any closer? You suggest we are looking for an important man with syphilis – there must dozens in the city, all of them no doubt reclusive.'

'There is more. If this is the same gentleman who killed Lou, and the same that questioned Mr Williamson, our Mr

Cullen has learned from a prostitute that he enjoyed giving and receiving a beating at his place. Not only that, but he *encouraged his fellows to watch*. What if this was the scenario at Colliver's coffee house that night? What if Mr Sampson's shouts of "I cannot" related to his inhibitions in this case?'

'Your reasoning is full of "what ifs", Mr Dyson.'

'You say so, but my individual research has offered more evidence in favour of it. My conversations with the gentlemen at the club (and I include my brief talk with Mr Poppleton) have suggested that the group favours the more extreme varieties of sexual endeavour. Indeed, they gave me a tract that seemed to describe their philosophy. You will note who the publisher is.'

Noah handed the tract to Inspector Newsome, whose face took on an expression of distaste as he read the first lines. He folded it and handed it back.

'Interesting. But what do we do without a name? His fellows – if they *are* his fellows – are unlikely to offer his identity.'

'Ah, that is where I have more information,' said Noah. 'Although the girl Mr Cullen spoke to did not know where the gentleman lived, you will recall that Charlotte told Mr Williamson about how the dead girls had visited certain charities for girls of their profession, and that their deaths were connected in some way?'

'Yes. An improbable suggestion.'

'Perhaps. Purporting to be a wealthy manufacturer looking for a suitable recipient of my munificence, I wrote letters to the secretaries of these charities asking for lists of their major benefactors and supporters in order that I could be sure they were respectable and deserving of my own considerable charity.'

'And?'

'Here are the replies: lists of some our most notable men and women. I have no doubt you recognize many of the names. But only one name appears on every list as a prominent supporter of "fallen women". I have circled it as you see.'

'Sir John Smythe.'

'Precisely. He is also a senior sponsor of the Society for the Suppression of Vice, though I cannot say I have heard the name before.'

'Nor I, though I find myself oddly unsurprised at the Vice Society connection. What does it prove that he is on the charitable lists of these bodies?'

'It proves that Charlotte was telling the truth,' said Mr Williamson. 'Or, at least, that the truth can be found somewhere in this web of unlikely coincidence. True – we still do not know why these murders are being disguised as such, unless it is somehow part of the unholy philosophy outlined in that tract.'

'I am afraid to admit that George is right,' said Noah. 'All we have is coincidence at present. We could locate and speak to this John Smythe, but I suspect he currently feels confident in his anonymity. We might guess at the others involved, but we are supposed to know nothing about him. I suggest we keep it that way for the time being. Instead, tell us what *you* have discovered, Inspector.'

'With so much untruth and subterfuge going on, I admit that I am as baffled as you—'

'Enough of that! What has the case of poor Nelly shown you about this case?'

'All right. Her body was found with an empty glass nearby. It smelled of gin and prussic acid. The cause of death was poisoning. Sexual activity had taken place.'

'Hmm. Hmm,' intoned Mr Williamson with a sombre air.

'I suppose that you see another connection with those girls and Katherine, George, but what possible connection can there be? Katherine's death was a fall; these are not. That death was years ago; these are much more recent.'

'We will come to that in a moment,' said Noah. 'In the meantime, Mr Cullen has told us about the chewed seeds he found. You might have dismissed them at the time, but I suspect you have revisited that clue as the only one you have. Have they been found on other girls?'

'Another betrayal from Constable Cullen. I see. Well, in fact, the body of Nelly also had seeds in the mouth. I have made enquiries and I must say that my findings have been most enlightening. The fruit in question is not an orange, as Constable Cullen thought, but—'

'A pomegranate,' said Noah.

'Yes. I see you have done your own research. But did you also discover that in ancient mythology a number of these seeds were consumed by Proserpine . . . also known to the Greeks as—'

'Persephone,' said Noah.

'Well . . . we have the same information, but where does it get us? Are we any closer to the Persephone of that letter? Are we any closer to the death of Katherine? Are we any closer to finding our syphilitic villain, or discerning the reason for these deaths of prostitutes? Do we know why Mr Sampson leaped from the window, and who the mysterious young man was? No – we know none of those things.'

'Perhaps . . . and perhaps not. Joseph the waterman told us something else that we have not revealed to you – most likely the thing that led to his death. He heard an unmistakable laugh coming from that room after Mr Sampson fell. Inspector

315

– I have heard that laugh ... at the Continental Club. It belonged to one of Tunnock's group.'

'Then we must go there immediately and arrest the man.'

'For having a distinctive laugh? You have already said that these men will not talk to policemen. Let us assume for the time being that he will be there at my meeting – the trap – with Major Tunnock. Of more relevance at this moment is how we locate Persephone that we may discover more about the connection to Katherine. What have you got, Inspector?'

'Very little. And I admit I am more confused than ever on this point. Persephone seemed initially to be an informant pointing us towards the perpetrators of a crime – now we discover that she is at the centre of some heretical sect or *cabal* that is killing prostitutes. What should I think?'

'Perhaps that our letter writer is aware of the group and took that name knowing that we were bound to investigate it, thus uncovering the true criminals,' offered Mr Williamson. 'We have, after all, deduced she is intelligent and has uncommon knowledge.'

'That is an intriguing idea, George, but does it help us? Who is she? Where is she? Is she as much a figure of fancy as her namesake?'

'Fortunately, she is still watching us,' said Noah.

'What? Have you had further communication from Persephone?' said Inspector Newsome.

'At the British Museum reading room. A book was brought to me that I had not requested. This led me to a second book and there I found this note.'

He who helps

I see that you are aiding Mr Williamson in his endeavours. I do not know you, but I thank you.

You are exceptionally close to the solution of this case. I urge you to continue in the direction you are heading and you will find the killers of Katherine, Mr Sampson and the other girls.

I can tell you no more.

Persephone

An atmosphere of fevered cogitation took hold of the occupants of that room. Assuredly, some of them had already spent some time considering the note's contents, but there was matter in it to occupy even the greatest investigator's mind in relation to this most perplexing of cases.

'So, Inspector – apply your detective skills to that,' challenged Noah.

'Firstly, have you reason to believe that this letter is from the same hand as the original?'

'The paper and the hand are identical, though I admit that may mean nothing,' said Mr Williamson.

'All right. It is addressed to "He who helps", which suggests she has been observing both of you since the first letter was delivered, but that she does not know Noah by name. However, she couldn't have known you would be in the library that day in order to leave a message in a book.'

'True,' said Noah.

'So we deduce that she, or one of her people, was following you and observing you in the library. Also, it is interesting that she makes a point of saying she does not know you, Mr Dyson . . . almost as if she *expects* to know everyone. And evidently she knows precisely where you are in your investigation to know that you are exceptionally close.'

'Indeed,' said Mr Williamson. 'But I wonder at this word "exceptionally". It is somewhat out of character with the

317

terseness of the original letter. Is it, I wonder, a veiled clue: that we are close to the solution but *with one exception* – that we have one key detail wrong?'

'A clue it may be, but it is not a helpful one. More telling is the final sentence: "I can tell you no more." Why not? Because she knows no more? Because she is afraid to tell more . . . because someone is preventing her by threat?'

'Or because she knows of the perpetrators but they do not yet know of her?' added Noah.

'Explain yourself on that point, Mr Dyson.'

'Everyone who has heard the name Persephone has responded in one of two ways: complete ignorance or blanched-face shock. It is my belief that our suspects know only of one Persephone: the mythological lady.'

'I do not follow your logic.'

'Then let me add this: when Mr Williamson challenged his erstwhile captors on the death of Katherine, their reaction was of genuine surprise. If they knew of our letter writer, might not they have already made a connection?'

'Not necessarily.'

'So what have *you* found with the entire apparatus of the Metropolitan Police at your control,' said a clearly emboldened Mr Cullen.

'Well, well – hark how the hen crows when playing with the roosters!'

'Gentlemen, please!' interceded Noah. 'It is fair question: have you any further intelligence on who Persephone might be, Inspector? You do have hundreds of men out on the streets to do your bidding.'

'In fact, I have made enquiries. It occurred to me that if she *were* a prostitute as Mr Williamson initially assumed, perhaps she could be one of those lofty types of Park-lane. That assumption would at least tally with her alleged intelligence, knowledge and classical pseudonym. Those women are quite unlike the married variety – they are repositories of rumour and gossip to make the very government blush.'

'And what have you found?' said Noah.

'There are a number of them, of course. And they are sur-prisingly reclusive. To the common populace, they do not exist except as figures in passing carriages, or as an equestrian glimpsed from afar at Rotten Row in the summer. To her accustomed audience, however – rich men with a taste for high class in every element of their lives – she is as conspicuous as the advertisements that plague the city.'

'Go on. Have you names and addresses?'

'I have addresses – the names are elusive. Here is the list. These women live in luxury that our Queen might envy. Approaching them is almost as difficult. They see only who they think can benefit them. Why, I have learned of one who has a retinue of servants in a unique livery, and a carriage painted with her own spurious coat of arms. I fear they will admit no investigator to their rooms.'

'It is worth us speaking to these women if we can, even if it is only to move further towards Persephone,' said Mr Williamson. 'We must attempt to find a solution *before* Noah goes to his end on Sunday.'

'So we have tomorrow to act. Let us formulate a plan,' said Noah. 'There are three names on this list of Park-lane courtesans. Mr Williamson is "dead" now and may be able to enjoy more freedom of movement, so I suggest that he pursues them. You, Inspector, are in a position to discover what you can about Major Tunnock and Sir John Smythe without actually venturing to that club. It is time we began to pursue the killers rather than *vice versa*.'

'Do you trust Mr Cullen to aid you in these endeavours?' said Mr Newsome.

'I trust him more than I trust you. Perhaps you will surprise me, Inspector.'

'What will *you* do, Mr Dyson?'

'Of all of us, I am perhaps the one in most danger. I will be pursuing my own investigation and trying to remain unseen to preserve at least some semblance of doubt in the minds of our suspects. If we have been successful, they may think I have been cowed by the death of Mr Williamson.'

'And if our researches unearth nothing of worth, you will still attend this obvious trap on Sunday? Are you not afraid that they know everything we know? Who knows whether that whey-faced fool Eusebius Bean was also watching you in the library?'

'It is a risk, but after Mr Williamson's encounter with them, I believe they will be more circumspect – and very likely more lethal. We are all in danger, but we have been followed before and lost our pursuers. I *will* go to my *rendezvous*, but certainly not alone. Be reassured that I have plans to turn the villains into your hands, Inspector, while providing all the answers we seek.'

'Tell me – what really interests you in this case, Mr Dyson? Why do you risk your life for a man who would once have put you behind bars?'

'The fact that you have to ask means you could never comprehend the answer, Inspector. We meet again on Sunday afternoon in this same place, if not before.'

TWENTY-FOUR

It had been an inadvertent comment of Inspector Newsome's that Noah had returned to later once he and Mr Williamson were alone.

'When the inspector made that comment about the unique livery, it struck a note,' said Noah. 'At the library, shortly after I received the note, I told you I glimpsed a figure fleeing – a figure wearing some manner of scarlet decoration.'

'A scarf, perhaps. A coloured handkerchief? It is hardly conclusive,' said Mr Williamson.

'What man do you know that wears scarlet in any form? A uniform jacket, yes – or perhaps some clerical garb . . . but a hat or a scarf or an epaulette?'

'I suppose so.'

'No – it seems to me that a man would wear such a thing only if he had been dressed by a woman: if he was wearing livery designed for and by a woman. How many women are there in London who would dress a man thus?'

'I can think of none. Black tends to be the fashion.'

'Quite. But these kept women of Park-lane *advertise* their power by such subtle means. In this way, they lord it over those matrons of the upper classes who must beg and wheedle their husbands for a show of luxury.'

'You know more about the subject than I, Noah. I am reluctant to admit it, but Mr Newsome was right upon one point: if Persephone is anyone, she is likely to be one of these women. They have the power, the knowledge, the education . . . Everything about our case points to this world of privileged immorality. Only the connection with Katherine's death is utterly inconsistent.'

'And that, George, is what you are to discover tomorrow morning.'

'I would rather *you* undertook the action in this . . . this particular adventure.'

'We have discussed this. You are dead to our observers; I, on the other hand, am their main focus as they methodically kill anyone touching on the case. And have you forgotten – it was to you that she first addressed her information. Of all of us, you are most likely to gain access.'

'I understand all of that, but . . . Hmm. Hmm . . .'

'I know: your interview with Charlotte went badly, but *she* is a different girl altogether, George. She is a predator and you were her prey. These Park-lane girls are also pretty – perhaps the most beautiful in the world – but they have no interest in a man like you. The most you have to fear from her is that her intelligence will quite eclipse your own.'

'Thank you, Noah.'

'These women are experts with men. She will see in a moment who you are, what you know, what are your strengths and weaknesses. She will see this and she will adopt a fitting tone. It is her unique talent to be the woman that every man feels comfortable with.'

'Hmm. We will see.'

'The challenge, of course, will be achieving an audience with her at all. If she wanted to meet, she would have engineered it already. Indeed, everything she has done thus far has shown an exceptional disinclination to be associated with any part or person pertaining to this case – though she clearly *is* associated. You will not be able to gain access merely by knocking on her door. And nor would Inspector Newsome, I fear. She probably has more power than he.'

'You have said that these women are often to be seen at the opera or theatre . . .'

'Yes, but they attend as male diversions: showing themselves to prospective benefactors. A man such as you would not come within ten feet of her silk dress.'

'Let us say I do gain admittance and present to her that she is Persephone. Notwithstanding the livery of her servants and our suppositions, there is nothing I can do to prove she is who we seek if she refuses to admit it.'

'And that, George, is where you prove your reputation and resolve as a detective. That is when you discover the truth behind Katherine's death. Tomorrow ends the uncertainty of seven years – you will succeed. You must succeed.'

'Hmm. Tomorrow.'

And the following morning did indeed find Mr Williamson alone in the post-dawn stillness of Park-lane. No traffic troubled that hallowed thoroughfare, whose balconies gazed from loftily haughty *façades* upon the hoar-frosted expanse of Hyde-park. A few words with a shivering sweeping boy had been enough to discover that those distinctively liveried foot-men emerged from a residence close to the corner of Mount-street that, superficially at least, appeared little different to its neighbours.

It hardly seems necessary to say that our investigator was not dressed in his habitual top hat and greatcoat. Strangers were conspicuous on this street of conspicuous wealth, so he was standing on the opposite side of the street beside a barrow of fresh fish and dressed in the garb of one associated with that piscine trade. Every now and then he would push the barrow further along and yell out 'Eels! Get yer eels' in a somewhat self-conscious approximation of the commercial demotic.

There were no customers. There was, however, a carriage approaching.

Mr Williamson busied himself with his semi-frozen wares so that the brim of his hat partially covered his face as the carriage passed . . . but he was able to see that it was a Metropolitan Police conveyance.

The carriage stopped outside the house by Mount-street and no lesser a personage than Detective Inspector Albert Newsome stepped down. He cast a rapid glance up and down Park-lane, not registering the fish barrow, and approached the street door, rapping sharply three times upon it.

Mr Williamson watched from under his brim and found himself entirely unsurprised that Mr Newsome had ignored their suggestion to stay away from this particular avenue of investigation. The door opened and a girl of impressively elegant appearance evidently asked the gentleman's business. He handed her a card, which she took, and the door closed with the inspector on the outside.

Minutes passed. Inspector Newsome breathed steam into his hands and stamped his feet. He rapped once again at the door, this time with increased vigour. More minutes passed. And the door remained stubbornly closed. With a final kick at the door and a muttered oath, a furious Mr Newsome strode back to the carriage and it set off, presumably back to Whitehall.

Mr Williamson could not help but smile. His approach would hopefully be more successful, albeit less conventional. He looked south towards Piccadilly and saw a burly figure approaching, also dressed as a purveyor of fish. As the man drew closer, both smiled and shook scaly hands.

'Was that the inspector in the carriage?' asked Mr Cullen.

'Indeed. He was just shunned most shamefully by the house girl.'

'I am sorry to hear that, sir.'

'Your smile says otherwise. Well, let us attempt this madness before he has time to return with constables or some manner of judicial order. Are you ready, Mr Cullen?'

'I am, sir . . . though I must say I feel uneasy acting without the authority of the law at my back.'

'You will become accustomed to that soon enough. Let us go.'

Mr Williamson wrapped five eels in newspaper and the two men approached the kitchen door of the house. He knocked at the glass and a young man in splendid scarlet-detailed livery opened it.

'Deliv'ry of eels for the mistress of the 'ouse,' announced Mr Williamson.

'We ordered no eels! Off with you, you malodorous cur,' said the youth.

Mr Cullen pushed the door inwards with sufficient force to knock the servant over. Before he could get up and shout, a handkerchief of chloroform had been pressed with great force over his mouth and nose and he had been dragged under a large oaken table upon which vegetables were waiting to be cleaned. The room was otherwise empty.

'Upstairs,' whispered Mr Williamson, making for some stone steps.

The stairwell emerged into a corridor, which was also mercifully free of servants. They briskly took the next flight of steps and tiptoed past a room that had just been used for breakfast – inside two women were clearing away the dishes and chattering so contentedly that they did not notice the shadows flash by the doorway.

To the next floor they proceeded, and were faced with a corridor of four closed doors. Mr Williamson, now breathing heavily from the exertion of the steps and the fear of discovery, tried the nearest door and found it locked. He crossed the corridor on shaking legs and pushed open the second, glancing inside at the breathtaking opulence.

'Empty,' he whispered.

To the third door.

The blood throbbing in his ears seemed to fill the very house with its boom, and his palms were sticky with apprehension. He turned the knob and pushed the door open . . .

. . . And there she was, sitting at her looking glass.

We will pause there for a moment, though I admit some readers may find the momentary halt infuriating. Much as I would like to continue with the remarkable discoveries made by Mr Williamson in the company of that incomparable woman of pleasure, I have a responsibility to another pertinent thread of my story, namely, that of Noah Dyson.

He had told Mr Newsome that he was going to pursue his own investigations while trying to remain unseen, which is precisely what he was doing. We find him in a cab on his way to a location already familiar to us on Albert-road, his mind working through the previous day's meeting with the inspector.

Mr Newsome was not to be trusted. He might be genuine in his attempts to capture the villains behind the Holywell-street case, but his attitude to his temporary accomplices was a matter of far less certainty. Mr Cullen had betrayed him, Mr Williamson had always been the better detective, and Noah himself was considered something of a threat. Such things could not be discounted in the sly machinations of that police-man's mind.

The cab stopped outside the asylum of Doctor Norwood . . . and Noah immediately sensed that something was amiss. Though the house itself looked unchanged, there was an un-earthly sound emanating from the garden at the rear: some-thing like a babble of conversation, but with the fraught inflection of utter derangement.

He walked briskly around to the garden and found his view blocked by the tall, thick hedge that had been cultivated there. The odd sound was louder: human voices but somehow changed, somehow disconnected. Undeterred, he parted its heavy frondage, snapping twigs aside until he could gain a view of what was taking place beyond.

And what he saw through that leafy portal was a piteous fracturing of the delicate structure of sanity that Doctor Nor-wood had worked so hard and so long to build. Immediately to Noah's right, a young man was in the process of haranguing a shrub that had evidently caused him offence, striking it blows with one hand while holding on to its twigs with another as if to prevent its escape. His eyes were quite expression-less.

In another place, a gentleman was attending to a painting

on an easel while conducting a sing-song monologue with himself. He was facing the house, but what appeared on the canvas was merely an angry effusion of red – an accumulation of paint so thick that it dripped on to the grass, and applied with such force that the paintbrush had lost all of its bristles and scored through the canvas to leave a ragged hole in the centre.

Yet another figure sat on the bench so recently occupied by Noah himself. This one merely rocked back and forth with his arms wrapped around himself in a cold and loveless embrace. He intoned some kind of repeated phrase that Noah could not discern with any clarity. A thin strand of spittle hung from his chin.

Aubrey Alsthom was nowhere to be seen.

At that moment, Doctor Norwood emerged from the house in a state of obvious distraction, looked around the garden and wiped his brow.

'Doctor! Here – I am at the hedge!' shouted Noah.

'Mr Dyson? Is it you? O, there has been a terrible tragedy. Aubrey has been shot!'

'Admit me at the street door!'

Noah raced back to Albert-road and up the stairs just as the door was opened.

'What happened, doctor?'

'He was in the garden, just doing his whittling . . . a series on the philosophers, you know . . . and there was a loud report . . . I was not there at the time but . . . Mr Josephson, an obsessive . . .'

'Slowly, doctor. Take a breath. You say there was a loud report. What happened?'

'He was shot through the hedge. They must have pushed

the pistol through and fired without anyone seeing them. Aubrey was hit in the abdomen.'

'Who did this? Was anyone else injured? Did anyone see anything? When did this happen?'

'Only Aubrey. Only Aubrey. Nobody saw anything . . . the hedge, you see: it is very thick . . . It occurred last evening just before the gentlemen retired. O, it has quite undone the others. They sense the anguish, you know. It is a quite catastrophic reverse in their treatment, quite catastrophic.'

'Is Aubrey still alive?'

'He is upstairs. The physician has said that nothing can be done with the wound. He has lost a lot of blood and is quite weak . . .'

'Take me to him – now!'

Noah followed Doctor Norwood upstairs and along the corridor to Aubrey's room. The young man was lying in bed with a bloodied bandage wrapped around his middle. His face was a pale, wax-like mask and his closed eyelids fluttered. The smell of blood was quite oppressive.

'Can he speak?' said Noah.

'I advise against it,' said the physician gravely. He was a kindly-looking old man who had obviously seen enough deaths to accept them, respectfully, as they came.

At Noah's voice, Aubrey's eyes had blinked open.

'Can you hear me, Aubrey?' asked Noah.

'The man . . . who asked me all the . . . questions.' The voice was a mere breath.

'Yes, it is I. You have quite the collection,' said Noah, gesturing at a shelf of whittled philosophers. 'I recognize Plato there. And Socrates, of course. That must be Aristotle. Who is the one on the left?'

'Py . . . Pythàgoras.'

'Of course. I am sorry to see you in such a condition, Aubrey.'

'Have . . . have you . . . come to ask me . . . more questions.'

'If you would not mind.'

Aubrey turned his head slowly to where Doctor Norwood stood.

'It is your choice, Aubrey. I no longer tell you what to do,' said the doctor sombrely.

There was a blink of the eyes where no energy existed for a nod.

'Search for . . . "Sir John Smythe".'

Aubrey's eyes partially closed, showing only the whites. His mouth opened slightly. Noah leaned close to hear the whispered response:

'". . . also at the Epsom Spring Meeting were Sir John Smythe . . . shooting at Glenfiddich were Archibald Harlow, Donald MacCaggan, Sir John Smythe . . . The Royal dinner party at the castle this evening included Lady Harriet Hereford, Sir John Smythe . . . Secretary of the Church Extension Fund will be Sir John Smythe . . ."'

'Stop. I think that is enough. One more question, Aubrey: when is the last entry on Sir John?'

'It was . . . 1843 . . . in a court circular.'

'Thank you. I will trouble you no more.'

'It has . . . been . . . my pleasure.'

The figure on the bed was paler than ever. The breathing was laboured and shallow. Noah looked at the bloody bandages about his middle and wished that he could take hold of the one who had wielded the pistol. Had it been the taciturn James Tattershall?

'Noah . . . I wonder if perhaps . . .' Doctor Norwood let his question hang above the dying young man.

Noah caught the inflection, discerned the thought, and nodded. He reached inside his coat and extracted a phial of the finest distillate of opium.

'You might want to leave us now,' said Doctor Norwood to the elderly physician, who had immediately ascertained what was to happen and was already reaching for his hat and bag. He left silently with just a nod to each of the gentlemen.

'Aubrey – can you hear me?' said Doctor Norwood. 'I am about to administer something that will ease your suffering. You will drift into a state of warmth and comfort. May you . . . may you rest in peace.'

Noah watched. Never had he seen a passing so gentle.

'You *will* catch the fellows that did this?' said the doctor after Aubrey's breathing had diminished into silence.

'You may have my word, doctor. And their ends will not be nearly so placid.'

TWENTY-FIVE

The reader has waited long enough. I will prolong it no further.

Her real name – the name she was born with – was Mary Wright. Young Mary was the daughter of a Clerkenwell clockmaker: a moderately educated man and an artisan of some local standing. Like her father, she had a quick wit and an enquiring mind, but she would never be a clockmaker. Rather she was required to bring money into the house by that most favoured of professions among families of limited means: the milliner's girl.

Was it a sin that she was such a pretty thing and instinctively knew it at a tender age? Was it a sin if certain gentlemen asked to walk with her before or after her hours at the shop? Was it a sin to offer them a kiss in return for money to save for nicer stockings or a ribbon for her bonnet? Very likely it was – but it was not long before she realized the opportunities of her power. By that time her destiny was inevitable.

Who knows what route she took from there? Not I. Perhaps she was seen dollymopping around by a procuress and offered a more certain income. Perhaps she spent some time in a brothel. It must have been the briefest periods, because she was soon visiting the supper rooms as an independent girl, now calling herself Marianne. She was better dressed, better educated and with far, far higher expectations.

And young Marianne had learned enough from the world of commerce and shop windows to know how she should be perceived. At those dancing places and sophisticated *soirées*, she made herself an object of desire that men could neither ignore nor resist. Her beauty attracted them, and her indifference made them mad with the obsessive need to possess her. She was a prize that all wanted, but she would yield only to the one who met her simple criterion: that the gentleman in question be both limitlessly rich and boundlessly generous.

In return, that lucky man would rise above his peers as her possessor and boast of having a woman to shame all others with her grace, beauty and learning. For let us not imagine for a moment that her only talent was an artful lasciviousness commensurate with the appetite of a male (though Marianne, now called Anna, was assuredly expert in this) – no, she was also expected to be a reliable foil in conversation: as adept with her Voltaire and Seneca as any club man, and as quick with a Shakespearean pun as any author. She was, in short, a woman self-created by the dreams of men: a cigar-smoking, champagne-drinking, morality-eschewing, Latin-quoting phantasy Venus.

Few could afford her. For all her attributes and attainments, she deserved a box at the opera, an apartment with a view of the park, stables, a carriage and footmen of her own, girls to dress her and enough incomparable dresses and jewellery to keep her the envy of every female eye in the city. Even then, it would have been foolish to expect that she would be loyal to one alone, though she would at least be dutifully discreet in her appointments with others who might ruin them-selves to afford an hour of her time.

And there she was before Mr Williamson and Mr Cullen . . . She did not turn, but looked at them in the reflection of her looking glass.

'Mr Williamson – I did wonder if you would visit. You may enter, but your man will wait outside if you please.'

If she was surprised to see two men walk into her room early that morning, she did not show it. Indeed, her expression was one of mild amusement rather than fear or consternation.

Her voice betrayed no geographical origin, but was an exemplar of intelligent enunciation. She was beautiful, cer-tainly, but in quite a different way from the beauty Mr Williamson thought he had seen in Charlotte. That had been the mere freshness of youth allied with an unsullied, untamed animal sensuality. No, this woman seemed somehow preter-naturally beautiful, as if she were a painting rather than a breathing entity. Her hair, free from headwear, was long and dark; her black eyes seemed to bore into him – and her form was silhouetted to affecting effect in a dress that – if he had known of such things – Mr Williamson would have recognized as costing more than Mr Cullen had been paid annually as a constable.

'Mr Cullen – will you wait outside and see we are not disturbed,' said Mr Williamson with a dry throat.

'We will not be disturbed,' she said with a wry smile, turning now to examine her visiter with a gaze that, it seemed to him, emptied his very pockets and counted the stitches in his coat.

'You know my name, madam. What should I call you?'

'You may call me Mary.'

'Is it your real name?'

'What *is* my real name? Does it matter? Mary? Marianne? Anna? Courtesan? Prostitute? Whore?'

'Persephone?'

'Shall we be seated?' Mary gestured towards the balcony window and a pair of handsome-looking chairs decorated with gilt and scarlet velvet.

Mr Williamson sat and placed his hat beside him on a table inlaid exquisitely with fine marquetry. He looked around the room and his eyes settled on a selection of fruit arrayed on a scalloped silver tray: strawberries, plums, grapes, a pineapple and pomegranates – none of which had been cultivated on these shores. The air smelled of some exotic perfume and there was a glass vase full of visiting cards above the fireplace. Were they the cards, he wondered, of men who had been accepted, or rejected?

Mary made to sit across from him, moving with a grace that denied she was executing anything as quotidian as actual steps. Barely a moment of the last decade had passed without her being an object of rapt attention, and she had made herself a work of art. Arranging her dress about her, she maintained a cool gaze that simultaneously mocked him and made him feel that he was the only man who had ever interested her. Fortunately, the interest seemed entirely cerebral.

'I saw you looking at my collection of cards, Mr Williamson.'

'Hmm.'

'It is beneficial to me that I have those records of those who have visited or attempted to visit. All would deny it, of course.'

'I am sure. If I may say so, madam, you do not seem at all surprised to see me here. You have made no denials; you have asked no questions.'

'The fact that you are here at all means none of that need

be said. There is a time for games, but this one would be neither amusing nor beneficial.'

'And yet you are the one who started it. You do accept that you are she who sent me that letter?'

'I will neither accept nor deny it, but you will know my answer.'

'I see that I have entered a level of society in which conversation is not what it seems, and where one may say nothing as eloquently as something.'

'Ha! You are a quick study, Mr Williamson. I apologize – such frivolity is my daily custom. The gentlemen enjoy it.'

'Hmm. The fact remains that you sent me a letter. It was pseudonymous, but you must have expected that the investigation would lead back to you.'

'In fact, there is no reason at all that it should lead back to me. I have absolutely no part in it.'

'You signed the letter "Persephone". The name is quite clearly the key to the Holywell-street case.'

'O, Mr Williamson – you disappoint me. You said yourself that the name was pseudonymous. I am no more Persephone than I am the Queen. Nor am I acquainted with anyone else you are investigating. Frankly, I am surprised that you were able to make a connection where none existed.'

'It was you who made the connection. We had no idea who "Persephone" might be. Two things led us to you: the assumption (born of ignorance) that the name was the *soubriquet* of an actress, or a pro . . . or another kind of lady, and your error of having us followed by men wearing distinctive livery.'

'I see. That is disappointing. I did tell them not to wear their uniforms at any time while engaged in that game, but, well . . . one cannot control everything, no matter how one tries.'

'Indeed.'

'The truth, Mr Williamson, is that your presence here may prove exceptionally difficult to me – perhaps even fatal. My men are not the only ones who have been following you. If the others followed you here, and if they have any concept why you came, my life may not be worth a farthing.'

'Madam – if your life is in danger, perhaps it is because we have spent many days running around the city chasing a phantasm called Persephone. Had your initial letter given details and names, three more people might be alive today.'

'It is cruel of you to throw that at my door. Cruel and unjust.'

'Perhaps it is cruel, but it is just. If you know more, you could have informed me and kept your anonymity.'

'If I had told you more, they might have discerned the source of the information and I would have been the first on that list of dead.'

'You credit them with great power and knowledge.'

'Am I not correct? What is your experience of the men you seek?'

'They have followed our investigation so closely that it seems they briefly became a part of it.'

'Quite. I am merely a woman; you have the Metropolitan Police as your ally.'

'But you are no street girl, madam. Surely they would not venture to kill one such as you, even if they managed to discern that you knew something.'

'Mr Williamson – how little you know! I may wear this diamond as large as a grape; I may own four horses and stables; I may wear dresses whose cost would feed a family – a family such as I came from – for a year and more; I may have my box at the opera . . . but what am I? Who am I?'

'Well . . .'

'I am nobody. I am a dream, a promise, a prize. I have no name; I am a member of no august society; I exist as long as my beauty does. Wealthy men admire me in private and abhor me in public. Wealthy ladies condemn me in public and envy me in private. My death would make as few newspaper words as those poisoned street girls – probably fewer. I am an angel to few, an embarrassment to many, and a threat to most.'

'Hmm.'

'Power, as I am sure you understand, is more than mere wealth, Mr Williamson. It is birth. These men you seek have power, and I know enough to fear them.'

'Who are "they"?'

'If you do not already know that, I fear also for your safety.'

'Madam . . . Mary – whatever prompted you to send that letter, let it guide you now. I understand that you are afraid, but you have started something that must be finished. You cannot withdraw. If your safety is already compromised, I see little advantage in saying nothing.'

'Ha! "Stepped in so far that, should I wade no more,/ Returning were as tedious as go o'er." Is that not it?'

'I beg your pardon?'

'Do you not read Shakespeare, Mr Williamson?'

'I find there is usually something else to do.'

'You are a curious man.'

'I am a man; I pretend no more or less. Who are "they"?'

'Perhaps I have not made myself sufficiently clear . . .'

'No – it is I who have not expressed myself adequately. Tomorrow we meet the men we believe to be behind the Holywell-street incident. By doing so, we put our lives at risk. Anything you could tell us about these people might be the difference between life and death ... perhaps *your* death. Three days ago, I was led into a trap in which I was drugged and questioned under the influence of opium. I have no idea what I revealed ...'

'If that is a threat, it is not a particularly veiled one.'

'It is a matter of fact. You have expressed a desire to aid me. Whatever the manner of that expression, I am still in need of the aid. Let us begin in another way: what is *your* interest? Why did you contact me? And, please, let us not speak of civic duty.'

'You leave little room for manoeuvre.'

'This is not a game, madam – one of those witty conversations at which nothing is risked. At least four people have been murdered as a result of this investigation: Mrs Colliver, Mr Jessop and a cab waterman named Joseph. Mr Sampson is another. And then there are the street girls poisoned with prussic acid ... Ah ... I see from your eyes that it is these latter deaths that are of primary interest to you.'

'Very clever. You are indeed a pre-eminent detective.'

'Tell me about these deaths.'

'Very well, Mr Williamson. Very well. You understand that in my position I hear many things. This chamber has been the scene of more secrets than any parliamentary anteroom or confessional. Men talk, and I listen. It is what keeps me where I am.'

'And you heard something that concerned you enough to contact me?'

'A man visited me. He was referred to me by ... well, never mind by whom. He was not typical of my customary visitors; frankly, I am more than the gentleman could afford. But he had persisted so often (via many routes) in trying to meet me, and it seemed he had managed to collect together the requisite funds . . . I was amused by his efforts and I deigned to see him for twenty minutes only.'

'No doubt to ruin him in so short a time.'

'O, Mr Williamson. Let us not descend to such things. Men gamble, men drink, men steal . . . their weaknesses are legion. Blame the man – not his weakness.'

'Hmm. Twenty minutes seems rather parsimonious.'

'Then you have never experienced what *he* did.'

'Hmm. Hmm. Proceed.'

'The gentleman actually took more of my time than I had intended. Poor man, he was trying to impress me with stories from his club. It seems there was a group there who had formed some manner of "secret society" calling itself . . . well, the Persephone Club. He spoke of it in tones of the utmost guardedness, unwilling at first to give me any detail, but said that he was himself to join this club. Well, Mr Williamson – I am not a woman to let a secret pass me by.'

'He told you more?'

'Of course! Have you discerned nothing about me? He told me everything! Or, at least, everything he knew. This Persephone Club was based upon a very particular letch: one that married carnal union with death.'

'I am not sure I follow. Do you mean they visited cemeteries?'

'More sinister than that, I fear. According to my gentleman visiter, the group would pay for a street girl and compel her to drink gin poisoned with prussic acid. In the interim between life and death – which time, apparently, they could measure by the dose – they would consummate their desire. The aim was to reach their end point as the girl passed into the next world.'

'Hmm. Hmm. Why did you not contact the police immediately upon hearing this?'

'In truth, I did not believe him. I felt he was trying to shock or impress me with some fanciful letch of which I had not heard. Perhaps he thought I would find him more interesting as a result.'

'So what changed your mind?'

'The girl found dead at Holywell-street. The details of her death made my blood run cold.'

'That death was not detailed in the newspapers. How did you hear about it?'

'Have we not established that I know many things from many sources? Besides, there is another fact that cannot be ignored – one that made me fear for my own life.'

'Must I ask?'

'The gentleman who visited me was Mr Jonathan Sampson.'

'Hmm. Hmm. You knew all of this and you did nothing.'

'On the contrary, I wrote a letter to you.'

'And what a circuitous path it has led to. Why me? With all of your supposed knowledge, did you not know that I was no longer an officer of the Detective Force?'

'I did know. But it was in that capacity – as a detective – that I hoped you would investigate. As you have guessed, I chose the name Persephone intending that your search for "me" – alongside any other evidence you could collect – would lead you to those men and their sordid little *clique*.'

'And the mention in your letter of my wife Katherine? Was that just a worm to catch your fish?'

'I hope you will allow me more respect than that, Mr Williamson. I would not lie about such a thing to trick any man. It was something Mr Sampson said. He did not mention Katherine directly, but he did talk about a death at the Monument.'

'Tell me everything. Omit not a detail.'

'When he saw that I was frankly incredulous at the details of this Persephone Club, he became quite conspiratorial and said he had an even greater secret. He made me swear on my life that I would not tell a soul . . . then he told me that the originators of this club had been responsible for a death from the Monument some years past.'

'Did you believe him?'

'I think *he* believed it. My impression was that somebody had passed it to him as a rumour, for he had no further details. Whoever had told him was obviously a person whose stories he trusted.'

'Then I must ask how you know it was Katherine.'

'After the Holywell-street incident, I realized that much of what he had said was very possibly true. I obtained old editions of the newspapers and read about suicides from the Monument. Not many have occurred, as you must know, but there was the young George Williamson at the inquest, fighting for justice against a wave of apathy. The mention of prussic acid seemed decisive.'

'Hmm. Hmm. So it is true.'

'You have my condolences. To lose one's wife is devastating enough, but . . . I hope that you will be able to prove the case, and bring the criminals to justice.'

'Yes. Madam – I must have names. Who is in this Persephone Club? Who did Mr Sampson speak about? Who was there atop the Monument?'

'Believe me – I would very much like to help you, but he did not mention a single fellow by name. Perhaps he, too, was afraid of revealing the secret. Or perhaps he did not know the names himself – I can hardly see such men telling a loquacious fellow like Mr Sampson so much about their secret club.'

'He gave not one single name?'

'None. Garrulous he may have been – yes, and eager to impress – but indiscreet he was not.'

'I see. Then we must pursue another avenue.'

'Mr Williamson – if you are going to ask me about the gentlemen who visit me, you must understand that I cannot answer. You are not a policeman, and I cannot be compelled to speak.'

'Calm yourself, madam. There are names that we know. I will question you on each to see whether you have any intelligence on each. If one of these is a visiter of yours, you will simply not answer and I will know not to proceed further. Is that agreeable to you?'

'If that will relieve me of the obligation initiated by my letter, then, yes, it is agreeable to me.'

'Very well. What do you know of a Major Archibald Tunnock?'

'Ha! The old fool! I have met him once or twice about town and hear much talk of him. He is a thoroughly debased fellow with a taste for very young girls, though apparently his "sword" is not as rigid as he would hope. His tastes do not extend much beyond the brothel, though they tend to spend much of their time there. I believe he is a member of the Continental.'

'Is he capable of those acts described by Mr Sampson?'

'Mr Williamson – if I have learned only one thing about men, it is that one can never know the extent of their capabilities. A man such as he, with such a long life of lasciviousness . . . I would think him capable of anything at all.'

'Hmm. What of Harold Jute?'

'Would he be the son of Jacob Jute?'

'He is a young man recently come down from Oxford – another member of the Continental.'

'I believe Jacob was an Oxford man also, but I know no Harold. Most likely he is rather too young and under-funded to appear within my world.'

'Hmm. In that case you may not know of another young man, a certain James Tattershall . . . Madam? Mary . . . what is it that animates you so?'

'That man is a monster!'

'What do you know of him?'

'More than I wish. I have met him on occasion – just passing at the opera or at the races – and each time I have felt that I am in the presence of evil. I have heard . . . terrible things said about him.'

'What things? Mary – this could be very important to our case.'

'He is violent. Like many men of his class, he likes sometimes to beat a girl – but he is not content unless he draws blood. I hear that there are many places that will no longer admit him. I quiver to think where else he is finding his sport. He is waiting for his title and inheritance, and when he receives it . . . well, his power will only increase.'

'So it is entirely conceivable that he would be involved in this club described by Mr Sampson?'

'He more than any man. I believe he could commit murder.'

'Very likely he already has. What do you know of Sir John Smythe?'

'Smythe? I know the name, but I have not been acquainted with the gentleman. Wait . . . I may have heard . . . Yes – I have heard that he has the very worst case of syphilis. He may even be dead as we speak. They say he has not been seen publicly for some years. It seems his lusts have had their revenge.'

'Do you know more about his character?'

'I have heard him described as a *connoisseur*: a man of sophisticated tastes . . . but I really do not know anything more.'

'What of the publisher Henry Poppleton?'

'O, everyone knows him! I mean, every girl with a higher grade of client has one or more of his books. His customers must include almost every gentleman in London. I believe he is also one of the Continental men.'

'Could he be part of this Persephone evil?'

'I would not think him capable of murder, but his curiosity is such that he would not be able to resist involvement. It is possible.'

'Hmm. These are the men we believe are involved in the death of Mr Sampson. The details of that death are still, how-ever, largely unknown to us.'

'Mr Williamson – you speak of "we" and "us" in your references to the case. In the interests of my own safety, how many people know what you know?'

'Very few, and all eminently trustworthy.'

'And the man in the library who received my note?'

'He especially. I am sure he was quite subtle in his be-haviour.'

'Can you be sure of that? Perhaps he was being watched and his observers saw my man as he did.'

'You may trust me. He is not easily followed.'

Mr Williamson stood and took his hat.

'I thank you for speaking to me. I believe that this case will be solved by tomorrow evening. No doubt you will hear of the details.'

'And my safety? If they know you were here . . . if you revealed something when they drugged you . . . are you not afraid that there will be another death?'

'Madam, I will take measures to see that that does not happen. Whatever you have become, I believe you have the goodness of womanhood within you still.'

'And you, Mr Williamson – however cold you may seem – have the warmth and honour of a man.'

'Hmm. I bid you good day.'

Mr Cullen was standing duty in the corridor. As the door opened, he turned to look inside the room once again. The immaculate female herself was sitting there with her hands folded in her lap. She did not look like a sin-sodden woman of pleasure. Indeed, but for her seeming vulnerability, he reflected, she could well have been a goddess.

TWENTY-SIX

The bells on that Sunday morning chimed weakly over a city rigid with cold. A dawn temperature of 21 degrees had rendered the Serpentine quite frozen, and multitudinous streams of black smoke rose vertically into the windless aether of a sky so pure and blue that it seemed to mock the grime of the metropolis below.

Later in the day, the Humane Society set up its tents in the parks to rescue skaters who had fallen through the ice and required a hot bath to prevent their deaths. For the mendicants and common poor, however, it was already too late; their blue-lipped bodies were found frosted and stiff in numberless alcoves and arches. Cobbles were rendered lethal to horses, panes became opaque with crystal ferns, and breath steamed thickly from every mouth. The city shivered.

By dusk, the temperature had risen to just above freezing point and the air was thicker than usual with the smell of smoke as the populace struggled to keep warm. At the residence of Mr Allan, Mr Williamson had taken it upon himself to resupply the fire with a shovelful of coal, causing sparks to billow up the flue as he did so. Seated close by were Mr Cullen, Noah and Inspector Newsome – all of them digesting the information recounted to them by Mr Williamson of his extraordinary interview the previous day.

'So, it seems we will have all of our criminals in one place this evening,' said Mr Newsome, both of his hands round a cup of tea.

'If they attend,' said Mr Williamson, retaking his seat. 'There is every reason to believe that they will not. They know that Noah has been collaborating with me, and with you also, Inspector. The fact that Aubrey Alsthom has also been killed is proof enough of how closely they have been observing us.'

'Perhaps if you had trusted me enough to inform me of that avenue of investigation . . .' said the inspector.

'It would have changed nothing,' said Noah. 'And you have already given us sufficient evidence of your treachery. Was it not you who was turned away from a certain address on Park-lane yesterday when we had all agreed that Mr Williamson would pursue that line of questioning?'

'I apologize for nothing. I am as keen as you are to see this case to its conclusion . . . And I might level the same accusation at you for your undisclosed visits to this lunatic.'

'On that matter,' said Noah, 'I have corroborated what we have all assumed: that Sir John retired from public life a couple of years ago, most likely due to his advanced disease. What have you discovered, Inspector?'

'I have made some enquiries and discerned much the same. This Smythe fellow was once a public figure: a notable benefactor and gentleman with many connections who has, of late, rather vanished. Some say he is dead. I have, however, discerned from . . . from a certain source that he pursues a life of secret vice among street girls. He has been seen by constables.'

'Hmm. The fact remains,' said Mr Williamson, 'that whatever we have discovered or suspect, I believe these men will not be at the meeting. Are they so foolish?'

'The same may be said of your appointment at the Murder'd Moor,' said Noah. 'They knew who you were, what you knew and who you had been working with – but they attempted to kill you all the same. Perhaps they will want to question me as they tried to question you. With me dead, they have only Mr Newsome to deal with, and we have already seen how easily the Metropolitan Police is manipulated by the Society for the Suppression of Vice. I would not be surprised if the whole thing was merely forgotten provided I could be successfully murdered this evening.'

'I will not let this crime go unpunished,' said Mr Newsome. 'And nor will Sir Richard when he knows the full extent of its ramifying evil – whatever the influence of these men and their connections.'

'Then he does not already know?' said Mr Cullen. 'How is it that I, a "disgraced" former constable, know more than the Commissioner of Police?'

'You, *Constable* Cullen, are indeed a disgrace. If you were of a higher rank, you would know that Sir Richard will not be burdened with supposition. He wants facts.'

'Gentlemen! Let us not begin this again,' said Noah, raising placatory palms.

'Yes, let us go over the plan before Noah leaves us,' said Mr Williamson. 'How many men will be accompanying you, Inspector Newsome?'

'Three of my specially selected constables will be on hand. Shortly after Noah is admitted, you and I will position ourselves in a carriage at the end of Princes-street, from where we will be able to observe the house on Bedford-row. Two constables will loiter out of sight at the front, and one on the alley at the rear. We will all pounce if the signal is given.'

'Good. Noah – I trust you have given sufficient thought to a signal that will be unequivocal?'

'Indeed. It is no use taking something into the house because they will most likely search me. When I feel that I have learned the information I need, or if my life is in immediate danger, I will simply endeavour to break a window with whatever comes to hand. That will be your signal.'

'It is not much of a signal,' said Mr Newsome.

'Perhaps not in St Giles's, where a breaking window can be heard almost constantly after dark. It is less of an occurrence, however, in the environs of Red Lion-square.'

'And if they take you below street level?' said Mr Newsome.

'I do not believe that a kitchen *rendezvous* is in the nature of these gentlemen.'

'Very well – it is your life. At the sound of that signal, I and my men will enter the building and catch either the men we seek, or the murderers they have sent in their stead – in which case we will proceed to the Continental Club or wherever else to collect the men on our list for questioning.'

'And what will be my role?' asked Mr Cullen.

'You will be hiding at the rear of the house with one of the inspector's men lest an escape be attempted from there,' said Mr Williamson. 'If that happens, you are to raise a hue and cry and prevent their flight.'

'Yes, sir. May I also ask what we are to do if there is no signal given?'

'We are to wait. Noah may be engaged in prolonged conversation if these men have attended. If, on the other hand, he is murdered immediately upon entering, then he will be dead and there is nothing we can do. We will enter the house after two hours. All we can do between this time and that is pray.'

'You can pray; I will have another cup of tea,' said Noah, looking at his pocket watch.

Sleet was blowing in on a north-east wind when Noah got out of the carriage at Bedford-row. Icy fragments spattered against his coat and stung his face as he rapped the knocker, wondering if this night would be his last.

The door was opened by Major Tunnock, his face already flushed with spirits.

'Mr Norman! So glad you decided to accept my, ah, invitation. Come in, come in out of that horrible weather!'

'Yes, I found the tract you gave me most intriguing,' said Noah, entering and handing his exterior garments to a servant. 'It is an altogether more sophisticated concept than one is accustomed to reading.'

'Indeed, what! I think you will find yourself among men of, ah, similar predispositions this evening. And here they are now . . .'

The major led Noah from the corridor into a large reception room at the front of the house that was thick with smoke: tobacco and the mildest scent of opium. Around the hearth – their figures illuminated by the flickering firelight – were seated some of that group from the Continental Club: the fresh-faced youth previously introduced as Peter, a nervous-looking Harold Jute, and James Tattershall. The latter gave Noah a dead-eyed stare and nodded a greeting. Eusebius Bean was nowhere to be seen.

Noah greeted each of the men in turn and was invited to

sit with them. A glass of sherry was pressed into his hand and a fine cigar lit for him.

'There is, ah, one more gentleman I believe you would enjoy meeting,' said the major, swirling his drink and inhaling the aroma. 'He is, in fact, the very gentleman who wrote the tract I gave you: a man of quite considerable, ah, standing and intelligence.'

'I have no doubt of that, Major.'

A connecting door opened and the man already known to us as 'J.S.' entered. His scarified face seemed to writhe and twitch as the light from the flames animated the disrupted skin. A sheen of soothing oils covered all, and Noah caught the unmistakable *bouquet* of lavender as the gentleman extended a smooth hand to shake.

'I am pleased to meet you, Mr Norman. I am John Smythe. The major told me that he had found a kindred spirit at his club, and I am always happy to meet a kindred spirit.' The voice was as Mr Williamson had described it: a wet, glottal instrument – a diseased faculty from which bubbled disease.

'As am I, Mr Smythe. I found your piece of writing most interesting.'

'Some would call it shocking or blasphemous.'

'Indeed they would. Such a document could put its publisher in gaol if the Vice Society were to see a copy of it in public.'

'Ah, Mr Norman – I believe you are jesting! We both know that the Vice Society chooses its prosecutions with care. Does one ever see magistrates and senior politicians hauled into court over such things? For, assuredly, it is men like they who purchase the majority of such materials. We at the Society catch only the smaller fish in order to justify our sponsorship monies.'

'"We"?'

'You must know that I am a major benefactor of that Society. Surely a man of your evident intelligence would not attend a meeting such as this without first doing a little investigation into the gentlemen who had invited him.'

'I admit that I have made enquiries.'

'Of course you did. And what did you find?'

'As you say: you are indeed a generous benefactor of numerous charities, with a particular focus on "fallen women". The major here is every bit the illustrious old soldier. And I believe I heard something about young Harold Jute volunteering at the Mendicity Society. Of Mr Tattershall there, I am afraid I know nothing.'

'I am sure James is glad of it. But what of you, Mr Norman? A supplier of "Oriental goods" is it? I take that to be opium.'

'The finest available in London. The correct refining of it is critical to the quality, as you must know.'

'Indeed? Why must I know such a thing?'

'I expect that a man of your standing is knowledgeable about all fine sources of pleasure. I can smell it in the air as we speak.'

'There is more to you than first observation would suggest, Mr Norman.'

'I hope so.'

'An interesting name: "Norman". Like the conquest, yes? Or, but for the sake of a single letter, it might be "Normal".'

'Or even "No man" – but I was never one for word games.'

'Excellent!' ejaculated Major Tunnock, putting down his glass to clap his hands. 'What good, ah, sport!'

James Tattershall maintained an almost unblinking glare

at Noah, stroking his cheek with a single finger as if contemplating a particularly taxing mathematical problem. The other men present, Peter and Harold, seemed to exchange glances of apprehension and doubt at the proceedings, but said nothing.

'Major – shall we tell Mr Norman what we plan for this evening?' said Sir John, pouring himself a drink from a decanter of sherry.

'Indeed! Indeed! Mr Norman – would it disturb you to learn that the philosophy described in that, ah, tract is in fact a reality?'

'I have always believed that any good philosophy must be a reality.'

'Quite so. Well, we gentlemen here are part of a, ah, fraternity – a society or a club if you, ah, prefer. Each of us has passed a test to become, ah, a member.'

'A test you say? What manner of test, and what manner of fraternity?'

'Have you ever seen a man die?' said Sir John.

'I have. And women, too.'

'It is a sacred thing, the passing from life to death. One might even envy those who make that journey.'

'I prefer life to death, especially my own.'

'And rightly so. But if one were to experience death *vicariously* through union with one who was passing from this world . . .'

The sound of a carriage drawing up outside caused Sir John to pause. The street door banged and voices were heard approaching the room – one of them female.

Noah looked at the gentlemen around him for a reaction. Peter and Harold seemed more anxious than ever; Major Tunnock twitched with an almost childlike excitement; Sir John looked at Noah with an ambiguous benignity . . . and

James Tattershall gave the slightest smirk – an expression that, on his face, seemed more chilling than any malevolent gaze.

The door opened and the servant who had taken Noah's coat presented a street girl who was clearly already mildly intoxicated. She was holding a pomegranate with a sanguineous bite taken out of it.

A pretty enough example of her kind, she looked at the men seated there and, perhaps sensing a danger beyond her understanding, ceased her smiling.

'O! I did not expect a party,' she said with her best pronunciation.

'You must be chilled to the bone, young lady. May I offer you a drink?' said Sir John. 'What have you been drinking this evening?'

'A glass of gin on a cold night such as this might be just the thing,' said the girl uncertainly.

'How apt. I have some gin just here,' said Sir John, opening a bottle and pouring a measure into a glass. Did he look sidelong at Noah for the merest second as he handed it to her? She raised it to her lips, not taking her eyes from that group surveying her with expressions that had started to make her feel vaguely afraid.

'*No!*' shouted Noah, springing from his chair to knock the glass from the girl's hand.

Gin spattered across the carpet and the glass clattered over wooden boards into the corner of the room. The girl blinked in mute surprise.

'What a curious reaction!' said Sir John with a smile. 'Have you some aversion to young ladies imbibing strong drink, Mr Norman? I would not have taken you for a temperance supporter.'

James Tattershall stood and approached the girl, who –

now utterly confused by the state of affairs – allowed her arm to be taken.

'Take her away,' said Sir John to the young man. 'We will use her later.'

Sir John followed the two to the corridor and locked the door behind them, putting the key into his trouser pocket.

Noah remained standing where he had dashed the glass to the ground. The major's demeanour had become significantly less jovial. Harold Jute looked as if he, too, would have liked to leave the room.

'Shall we dispense with the *charade* now, Mr Dyson?' said Sir John. 'It was mildly amusing while it lasted. Please retake your seat.'

Noah did as bidden, no sign of fear in his movement. He waited for Sir John to take a seat opposite him by the fire.

'Is this how Mr Sampson met his end at Colliver's coffee house?' said Noah. 'You were there, of course. Joseph the waterman smelled those fragrant unguents you use to alleviate your pox.'

'It is a pity about that poor old gentleman – a pity that his urge to talk was as acute as his olfactory sense. But these things will happen when one blunders into the unsafer regions of the city . . . or into other areas were one has no business.'

'Mr Tattershall does have the look of a murderer about him. I assume it was he who murdered the old gentleman. Was it also he who killed Mr Jessop, Mrs Colliver and Aubrey Alsthom? Was it he who threw Mr Sampson through the window that evening on Holywell-street?'

'Jonathan Sampson was a *dilettante*. He professed an interest in higher thought, but when the time came for him to be initiated, he could not embrace the philosophy.'

'So he was thrown to his death, shouting "I cannot".'

'He was garrulous. He would have told others in that bragging manner of his . . . just as he told that refined lady of Park-lane. O, yes – you need not attempt to hide your surprise. Inspector Newsome was seen there yesterday and suddenly it all started to become clear. We know that Jonathan visited her once, and it would have been just like him to tell her about us to impress her with his worldliness. That is clear now.'

'Who else was there in that room on Holywell-street? There were four glasses.'

'I must say, your investigative pertinacity is impressive. Even now, you persist. Very well – I have no reason not to tell you. I was present, as was James, Mr Sampson, Mr Poppleton and our Mr Jute there. Harold did not drink – a weak stomach as usual.'

'And the girl?'

'A girl. Some girl – it matters not.'

'She was a girl called Lou whom you had seen on a few occasions previous to her death . . . to earn her trust, I wonder? A girl, no doubt, who had partaken of the pomegranate's flesh, just as Persephone did . . . and those other girls less divine in nature: Kate, Mary, Nelly. All of them your victims.'

'My, my – your researches have been quite thorough. You evidently made good use of your time at the reading room the other day.'

'So you did have your spy watching me. I am not surprised. How is Eusebius? I expected to see him here.'

'Eusebius is not the kind to appreciate a gathering such as this.'

'I wonder if James has killed him already? Eusebius may have been a simple sort, but I am sure he had put the story together long before I did. And I think we all know he would not have withstood an interrogation.'

'What possible benefit is there for you in discussing these things, Mr Dyson? You will not be speaking to anyone about them.'

'Call it curiosity. Call it perversity. I have come this far.'

'Perhaps you think you will take this information and use it against us? Even if you were to leave this house, do you think anyone would believe you? There is no evidence, no witnesses. Who are *you*? What power do *you* represent?'

'Think of me as one of the Eumenides.'

'Ha! I may doubt your power, but I applaud your classical reading. You are one of the Furies of Greek mythology, yes? My retribution in human form? How amusing.'

'I will take your evasion as an admission that James is indeed the murderer.'

'I must say, I am tiring of this conversation.'

Sir John's face had now become quite moist and reddened. Perhaps it was the heat of the room, but his countenance was glistening with an admixture of perspiration and the emollients upon it. He might have been a life-sized waxwork standing there too close to the fire.

'You could have killed me many times, Sir John. Perhaps that was the intention when I was struck at Mr Poppleton's shop. Or perhaps my fleeing from the library was another lost chance for you. How close did I come to death on those occasions? Should I be expecting the opium pipe to be brought out shortly?'

'You really are rather tiresome, Mr Dyson.'

'One more thing, Sir John,' said Noah, reclining insouciantly in his chair as if *he* were the host and this were some genteel *soirée*. 'What is this about the woman pushed from the Monument? You may recall that Mr Williamson mentioned it to you when you forced opium upon him.'

'Mr Williamson?'

'The same. He has described your voice and that of Mr Jute to the police. In fact, you may have read of his interment recently – or rather the interment of his empty coffin. He survived the razor-wielding bully in whose care you left him.'

'Hmm.' Sir John dabbed at his face with a kerchief.

'Oddly enough, that is just what Mr Williamson said. He said that you, Sir John, were quite nonplussed by the mention of the incident at the Monument.'

'Who can remember the events of seven years ago?'

'It is oddly coincidental that you refer to the period of seven years, is it not? Evidently somebody had told Mr Sampson about it. Let me refresh your memory. Three men ascended the Monument shortly after Katherine Williamson on that day. At the top, they engaged her in conversation, no doubt mishearing her name in the wind as Kathleen. Then they offered her gin poisoned with prussic acid. How or why she went over the railings is a matter of conjecture. Perhaps she was pushed as part of some lunatic experimental "philosophy". Perhaps she was already dead and fell. But those three gentlemen had intended her to die: they had brought with them a suitably annotated Bible and materials for a suicide message. In the *mêlée* that followed, they were able to walk away without being noticed. I do not know who those three men were, or what compelled them to enact such a wicked act, but I feel sure that one of them was you, Sir John.'

'A pretty story, but one that has no bearing on anything.'

'No bearing you say? But for that particular murder, your recent activities might have remained quite unnoticed. It might have been quickly and wrongly investigated by the police under your remote supervision. But news of it reached Mr Williamson, the husband. Then the husband reached me –

and I felt obliged to repay a favour once done me by that gentleman. Then my good friend Benjamin was assaulted by the ruffians at Freepass-alley, adding further impetus to pursue the criminals. And now here I sit as a result of that event which has "no bearing" . . .'

'Indeed, Mr Dyson. Here you sit. Inside a locked room with men whom you imagine to be murderers. For all of your clever deductions, you have made a bad decision in that respect.'

The lock of the connecting door rattled and James Tattershall entered. His face was a mask of impassiveness. And he was carrying a pistol.

'You are a dangerous man, Mr Dyson,' said Sir John. 'I am reluctant to leave you alone with the ambiguity of a razor. A bullet is more suitable for a man of your kind. Mr Williamson will follow, and soon we will be rid of this whole graceless mess.'

'The same gun that was used to kill poor Aubrey Alsthom, I presume?'

'You are an odd one. Even as you stare death in the face, you sit quite calmly by the fire there.'

'Sir John – you talk about proximity to death; you decorate your childish "philosophies" with classical allusion to lend them a veneer of authority. *I* have lived with death. I have waded in gore and walked among the cerements of the grave. I have felt hot blood fresh on my hands and the life ebbing from a body in its dying spasms. There is no mystery, no poetry, no deeper meaning in death. Only in your fancy do you pretend otherwise.'

'You will discover soon enough. Goodbye, Noah Dyson.'

James Tattershall raised the pistol . . .

TWENTY-SEVEN

Snow was falling thick and silent now, smothering the gas-lights like drifting duck-down. Inside the carriage, Mr William-son wiped the condensation from the window and breathed upon his hands. Mr Newsome sat opposite him looking at a pocket watch.

'It is almost two hours,' said the inspector.

'I can see almost nothing in this confounded weather. Your men must be half-frozen.'

'I expect so, but they are used to being out in all weathers. Do you ever miss walking the streets, George?'

'I still walk the streets, but no longer as a policeman. You saw to that.'

'What was I to do? You abetted a prisoner in his escape from gaol. How could you remain a detective after that?'

'I acted in the interests of a greater justice than the one that had gaoled him there.'

'Who are we, as mere servants of the law, to make such decisions?'

'An apt question – and one you might turn upon yourself.'

'I fear that *you* are the one who has learned no lessons. You are still associating with criminals.'

'I am still pursuing justice . . . Listen! Did you hear that?'

Had there been the slightest sound of breaking glass, half-muffled by the weather?

Mr Williamson opened the carriage door and squinted through the snow.

A chair crashed through the window beside the door of the house they were observing, carrying a billowing curtain with it and becoming lodged in the frame. A gunshot cracked into the night. A heartbeat – then another shot.

'Let us go, Inspector! Rally your men!'

Mr Newsome made no attempt to move.

'Inspector? That is the signal – let us take the criminals!'

'I think not.'

'What!'

'Why hurry into a house where pistols are being shot? We have men at the rear and men in front. Anyone fleeing will run into their arms.'

'But . . . Noah . . .'

'Did you really think I would risk my life or those of my men for one such as he? Indeed, it is all the better if he has been murdered. Then I would have a certain conviction rather than a fabric of supposition to wage against their immunity of wealth and power.'

'You have planned this all along.'

'Is not planning one of the detective's greatest tools?'

Standing with one foot upon the carriage's iron step and one foot in the settling snow, Mr Williamson looked with loathing upon his former superior, who reclined with a smirk upon the leather seat. And he made his decision . . .

The carriage door slammed and he was half running, half sliding along Bedford-row to the street door. He bashed on it madly with a fist and looked around to see where the inspector's special constables might be. They were standing well away from the house on the same side of the street where the residents might not see them. No doubt they were waiting for a word from the inspector himself.

No answer.

He listened intently for any sound of Mr Cullen's cries at the rear, but there was only the maddening silence of accumulating flakes and the thud of blood in his ears. He wondered whether he should run around to the rear of the property. Frustration burned in his eyes. Something had to be done.

The window with the chair lodged in it was too far from the doorway to peer through, and railings barred his way. He grabbed a broom that had been left propped in the doorway and used the handle to smash a pane so that he might push the curtain aside and look in.

He saw the legs of a man lying immobile on the floor. There was blood on the carpet around the body.

'Noah? Noah – is it you? Can you hear me! Move your legs if you can hear me!'

Nothing. No movement or reply.

Mr Williamson went back into the street and looked frantically towards each end of Bedford-row for signs of activity. There . . . at the south end: two figures were ascending from below the street and running madly towards Brownlow-street, that narrow aperture connecting with Holborn. They were escaping.

He raced back to the carriage and wrenched open the door. 'Inspector – two of them have escaped on foot. The houses must be connected below the street. We must pursue before they have a chance to disappear.'

'I think not. As you have said, we know who they are and

where to find them. Why chase across the city in this weather? Let us wait to see whether the street door opens. We have constables ready.'

'We do not know who those two escaping gentlemen are. They may be entirely different but connected criminals!'

'Or two gentlemen late for a show. I will wait, George, and so will my carriage.'

Mr Williamson looked back at the house. Was that Noah dying inside? Was he already dead? Were those running gentlemen the same who had murdered his wife?

'D—— you, Albert Newsome! I follow justice alone!' shouted Mr Williamson, and he was off running hazardously over the snow towards Brownlow-street.

He emerged into Holborn, where a cab was parked just a few yards away.

'Did you see two gentlemen emerge from here a minute or so ago?' he shouted to the cab driver. 'They were running.'

'Aye. Got a cab. They won't be goin' nowhere fast in this weather though, and no mistake. Though the way he's lashin' the 'orse, they're in a right 'urry.'

Mr Williamson climbed into the cab. 'Pursue that carriage with all haste! Catch it and there is a sovereign for you.'

They set off with a lurch.

The streets were virtually clear of traffic due to the weather, but it seemed both of the cabs were possessed by some demonic force. Whips cracked, equine nostrils snorted and hooves skittered over the stones, each vehicle risking a fall in the worsening conditions but neither making the least attempt at caution.

Holborn passed in a blur, its occasional human forms hunched and cowering into malformed shapes. Holborn-hill was becoming a pale sepulchre, made ghostly in its valiant illumination. On they raced, the distance between them un-changing and the flakes flashing about them in icy vortices.

And then, even above the rattle of wheels and the muffled clop of hooves, they all began to hear it:

Something like a colossal moan expressed from innumer-able throats; something like the plaintive cries of thousands; something, indeed, one might expect to hear from the very fields of the damned: a cacophonous chorus of anguished and bestial cries punctuated by individual wails and yelps.

'Smithfield,' muttered Mr Williamson.

As if in response, the carriage pulled to an abrupt halt.

'Can't go no further,' yelled the driver over the noise. 'The other carriage has stopped and the gents has bailed out!'

Mr Williamson stepped down to behold the scene on upper Farringdon-street. A drover with dogs was leading a flock of sheep around the stopped cab across the thoroughfare and up towards the market. The animals bleated *en masse*, raising clouds of steam and pungent manure as they trotted blindly through the night towards their waiting pens at the market.

'Which way did they go?' shouted Mr Williamson to the driver.

'Up yonder – up the hill with the animals!'

'Here is your sovereign.'

'Are you goin' up there amidst the sheep?'

'I am.'

And Mr Williamson pushed off through the beasts' snowy fleeces towards the market, his coat collar pulled up and his shoes sliding in the reeking slush of ordure and ice. The close thoroughfare reverberated with animal cries and flowed inexorably towards Smithfield.

Into Cow-lane he progressed, pressing close against the wool of the sheep and being driven relentlessly along. Pigs joined the procession from another direction, grunting and snuffling their bristly hides against his legs . . . and up ahead . . . was that two top-hatted figures also caught in the ovine–porcine cataract, turning around now and then to look behind them?

'Stop! Stop those men!' shouted Mr Williamson, but his voice was dumb, dissipated in the whirling flakes and deafening babel. There was nothing to do but proceed at the pace dictated by the herd.

Minute by agonizing minute, the animals moved: cloven-footed and emanating the thick stench of manure. His hands grasped at rough, greasy wool for balance and they moved ever closer towards the end of that narrow artery. Slowly, mercifully, the buildings began to open and Smithfield market presented itself in a scene that, even in the heat of his pursuit, made him momentarily stop and wonder at its horror.

The vastness of that city-walled plain was a veritable inferno of torches blazing above endless ranks of pens in which 40,000 beasts writhed and shifted like waves in a swollen sea of flesh. Swine, sheep, calves, bulls and the ever-present yelping dogs sent forth billowing clouds of steam from their expirations, evaporations, evacuations and execrations against a bloody fate. It was scene from before civilization, from before history and the settling of cities. It was a scene of madness seen through the ceaseless swirls of snow now lashing and enveloping the marketplace. The phantasmal light of the gas flares at surrounding establishments cast a sickly glare over all. The noise was a palpable vibration.

He could not see the two top-hatted men.

Where to begin amid such chaos?

Two constables in oilskin capes were sheltering in a doorway close by and he ran to them.

'Constables – two gentlemen came this way,' he shouted. 'They were wearing top hats and were not dressed for the market. Did you see them? They were most likely in a hurry.'

'What business is it of yours?' returned one of the men, a surly sort with his hand on his truncheon.

'They are murderers!'

They looked at each other, sceptical.

'Listen! I was once a policeman. I was Sergeant George Williamson of the Detective Force. Which way did they go?'

The name stirred something in the constables. They looked anew at the agitated gentleman before them, his legs soiled with manure and his reddened and pox-scarred face wet with snow. Could this man really be the great Williamson?

'You will answer to Sir Richard Mayne himself if those men escape me!'

'I think they went that way,' replied the surly one, gesturing towards the corner of the market leading off towards West-street.

Mr Williamson took off at a trot, urgently scanning the crowds for the fugitives. Grotesque *tableaux* assaulted his senses: here a blue-aproned buyer with his spittle-sticky fingers in a calf's mouth; here the flash of a switch and the moan as it pierced a bovine hide; here the flashing heat of the brand and the stench of burned hair; here a flaming torch illumin-ating the lumpen impassivity of a drover; here the bared teeth and darting legs of the sheepdog . . . and there, two figures rounding the corner of West-street . . . one of them with his hat knocked off and a bare cranium exposed to the elements.

He arrived at that corner just as a drover was leading a number of calves to the slaughterhouse district. Even there, at the market's edge, the metallic tang of blood and fresh death was thick in the air. The animals sensed it; they smelled the hideous effusions of the bone-boilers and tripe-dressers . . . and they sent up moans of distress. Their eyes rolled back and their hooves hammered nervously through the filth.

Onwards he hurried, slipping ahead of the herd now, and driven by a goad more piercing than that wielded by any drover. The two men – around twenty yards in front – looked back phrenziedly and he saw their faces: one with a moustache, the other seemingly disfigured. Then they were gone.

It was futile to shout over the din of the animals. All he could do was chase towards them through the freezing mud before they could lose themselves in the labyrinthine yards and alleys.

At the place where they had vanished, he turned and looked down a narrow, twisting passage whose very walls seemed to glisten and steam with freshly butchered flesh. Perhaps three hundred carcases hung on hooks all along that hideous nook, leading towards a place where the poleaxe was wielded and knives parted muscle from bone. He gulped a breath and started to run.

It was a charnel parade of horror. All about him, bones glared white; yellow fat hung from flesh so recently alive; glutinous things dangled from cavities once vital with organs. There was a sweet, steaming smell of death that clogged his throat and forced him to breathe lest he vomit. This was the very throat of the city: moist, ravenous and corrupted beyond redemption.

He stopped, panting, and rested his hands on his knees. There was no sign of them – only a choice of two alleys. He looked for footprints, but the ground was so churned with slush and soil and two-toed treads that there was barely a trace to read. With no lamp to hand, he was venturing into an area of darkness to rival any subterranean chamber. His breath billowed about him in the falling flakes.

There . . . was that a footprint? A slipshod sliding arc where a man had almost fallen? It pointed towards an alley into which an onrushing herd was now being steered by lashes of the switch and the unintelligible oaths of the drovers. They would block the thoroughfare and leave no escape for the villains. He ran ahead of the cattle.

The alley narrowed and began gradually to descend, channelling the beasts into a smaller and smaller area so that they would eventually pass in single file through an aperture from which they would emerge only as joints and cuts:

The slaughterman's killing pit.

Mr Williamson felt the herd at his back as he searched for his fugitives. Cows began to surround him. Hides pressed closer and closer in upon him. He dug his elbows into the bodies in an attempt to lift his feet clear of the crushing hooves. The reek of blood was thick in the air; the bovine chorus of despair was horripilating. Where were the two men?

There was a strangulated cry. Cattle ahead seemed to stumble. Mr Williamson strained higher to see above the steaming masses. All moved ceaselessly forward.

Then, a body . . .

It was one of the men: dead or dying, his mortal form mangled and soiled almost beyond recognition by the innumerable limbs passing over him and crushing the life from his frail frame. There was a moustache . . . there was the dull glint of a medal . . . there was a mouth splashed with filth and open in a soundless scream of outrage at a life extinguished in the scatological mire.

The other man must be close.

But closer still was the tunnel.

Single file now. He struggled to maintain balance and stay clear of their legs. They descended deeper into the earth.

And there was the slaughterman himself: his bare, thickly muscled arms raised above his head . . . his eyes staring life-lessly at the spot on the hairy scull before him . . . his entire form bespattered with steaming gore. He brought down the poleaxe with a tremendous swing upon the animal's head and, even before it could fall, his accomplices had pushed it from the side so that it toppled still further down into a cellar to be divided by the waiting knives.

And there . . . another man's arm reaching up between bodies! The fugitive risking his life to stay low among the hooves.

'Stop! Stop there! There is a man among the cattle,' yelled Mr Williamson, his voice utterly lost.

There was no stopping the flow.

The poleaxe fell. The bodies rolled. The herd moved on.

'Stop! You there – slaughterman! There is a man hiding there!'

The poleaxe went up. The eyes stared at the spot on the hairy scull. The poleaxe came down . . .

A human head of pale, mottled skin was where the cow's forehead should have been. Weak brown eyes stared madly. A mouth opened too late to make a sound.

The axe drove into the delicate scull with as little hindrance as if it had been striking a hen's egg. And the slaughterman's eyes widened in amazement.

Unspeakable matter splashed across the heaving, protesting bodies of that hellish space.

A human form rolled into the blood-puddled pit.

And for an instant – for the merest few beats of the heart – it seemed to Mr Williamson that everything stopped: that there was no miasma of blood and urine, no ceaseless bestial clamour, no blizzard lashing the soot-blackened city. For that instant, there appeared to be a silence that suggested even the ignorant beasts had recognized the outrage of the scene and had paused, startled, at its horror.

The moment passed. Gore-bewrayed reality returned. Mr Williamson looked down to see that he was ankle-deep in blood.

TWENTY-EIGHT

For twelve hours the snow fell: a relentless, soundless assault through the night. It coated roofs and clogged gutters; it carpeted roads and blocked bridges; it drifted over steps, masking their form; it insinuated itself into alcoves and arches; it disguised the familiar with immaculate accumulations; and it transformed the charred metropolis into a pristine field of featureless white.

By morning, household curtains twitched and extra coal was put on fires. Shops stayed boarded against the still invading flakes. The chimneys of Southwark gaped emptily at the sky. All trace of human life was absent from the *tabula rasa* of the city.

By midday, the snow had stopped. Tentative patches of blue appeared in the sky. The temperature dropped again. Three feet of coverage muffled the sounds of the people emerging into that alien landscape to find themselves in a London that had momentarily become a wilderness as remote and inaccessible as any highland glen. But human industry persevered as it will. Within hours, boys were out with shovels and brooms cleaning the major thoroughfares. Inundated carriages were reclaimed from their frigid cocoons, and, by dusk, a number of shops were open, casting their eerie gaslight over the pallid streets.

And at one particular residence, Mr Williamson sat sombrely in front of the fire, staring into the flames and warming his stockinged feet. He was wearing the same clothes of the previous night's activity, the ordure of Smithfield now crusted and congealed upon his legs and his saturated shoes curling slowly in the heat of the hearth. Snoring on the floor beside him was the hefty form of John Cullen, his trouser bottoms steaming where they came closer to the fire.

After the slaughter pit, and the necessary extrication of the corpses from the filth, Mr Williamson had trudged back to Snow-hill in the hope that his cab had remained. It had not, but another late-running (and particularly irascible) cabman had been persuaded to take him back to Bedford-row and the scene of the *rendezvous*. Mr Cullen had been waiting at the street door of the property.

'My G—, sir! What has happened to you? Are you hurt?' said the doughty ex-constable on seeing the reeking and bloody figure in the snow before him.

'I am uninjured. Have you been inside? What has happened here? Has the inspector been inside?'

'Yes, sir. I gained entry shortly after the gentlemen fled. Inspector Newsome has recently left. He went into the house, looked around and left in a black humour with his men. He said he would send the surgeon.'

'The surgeon? Let us go inside.'

They entered the room that Mr Williamson had glimpsed through the broken window. The body was still on the floor and had evidently been turned over to discern his identity. Neither of the investigators recognized the body as Peter, the young man who had been sitting alongside Harold Jute.

'A gunshot to the chest. And there is another, sir – here behind the sofa.'

They stepped round the furniture to look upon the other form.

'Harold Jute,' said Mr Williamson without emotion. 'Where is Noah?'

'He has gone, sir.'

'Gone where? What happened here? Tell me everything.'

'I told Inspector Newsome and he—'

'I am not Mr Newsome.'

'Yes, sir. I was waiting at the rear as arranged. I admit I was bored and so I strolled along to where the pump is: opposite Brownlow-street. It was there I saw two gentlemen running. I did not know what to do, so I waited . . . then I saw you, sir, running after them and I discerned that an escape was in progress.'

'Very astute.'

'Well, I called the other constable and we went around to Bedford-row. There was a kitchen door open and a scream coming from within, so we charged down the stairs and . . . a girl had had her throat cut. That was when we encountered the other gentleman.'

'Which other gentleman?'

'I did not know him. He hit the constable with something that sounded like a metal rod and the wounded fellow took me to the ground as he fell. I . . . fear I allowed the murderer to escape as I struggled to right myself.'

'Never mind that. What of Noah?'

'Once I righted myself, I saw that the kitchen of that building was curiously connected by a doorway to the next house, and that to the next. Evidently the men had passed under three buildings to escape at the end of the street. I walked through to where I knew the villains' house to be and discovered these two bodies here. The two constables from the front appeared shortly thereafter with Inspector Newsome. It seems Noah had exited from the street door and called them in to apprehend the villains. Of course, there were none alive to apprehend and Noah ran off before they could discover this.'

'It must have been James Tattershall who escaped you.'

'If he was the man with the metal rod . . . I am afraid he has.'

'Hmm.'

'What of the other two? They who ran down Brownlow-street?'

'Dead. One trampled by cattle, the other's head cleaved open by an axe.'

'O . . . I see.'

'Did the inspector say anything about where he was going?'

'No, sir. He looked quickly around, asked me about my entry into the building and then he left. He may have shouted something about the Continental Club to his driver.'

'Fool. As if Mr Tattershall would return there.'

'What do we do now, sir?'

'No doubt Noah will contact us. I am of a mind to go home. I find myself extremely tired.'

'And the bodies, sir? What shall we do with them?'

'We will leave them for the surgeon. No harm can come to them now.'

And thus it was that the two men ventured south through the snows to the coldness of Mr Williamson's empty home, where we recently saw them by the fire.

The reader will ask, however, what became of Noah Dyson on that eventful evening: how he had escaped the bullets, where he had rushed after leaving the house, and what had kept him as the snow fell thickly. Good questions all, and I would expect no less from the perspicacious handler of these pages. Since we are in the final chapter, and the covers are the boundaries of this world, I have little other option but to answer.

Or rather, I will let Noah do the speaking, for he arrived with Benjamin at Mr Williamson's house shortly after lunchtime on that Monday. Both seemed subdued and looked tired as they took the seats offered to them and accepted cups of tea from the solicitous Mr Cullen.

'I am glad to see you alive, Noah,' said Mr Williamson.

'By which tone I understand you are mildly discontented I have not come to you earlier,' said Noah.

'It is rather a long time to wonder whether a man is alive or dead.'

'I was sure that Mr Cullen had advised you of my escape.'

'Indeed he did – but to where, and why?'

'Very well. There is no secret about it. The fact is simply that I have been busy in the name of justice. Before I tell you the story of my recent hours, perhaps you would first like to read this.'

Noah took a piece of folded paper from his jacket pocket and handed it to Mr Williamson. The smeared bloodstains on it, though now dry, were unmistakable.

For the attention of the Metropolitan Police

I, James Tattershall, resident of The Continental Club, Pall Mall, do hereby offer my full and frank confession before the witnesses Mr Dyson and Mr Benjamin Black to the murder of Mr Jonathan Sampson at Colliver's coffee house, Holywell-street, and sundry other murders . . .

'Benjamin *Black*?' said Mr Williamson, looking up from the sheet.

'His own conceit,' replied Noah for his friend. 'In truth, he has no surname; he chose that one just for the occasion.'

'Apt. Am I to presume that this confession was actually written by James Tattershall?'

'He did not write it – Benjamin did. Young James, however, supplied every detail within and signed his name at the end. The signature is a little uneven, but legible and genuine. The gentleman had undergone a thorough interrogation by that stage.'

'I do not want to know how that was effected.'

'Indeed you do not,' said Noah, rubbing his knuckles. 'He was very reluctant to speak, but we managed to persuade him.'

'Is the full confession as detailed in that first paragraph?'

'Everything he knew; everything we could wish to know: all of the murders, the members of their disgusting little group (Poppleton among them, unsurprisingly), the incident at the Murder'd Moor, the Vice Society connection and the role of Eusebius Bean . . . everything is laid bare. Also the truth about Katherine . . .'

Mr Williamson nodded and returned his attention to the text, evidently skimming quickly through to the part he was looking for. His jaw set as he did so but his hands remained steady. The other gentlemen avoided looking at each other as he read.

. . . Another crime committed by the members of the club (though not by myself) was the murder of one Katherine Williamson. It was in 1839 when Sir John Smythe was first formulating his philosophy. He and his fellows were interested in testing the effects of prussic acid and

contrived to do so in a manner where the effects would be judged a clear suicide on the part of the victim.

    Sir John and two fellows not known to me ascended and engaged the lady in conversation, offering her a jolt of gin on account of the chill. Then one of them timed the period before her inevitable death and Sir John threw her over the parapet. A Bible and hastily written note were left to further suggest suicide.

    It was following the furore about the incident (and the attendant risk of discovery) that the decision was taken to use prostitutes exclusively for further experimentation, though the very public nature of the event was something that had always added to Sir John's enjoyment . . .

'Hmm. Hmm. An experiment. Killed for an *experiment*.'

'That is what James told us – what Sir John told him. There is no reason to disbelieve it.'

'An experiment . . . as one might do on an animal.'

'George – these were men with no moral core: animals themselves. I believe they have all received what they deserved, if I am to believe what I hear of recent events at Smithfield.'

'I exerted no justice in those instances.'

'Perhaps not, but justice was done. I can think of no better end for Sir John and that old lecher Major Tunnock.'

'And what of Mr James Tattershall?'

'A strange thing. You will not yet have read of it in the newspapers, but a young man will be found at the foot of the Monument stairwell this morning. A most unusual case. The young man in question seemingly smashed in the lower door shortly after dawn when the blizzard was still raging. Nobody saw anything due to the awful weather, and any other footprints were obliterated in the downfall. It seems he tried to gain access to the platform but could not. Then, inexplicably, he was precipitated down the centre of that formidable spiral staircase, striking it over and over as he rushed headlong to a most grisly death. True, the injuries are not *entirely* consistent with a fall, but . . .'

'I . . . I do not condone murder, Noah – whatever the circumstances. It would not be appropriate for . . . for me to thank you.'

'I know, George. We must assume, as will others, that James was so burdened by his sins that he could no longer live among us. I understand that another copy of the confession you have in your hand might be found inside his coat.'

'It will not be in his handwriting.'

'Quite, but it would not be the first time a note found after an apparent suicide was taken to be true for want of contradiction. I trust Inspector Newsome will soon come into possession of that confession. If he does not, I will say I found this one at Bedford-row. I think we can trust the inspector not to enquire too closely into where his evidence comes from.'

'Hmm.'

'But what happened at the house?' said Mr Cullen. 'We heard shots, but neither of the dead men was you. How was that possible?'

'The events unfolded in the most unpredictable manner. James had entered the room with a pistol and was to shoot me there and then. It was your Harold Jute, George, who saved me.'

'Jute? I cannot imagine it, knowing what we do about that Judas.'

'He had been uncomfortable all evening. Like the late Mr Sampson, Mr Jute did not, I fear, have the stomach for what his acquaintances did. He began to protest at yet another death and started to argue for my release. And James shot him down with as little hesitation as if he had been a bird. I believe the killer did not even flinch at the sound.'

'And the other man?' said Mr Williamson.

'His name was Peter. No sooner had James shot Harold than Major Tunnock extracted a pistol and shot Peter where he sat. The poor fellow had not even said a word. Perhaps something had been said beforehand about the resolve of these two. Perhaps that is why they were in attendance at this most unusually confidential meeting.'

'This still does not explain your escape,' said Mr Williamson.

'Well, I clearly found myself in a most fortuitous situation. Both men had discharged their weapons and needed to reload. I picked up a vase and threw it at the window, where the curtain absorbed most of its velocity. They were quite stunned and merely stared at me. Then I threw the chair and calmly explained to the gentlemen that it had been a signal to Inspector Newsome of the Detective Force, who was outside at that very moment. Major Tunnock sneaked a look and perhaps saw you or the constables lurking. Whatever he saw, it was their signal to flee rather than be caught with guns and two dead bodies. James silenced the other witness: the girl.'

'A terrible mess,' said Mr Cullen.

'Indeed. I must admit that I could not have imagined the houses were joined through the kitchens. They must have expected just such a raid one day.'

'Did you manage to speak to either of the shot men?' said Mr Williamson.

'Peter was quite dead; Mr Jute could only mutter a single word over and over.'

'"Sorry"?' offered Mr Cullen.

'No – "Father".' Whether paternal or divine, I think we may assume a degree of guilt in poor Harold.'

'The question remains how you managed to locate the fleeing Mr Tattershall with such ease,' said Mr Williamson.

'As you all know, Benjamin was waiting at the Park-lane residence of our grand lady of pleasure lest anyone attempt – on that night of all nights – to sever another link to that perverted brotherhood. I guessed that James would go on just such a mission.'

'A lucky guess,' said Mr Williamson.

'Perhaps. Or rather a decent expectation based upon his killing of all others who had spoken with us. Mr Tattershall did indeed go to Park-lane, where he burst into the building and upstairs . . . to discover Benjamin's fist in his face where a beautiful lady should have been. The rest you know, or can imagine.'

'Hmm.'

'So the case is solved,' said Mr Cullen.

'I suppose it is,' said Noah. 'Perhaps not to everyone's satisfaction, and at a great cost to innocent lives, but we do have a conclusion.'

'Do you realize, gentlemen, that this is the second such time that we have worked together to solve a difficult and dangerous crime?' said Mr Cullen. 'It rather seems we have an aptitude for it.'

'Are you attempting to make a point?' said Mr Williamson.

'Well . . . have we not solved these crimes where the Metropolitan Police have been unable to do so under their own power? Have we, together, not demonstrated skills that, though they are considerable in isolation, are increased when combined? Might not we agree to work together again when another case occurs – one that has mystified the police, gripped the newspapers and called out for justice? Might not we become a Force in ourselves? A Force of uncommon detection?'

The gathered gentlemen looked at Mr Cullen, then at each other. All seemed amused – whether at the absurdity of the idea, or at its odd attraction, one might not have said.

'Would anyone like more tea?' asked Mr Williamson. 'Mr Cullen – will you oblige? I believe we have identified this as your particular skill in the uncommon Force of which you speak . . .'

That might have been a fine place to end our story, but the reader will be asking what became of Inspector Newsome's snow-blasted carriage race to the Continental Club on that previous evening, and how far along the road to justice *that* investigator had proceeded. Indeed, those were just the kind of questions also being sought by Sir Richard Mayne as he gazed with disapproving eyes at the detective before him that same day at Scotland Yard.

'Would you like to explain yourself, Inspector? Not only do you attempt to gain access to the Continental Club, but you do so with intemperate violence unbecoming of a detective. Can you imagine how humiliating it is for me to have constables called to arrest an inspector?'

'Sir – I was pursuing a fugitive named James Tattershall: the man who murdered Jonathan Sampson, Mrs Colliver, Mr Jessop and a number of others touching on this case. He is a resident at the club.'

'Wait – I feel I have missed something. What makes you think he was the murderer? We have not spoken of this man before.'

'You will recall that Mr Williamson was helping me briefly

with my enquiries. Well, it seems the waterman on Holywell-street – he who was murdered – had heard an unusual laugh immediately after the incident. By a stroke of luck an . . . an acquaintance of Mr Williamson was able to link the laugh to this Tattershall and learn that he was a resident at the club.'

'A laugh? That is hardly conclusive. Were there no actual witnesses to justify your insensate rush to the Continental Club?'

'No, sir. However, James Tattershall was found at the foot of the Monument stairs earlier today. He was dead. Upon his person was found this letter – I am afraid it is somewhat soiled but its contents are quite revelatory. If you would care to read the first paragraph . . .'

'Whatever it says, you obtained it *after* your reckless assault on the Continental. Here – let me read it . . . Wait . . . is this "Noah Dyson" the same who was involved in that recent case . . . ? Is he that escaped convict who goes about with the Negro fellow? Inspector – if I find that you have been colluding with criminals . . .'

'Sir – if these men have participated in any part of this investigation, it has been without my knowledge. It is pure coincidence that their names appear. Please – read the rest of the document.'

Sir Richard applied his keen attention to the stained sheet and his face passed through a range of expressions as he did so: from grim focus, through shock, to disgust and finally to surprise.

'Katherine Williamson, too? So George has been right all along in his suspicions. Has he seen this document? Have you informed him of the news?'

'I will, sir. But you see: James Tattershall *was* our villain.'

'What of these other men he names?'

'Two were found dead – shot – at a house on Bedford-row. Two more died in quite horrible but inexplicable circumstances at Smithfield last night.'

'Do you not find all of this extremely suspicious, Inspector? All of the conspirators dead in a single night, two of them apparently murdered? A confession found upon a man who died in the same way as one of his group's victims?'

'It is indeed all highly questionable, sir, but the case is indubitably complete – all answers provided. Let us also remember that this was a group who made a fetish of death. Perhaps they chose their own ends. Of more concern to me are the references in that document to the Vice Society and the spy Eusebius Bean.'

'Yes. I would prefer not to discuss that, and I would caution you from mentioning it to anyone at all. This is a matter for me to take up at a much higher level. If indeed the Society has been manipulating this investigation – rather than one immoral member – then discussions must be had. What do we know about the whereabouts of Mr Eusebius Bean?'

'Nothing, sir. He has not been seen for some days.'

'That bodes ill. It seems nobody connected to this case returns once they have vanished. I will put out a notice to all watch houses.'

'Quite. It has been a strange case, but I hope we can take some comfort from its conclusion and not gaze too closely at the details.'

'At present, I am inclined to agree.'

'Well, I have matters to attend to and I am grievously fatigued. May I be relieved, Sir Richard?'

'Not quite yet. There is one more question that needs to be answered. I wonder if you can explain the purpose of this ledger that was found locked in your office.'

'I . . . I have never . . .'

'It appears to be a surveillance catalogue detailing the movements of a number of highly notable personages and their visits to certain establishments. I wonder how such information was gained, and on whose authority? Is that a question you can answer?'

'I . . .'

'Do you realize what levels of illegality, treachery and deceit this ledger constitutes, Inspector Newsome? Do you realize what you have done?'

'How . . . ?'

'I received a letter informing me that you were running an unofficial group of constables who apprised you of this information in return for you turning a blind eye to their particular schemes. All of those men have been identified and dismissed in shame. On the assumption that this knowledge must have been stored somewhere, I had your clerk brought before me and the truth came out. Now – what penalty are you to face?'

'Sir . . . I . . . Who sent that letter? May I see it? I fear it is a fakement.'

'That is hardly a concern of yours at this moment. It was anonymous. It may have come from any one of the properties you were observing, or from any one of those people who perceived themselves observed. It matters not. What matters is whether you go to gaol.'

Sir Richard folded the letter and returned it to his pocket. In fact, it was not anonymous at all. In addition to being a denunciation of Mr Newsome, it was also a letter of resignation from one Mr John Cullen, previously a constable of Lambeth.

*

And so we come to the end of our story. Let us finish where we began, gazing down upon the metropolis from the chill aether of the Monument's viewing platform.

It remains mostly white down there, an immense page writ with the black letters of a million lives. Trails of smoke trace lines, ash heaps make blots, the river churns ice angrily against the bridges' buttresses in an endless flow. Life continues, and the snows slowly thaw to reveal the grime: the truth hidden below.

What is this commotion here, as a group of road-sweeping boys attempt to move a 'ball' of snow near Lincolns-inn-fields? Why, it is the body of a man frozen quite blue, an obscene collar of scarlet snow about his severed throat. He must have been killed just before the snows and buried where he fell. Poor Eusebius Bean – his loyalty to men more powerful and prescient than he ended thus, another victim of that pernicious case.

And what is that noisily chattering group there on the Southwark shore: a number of dock workers pulling a figure from the freezing waters and laying its sodden form upon the mud. Does anyone know his name? Yes – he is none other than the mariner Ned Coffin: the only Holywell-street witness unaccounted for. By the looks of his bloated and rotting corpse, he has been in the river for some time. In fact, during that entire period when the constables of the city were urgently seeking his testimony, he had been dead the whole time, having toppled into the waters that very same night owing to a surfeit of rum. Such are the vagaries of fate.

Looking further afield, we see a man standing over a freshly dug grave at one of those airy new burial grounds at the edge of the city. The soil is dark against the snow and the bare black branches rake the frigid wind. We cannot see the man's face, though he is rather slight in build and his legs are a little bowed from his years of walking the city streets. He wears a black coat and a top hat. The name on the gravestone, which nestles in consecrated ground, is newly chiselled: Katherine Williamson.

There is one more. He is passing from Ludgate-hill past the blackened visage of St Paul's and into the darkness of Paternoster-row. He is an author clutching his latest work, holding it to his chest lest he slip and soil those precious pages. This time he will be lucky; this time the publisher's reader will advise the publisher to print a thousand copies with all haste; this time the faceless author will succeed where countless others of his kind have failed, for his work is as broad and as complex as the city that urged it, as dark and as malodorous as the alleys in which it was bred, as incisive as the razor's slash, and as characterful as the lunatics that haunt these alien streets.

It is I.

Acknowledgements

Moniczka – sorry for leaving you alone so often
Monika Wolny – first reader and best critic
Jennifer White – still holding the card
Diana Cecilia de Graff – Dutch angel
Malcolm and Angus – for the energy when I had none
Nicholas Pearson – for the unpaid work
JW – unsolved death, 1849
MB – suicide, 1839